Giovanni Anthony

DEDRA

DEDRA

Giovanni Andreazzi

VANTAGE PRESS
New York

Excerpts from the song, "Navajo Rug," by Tom Russell and
Ian Tyson used by permission.

Published by Vantage Press, Inc.
516 West 34th Street, New York, New York 10001

Manufactured in the United States of America
ISBN: 0-533-14602-X

Library of Congress Catalog Card No.: 2003092523

0 9 8 7 6 5 4 3 2 1

To my ninth grade teacher, Mrs. Ruth Williams, who taught me the value of reading; Fred Hamlin, who showed me how to write; and *Mad Magazine*, which gave me my sick sense of humor.

DEDRA

PART I

One

Like an octopus propelling itself through the murky depths of the oceans with a blast of water from its pouch, he belched, jerking his head back with the force of the out-rushing air. He had just finished one of his favorite meals, a bagel sandwich. The sandwich consisted of a bagel, mustard, lettuce, and a slice of his special store of wild game meat. The meat was the size of the bagel and even had a hole in the center where it was de-boned. This specific slice of meat had an Oriental flavor, not one of his favorites, but a good one nonetheless.

He had just set his fifth wheel up at the state park, unhitched his Dodge extended cab diesel, and was now enjoying the leisure time before he set out to do the two things that pleased him most. After winning the lottery jackpot of $84 million five years ago, he was not shackled by a job or any other monetary worries. This freed him to do as he pleased, which consisted mostly of relaxing at his mountaintop secluded "mansion" home near South Royalton, Vermont, but today, this week, this month, he had work to do. Not so much work, but pleasure. A sort of pleasure he was getting to be an expert at after five years of honing his skills.

First, he needed to get the kinks out from driving two days and nights from his mansion to this park near Dallas. Except after a long trip, he slept little, getting by on three to four hours a night as was his custom these past five years or so. He liked the night, identifying with the many cats he kept as guests back in the mansion. First, he stretched in preparation for his bike ride. He loved to ride and to run. Sometimes he got lucky and was able to combine business with pleasure, meeting one of his victims along a bike route. This made his work a little easier and quicker, the quicker the better. He did not like the exposure or the separation from his guests. After all, the cats had to fend for themselves when he was working, something they let him know about upon his return by incessant mewing while shaking their tails in the air.

He was, by many standards, a very good-looking guy. His facial bone structure gave him a chiseled look with a sharp nose and jutting dimpled chin. He had deep-set, blue eyes and dark, wavy, long hair, which women loved to run their fingers through. His skin was tan and covered lightly with body hair. At six-feet two-inches tall with a 180-pound athletic build, he had no problems attracting women.

Donning his helmet, riding pants, gloves, and special shoes fitted for the clipless pedals, he took his bike out from the storage space just under the bedroom and above the gooseneck of the fifth wheel. He aimed the bike toward the circular road of the campsite he had chosen. It was one of the more secluded sites, surrounded by trees and not in direct view of any of the other nearby sites. Mounting the bike, he started out slowly, warming up by putting the bike in its lowest gears and spinning at a moderate pace. On exiting the park via a back trail, which he noticed from the park map, he headed across the dam that held back the reservoir water, picking up speed. His lean build was well suited to biking. He prided himself on keeping an athletic build, with muscled thighs and moderate upper body strength. Riding and running helped keep his weight down, since he did consume a fair amount of animal protein. If it were not for this exercise regimen, he would weigh far more than he did now. Also, at thirty-nine, he was plagued like many his age with the inability to burn off what he used to as a youth.

It was late October, and a cool front had come through the Dallas area the night before. It rained like hell, cleaning the oil and dirt from the roads. The storm also chased the summer humidity from the stifling days that typify the DFW area. Otherwise, he would not be able to ride very far, since he was not acclimated to hot, humid, Dallas weather. The trees and grass looked especially green, having been cleansed of dust and grime. It would be a pleasant day to ride.

Crossing the dam, he entered a main road, one he had committed to memory from the mapping program on his portable computer. He also had a GPS connected to the roof of his truck and a portable one he used as needed. Money bought the best toys. He noticed a bikes-on-roadway sign, always encouraging, since if he did not get lucky, at least he might meet up with another rider to take some of the boredom away from the routine. A half an hour into the ride, two riders passed him going the other way on the other side of the road. He continued on a little further, did a U turn at the break in the median, and shifted gears to increase speed. There would be no problem catching them; he had every confidence in his ability to ride with most amateur riders.

Long before he got close, he noticed they were women and got excited at the possibilities. He laughed to himself, thinking of all the hype lately about the new wonder drugs to cure male impotency. He had no problem getting a hard-on. People that can't get it up should leave it down was his philosophy, and why give the drugs to people who can't afford them? If they can't afford to buy the drug, they can't afford the results of fucking anyway. If Medicare started to fund Viagra, just imagine the flood of babies nine months after those limp-dicked, low-income assholes got their hands on free hard-on drugs. More and more babies will be on welfare, using the money he had to pay from his hard-earned winnings. Shit on them!

Approaching from behind, he was cautious to make sure he selected the right person. He liked his women on the thin side. They can be attractive or butt ugly, but a nice thin body was a must. An athletic build helps, but was not a necessity. That old saying, the closer to the bone the sweeter the meat, was true. He pulled up behind the two.

"Mind if I ride with you for awhile?" he asked.

They glanced around briefly.

"Okay," the one with the red hair flowing out from under her helmet responded. "But do you mind taking the lead, since there is quite a headwind today."

"I appreciate it, and I will," he said. "I'm new to the area and hate to ride alone." Most bikers were willing to share the ride with others, especially with a strong rider. With a strong rider leading the way, the other riders stayed close behind and used the draft created. The elimination of the head wind, or draft, allowed the following bikers to go faster and with less effort.

He sprinted around them and slowed so that they could draft

him. Had they said no, he would have ridden past them. If they looked promising, he would have gained distance and dropped some special items on the roadway that he knew would provide an opportunity to help a maiden in distress who just happened to get a flat tire. Although adding to the weight of his own bike, he carried a variety of emergency equipment, both for his own use and to repair the damage done by those demons of the roadway that happened to jump up and bite the tires of some unsuspecting fair lady.

He was always amazed by how much people told a perfect stranger about themselves in such a short time. People seemed to want to let others know their deepest, darkest secrets. Within thirty minutes, he would know such things as marital status, education level, number, if any, of children, where they worked, what kind of car they drove, and on and on. This was usually more than enough information for him to make his decision.

As the head wind shifted to a side wind, they approached his left side, taking advantage of the block his body provided. This allowed them to talk without shouting.

"I've not ridden here before," he said, hoping to inform as much as to get a conversation started. Continuing with, "It's a lot flatter than where I'm from."

"Where is that?" asked the red-haired, athletic-looking biker.

"Southern Ohio," he lied. He had different scenarios to mislead any future investigations. "Southern Ohio is hilly and has many side roads to challenge the thighs," he continued. "There is a fair amount of car and truck traffic. I have to be on guard so I don't end up a road taco."

Trying to entice a response, he said, "My name is John, by the way." Of course this was not his real name.

"I'm Alice, but I go by Ali," the redhead responded.

"I'm Trish," the other biker said, not wishing to be left out of the conversation.

"How often do you ladies ride?" he asked, trying to sound gentlemanly and polite.

"Usually four times a week," Ali said. "As a minimum, we ride every Saturday and Sunday."

"I try to get in at least that amount of riding also, but it gets difficult because of my travel schedule."

"What do you do?" Ali asked.

"I'm a computer troubleshooter." (Another lie) "I fix problems clients have with our computer systems."

"So you are a computer geek." Ali said.

"Hey, Ali," Trish said. "Maybe he can fix your computer."

"I could try. What's the problem?"

"No problem really. I want to upgrade what I already have so I can surf the net better and faster."

"I can help. That's exactly why I'm here. I'm speeding up several computers in an attorney's office in North Dallas."

"I don't want to impose, but if you are serious, you could follow us back to my apartment and take a look at what I have now, and then tell me what I need to do," said Ali.

"Sure, I can always mix business with pleasure. Right now, I'd like to hammer a bit, wanna draft me?"

"Sure, let's go."

"You two go on ahead of me. I'll give you a call this evening, Ali. I don't want to ride too hard today," said Trish.

Leaving Trish behind, he and Ali picked up the pace by spinning and shifting into higher and higher gears. He was not surprised she was keeping up with him. He was a good judge of the abilities of others by looking at their physique. They continued on for another five miles at twenty-plus miles per hour, sometimes pushing thirty. She was a good biker after all. He noticed she was standing on the pedals every once in a while. He slowed the pace a bit so he wouldn't lose her. They continued on for another five miles without saying anything, since all of their efforts were devoted to getting enough oxygen to keep their aerobic level high.

Finally they came to a more populated area and had to slow for traffic. She pulled up next to him and started grilling him.

"You live in Ohio." Making an assumption, she asked, "Did you go to college there?"

"Yes, Ohio University, in Athens, Ohio. I majored in engineering with a secondary in business." This story was well rehearsed, as were the others. He added to the stories from time to time, but the basis was always the same.

"When was this?"

7

"I graduated six years ago and have been working with the same company ever since."

"So, you are in your late twenties then."

"No, early thirties. I spent four years in the navy before going to college. I needed the GI Bill to help me get through."

"Your parents didn't help out?"

"No, my dad died when I was ten, and although I have no brothers or sisters, my mom couldn't afford to pay my way. In fact, she lives with us now, since she barely earns enough to get by on her own."

"Us?" was the cautious response.

"I have a dog, and no, I'm not and never have been married."

"So, you work for a computer company in Ohio?"

"Yes, Dayton," he said, growing weary of her questions.

"I've been to Dayton, and it isn't very hilly," she said. "Where do you ride in southern Ohio?"

"In and around Dayton, but on weekends, I ride farther south and down around the river, and it gets hilly. When were you in Dayton?" He knew sooner or later he would run into someone who could question the veracity of his stories. There was always someone else if Ali became too suspicious.

"Three years ago at a seminar. It was winter, so I didn't see much of Dayton except the airport and the hotel."

"What type of seminar?" he asked.

"Retirement planning," she said.

"A little young for retiring, or are you independently wealthy?"

"It was to learn. I'm an investment counselor."

"Should we slow down and wait on your roommate?" he asked, trying to determine if she lived alone.

"We're not roommates. We live in the same complex. Besides, we are almost there. Take a right at the next light. Have I taken you too far out of the way?"

"Sort of, but I have the rest of the day to get back to the Hilton."

"You are in a hotel with your bike?" she asked.

"Yes, I have a suite with plenty of room. I need to bring a lot of my stuff with me and am able to take the time to drive to each assignment. This way, I can eat healthy food, which I prepare in the suite, ride my own bike, and take my time getting from job to job."

They turned right at the light. "Make a left, and I'm in the apartment complex on the left side," Ali said. "Let me go first so the security guard will let us in."

"Hi, Ali," greeted the security guard as they approached the entrance.

"Hi, Tom. This is a friend of mine," she responded as they entered through the security gate. She led him to the back area of the second group of apartments. "I live right over here," she said, making a left toward the apartments with a big 307 written on the side of the building.

He was not concerned about being recognized, since the bike helmet and sunglasses was an ample disguise for anyone seeing him enter the apartment area with her. The same went for Trish, who never even saw him straight on or standing for that matter. Yes, he would be difficult to describe later if it came to that.

She got off her bike. Her Sidi clipless shoes made a clacking sound as she made her way to a bottom entranceway. As he got off his bike, he made a similar sound, as if they were both from Holland and wearing wooden shoes.

"Aren't you afraid I will rape and pillage you?" he said, jokingly, but considered the possibility.

"No, my roommate will protect me should it come to that," she responded as she opened the door.

He was about to ask, "What roommate?" when immediately, a large form filled the entryway. A German shepherd peered first at her and then menacingly at him.

"That's okay, AJ," she said to him. "This is a friend," and she gave the curious dog a pat on the head. Immediately, the dog started wagging his tail and sniffed at him as if to categorize his scent, at the same time storing it away for future recall.

She pulled her bike in through the entrance while he leaned his against the wall of the small porch leading to the door. "Come on in," she beckoned with a jerk of her head. He took off his shoes and made his way through the entrance. He was not afraid of animals. In fact, he liked them all. He had a natural way with them that he did not understand. He liked to believe it was

9

the animal in him that they recognized and respected. On taking off his biking gloves, he licked the back of his hand and presented it to AJ as Ali closed the door behind them. He learned somewhere that this was the way to get a dog to accept you as part of the pack. It seemed to work, as AJ first sniffed then licked the saliva from his hand. According to the rules of dogdom, he was now a part of the pack.

"Would you like some water or power drink?" she offered.

"No, thanks. I really need to get back to the hotel before it gets too late. I have a few phone calls to make before dinner. Where's the computer?" he asked. Hoping to get out of the apartment quickly before Trish got back to the complex.

"Over here in my office. I want to have a faster modem installed and some more disk space," she explained, as they walked toward the rear of the apartment. AJ followed close behind.

When they got to the room, he noticed how neat and organized the room was. He walked over to the computer and looked at it. It was a generic type. Someone's homemade that he could easily upgrade. Not only was she a neat person, but a practical one having saved a bunch on a computer by not buying a brand name.

"I can easily help and probably won't charge you more than a dinner date," he offered.

"You're quick," she responded, "but I'm willing to pay for the parts and your expertise."

"No, you don't have to pay," he repeated. "I have the necessary modem and hard disk back at the hotel," he lied for the umpteenth time. "I took it out of a system last week and can put it in yours rather than toss it. It won't be the latest and greatest, but there is nothing faster as far as the modem, and you don't need anything larger than the hard drive I have, so what do ya say to dinner?"

"After you upgrade my system, we'll talk about it," she teased. She did not want to appear too anxious. She liked this guy, and she was not seeing anyone at the moment. "When do you think you can do this?"

"Tomorrow would be fine," he responded, noting he would have to get the parts before he could fulfill his end of the deal.

"What is your phone number? I'll give you a ring when I'm free with my appointment."

"Let me write it down for you," she said, as she pulled a sticky note from a drawer beside the computer. This was not necessary, since he already memorized the number from the empty wireless phone cradle next to the computer. He also noticed a caller ID and answering machine adjacent to the phone. He carefully avoided touching anything in the room.

"I should be done about 5:30 tomorrow. Will that work for you?" he asked, as he took the sticky note from her and put it in one of the three pockets on the back of his biker shirt.

"That should be fine, and if I'm not home yet, I have the answering machine on all the time," she unnecessarily responded.

"Cool," he said, as he put his gloves back on and headed for the front of the apartment. "Do you like Italian?" he asked, carrying the tease back to her.

"I'll let you know tomorrow as soon as I make up my mind on whether your upgrade was worth it," she replied.

"See ya tomorrow," he parried as he opened the door and walked out of the apartment. "Later, AJ," he said to the dog, which responded with a wag of his tail.

As he was getting on his bike, he saw Trish riding into the complex. He waved as he headed out on the opposite side of the street. He knew they might be able to identify his biker clothes if he kept them long enough to be found. But as before, the clothes would be incinerated, helmet and all, before she was even missed. He bought his biker clothes from stores throughout the country and never in the same place as he found his victims. If everything is random and there is nothing to be found or traced, then it sure makes it difficult for the cops. It's like tracking an animal without a trail, without a clue, without knowing what the animal looks like.

He picked up the pace as he headed back toward the park. He could not believe how quickly he was able to find just the right woman this time. Other hunting expeditions took days, and a few took weeks, to track down suitable prey. Nothing like a quickie to get him back to his quests. *Maybe this is getting too easy*, he thought.

He rode back across the dam to the state park, taking the back way in through the wooded area. He needed to find a computer store and get the necessary parts. He dismounted, opened the keyed storage compartment under the fifth wheel, and stored the bike neatly away. He opened the door, entered, and cleaned up from the hard day's ride. He ate another bagel sandwich, drank a glass of Carlo Rossi Paisano wine, climbed up the stairs to the queen-size bed, and caught up on some of the sleep he lost during the trip from Vermont to Texas.

While he slept, Ali and Trish exchanged thoughts about him. Ali told Trish how good-looking he was without his helmet and what a cute butt he had. Trish was jealous and told Ali so.

Unlike the stereotypical redhead, Alice was not fiery. She was frail as a child, but as soon as they could, her parents got her into sports. She loved karate, which gave her confidence and a nice body tone. She was not beautiful, but she was attractive and smart. As a teenager, she was more interested in soccer and cross-country running than the opposite sex. She was a mediocre student with a C average and no interest in higher education. After high school, she got a job in a bank as a teller, but wanted something more.

She saved up enough to attend some seminars on investment banking and retirement planning and decided those were the fields for her. She stopped the karate classes after she got her first-degree black belt and took up biking as a gentler way to stay in shape. She occasionally taught karate at the local school, just to keep up with the sport.

Her sex life was typical, but she did not fall in love easily. She did not know what type of man she was attracted to. As a consequence, she dated every chance she got, trying to find someone she was compatible with. Born and raised a Texan, she did not travel much except on business and to seminars. She was slowly settling into a mundane lifestyle when he found her.

Two

The next morning, Monday, he awoke at four. If he had any dreams the night before, he did not remember them. His dreams plagued him ever since he could remember. They used to scare him, but not anymore. He brushed his teeth and put on his running clothes. It was still dark, and he rode his bike only in broad daylight. He stepped outside of the fifth wheel and did some stretches for his hamstrings and quads. The park was nearly empty, and those trailers he passed were dark.

He took off at a leisurely pace and, after a quarter-mile, he stepped it up to eight-minute miles. He was capable of seven-minute miles, but wanted to run ten miles today. The air was still fresh and had not yet taken on the pollution that starts most clear windless mornings in the Dallas area. An hour and a half later, he was back at the fifth wheel, doing another set of stretches. He had planned his day during the run.

After cleaning up, he took care of several "housekeeping" chores. The first was to check on his computer at the mansion. To do that, he went to the nearest airport, in this case, DFW. He belonged to several private airline clubs, and in addition to getting a drink or two, he could hook up his laptop and connect to his base computer in Vermont.

He drove to the airport and parked at the terminal parking. He walked to the terminal and went through the security checkpoint, stopping momentarily to get the computer checked out. He then proceeded to the Admirals' Club, next to the American Airlines gates.

"Hello," he said to the hostess, showing her his card.

"Good morning" was her perfunctory reply as she checked the expiration date on his entrance card. "Do you need some assistance with your flight?" she asked.

"No, thank you," he said, as he proceeded past the desk,

then into the lounge area.

He went to the bar and ordered a vodka martini, shaken not stirred, and thought of the James Bond character. He paid for the drink and went to the business side of the club where there were individual cubicles set up with telephones. These provided the privacy he needed to do his work.

He turned on the computer and connected the modem and waited for it to warm up. When the screen was stabilized, he clicked on the PC "Anywhere" icon, and it responded with the familiar screen he had used so many times before. Connecting to his computer was easy enough, but to make it untraceable to him or his location, he went through a calling card service that he had purchased with cash at a convenience store along the way.

Connected, he now started to download his e-mails, financial information, phone calls, and environmental information about his house. Awhile back, his mainframe had shut down. He now had redundant systems, which enabled him to do all the necessary functions he normally did when he was home without interruption. He paid bills, answered e-mails, listened to phone messages, reset all the equipment. If anyone were to check up on his whereabouts during this week, they would find computer records indicating he had been home the entire time. At least, there would be confusion, since it would appear he was in two places at one time. He did not want to get caught. That would spoil his fun.

He also accessed the cameras he had set around the house to check on his guests and to see if everything was secure. They were lounging all over the mansion. It was fun to remotely watch their actions. He amused himself while sipping on his martini. Everything seemed to be in order. Even the outside appeared undisturbed. He had the security system set to call him if any of the sensors leading up to the house and around the house were disturbed. He could then connect to the computers and check the seriousness of the intrusion for damage control or evasive action. Video recorders kept a record of the situation inside and outside if an alarm had been tripped. He could replay the tape to catch up on the action if he was away from his laptop when the beeper went off.

He had a little time left, so, still connected to his home computer, he logged on to an Internet chat room. He liked the chats, occasionally spending his spare time at home and on the road logged on, chatting, or just watching the others. One of his victims was contacted in a chat room. Although he wanted to change his methods with each victim, he could be enticed to try this method again. He realized there was a danger with connecting in a chat room, but it was the easiest. He lingered in the chats for about an hour. Then, realizing it was getting late, he reluctantly shut down the programs, put away the laptop, and got ready to leave the Admirals' Club. He had one more job to do before he went on his date.

He picked up the phone and used his card again and called the local animal shelters. Usually there was no problem finding what he wanted. However, it took three calls before he located a shelter that had a kitten that was less than a year old and had been spayed. This done, he left the Admirals' Club, located his truck, and left the airport through the south gates, paying cash. He noticed that sometimes they recorded license plate numbers. However, his license plates were phonies so there would be no record of his having been there. He left the airport and headed for the animal shelter.

Ten minutes later, he pulled up to the animal shelter. A small wood-framed building, which had "Your Best Friend Animal Shelter" painted in black on a wood plaque above the door of a long, wood building with several windows lining the south side. The north side had chain-link dog runs with several dogs with wagging tails watching him arrive. At the west end, or the back of the facility, he recognized the tall metal pipe pointing to the sky as the exhaust from the incinerator. He had one at his mansion in Vermont, although none of his cats would ever see the inside of it. He entered the shelter and went to the office, where he found a man behind a desk, reading a paper.

"Howdy" he said with his best attempt at a Texas drawl.

"Hi" the caretaker said, without looking up from the paper. He finally looked up and smiled, showing two gold-capped teeth from under a bushy unkempt mustache. He stood to shake hands, revealing that he was a short Hispanic and appeared to be in his late forties, although it was hard to tell. He had on a pair of baggy jeans and a white shirt, which, despite his working in an animal shelter, was clean and had little wear.

"What can I do for ju?" he asked, without proffering his name.

"I called about a kitten just a few minutes ago. Can I see her?"

"Chure, chure, ju come with me." He went through a door to the back section. Inside, there were cages from which emitted incessant barking. The cats looked out from their cages forlornly, some of them crying, but they could not be heard above the din caused by the dogs. "This tabby, has been spayed. Her owner brought her in two days ago when chee found out chee was allergic to cats. One more day, and we will give her the gas," he said, gesturing to a door in the rear of the building where the incinerator was kept. "We can't keep that many animals here, and we can't afford to feed them. Almost all the animals here will be gone in a week, replaced by new ones brought in daily. It's a chame that these pets once had owners that they were attached to and then thrown out like so much garbage," he said, displaying concern unexpected from a Hispanic male.

He heard all this before. At least his mission does some good for these poor animals. The rest of his cats will accept this one as they had accepted the others.

"If this is the only one you have that is spayed, I'll take her. She looks healthy enough."

"Okay, there is a vet down the street that can look her over for ju and give any vaccines, free of charge. Just show her the papers I will give ju. If chee is seriously ill, ju can bring her back."

"Thanks," he said, as the caretaker opened the cage and took the cat out and handed it to him. They then went to the office, closing the door on the noise, although not shutting it out entirely. Presented with some papers to fill in, he used his fake Texas driver's license, which the caretaker verified with the completed form. Chances were the form would be only used for statistical purposes, since animal shelters were glad to place some of the pets in homes rather than gas and incinerate them. It didn't matter, he would be long gone in the morning.

"*Muchas gracias y que is la nombre del gato?*" he said with what little Spanish he picked up in high school.

"*De nada* and the cat's name is Puss," was the response with a golden toothy smile at the *gringos* butchering of the caretaker's native tongue.

"I believe I'll rename her Tejas," he said, as he walked out the door, carrying the wide-eyed cat.

He next went to the CompUSA store that he noticed on his drive to the airport. He got the modem and hard drive and paid cash. He then returned to the state park and introduced Tejas to the fifth wheel, especially the litter box, food, and water bowls. Tejas seemed to take to the surroundings with ease and prowled the inside perimeter. He usually did not pick up the new cat until after he had the girl well in hand, but he was so confident of success, after so many times, he jumped the gun.

Using the cell phone and calling card, he called a local restaurant he located on the Internet earlier that afternoon. It was expensive, out of the way, and he was sure Ali probably had never been there before. He made reservations for 8:30. This would give him plenty of time to fix her computer. It was 4:30 when he called Ali. Her caller ID would register unavailable for his name and number or possibly some connecting telephone link in Georgia or Kansas. This would not help the cops when they started looking for clues. The phone rang four times, and the answering machine came on. He left a message, telling her he would be there at 6:30. *She must still be at work*, he thought.

After a shower and shave, he put on a plain, blue, long-sleeved shirt, blue trousers, and khaki tan suede jacket. No tie, since he wanted to present a business-casual look. Nothing to attract attention. He got something special for AJ. A doggy treat laced with some arsenic. Enough to kill a horse; he did not want to leave any witnesses. It would be cruel to leave AJ to the fate of the animals in the shelter when his master did not return that night. He could also starve to death if no one decided to miss Ali for a week or so. He was not going to be cruel to animals. He also made sure he had the tranquilizer, Rohypnol, two two-milligram tablets. One was sufficient, but two was sometimes necessary. He put on a silver-gray Charlie Hunt felt Cattleman hat. The wide brim would cast a shadow on his face and hide his hair.

He drove to DFW airport in his truck, parked at the remote

parking, and took the shuttle to the terminal. He then took the rental car bus to the rental car area and picked up a nice Lincoln Town car without reservations. He used his phony driver's license and a fake credit card not in his name. When he returned the car, he would substitute cash. That way, no one would know who rented the car, and it certainly could not be traced to him.

He drove to Ali's place with the hard drive, modem, Rohypnol, and doggy treat. "This is all too easy," he mused.

He arrived at Ali's apartment a little before 6:30. The security guard, not Tom this time, let him in after checking with Ali. He kept his face looking down, letting the hat brim shield his face so the guard could not get a good look at him. Parking in one of the visitor's spots as close to her door as possible, he took off his hat and jacket and got out of the car as soon as he was sure no one was close enough to positively ID him. When they left the apartment later that evening, it would be dark and so would not worry about being seen. Eyewitnesses were always notoriously unreliable. He was careful to check yesterday for any outside security cameras as he rode his bike out of the area. If there were some, he would have aborted this mission.

AJ did not make any noise when he rang the doorbell.

"Just a minute. You're early," Ali chastised from behind the door. A few seconds later, the door was opened, and AJ stuck his head out to greet him. Ali was in jeans and a large T-shirt. She was bending over to replace a well-used running shoe on her left foot with a slipper matching the one on her right foot. Her long red hair hung down over her face. As soon as the door was fully opened, he noticed that AJ was wagging his tail.

"Hi, AJ," he said, getting a more enthusiastic wag.

"Do I get a greeting?" Ali said, letting go of her slipper and standing up.

"Yes, hello, Ali," he replied. "Reservations are for 8:30, which should give me plenty of time to work on your computer."

"I just got back from a walk with AJ. I plan on getting ready while you work on the computer. Just in case I decide to go with you, what restaurant did you have in mind?"

"Marsala. It's off of 360."

"I've never been there. What kind of food do they have?"

"The hotel recommended it," he said, anticipating her next question. "They said it's a mixture of French and Italian. I checked, and it's not coat and tie, but the concierge at the hotel said it was not a shabby place."

"That's good to know. I'll be getting ready while you work on the computer. AJ will keep you company, I'm sure." At the mention of his name, AJ perked up his ears.

"All right, I'll get started. Come on, AJ." The dog jumped to its feet with tail wagging. He bent over and scratched AJ behind the ear.

He followed her to the room containing her computer, followed by AJ, who was still wagging his tail. "I need to wear these antistatic gloves," he half-lied. Actually, an antistatic wrist strap was necessary, but latex surgeon's gloves masked fingerprints. So far, he had not touched anything other than the dog, and getting a latent from fur was nothing to worry about.

"Fine," said Ali. "I'm going to get ready." She left the room; however, AJ kept a diligent watch over the proceedings. Perhaps he could smell the "treat" in the pants' pocket.

A half-hour later, he was ready to test out the new components. He loaded the necessary software and started some diagnostics tests on the modem and hard drive. The new hard drive would be a slave to the system to load any Internet files or MP3 music files. Another half an hour, and he was ready to test the connection to the Internet. Just then, Ali appeared.

"I thought you were an expert. It's taken an hour, and you aren't through yet?" she said, with a tease in her voice.

She had on a dark green dress, accenting her red hair. She stood, adjusting her left shoe on a bent knee, bracing herself against the wall with her other hand. Her shoes were dark green half-heels but still made her calve muscles show. She had a very nice, thin body, which was one of the prerequisites. She looked good enough to eat, on rye.

"Wow, you look great, and I've been through for forty-five minutes. AJ and I have been napping, waiting for you to get ready."

"Oh, yeah, right. You're still wearing your gloves."

"I was working so hard, I forgot to take them off. Now, you sit down and log onto your favorite porn site and see how fast it

19

loads up the naked men pictures," he said, while taking off his gloves.

"Funny, funny," she said. "If you want something to drink, help yourself to the fridge."

"I'm saving my thirst for some wine at dinner, but I will have a little drink of water and a visit to the bathroom if you don't mind. You have thirty minutes to play since the place we are going to is about thirty minutes from here."

Followed by AJ, he went into the bathroom but did not let the dog inside. Something bothered him about letting an animal see him excrete his bodily fluids. He put the gloves back on and took a piss in the sink. He did not want to splash any evidence around the bathroom. Flushing the toilet for effect, he rinsed the evidence down the drain, carefully rinsing the sides of the sink. He dried the gloves, then went to the kitchen, found a glass, and poured some water from the faucet. He drank from the glass pouring the water into his mouth so his lips would not leave a lip print. He then took off the gloves by pulling one inside the other as a surgeon would do.

His only dilemma was when to give the dog his goody. If he did it now and did not get a chance to give Ali her treat at the restaurant, the dog would be dead when she got home. Then there would be no chance to slip her the drug at the apartment. There was always the chance she would not invite him in for a nightcap anyway, so he took the treat out and gave it to AJ. AJ crunched the bone-shaped treat and swallowed it in about five seconds. Wagging his tail, he licked the hand that fed him and looked around for more.

"Good dog," he said, then turned toward the room with the computer. "Are you about ready? I'm starving."

"Just a minute," she shot back.

He gave AJ a pat on the head as they left the apartment. AJ wagged his tail one last time as Ali shut the door. It was dark, and no one else was in the lot.

"Over here," he said, as he pointed the way to the Town car.

"Ooh, nice," she said admiring the Lincoln. "Do you drive this to all your jobs?"

"No, it's a rental. I didn't think you would want to ride in a truck to a nice restaurant." He opened the door for her and closed it as she slid in. He admired the smooth way she moved. They made small talk as they drove to the restaurant. She thanked him for the work he did on the computer and said that she was surfing much faster now. She thought this would do until she could afford a cable or DSL connection. She offered to pay, but he refused, saying that he used parts he was going to discard anyway. About the time they arrived at the restaurant, AJ, back in the apartment, was foaming at the mouth and starting to convulse. He would not suffer too much longer.

The Marsala restaurant was just off spur 360. It had a dimly lit parking lot with only a few cars. The inside was small, and the maître d' met them just inside the door. He was dressed in a black suit and bow tie. Marsala looked like an extremely dressy place, but the patrons just leaving were in jeans and cowboy shirts. So this was a place you could dress up or down. From experience, he knew the dressier you were, the more likely you were to tip big, and the better the table you would be seated at. There was a bar just inside the entrance, but no barstools could be found. The tables were neatly arranged, and the place settings were top notch. Roaming from table to table were two men, one with a mandolin and the other with Spanish guitar, serenading or otherwise annoying the patrons. Since they were not formally dressed, they were seated in the informal section. The table they were seated at was in a secluded corner and lit, as were the other tables, by candlelight. The overhead lights were dimmed so that you could see the person you were with, but not very well the people at the table next to you.

"I'm impressed," she whispered as soon as the maître d' walked away. Immediately, two men appeared and removed the extra place settings, poured water, and made a fuss with the remaining items on the table. "I didn't even know this place was here, and I drive by here several times a month. I feel like I should have dressed up more."

"Don't worry, you look fine. More than fine actually, and the way the candlelight reflects on your hair is hauntingly beautiful. And what would the lady like to drink?" he said in his best wine-steward voice.

"I would like a shooter and Coors chaser," she mimicked with a drawl. "Actually some white wine would do."

"Garçon, a gallon of your best wine," pretending to order. She laughed as they finished their little banter. The waiter approached their table, and their evening of wining and dining began, one of many to come for him, her last.

After the meal, as if it was planned, she excused herself to go to the ladies room. As soon as she was through the door, he took the Rohypnol from his jacket and dropped it in her half-finished glass of dessert wine. He carefully swished it around so that it was all dissolved. He decided two milligrams would be enough. He then signaled for the waiter to bring their check. He wanted to make sure they were in the car in twenty minutes when she would start losing her psychomotor abilities. He made a mental note to get more of the drug the next time he was this close to Mexico. It was easy to walk into a Mexican pharmacy, pick up what you wanted in the way of prescriptions or drugs, and stroll back across the border with your booty. Illegal drugs were a little more difficult to get, but if you asked, they were available.

Fifteen minutes after she returned and finished the last of her wine, they were on their way out to the car. He let her in as before, but noticed she now did not move so smoothly. The combination of drugs and booze would have her out by the time he got her to his truck at the terminal.

On the way to the airport, Ali was not passing out as he had hoped. She was woozy, but not slipping into a comatose state. Perhaps she had Rohypnol in the past or was metabolizing it slowly because of the meal. This meant she probably needed another two milligrams. He pulled over to the side of the road and gave her another pill with a drink of water from a bottle he had stored in the back seat. Barely aware of her surroundings and not aware of what she was doing, she swallowed the pill. Ten minutes later, as he pulled into the parking space next to his truck, the effect he wanted was taking place. She was completely slouching in the seat and would have dropped slowly to the floor if she were not wearing a seat belt. He could now leave her in the truck while he turned in the rental car.

By the time he turned in the rental car, exchanged cash for his credit card receipt, and returned to the terminal to pick up his truck and Ali, it was 10:30. It would be a long day for him. He needed to get back to the state park, hitch up the fifth wheel, and get Ali settled in. The gates at the state park closed at 10:00, but he had been given, as all campers were, the combination to the lock.

Thirty minutes later, he backed into the campsite under the fifth wheel. He was able to reconnect the trailer to the truck and disconnect the electricity in less than fifteen minutes. The sewer and water hook-ups were disconnected before he left to go to Ali. In her stupefied state, Ali was barely able to stumble out of the truck, but with his assistance, they made it easily. The campsite was dark and surrounded by trees; therefore, isolating him from the other campers. At this late hour, no one was awake anyway.

He got her up the stairs to the bedroom and laid her out on the bed. He tied her hands and feet to the cleats he had installed at the head and foot of the bed. She was semiconscious as he prepared the needle and the tube that he used to drain blood from her arm. He watched as the blood drained from her arm through the tube and down to the plastic milk container on the floor. When it was three-fourths full, an amount arrived at from past experience, he stopped the flow with a clamp. She was now in a deep sleep/coma and would stay that way for the trip back to Vermont. With the exception of her panties, he stripped off her clothes and tossed them in a bag in the closet with his helmet and bike clothes. He then covered her with a blanket and put pillows over her arms. If he were ever stopped, it would appear to the police that she was just asleep. He let Tejas out of the bathroom when he dumped the blood into the holding tank. He took a bleach bottle from behind the toilet and filled the milk container, then poured that too down the toilet. He picked up the purring kitten and took her out to the cab of the truck with him.

He started the diesel, which made a racket, but he was not concerned about waking his neighbors. The sound of a truck was not a cause for concern in a state park. He drove slowly to the entrance to the park, opened the combination lock, and let himself out of the park. After locking the gate, he got in the truck and started the trip back to Vermont and his mansion. It would be a long drive, and he would not stop except for diesel fuel and to check on his cargo. Once safely on the highway, he reminisced about the construction of the mansion.

Shortly after collecting what was left after taxes of his $84-million lottery winnings, he started construction of his mountaintop hideaway in South Royalton, Vermont. He selected the location because it was isolated. Construction was expensive because of the location of the land being at the top of a 1,700-foot mountain. Concrete for the foundation had to be lifted by helicopter, as did all the building materials. The lack of a local contractor to build such a house meant that he had to pay a premium for a construction firm from Burlington. The architect was also from Burlington, the closest town of any size. Because of the location and relative size of the house (4,000 square feet), the locals called it a mansion. Soon, everyone involved in the project referred to it as a mansion. Locals were hired as needed by the construction company, two of which, Wayne and Bill, became hunting buddies of his.

During construction, he lived in a fifth wheel garaged in the barn at the base of the mountain. This allowed him to closely watch the progress of the work and to add certain touches to the mansion that he wanted. The barn was soon converted into a garage for the fifth wheel and a place for a generator and propane storage. All the utilities for the mansion went through the garage.

To minimize the concrete needed, all the construction was above ground with the exception of the tunnel. An oversized garage was constructed at the top on the north side of the site and served as the main entrance. There were other utility doors at the screened-in porch on the south and west sides, but these were seldom used. The garage would be used to house his truck and the Hum-Vee he purchased during construction. After entering through the garage, there was a long corridor, near the end of which, on the left, was the entrance to the butcher shop. He told the architect that he was an avid hunter and wanted a room to process his kills. The shop had a large walk-in freezer that shared a wall with the garage. The shop was thirty feet square, tiled on the floor and up four feet on the walls. On the back wall opposite the freezer was an incinerator that could hold a hundred pounds and could turn the contents into ashes in under an hour. The room had all the necessary tables, saws, and racks to butcher a nine-hundred pound moose.

At the end of the corridor was the entrance to the house, the door of which opened to a short flight of stairs directly up into a gourmet kitchen complete with a subzero refrigerator, gas cook top, and electric oven. To the right was a large living room facing south and west. The wrap-around, screened-in porch had sliding glass windows, was heated, and could be used during all seasons. Under the living room and kitchen was an exercise room adjoining a large room with lots of windows facing south. When necessary, he isolated his cats in these two rooms. They would follow him there like the pied piper when he opened cans of food and rang a little dinner bell.

On the northeast side of the kitchen was a door leading down to the computer room, the heart of the house. Everything in the house could be controlled from there. In the southeast side of the kitchen was a spiral stairway leading up to the bedrooms and loft overlooking the living room. All the levels had full bathrooms with a Jacuzzi in the master bath. The master bedroom had a hidden escape hatch leading down to the computer room.

In the computer room, a trap door led down to an underground tunnel, which ended on the south side of the mountain 300 feet away. At the base of the mountain, below the tunnel outlet, was another old barn that came with the property. He explained to the architect that this was his only way out should something happen to the house. It was the first thing built and soon was covered up by the time the framers, which included Wayne and Bill, started the vertical construction. None of the locals knew of this tunnel.

The property had sensors, cameras, and speakers located at various locations in the woods. They were connected to the computer which fed sound and video to monitors throughout the house. The house and grounds were completely wired. Anyone attempting to hunt or approach the house would be detected and warned to leave immediately. He did not want any surprises. In the end, the house with all the furnishings cost a little over three million. He had a lot left over for play.

During construction, he became an unlikely friend with Wayne. Wayne's sidekick, Bill, tagged along as they went hunting. Their hunting trips were just an excuse for the butcher shop he had installed. Since all the locals knew about it, he had to use it or suspicions would be raised. Besides, hunting with Wayne and Bill helped pass the time between his real hunting trips, and they were a source of amusement. Having come from the same humble beginnings, he felt more akin to Wayne and Bill than any of the other people who had as much money as he had.

Three

He left Dallas on I30, heading east. Pulling the fifth wheel with the big Dodge diesel was smooth and easy. He set the cruise control as he passed sixty-five miles per hour, the speed limit. Both fuel tanks were full with fifty gallons of diesel. At fifteen miles per gallon, he could cruise 700 miles before refueling. That was enough to get him to the other side of Nashville. Then one more stop in Harrisburg, and then, on to Vermont.

He selected a CD from the twelve on the changer hidden in the back of the extended cab. Four seconds later, the six speakers were booming the sound of the Rolling Stones, "Under My Thumb." He sang along to help quell the boredom. Tejas finished inspecting the inside of the truck. He had a litter box on the floor of the passenger side. She got in it once but got out again and crawled into his lap. He petted her with one hand as he steered the truck along. He soon got into the rhythm of the road and did not slow down until he got to the other side of Little Rock.

Time to check on his cargo. The sky was starting to glow with the first hint of the rising sun when he pulled into the roadside rest. He picked Tejas up and carried her to the fifth wheel. She went immediately to the bowl where water and milk were waiting for her. So smooth was the ride that barely any had splashed out.

He went up to the bedroom and noticed that Ali was semiconscious and tugging at her bindings. He needed to draw some more blood. He slid the bedroom door closed to keep the cat from interfering. He uncovered her and removed the pillows from her arms. The tube and needle were still in her arm, so it was an easy matter to take out another half a pint. This should be enough to get her the rest of the way to Vermont. When the blood was drawn, he took the needle out of her arm, replaced the protective cover over the metal tip, and coiled it with the hose. He placed them into the bag in the closet with her clothes and the bike clothes. He then re-covered her with the blanket and pillows.

He opened the bedroom door and went to the kitchen. Tejas was watching him with curiosity until he started to open a can of cat food. She then rubbed his leg meowing in anticipation. After he fed her, he opened the freezer and took out a frozen bagel sandwich, started the generator to the fifth wheel and popped it in the microwave for two minutes. When the microwave beeped, he turned off the generator. Deciding to let Tejas ride it out in the fifth wheel, he returned to the truck. Pulling back out onto I-30, he munched on the sandwich. He pulled a diet cream soda from the cooler in the back of the cab and settled down for the ride to Nashville.

Just before Nashville, he saw a sign for a roadside sanitary dump at the next exit. Dumping the sanitary tank sounded like a good idea and what better place to get rid of some more evidence residing in the fifth wheel holding tank. Even though by now the bleach had done its work sloshing around in the tank with the blood. He slowed the truck and exited the highway. It was almost noon. He was making very good time, and he could use another sandwich. The dump station was a mile south of the interstate located at a truck stop. *This is two birds with one stone*, he thought. *I'll fill up with diesel while I'm here.* He pulled alongside the dump station, got the hose out of the bumper storage location, and connected it to the black water dump valve. After inserting the other end of the hose into the dump station sewer connection, he opened the dump valve on the fifth wheel. He went into the trailer and connected a flush hose to the sink in the bathroom, opened the toilet valve with the foot pedal, and flushed out the tank with fresh water. It wouldn't get all the blood out, but there would be very little left. After disconnecting all the hoses and restoring them, he was ready to fuel up.

He paid for the fuel with cash. He pulled over to the parking area and went back to the fifth wheel. He checked on Ali. She was still alive, tied up, and in a stupefied state. He started the generator, fixed another bagel sandwich, and was getting ready to go back to the truck, when he heard a knock on the door.

He opened the door to an officer.

"I'm Officer Dan Blocker. I noticed the license plate on your trailer is hanging by the corner. You better fix it before you lose it."

"Thanks, officer," he said, trying to keep his heart from bursting from his chest. "I'll do it right now."

He walked to the back of the fifth wheel with the officer to look at the plate.

"I thought I saw a curtain moving, too. Just make sure no one is riding in the trailer while you're driving. Not only is it against the law, it's dangerous," officer Blocker said.

Rounding the back of the fifth wheel, he responded.

"That was probably my cat peeking out the window. She likes it better than the truck."

"No law against that," the officer said as he headed back to his cruiser.

After reattaching the license plate, he left the truck stop and resumed the trip back to Vermont. Had the officer checked with DMV on the plates, he would have found them legal. They were on the fifth wheel when he bought it from a man whose wife had just died. The old man told him the plates and inspection were good until February.

Fueling up again in Harrisburg, he started the last leg of his trip. He checked on Ali two more times and found her in a deep coma with Tejas nestled on top of the blanket in the Y formed by her outstretched and bound legs.

Returning to the South Royalton area at 4:30, it was easy to go undetected. Only the farmers got up that early, and there were precious few of them left in what was once a prime milk state. He had to pull the RV into his barn-sized garage at the base of the mountain to transfer Ali from the RV to the truck unseen. After pushing the remote control, the large doors opened, and the truck and RV easily slid into the sixty-foot-long space. Remotely closing the doors, he slipped out of the truck using the headlights and automatic garage door lights to see his way back to the RV.

He opened the door and stepped in, flicked on the lights, and moved to the bedroom above the bed of the truck. The scent of her excited him. She was still unconscious and would be for some time. He easily lifted her and carried her out of the RV and into the back of the extended cab of the truck. She was his now, and it would not be long before the transformation took place.

He then lowered the stabilizers for the fifth wheel and threw the lever disconnecting the two vehicles. He reentered the RV and moved to the couch where the kitten was softly mewing. He gently lifted the tiny body and caressed her. Her fur was similar in texture to Ali's hair, and soon, they would be one. He retrieved the bag of clothes from the bedroom closet and carried them with the kitten to the truck. He tossed the clothes in the bed of the truck and climbed into the driver's seat, used the second remote to open the opposite door, and drove the truck out of the barn to begin the steep ascent to the top.

When shifted into four-wheel drive, the Dodge had more than enough traction to crawl slowly at grades approaching twelve degrees in some places. It was an unpaved path, overgrown with brush. Tree branches brushed the top and sides of the truck, making eerie screeching noises. Anyone attempting this sojourn at night would not easily find the way because of the lack of markings. Only the ruts gave a hint of which way to go, and in several places, there were ruts going in different directions. "Soon, Tejas, you will be with the rest of my guests," he softly whispered to the cat.

The trip took the better part of ten minutes of low gear on the rise to the top of the mountain. He was not in a hurry and did not want to make a lot of noise or make any mistakes that would draw attention. The kitten had fallen asleep, and his victim was not stirring. By now, the drug had worn off, but having less than half of her blood remaining kept her comatose. At last he reached the top, where there was a clearing and a large door leading into the oversized, two-car garage. He pulled up next to the keypad and entered the code to open the motorized left door. He drove the large truck in and pushed the buttons on a second keypad to close the door behind him.

As he got out of the pickup, he grabbed the bag of clothes and cradled the kitten in his arms like a sleeping baby. He walked to the south wall of the garage and unlocked a door leading into the hallway. He walked down to the end of the hallway and unlocked the door to the butcher shop. Lights turned on automatically as they did in the garage and hallways. Several drains in the tiled floor looked like gaping mouths with steel cobwebs ready to accept whatever they were fed. Next to the incinerator, there were a litter box and a small pet's bed. He placed the kitten in the bed, the clothes next to the incinerator, and returned to the garage for his other possession.

Grabbing the girl gingerly, he lifted her onto his back for the return to the butcher shop. He laid her on the cold slab of the large table, and he thought he felt her shiver. She seemed to shiver again as he removed her panties and tied her limbs to the table legs. It was almost time to begin, and he was getting anxious. He did not want to go into the main house just yet. He would not be able to restrain himself from greeting the rest of his guests and introducing Tejas to them. Doing so would take time and delay him from completing the task at hand. Anything could happen at this critical time. Once when he delayed too long, one of his victims woke up briefly to stare directly at him. This scared the hell out of him, and he had to choke her, which was easy because of her weakened condition, but experience is one way to learn, especially in an area with no written instructions.

Everything he needed was placed on the table which, he learned from experience, made the most efficient use of his time. He inserted a needle and tube into Ali's arm and proceeded to drain the rest of her blood into a plastic container on the floor. As the last of her life was drained from her body, she started to twitch. Her twitching caused him to remember the Philippine nuns in Catholic school.

On Saturdays, he cut the grass at the church. One Saturday, he was going to the storage shed to get a can of gasoline for the mower. While in the shed, he heard the nuns in the yard of the adjacent convent. He could see them through a crack in the wooden shed. They were holding a chicken down on a block of wood. Slowly they cut the chicken's throat, bleeding it to death. The chicken's muscles were tensing and quivering in a death dance. He found out later that bleeding the chicken was part of the ritual to make chicken adobo, a favorite Philippine grilled dish.

When death came to Ali, it occurred just like the chicken.

31

The technical term was exsanguination, or bleeding to death. He now had to act quickly so there would be little chance for spoilage. The fifty-five-degree temperature of the butcher shop helped. Draining the blood, in addition to causing death, helped to minimize the mess that would come shortly.

When he was certain she was dead and blood had quit draining, he donned the butcher's apron and latex gloves from a drawer in the butcher table. On his left hand he placed a fisherman's glove made of steel mesh. If the knife slipped, it would not cut his holding hand. He picked up a very sharp butcher knife from the table and proceeded to cut the carcass from the breastbone to the anus. The kitten was moving about now, checking out her new surroundings and, no doubt, smelling the blood and other odors which butchering produces.

While removing all the entrails carefully so as not to release any of the contents of the intestines, he softly sang an old Buddy Holly song, "Peggy Sue." The intestines were placed in a large pan to be loaded into the incinerator at the far corner of the butcher shop chamber. The liver, kidneys, and other organ meat, except for the heart, were placed on butcher's paper, removed from the large roll at the end of the table and wrapped and placed in the large chill box. The heart was set on the table by itself. She was no longer a being, but only a thing to be disassembled.

He skillfully cut at each joint while the kitten moved about the shop, checking every corner and batting at any loose object. All the joints were cut free in less than thirty minutes. Some were set inside the chill box, but the arms and legs were left out. The head was placed beside the intestines in the pan. He carried the pan to the incinerator and placed the contents into the firebox. After the door was closed, he pushed the button starting the fire and exhaust fans. Soon there would be nothing but ashes, which would be sifted through to remove any fillings, teeth, or other objects not burnable.

Returning to the table, he took the limbs and placed them in the freezer. These were easier to cut on the band saw when slightly frozen. The torso was to be cut into small portions before freezing, so he set about this task. He made rump roast, leg of Ali, ribs, and shoulder packages. The fingers and toes were separated and placed in special packages to be used as "finger

32

food." These he liked to cook Buffalo-wings-style and keep for snacks while watching movies or while driving.

Having attended to all of the parts fit for human consumption, he now picked up the heart and set it on a plate. This he lowered to the floor and immediately got the kitten's attention. The kitten approached the still warm heart and not having eaten much all day, started to feast. It was too large an object for the kitten to consume at once, so she pulled at the meat and held the rest of it back with her small claws. Making a crunching sound, the kitten tore small pieces from the organ. Pieces small enough so that it could chew and swallow.

Soon the kitten was sated. He picked it up and held her high in the air changing its name to the name of the victim as he had done so many times before. It was like a scene from Alex Haley's book *Roots* when Kinta Kunte's father held him up in the air to be named. When he set the kitten down, the new Ali just purred and cleaned her paws and face. "Ali, how do you like your new name?" he asked. A muddled mew was the response. Later, he would stamp the name, date, and the state on a tag to be placed on a collar and then around the kitten. He needed a way to remember all his "guests'" names. He placed the kitten back in the bed and removed the remaining pieces of the ripped heart from the dish and placed it back with the other organs. He then ground them into one pile and set them in a large bowl.

By now the arms and legs of the victim would be partially frozen. He removed them from the freezer and, using the band saw, cut them into one-inch slices. He set all but two of the pieces back on the paper, wrapped them, dated the package, and returned them to the freezer. All of the cutting done, he washed down all the equipment with the hose and a mild bleach solution. The bleach erased the blood traces, so if the police ever got this far and tried to use the blood-illuminating chemical Luminall, nothing would be seen. He took off the apron and the latex gloves and placed them next to the bag of clothes. Tomorrow they too would be incinerated.

Done processing the body, he picked up the kitten, the two arm slices, and the ground organs and walked down the corridor to the main part of the mansion. Lights turned off behind him and on in front of him as he walked along. At the end of the tun-

33

nel, was another keypad, on which he entered the code, which opened the door to the house. Immediately, there was a din of meowing as his many guests came to greet him. He placed the newly named Ali on the floor so they could get used to her, and next to her, he placed the organ meat. The cats immediately began to consume the meat and soon there would be nothing left of the parts of the woman that had once been so vital to keeping her alive.

He left all his guests alone and went to the kitchen-dining area of the house. It was midmorning now, and the automatic blinds had opened, letting in the sun to passively warm the house. Everything in the house was controlled by the computer, safely humming away in the room below the kitchen.

"CD on," he said, and immediately, the computer mapped his voice, determined it was a valid command coming from the right set of programmed vocal chords, and turned on the audio CD player.

"Frank Zappa, random, all." The computer now instructed the 200 CD jukebox to randomly play all the CDs matching the criteria stated.

He went to the gourmet kitchen, set the arm slices on the counter next to the gas burners, and took down a non-stick Scan-pan skillet from its rack over the range top. He placed the skillet on one of the burners and turned on the gas. There was a crack, crack, crack sound as the automatic lighter started the flame. He took a package of bagels and some butter out of the freezer, cut off a piece of the butter, and placed it in the skillet to melt. He then took two bagels out of the package, placed them in the microwave, set it on thirty seconds, and put the rest back in the freezer. By now the butter had melted, so he clarified it before placing the two arm slices into the skillet.

The microwave turned off, and he took the bagels out, opened them, and placed them in the toaster. He was very hungry from the long drive and the night's work. He salted and peppered both sides of the meat slices, and they sizzled, cooking quickly. When no more blood bled through, he removed the meat and placed it on the butcher block. He pushed the arm of the toaster down to start the bagels. He had done this countless times before and had the timing down to the second. He took a sharp knife and neatly trimmed the bones out of the center of the slices so what remained on the block was a piece of meat the size of the bagels with a neat hole in the center.

The toaster popped up as he finished. He placed the meat on the bagels. No other items would accompany these bagel sandwiches. He preferred his first meal of the victim to be pure so that he could taste and savor every bite. He crossed the room to the open area facing south on a magnificent view of Vermont and sat in the Lazy Boy recliner. He knew he soon would be covered in cats and sound asleep. He slowly devoured the two sandwiches, enjoying the flavors of his latest victim. Slowly, one by one several of the cats found him and leapt up on his lap to jostle for a comfortable place to rest. Many of them were still cleaning their paws and faces.

No longer hungry, he let his exhausted mind and body drift into a warm and relaxing state, knowing he was safely at home and in the company of his guests. They were glad to see him once again. He was their provider, and they were loyal to him. If it were not for him, they would still be prowling the streets or worse, the ashes in some shelter's incinerator.

He smiled as he listened to the Frank Zappa music. He grew more tired as the songs progressed and then he slept, they slept, Both Ali's slept, one peacefully.

He dreamt.

Four

He dreamt of his childhood and some of his earliest beginnings. Of his paternal grandmother, who raised him, and of his sisters, who were raised by an aunt, his mother's sister. His grandmother loved him as she did her son, who she said looked like him when he was a boy. His father was killed in an industrial accident and his mother went insane soon after. Wards of the state, he and his siblings were separated because neither the aunt nor the grandmother could afford to raise them together.

He was a good student, not excellent, but he studied hard and got average grades. He was not a very popular boy. His grandmother could not afford a lot of clothes for him, since she was living on her dead husband's pension from the steel factory and Social Security survivor's benefits. His grandfather got emphysema from inhaling steel mill by-products and welding fumes in an era when there was no OSHA laws to help the workers. Grandpa died from lung cancer shortly after he retired.

He was not popular with the girls in the school and therefore became shy and introverted. His grandmother tried to make him more popular by baking cookies and sweets for all the occasions in the school, such as Valentine's Day, George Washington's birthday, and other causes for celebration. This did not work and actually made him withdraw even further. On Valentine's Day, his grade school class exchanged cards using names drawn from a hat. It was the teacher's way of ensuring all the children, not just the popular ones, got a card. He was ecstatic when he drew the name of the prettiest girl in the class and she his. He spent several hours making a card, the best card he could, for he thought this may be a chance to befriend another person and one of the opposite sex. Although his sexuality was just developing, he sensed this was an important event in his life.

Valentine's Day came, and they exchanged cards. He read

36

the front of the card, which had hearts and the usual blurb about being a Valentine on this day, he then anxiously opened it up. Inside, where it had "will you be mine" was the single written exclamation "**YUCH!**" in bold letters. To make matters worse, she told him he had dirty ears when they exchanged the cards. She did not realize how devastating this could be to a boy who was already shy and starting to form opinions and mind sets about women. That night, the voice started.

The voice came at night as he lay in bed trying to get to sleep. Before the voice started, his ears started ringing and the room would retreat from him. Everything would appear as if looking through the wrong end of a pair of binoculars, like tunnel vision. It was a zooming-out motion, as if he left his body, as if he backed away from the bed into a corner of the room, as if he were a stranger to himself, and then the voice began. It was a loud voice, singular and commanding, heard over the ringing. Almost like the drill instructors he would meet in his later days in navy boot camp.

It was an evil voice. He remembered listening to hear if any other voice would come. Like the voices of good and evil, but there was no other voice, only the bad one. The voice wanted revenge. Revenge for the death of his father, the insanity that was his mother, and the Valentine's Day yuch card.

He was transferred to Catholic school when his grades started to falter. The voice made him withdraw. He did not get along with the other children. He was poor and different. When he did socialize, it was with the boys who were also different, the ones who were left back a grade or two. After a few whacks across the knuckles and other disciplinary tactics, his grades returned to the high averages, nothing to boast about, but they got him into college after four years in the Navy.

He even became an altar boy at the urging of his grandmother. He served mass on weekdays and occasionally on Sunday. He was an altar boy until the day it happened. After the last mass of the day, one Sunday, the priest had asked him to have lunch with him in the rectory. A quick call to his grandmother, and the okay was given. Sunday afternoon dinners were not a ritual at his grandmother's house like they were at so many of his friends' houses. Therefore, he did not mind eating with Father

Cunningham. The priest had more than lunch in mind though. After lunch, Father Cunningham invited him to watch the football game with him, which seemed like a better way to pass a rainy Sunday afternoon than listening to his grandmother snore in her easy chair. The sofa in the rectory was not very large so he had to sit close to the priest. He remembered Father Cunningham's hands. They were large hands, hairy, but a pale white, and immaculately manicured. He remembered those hands and how the left one looked resting on his own knee.

What was the father doing? Priests were celibate, he knew that, but wasn't exactly sure what it meant. In his small town, there were no lessons on stranger danger, no registered sex offenders, and no sex education classes. You learned about sex from your friends. Since he had no sexually active friends, he learned very little. Like most of the young boys, he played with himself, jacking off in bed at night. He came in handkerchiefs or Kleenexes. Tossing them in the laundry or the trash the next morning. Having a grown man place his hand on your knee and then slowly moving it up your leg toward your penis was a shock, especially if that man was the priest you assisted at mass two hours ago. When the priest started to stroke him through his pants, he stared straight ahead at the football game, not hearing a word. The ringing began and the tunnel vision returned. The TV got small and distant as the voice came to him and told him this was wrong. "This just isn't something two people of the same sex do to each other unless they are queers," the voice said. "Is that what you are, a queer? A goddamn, fucking queer?" He had heard the word before and knew it was not good to be one.

"I gotta go home now," he told the priest.

"Why such a hurry?" asked the father.

"I forgot I have a test tomorrow and need to study" was the only response he could think of.

"You keep this between us," menaced the priest.

"No fucking shit" said the voice as the TV returned to normal. He got up and left, remembering the experience for eternity. That memory shaped him for life. He looked at sex with a distorted view, as if through the warped mirrors of a carnival fun house.

His sexual experiences after that consisted of whores at some of the ports his navy ship pulled into. It was not a satisfactory experience. Something was lacking. The voice told him to do in the whores, but he did not. The voice got louder on the nights he returned from drinking and whoring, castigating him for allowing the bitches to live. After awhile, he learned to ignore the voice. He also quit whoring around, since they did nothing for him.

Tossing and turning in his sleep, he continued to dream. It was like this after every one of his trips so far. In his dreams, he relived his past, hoping that there would be a different outcome, but the dreams were always the same, and the present never changed.

Five

He awoke. He walked to the window and looked out at the last bits of foliage clinging to the oak trees on the side of the mountain and at the hills across the valley. It was early November and the start of hunting season. Hunting defenseless animals was not his bag, so to speak, but he liked the camaraderie of the fellow hunters, the clean, fresh autumn air, and the exercise of the hunt. He shot a few deer on the past hunts; however, he generally aimed low so as to scare away the prey. He accepted the ridicule for his poor aim and put on a disappointment act to let the others believe he really wanted to slay Bambi's mother or father. Hunting was not wrong; it was just not for him, especially having just returned from a more successful hunt. Besides, the hunting show he put on was to justify the butcher shop.

His guests were stirring throughout the house as they always did. He looked for the newest member of the pride, found her, picked her up to cuddle her. "My sweet Ali, how are you adapting to your new environment? Have you met all your sisters, found the food and litterbox?" The kitten mewed contentedly as he scratched her jaw. She began to purr loudly. He carried her into the kitchen, opened the refrigerator and gave her some liver left from the night before. He went to the butcher shop, opened the incinerator, and shoveled out Ali's ashes. He tossed in the bike and butcher clothes and started the incinerator. On sifting through the ashes, he found nothing had survived the intense heat. He took the ashes to the garage and placed them with the fireplace ashes to be tossed in the woods.

When he returned to the living room, the phone started to ring. He let it ring one more time to check the caller ID. It was one of his hunting buddies, Wayne.

"Know what day this is?" Wayne asked, when the phone was picked up, not even allowing for the obligatory hello. Wayne knew that if the phone was picked up before the fourth ring, he was home and willing to talk.

"Whatever the day, it's very fucking early in the morning, ass wipe," he responded.

"Yeah, and like you forgot about huntin' season and all those fat-assed bucks out there waitin' to taste lead?" Wayne said.

"Somehow, I knew one of you nature lovers would remind me. I got in late last night, but I got enough sleep to beat your sorry ass in the hunt," he said.

"Yeah, well what time are you gonna pick us up so we can be the first on our block to eat fresh venison? Bill and I are ready," said Wayne.

"How about within the hour. I have to shit, shower, and shave. Also have to feed my pussies and get the Humvee out and warmed up," he said.

"Okay, you sorry-assed som-a-bitch. Beside, what choice do we have, since you have the only vehicle that can get us where the big ones hole up. See you when ya get here," said Wayne.

He hung up the phone and headed to the master bedroom to complete the three "S's." On lathering up in the shower, he slowly caressed his penis until it was hard and upright. He stroked himself slowly, and at the moment he was ready to cum, he squeezed his sphincter muscle as tight as he could to feel both pain and pleasure at the same time. He often did this. It kept him tight in the groin, and the act of jacking off kept his prostate small. If you don't use it, you lose it, as the old adage goes.

Completing the morning routine in less than twenty minutes, he was ready to get some breakfast. A bagel sandwich would do nicely. This time he added an omelet to the meat he fried. *This will get me through the morning*, he thought. Wayne and Bill were always good for the beer and sandwiches for the remainder of the day. He poured some decaf coffee he had set up the night before to automatically come on at 6:00. He added some to the thermos without anything else. "I like my coffee like I like my women." he used to say in the navy, "black and nasty." Well, now there was some truth to that, since he did like the dark meat every once in a while. It went well with rye bagels and a slice of jalapeno cheese. He took the remaining organ meat out and put it on the floor for the cats.

After grabbing his weapon on the way out the door, he said "Set alarm," giving him forty-five seconds to get in the Hummer and exit the garage. The Hummer started with a roar, the garage door opened, and he left the security of his mansion to go on the obligatory hunt.

The air was cold on the mountaintop, but not freezing. Not yet anyway. Winter was not that far off, and he needed to prepare soon for the coldness of it and the sometime isolation. The worst part was in late December until late February. He would have no problems plowing his way up and down the mountain with the Hummer. It was a monster vehicle for a monster winter. He was often called on by his neighbors in the valley to help them get their cars out of some deep drifts. He was glad to oblige. Must be a good neighbor in this part of the world.

Letting the Hummer crawl down the mountain at its own first-gear pace, he was on the road in about ten minutes. Wayne's house was about ten miles away, and he would make it just within the hour he promised. Wayne's wife, Lulu, was always glad to see him and constantly tried to "fix him up" with one of her friends, relatives, and anyone else she knew. Like nature abhorring a vacuum, married women did not think it natural for a man to be without a mate, suitable or not, especially a man with sooooo much money.

The problem with Lulu's acquaintances and most of the other women in the area was that they did not make very good intellectual partners. If he was interested in marriage (he was not), he would look elsewhere, thank you very much. Besides, marriage would really cramp his style. Finding a woman who likes cats, especially forty-nine of them, if he made it that far, would really be tough. Oh, well, a bachelor-for-life was his goal.

He pulled into Wayne's poor excuse for a driveway. Almost all driveways in Vermont were of the rocky road variety. *We ain't talkin' about smooth as ice cream either,* he thought, but Wayne's was in an especially sorry state. Wayne bounded out the door, all 250 pounds of him, with Bill, his opposite. They looked like Laurel and Hardy, except for Wayne's large red beard. Bill was clean-shaven, but chewed tobacco, causing him to have a trickle of brown saliva flowing down one side of his mouth or the other. Lulu waved enthusiastically from the door of the double-wide, no doubt thinking of how he would look next to one of her bovine buddies waddling down the aisle after getting hitched. It looked like Lulu was putting on her winter weight, which somehow never seemed to melt away with the winter snow. As Wayne was quick to say, she kept him warm on a cold winter's night, and it was a new wrinkle every time they made love.

Wayne and Bill both had more sense than they had teeth. The poor dental care in Vermont used to bother him until he figured out that there was no fluoridation of the town water supplies and well water did not have any natural fluoridation, as in some other parts of the country. Also, dental care was expensive and not a priority for poor people in rural Vermont. Hunting dogs received better attention than the family; therefore, most smiles in these parts were toothless.

Wayne got to the door before Bill and moved his great bulk into the passenger's side. Bill got in the back, carrying both their rifles. The Hummer did not even move an inch either way with the two of them on board. Wayne waved to his "honey" as they pulled away and turned to his left.

"How's your love life, you rich fart?" he said.

I guess small talk was the order of the day.

"I'm handling my love life quite well, you piece of shit, and is the old lady still pregnant and barefoot, dumbass?" he said, hoping they would change the subject. "And how you doin', Bill?"

"I'm doin' it," Bill said.

Bill was not as smart as Wayne, which meant the two of them couldn't discuss much other than football or hunting. This was all right, since in the woods, you didn't talk much anyway. However, getting there was going to be an intellectually challenging change of pace.

"Catch me up on the latest," he said, as he steered the Hummer back onto the highway and headed south.

"Well," Wayne started, "for one thing, you're headed in the wrong direction. We staked out a place up in the Northern Kingdom, where there are some eight pointers. So get this piece of military crap turned around."

"Yeah, eight pointers," echoed Bill.

Oh, deliver me from deliverance, he thought, as he made a U turn, eating six feet on either side of the road with the Hummer's large mud tires. Soon it would be time to put on the snow tires with metal studs so he could go anywhere in ice or snow.

"Ooowee!" hollered Bill. "It sure is fun to ride in a $50,000 Jeep!"

"A hunerd thousand" corrected Wayne. "Hell, the tires on this piece a shit cost more than the rusted-out old truck you own. Hey, good buddy, Lulu's niece is coming to visit for a few days. She is tryin' to forget her daughter, which turned up missin' last year."

"How can she turn up if she was missin'?" intoned a serious-minded Bill.

"Shut the fuck up, numb nuts!" countered Wayne. "I was talkin', so quit showin' us how stupid you can be. As I was sayin', she is comin' for a visit over Thanksgivin' an don't know nobody up here. She is kinda depressed over her daughter's disappearance and talks about it all the time. She needs somebody to take her mind off of it and show her a good time. Naturally you came to mind, since you are the only single guy in these parts worth a shit, so how about it? It would make the ol' lady happy?"

"What is her marital status?" he asked. "I don't mess around with married women. I have some morals even though most people here don't think so. Also, what does she look like? I don't want to have to roll her in flour and look for the wet spot if ya know what I mean."

This brought a laugh from both Wayne and Bill.

"She's been divorced for 'bout twenty years, and she ain't fat," answered Wayne. "As a matter of fact, she is downright skinny. She is kinda good lookin' for her age, too. Before you ask, she is in her mid-forties, is short, and has big titties. I can't help starin' at 'em, which gets the ol' lady pissed. Anything else you want to know, you will just have to meet her and ask her yourself."

"Where is she from?" he asked.

"She can tell you that and all 'bout her daughter when you come to dinner on Thanksgivin'. So how about it?"

"I'll think it over. It beats sittin' at home and beatin' my meat." This brought another howl from the peanut gallery. Merging on to I-91 at Norwich, he asked, "What kinda music do you want to hear? I'm tired of listenin' to you two anyway, and we got at least another hour to go."

"How 'bout some C&W or some Blue Grass?" asked Bill.

"Country it is," he replied. He picked up the remote for his multiple CD/MP3 player, pushed the buttons for George Strait's "Chill of an Early Fall" album, and pushed random. "Milk Cow Blues" started playing over the Bose speaker system. This satisfied his companions, so he could ride the rest of the way in peace. He really did not mind their company, but he liked to have some time to reflect about his latest adventure and plan the next. Winter was always a good time to get out of Vermont, at least for awhile. Besides, he had twenty-five more states to add to his magnetic map he kept in the fifth wheel. He wasn't going to use Hawaii.

The Hummer roared up I-91 toward the Northern Kingdom. For an expensive vehicle, it was noisy at high speeds. It wasn't meant to be comfortable, just to go anywhere, and this was a good state to do that. Forty-five minutes later, they got off the interstate at Newport and headed east. He did not know this part of Vermont, but Bill did, having hunted here many times. The area was filled with lakes and, of course, lots of trees. An excellent place to hunt.

Bill guided him up dirt roads and logging trails. He kept an eye on the GPS system, which pinpointed them on the map he loaded from the CD-ROM on his main computer. There would be no problem getting back, even at night, without any help from Bill.

At last they reached a point where even the Hummer could not proceed. The road ended, and there were trees no further than three or four feet apart. Some of the larger pine trees had low branches that touched the other trees. It was time to hunt.

"Let's go!" said Bill.

They stepped out of the Hummer and retrieved their rifles from the back seat. Not talking now was the order of business. It was extremely quiet in the woods, and deer had very good hearing. Bill led the way, followed by Wayne. He followed them both. They skirted the "no hunting" signs posted on the trees. Recently there were a lot of people in Vermont posting their property to prohibit hunting. This usually did not stop the hunting, especially with this group. They had no intention of reporting their kills. If they got caught, he would simply pay the fines for all of them. To lessen the chance of getting stopped on the highway, they would change out of their camouflage suits and hide the deer in the back of the Hummer. They would then return to his house, where they would butcher their kill and get rid of the evidence.

"I'm going to set up over there next to that old maple stump," he whispered.

"Good," whispered back Wayne. "Bill and I are going to go a little further on. We'll pick you up on the way back."

He went over to the stump and sat down, leaning his back against it. He had no intention of shooting a deer today. He really did not like to kill an innocent animal. He was an excellent shot and could, however, hit anything he aimed at. He listened to the sounds of nature. The wind was gently rustling what few leaves remained on the trees and whispered through the tops of the pines. There were no branches at the bottom of the trees except for the dead limbs of the many pine trees. A lack of sunlight at the floor of the forest meant that all the trees had to shoot straight up to survive. As a result, there were a lot of trees, but they were skinny and tall with all their vegetation at the top of the forest. Someone had cut down the large maple whose stump he rested against. Probably for its lumber as furniture, or just for firewood. It was a large stump about five feet in diameter. With his camouflage hunting gear, he was hidden on all but one side.

He reminisced about the first time he went hunting, at age eight, with his uncle. His uncle was one of the earliest male role models he had. A piss poor role model at that, he found out later, after his uncle and mother's sister divorced because the bastard would come home drunk and beat her. His uncle used to hunt rabbits, and this time, decided to take him along. There was another man with them, and it was the first time he heard an adult say fuck, only they covered up with "fix" as in "...well, fuck her, I mean I'll fix her." They had a hunting dog that had to ride in the trunk of the car. They said it was better for the dog, since he was bred for hunting, and riding in the front with his owner would ruin him. When they opened the trunk to let him out, there was a cut on the dog's nose from being bounced all over in the back.

It was a good day to hunt, unless you were one of the three rabbits they shot. He observed that it wasn't much work, since the dog found the rabbits and then ran them around in a circle until they got close enough to shoot. He didn't have a gun, but he liked the fresh air and the way things smelled and felt in the woods. He observed with great curiosity what happened after the rabbit was shot. The way the dead rabbit looked. The way the chest and stomach were cut. The way the rabbit was swung between the legs to remove the innards. Most boys his age would have winced a bit, but he did not. Later, when, eating the rabbit, he wondered if it was all worth it. The meat was tough and had buckshot imbedded in it. Besides, there wasn't much meat there anyway.

Still thinking of that first hunt, he nodded off and woke about twenty minutes later. His senses were alert almost instantly, a sign that there was something threatening near by. The hair on the back of his neck bristled. He did not move, breathing very deliberately, not moving any other muscles. His gun lay across his lap with his knees drawn up. He had his right hand on the breech. He carefully moved his left hand to the barrel so that he could swing the weapon if it were necessary. From the right, he sensed, more than heard, a faint rustling. Turning his head ever so slowly, he saw a movement. The rifle would have to be swung around if needed, and he was prepared to do that. Then he saw what had caused his concern.

It was one of the largest bobcats he had ever seen. Or perhaps it was so close, it only looked large. The cat was advancing, not on him, but on an unsuspecting turkey not twenty feet away. The turkey would live perhaps until hunting season in the spring, for, as the cat moved fully into view of him, it too sensed danger. It was not necessary to fear him, because he would never hunt a cat, no matter what species. The cat must have sensed this, for as it turned its head and saw him, it did not flee. Their eyes locked onto each other for what seemed an eternity, both taking in the encounter as a rare and exciting event. Both were breathing very slowly, both staring into each other's soul, both not moving, both in wonderment of the other.

Then, as quietly as it came, the large cat moved backwards, forgetting the turkey, which by now was also moving away. When the cat was out of sight behind the stump, he slowly got to his feet to see where it was. It was gone. He would never see it again, but would remember this encounter forever. The turkey now noticed the hunter and took flight, landing on the top of a tree forty feet in the air. It was impressive to see the large bird take flight and perch out of danger. He decided to move on now and stalk some other prey

He picked up Wayne and Bill's tracks with ease. They created large footprints and disturbed leaves as they went farther into the forest. He caught up to them in about five minutes, but they did not notice him, as was his desire. They were perched on hunter's stools, staring at a path that was obviously used by deer to go back and forth to wherever deer go when they are not sleeping. There was a pile of corn in the middle of the path, obviously placed there by Wayne. He probably placed feed there before to ensure the deer would come by and be easy to kill.

He flanked them, being as quiet as the cat he encountered. He made a wide circle, knowing they would not move from their chairs. He crossed the deer path and was opposite them 180 degrees from his previous position. They still did not see him. He got down on one knee and lifted his rifle to his shoulder. He drew a bead on both men, one at a time, and made a soft click-click sound with his tongue. *You've both been shot*, he thought to himself, *Now lay down and bleed to death, as you would have the deer do.*

Just then an eight-point buck strode cautiously down the trail. He must have caught the scent of the men, but he was, at the same time, hungry. Obviously, he did not sense the danger as he approached the corn. Behind him in the distance were four does waiting for the buck to advance before they followed. Wayne noticed the buck before Bill and signaled to him. Bill saw the buck and then noticed the does further down the trail. Both took aim, Wayne on the buck, Bill on one of the does. As the buck bent down to eat the corn, two shots rang out. The buck dropped almost where he had his mouth eating the corn, and one of the does lurched back and started to run. She was fatally hit, but still had the will to live. She would soon bleed to death, leaving a trail of blood the hunters would follow to where she lay. The other does took off, running in all directions with Wayne firing at them unsuccessfully.

Wayne checked his kill and was satisfied it was not going to jump up and run away. The two of them then went after the doe, following the blood trail into the woods.

He approached the buck and said what amounted to a little prayer, thanking the buck for giving up its life for food. It seemed the buck gave its last breath in answer; however, he was sure it was killed almost instantly when the bullet struck its heart.

He went back down the trail toward the stump, turned around, and retraced the trail back to where the boys had been sitting. They were returning from the woods, dragging the doe by the hind legs.

"I heard the shots and decided to see if you two had any luck or had just stumbled over a log and shot each other by accident," he said.

"We got ours for the day," Wayne answered.

"Where's the other one?" he asked, pretending not to see the buck.

"Over there," Bill answered. "Wayne dropped him where he was shot. Pretty good shootin' wouldn't ya say?"

Not from the way you had set him up with the corn, he thought.

"Boy, I'll say. Let's get them gutted and back to the Hummer so we can butcher them at my place before the warden finds out."

They then field-dressed the deer and, tying them to poles, carried them back to the Hummer. He in the middle, shouldering the buck in front and the doe behind. Wayne led the way with Bill carrying the other end of the doe. After loading the deer in the back of the Hummer, hidden under a tarp, they took off their camouflages and climbed in for the trip back. They arrived at North Royalton at 7:45 P.M. Now the work began.

Six

The loaded Hummer traveled up the access road to the house with ease. After pushing the button on the automatic door opener, the three hunters and two unfortunate deer entered the garage. Bill was asleep, and Wayne was nodding his head in semiconsciousness. As the Hummer came to a stop and the garage door started its descent, Wayne became alert. "Are we there yet?" he asked.

"Yeah, sleeping beauty, we're here. Get Bill up, and let's get started with the task at hand."

Wayne jostled Bill, who looked at the two of them as if they were complete strangers. It reminded him of the old computer lingo of erase, cycle, store as Bill's small memory bank got ready for some new data to replace the old.

"Wha' Wha'," Bill said as he started to realize where he had been. The memory bank was too empty to realize where he was at present.

"Let's get them deer outta the back and onto the chopping block," Wayne said.

"Okay," was Bill's only response. The two of them stepped down from the Hummer and went to the back to unload the deer. He went to the entryway, which led to the tunnel and the butcher shop. Before opening the door, he told the computer to turn off the security and other defensive systems, barely audible to Bill and Wayne. The computer responded loud enough for Wayne to hear.

"Why do you need a security system way up here on the top of the mountain?" Bill reacted. "After all, this is Vermont, and no one locks up their house let alone has a security system."

"It's an old habit of mine, having lived in a large city, and I do take extended vacations. That's why," he shot back.

He went back to help the two as they struggled with the

first deer. The three of them made their way into the butcher shop and placed the first of the animals on the stainless steel table, which had seen action just yesterday. The second deer was no less ceremoniously dispatched onto the floor beside the table.

"Everyone in the village wondered why you had this installed in your mountaintop mansion. We still wonder why you went to all this expense for cuttin' up critters one or two times a year," Bill queried.

"Who says I only use it during one or two hunting seasons?" he responded. "Beside deer season, there is bobcat season, turkey season, and outta season."

This brought a hoot from Wayne and Bill as they went and got the knives for skinning the deer.

"You can't take these deer to someone else for cuttin' up. They're illegal as hell," he continued. "They haven't been tagged, and we poached them from posted property. That's why I have my own shop and the incinerator to get rid of the telltale remains. Also, I can afford it in my mansion as you call it. What else am I gonna spend my hard-earned winnings on, you nosey fuck, you?"

"That's why you need a wife to help you spend some of that money, you filthy rich bastard," Wayne responded. "Hell, you got too many toys for one man to enjoy. What you need is some-one to do your cuttin' in here as well as in bed."

"Yeah, you need a wife," intoned Bill.

"So how's about Thanksgiving dinner?" Wayne prodded. "I'm pretty sure this woman ain't had none in quite a while. She might be the one to clean out your pipes, and I don't mean the ones you put that funny weed in. Speakin' of which, you got any of that special stuff you got growin' in the back?"

"Of course," he said. "As soon as we get these two disposed of, maybe I'll share some of it with you." He didn't smoke very often, but after the day with these two, he felt the need to loosen up. Besides, the image of that big cat kept coming back, sending chills up and down his spine.

The three of them worked on the deer. Cutting up most animals was about the same. The only difference between deer and his victims was the skinning. After the meat was neatly packaged, the remaining carcass, skin, head, feet, and the unusable parts were placed in the incinerator and the mess all cleaned up. It was a shame to destroy the antlers from the buck. By the time they were finished, it was almost 9:00 at night. With all the deer blood they splashed around, he would dare any pathologists to find any DNA that was identifiable as human.

"Let's have some dinner and smoke some dope," he said. "Do you need to call your ol' lady to tell them you'll be late? That's something I don't have to worry about and don't want to. However, tell Lulu I'll be there for Thanksgiving since you won't leave me alone if I say no."

"No, she knows I'll be late," Wayne said. "Hell, we do this routine enough times a year for her to know we'll be back when we're back. Lulu also knows I'll be workin' on your visit for Thanksgiving, so she'll forgive me if I get back real late."

They all three trudged into the main part of the house after he insisted they remove their shoes. Wayne and Bill both did so, as if they were proud of the holes in their dirty-looking socks. He didn't understand why they could afford the best hunting dogs and keep them fed while they themselves go without. Oh, well, "the good lord will provide," as Wayne was apt to say. The dogs must have had a better lord than the humans.

They were greeted by the cats, which mewed, purred, and rubbed themselves against their pant legs. He knew Wayne and Bill only tolerated cats, but if they wanted his friendship, if you could call it that, then they must put up with his house guests. In the kitchen, he got out some real hamburger, frozen French fries, and some homemade brew for the two hunters.

"Here," he said to Wayne, "fry these burgers up while I go and get some weed.

"Bill, you're in charge of the fries, and don't burn my mansion down." He wasn't worried though. The vent hood extinguishing system would take care of any fires started on the stove.

He went up to the master bedroom and retrieved his pipe, some weed, and two ready-made joints for his companions. On returning, he handed the joints to the two short-order cooks and stuffed his pipe. He was a recreational smoker and saw no harm in marijuana when used responsibly by adults who could afford it. He grew his own out in the woods, monitored by the security system.

By the time the fries and burgers were done, they were feeling great and had the munchies. Apparently, so did the cats, which were on the tables and counters, looking for a handout. They had their own food, but they still liked people food, real or otherwise.

"How do you stand these cats?" asked Bill. "God, they're everywhere and then some. Look at here, there is hair in my burger."

"It ain't the first time you had a fur burger, then ain't it," stated Wayne, laughing at his own joke. It seemed funnier when you were high.

"Where'd you get 'em all?" Bill, ignoring the joke, continued.

"I like to feel that the cats are guests in my home," he explained. "I get one on each one of my trips and name them for the city I get them in or for one of the women I meet along the way. They remind me of the places I've visited. Does this woman I'm to meet on Thanksgiving like cats? Otherwise, I'll have to boff her at your house."

"I doubt you'll get to boff her at all. Though she needs it," responded Wayne. He tore off a piece of his burger and handed it to the closest cat. He nearly lost a finger as the declawed cat pulled his finger into its mouth to get the meat before one of the others got to it. "Damn, that hurt. Look, it drew blood."

"That's what you get for feeding a strange pussy," he responded. "Maybe you'll get cat-scratch fever. That's the bad news. The good news is you'll then be immune for life and can play with all the nasty pussy you want."

They all laughed as they finished their burgers, fries, and joints. "Well, I better get you two back to the trailers before you turn into pumpkin heads," he said. "I'll clean up the paper plates and plastic forks when I get back. The cats will clean the floor and anything else that got food dropped on it." As he said this, one of the cats was playing with the frayed edges of Wayne's left sock and licking his protruding toe. "It looks like you won't have to bathe that part of your body tonight. Just don't let your wife lick your toes or she'll know you had some strange pussy today."

They retraced the way back to the Hummer, picking up some of the deer meat on the way. Wayne and Bill would be able to feed their families for a month or two on the contents in the butcher paper. Upon them both offering him some of their bounty, he thought, *No thanks, I've got some "dear" meat of my own.*

"You two shot them, I didn't," he said. "But I'll keep the rest of your kill safe and sound for you in the freezer. If I get snowed in for a week or two, I'll take you up on your offer."

The trip back to Wayne's double-wide was quiet. They took the truck with Bill sitting in the back of the extended cab and Wayne in the front. Bill went to sleep almost immediately, probably from the three hamburgers he ate and the joint he smoked, but most likely from lack of brain-wave activity. Wayne began nodding off as soon as Merle Haggard started singing, "I think I'll just stay here and drink," from the CD of the same name. He was not feeling tired, although it was going on midnight when he got them back to Wayne's.

"Good night," Bill said, as grabbed his packages of meat and went to his car.

"You'll be okay?" he asked.

"Sure" was the reply and the last words anyone heard from Bill.

"Well, I'll see you on Thanksgiving, Wayne," he said.

"Yeah, see ya," said Wayne. "The wife will be thrilled that you are comin'. You know how she likes ya."

"Glad to help out, good buddy," he said, as they both watched Bill pull out onto the highway and head for home twenty miles down the road.

He backed out of the drive and headed in the opposite direction of Bill. He had gone about a quarter of a mile, when his ears started ringing. The tunnel vision returned. Suddenly everything in front of him got small. At the next driveway, he turned the truck around, turned off the headlights, and raced after Bill. "Get him," the voice said.

He caught up to Bill easily because Bill was driving very deliberately and slowly, conscious of his tired and inebriated state. He probably never noticed the black truck inching up from behind. The road went up and down hills winding around the small stream thirty feet below on the right.

Out of the black Dodge windshield, the view was distant, but he was only inches behind Bill's car. Bill was weaving and taking every turn too wide. On the next sharp turn to the left, the voice said, "now." All it took was a push from behind. Bill, his car, and his deer meat went over the side of the road, hit a rather large cottonwood tree, and almost immediately burst into flames. That was good, since all the evidence of poaching, drinking, and smoking would be lost in the incinerated mess.

As the view returned to normal size, he looked in the rearview mirror to catch a glimpse of the fiery mess that was Bill. Looping onto a dirt road he knew would take him back in the opposite direction toward his mansion, he smiled. "Well, that was fun," he said to the voice, but the voice was silent. Bill had no family, so only his friends would grieve. There would be no investigation, since it was apparent his undoing was his own fault. Of course, he would pay for Bill's funeral and burial, being such a good buddy and the only one Bill knew who could afford it. Such a good friend he was.

There was no religious service, since no one had ever seen Bill attend a church. Some of the people Bill worked with came to the funeral home as did Wayne, Lulu, and Lulu's sister Elsie. He paid the expenses and drove the Vietnam vet, Bill, to the VA cemetery in Montpelier in the back of the Hummer. Wayne and Lulu rode in the front. Bill would have wanted it that way. There was no chaplain to give Bill a religious sendoff, so he volunteered to say the last words. There were a few old soldiers there at the cemetery and the crew that would push the earth over Bill. It was a shame that all who would remember Bill was this small cadre of mourners. After today, no one would visit the small cross marking his grave, save the old soldiers placing flags every Memorial Day.

He stood in front of them all, before Bill was lowered, and said a poem:

This soldier who has no wife or kin,
Is laid to rest in the earth herein.
But he has blessed us here on earth,

With his laughter and his mirth.

So we bid farewell on this sorrow-filled day.
The angels will guide him, they know the way.
Through heaven's gate to the Promised Land.
Good-bye to you, Bill, our dearest friend.

They tried unsuccessfully to dry their eyes as the bugler played taps when the casket was lowered. Bill's flag was folded and given to Wayne. Returning to South Royalton in the Hummer, no one uttered a word. After he dropped Wayne and Lulu where they left their car at Elsie's, he went for a ride. He thought about all the bad he had done and wished it could all be reversed. He stopped at a pullout along the side of the road when the tunnel vision occurred and the voice started. "Don't get sentimental on me, asshole," the voice boomed out. "You've got work to do."

Seven

Dedra Mayfield did not remember much about her father. Her mother, Deanna, liked it that way because he was a drunk and a womanizer, leaving his wife and daughter alone many a night. Deanna divorced him when Dedra was four and moved to Florida when Deanna found a good-paying job there. Deanna did everything with Dedra, trying to make up for the father she didn't have. When Dedra was old enough, Deanna got them both roller blades, and they learned together. Deanna was there when Dedra played in her first soccer game. Deanna was there for Dedra's first softball game. It was no surprise that Dedra grew up liking sports. She biked, she ran, she played tennis.

Dedra did have faults though. Dedra, like her mother, was pretty, with a nice build. She inherited her blond hair from her father, but her almond-shaped face with turned-up button nose was all Deanna. She also inherited Deanna's breast size, which blossomed early. The boys buzzed around her like bees on the sweetest blossoms. Without a father figure to guide her, she ran off with older boys two summers in a row, but came back after they treated her badly. She received a strong lecture from Deanna, but shrugged it off. Like her mother, she was stubborn.

Deanna wanted Dedra to go to college. Dedra seemed to want that too, because she was always a good student. She studied hard, and in her senior year of high school, she was accepted at the University of Florida. Deanna had saved enough for the tuition supplemented by a partial soccer scholarship. It seemed Dedra was on her way to becoming a productive member of society. Except Dedra still had a fascination with older men. They seemed to understand better. She ogled after her college professors. She also got in the Internet chat rooms and was wooed by the older men that were looking for an opportunity to meet younger women. That is where she met her fate.

Deanna had left her daughter's room just as it was February 1996, almost two years now, when Dedra was reported missing. It had been a long, agonizing period of phone calls, conversations with Dedra's closest friends, and dead-end trips to places where she thought Dedra may have been. It was not the first time Dedra checked out; however, she would always return with a story to tell, an adventure, which brought a stern lecture of concern from Deanna. Even as she opened the door to Dedra's room, Deanna's heart sunk with the pain of losing her daughter. A pain no one could understand unless one had been there. She did not look forward to spending the upcoming holidays alone again, crying for the one she loved.

The room seemed dark and dank, although there was ample light coming in from the south window. The bed was still covered with the flowered bedspread Dedra's grandmother made for her when she started college three years ago. Other than the computer and the secretary's desk in the corner, the room was pretty much devoid of any other articles. The computer was retrieved from Dedra's dorm room after it was obvious she was not returning from the semester break. Dedra, was an outdoor type and most of her athletic gear was kept in the closet. Her bike and helmet also retrieved from her dorm room were kept in the garage.

Deanna had looked on the computer for notes, schedules, letters, or any other hints that would have indicated where her daughter had gone before she disappeared from the face of the earth. There were none, but recently, Deanna discovered chat rooms, which she noticed was where people could meet electronically. She discussed her daughter's disappearance with her newfound cyber buddies, many of whom were sympathetic and tried to help. One suggested she check for files that record chatroom conversations that her daughter might have used to save her most intimate conversations. So, she was turning on the computer and hoping that there may be some clue, some hope, some bit of information that might point her in the right direction.

She knew that if she did find a pointer, she would best do any follow-up on her own. Her experience in reporting Dedra's disappearance to the police was disappointing, especially with Dedra's past history. The police did not want the computer unless there was homicide to investigate. A missing adult without any evidence of a struggle or foul play did not warrant anything more than a filing of a missing person's report.

The computer hummed to life, taking its time. Two hundred megahertz was a fast machine in 1996, when it was purchased at the start of Dedra's sophomore year, but was painstakingly slow when compared to Deanna's newer gig. After the Windows-95 screen came on, she clicked on the Internet Explorer icon to get to the yahoo screen. The first thing she needed to find was what chat name or names her daughter was using. This was easy, since the programs in Dedra's computer remembered all the old names and passwords logging her in under Dedra's Yahoo. The computer may have been slow, but it did not forget easily. She found two names that Dedra might have used. One was "floridasunshine25" and the other was "orangejewce2." Apparently, there were other chatters with the same names but different numbers.

Next, she had to check the friends' list. This was not as easy. The list was long. Dedra must have been very popular in the chat rooms, but then so would any young woman with her personality and a desire for adventure bordering on danger.

She tried several times to locate files that may have yielded clues. Not having any success, she decided to call her next-door neighbor, Joe, who was somewhat of a nerd with computers. Joe had a daughter Dedra's age and was sympathetic to Deanna. He was also a bit of a letch, making it known that if there was anything Deanna, or Dee, as her friends called her, needed, he would be there to help. He emphasized "anything." The stigma of being a divorcee hung over Dee like perfume on a cheap date. Dedra and Joe's daughter grew up together, went to the same public schools, and dated some of the same boys. Their friendship waned when Dedra went to the University of Florida. Therefore, Joe's daughter knew nothing about Dedra's personal life after that.

Joe was home and came over ten minutes later. He smelled the perfume of loneliness even across the yard, although there was a serious tone in Dee's voice.

"Hi, Joe," she said as she opened the front door. "Thanks for coming over on such a short notice. I'm checking up on some new leads on Dedra."

"Glad to be of help," said Joe.

She showed him what she had done so far and told him what she was looking for.

"What next?" intoned Deanna.

"Let's do a search using all the names you just found," Joe said.

"Guide me, oh, omniscient one," Deanna said, but regretting saying that, since it could be interpreted that she wanted to play.

After loading up the search program, Joe and Deanna sat back and watched as the computer plodded through all the files and folders for matches to sunshine25 and orangejewce2, coming up with a dozen or so possibilities.

"Okay, let's open them and see what they can tell us. But first, let's save them on a disk. I don't trust this old machine," said Joe.

"That's one thing I can do on my own," Deanna said.

After saving the files, Deanna double-clicked on one of them, and a note pad immediately came to life displaying the contents. One by one, the contents of her daughter's chat room conversations came to life. They were long and hard to follow on the screen, so Joe suggested they print them out and look at them in hard copy. It was amazing the old black-ink only printer worked, but it was slow, spitting out the paper, sheet after sheet, at two pages per minute.

"Thanks, Joe. I can take over from here. Besides there is a ream of print outs here. Some of them may be private, so if you don't mind, I would like to look at them by myself."

Joe looked dejected as the perfume faded, but reluctantly headed out of the bedroom with Dee close behind.

"If there is anything else you want, anything, please don't hesitate to give me a call," Joe half-pleaded.

"Don't worry, you will be the first one I think of." She, again regretting saying something that might give him encouragement, but she would deal with that later if it ever came up.

As soon as Joe left, she went back to the bedroom and sprawled on Dedra's bed with the printouts. A soft billow of dust filled the air from the untouched bedspread. She vowed that soon she would get rid of all items in this room, Dedra or no Dedra.

Looking through sheet after sheet of chat room conversations, she came across one that looked worth analyzing. It must have been a private chat room, for there were only two identities involved in the conversation.

orangejewce2: hi
man_iac: hi, how are you today
orangejewce2: doin better after the test we had today
orangejewce2: where are u?
man_iac: in the sunshine state
man_iac: not too far from you
orangejewce2: oh, really!!!
orangejewce2: so what are you up to?
man_iac: about 6 inches goin on 8
man_iac: no, not really, gettin ready to ride
orangejewce2: Lol, your bike or something else???
man_iac: rotflol
man_iac: the bike of course. So when are we gonna ride?
orangejewce2: as soon as my mid terms are over
orangejewce2: and as soon as you give me some references
man_iac: I got your references hangin'
orangejewce2: Lol, that we will have to see
orangejewce2: the proof is in the puddin
man_iac: I don't do puddin darlin, I will do jello though
orangejewce2: why don't you check back with me next week
orangejewce2: mid terms will be over and we can get together
man_iac: ok, I have a great place we can ride
man_iac: I can rent a tandem if you don't think you can keep up with me
orangejewce2: can you keep up with me? After all you are an old fart
man_iac: don't worry, just bring those legs of yours
orangejewce2: they go where I go
man_iac: won't your boyfriend get jealous?
orangejewce2: we broke it off two days ago

orangejewce2: besides, I dig older men
man_iac: no problem here
man_iac: I'm about as old as it gets
man_iac: without going over the hill
man_iac: and did I mention that I
man_iac: am filthy rich
orangejewce2: many times, so why do you travel in
orangejewce2: what do you call it, a five wheeler?
man_iac: a fith wheel
man_iac: fifth
man_iac: spelling ain't so good today
orangejewce2: so why don't you travel in your own jet
orangejewce2: or fly first class everywhere??
man_iac: I don't like to fly
man_iac: I can go at my own pace
man_iac: I keep my bike with me
man_iac: and it is a bit more private
orangejewce2: so you can entertain
orangejewce2: all your lady friends
orangejewce2: wine and dine them
orangejewce2: between satin sheets
man_iac: believe it or not
man_iac: I ain't got nobody
orangejewce2: oh, poor baby
orangejewce2: and me ain't got nobody either
orangejewce2: sounds like we ought to put our nobodies
      together
man_iac: and see what pops up?????
orangejewce2: Lol, will it be 6 going on 9???
man_iac: maybe more for nobodies
orangejewce2: we'll see
orangejewce2: you don't waste any time
man_iac: old farts ain't got much time
orangejewce2: 39 ain't old
man_iac: you're only as old as she feels
orangejewce2: Lol, you're funny
orangejewce2: that's why I enjoy our little get togethers
orangejewce2: can't wait until I meet the man in person
orangejewce2: are you as good looking as the picture

orangejewce2: in your profile?

man_iac: better, and the body ain't bad either

orangejewce2: as I said before, we'll see

orangejewce2: u won't mind if I change my mind

man_iac: before or after seeing me

man_iac: in the raw

orangejewce2: Lol

orangejewce2: you are assuming something

orangejewce2: assume means making an ass out of u and me

orangejewce2: get it???

man_iac: I got it ass-u-me but did you know

man_iac: that assumption is the mother of all fuckups???

orangejewce2: Lol

orangejewce2: I got to go study for tomorrow's test

orangejewce2: english composition

orangejewce2: I want to be a great writer some day

man_iac: well, I can give you something to write about

man_iac: not home of course

man_iac: but some great experience and I do mean great

orangejewce2: Lol

orangejewce2: so, next Tuesday it is???

man_iac: to meet or what

orangejewce2: no

orangejewce2: to set up our rendevouz

orangejewce2: I don't know how to spell that word

man_iac: another great writer is born, its rendezvous

orangejewce2: Lol

man_iac: ok, next Tuesday, same place same time

man_iac: my heart will beat on

man_iac: and so will my . . .

orangejewce2: Lol

orangejewce2: do what you have to

orangejewce2: but at least think of me

man_iac: but of course, who else

orangejewce2: don't get numb riding that bike either

man_iac: don't worry, see ya

orangejewce2: bye

man_iac: bye

Dee took a deep breath. There was something here after all. She started leafing through the other printouts, hoping she would find the Tuesday chat session. Five pages down in the stack, she found it.

man_iac: hi, how did the exams go?
orangejewce2: hi, pretty good. I think I passed them all
man_iac: great, I remember the feeling well
man_iac: although it's been awhile
man_iac: not that it's been that long ago
orangejewce2: when do we ride
man_iac: what, no foreplay? Just ride me and get it over with?
orangejewce2: Lol you make me feel good
man_iac: you think that was good, just wait
orangejewce2: can't, when and where?
man_iac: can you meet me at the hawthorne state rail trail
orangejewce2: sure, I know where that is
orangejewce2: I've ridden it before
man_iac: me too, just the other day
orangejewce2: what do I need to bring?
man_iac: just your bike, your water, and your bod
man_iac: I will provide the entertainment
man_iac: unless you want to ride ahead of me
man_iac: then I will be the one entertained
orangejewce2: lol
orangejewce2: you didn't say when?
man_iac: tomorrow morning too soon?
orangejewce2: no, about 8
man_iac: 8 is great see ya
orangejewce2: see ya
man_iac: bye
orangejewce2: bye

She was shaking after reading this. "If I find this maniac, maybe this will be the missing piece," she said out loud. There were only two more chat sessions recorded. The last one made her head spin.

65

Fairhairedgal: hi
orangejewce2: hi I have some news
orangejewce2: I have a date tomorrow morning
Fairhairedgal: with the old man?
orangejewce2: yes, and he's not that old
orangejewce2: anyway, he's rich and not bad looking
Fairhairedgal: how do you know what he looks like
orangejewce2: he posted his picture in Yahoo
Fairhairedgal: and that is his real picture??
Fairhairedgal: please be careful
orangejewce2: I will
Fairhairedgal: where are you going with him, to a bingo parlor?
orangejewce2: lol don't be silly
orangejewce2: we are riding the rail trail
Fairhairedgal: and then??
orangejewce2: whatever, you know me
Fairhairedgal: yeah, miss danger herself
orangejewce2: you only live once. Besides, he is rich
Fairhairedgal: yeah, and I'm your fairy godmother
orangejewce2: I'll find out tomorrow
orangejewce2: if he's riding a cheap bike, that will tell me
Fairhairedgal: he could steal a bike
orangejewce2: gotta run, I'll tell you all about it tomorrow
orangejewce2: see ya
Fairhairedgal: later, girlfriend

She put down the printouts and went back to the computer. She logged on and went to Yahoo, did a search for man_iac, and waited for the results. There were no matches. She went to the chat rooms and did a search. Again nothing. What did she expect? If he was the one responsible for Dedra's disappearance and was smart, then he would have long ago deleted the name and his profile. *So close*, she thought.

She looked up the name of the Sergeant who filled out the missing person's report on Dedra. It was a long time ago, but she would let him know of the new evidence she found. She found his card still tacked to the corkboard magnet on the refrigerator. After dialing the number, she got through on the third ring.

"East precinct police station, Sergeant Messina speaking" was the response.

"Hi, this is Deanna Mayfield. May I please speak with Sergeant Howard?" Dee asked.

"Sergeant Howard is now Detective Howard. At least, he was when he transferred to Orlando in April. Can I help you?"

"Yes. Who has taken over his cases?" asked Dee. "My daughter was reported missing in February last year, and I may have some more information about her."

"Ms. Mayfield, let me have the missing person's name and your phone number, and I will have the officer who took over for that case call you back," said Sergeant Howard.

"Deanna Mayfield and my number is 555-1233."

"Thank you, ma'am. Someone will get back to you shortly."

"Thank you, officer," Dee said, pushing the off button on the wireless phone.

No sooner had the phone been turned off and set down on the kitchen table, it rang. She let the answering machine pick it up. It was her aunt Lulu in Vermont. Carrying the phone, she walked to the living room debating whether or not to interrupt the machine. Lulu was longwinded and would make sure she got to the end of the tape before she hung up. Saying "what the hell" to herself, she picked up the cordless, pushed the receive button and interrupted Lulu's message.

"Lulu, hi. It's me."

"Hi, Dee," Lulu said using Deanna's nickname. "How have you been? We haven't heard from you in quite a while. Is the pain any less?" referring to Dee's loss.

"I'm about the same, still hurting, chasing leads, and hoping Dedra will call any day telling me she's been on the adventure of her life" was the response. "How have you and Wayne been?"

"Poor but happy," Lulu answered, recognizing her own unfortunate position in life. "We get by and measure our joy in our children." Lulu regretted the comment as soon as it came out. "I'm sorry, Dee, I didn't mean to bring up that subject. Me and my diarrhea of the mouth."

"Don't worry, Lulu. I live with the thought daily. I think the crying is finally tapering off."

"Why don't you think about what we discussed last month. About coming to Vermont for one of the holidays. Thanksgiving would be good. It's not too cold then, and there usually isn't any snow to worry about. We were able to get that rich friend of Wayne's to come over, too. I think the two of you would be good together."

Lulu was usually very insistent, and Dee was about ready to get away from her torment, this house, and the memories. At least for a little while.

"Why don't I give you a tentative yes for now, and I'll let you know if I later change my mind. I'll call the weekend before Thanksgiving and let you know my schedule."

"That's great," responded Lulu. "I can't wait to tell Wayne. And I'll put some pressure on that rich bastard, I mean bachelor. He is quite a catch and a looker to boot."

"If you have to twist his arm, it probably isn't worth it. If I come, it won't be because he is or isn't there. Lulu, I'm waiting on another phone call, so I'll need to call you back later. I'm chasing another lead on Dedra. You give my love to Wayne and the kids, and with any luck, I'll see you on Thanksgiving."

"You take care, and please, make every effort to get here." With that, Lulu hung up and Dee placed the receiver back on the coffee table.

She went to the calendar and noticed that it was three weeks until Thanksgiving. She thought that maybe a little tender love from the right man might help her through the holidays. She hadn't been with a man for almost three years. She looked out the window. The weather was nice and she hadn't had her run for the day. *Maybe I'll take Dedra's bike out for a spin instead of jogging,* she thought. *I might even meet mister Man_iac along the way. Every man on a bike will be a suspect now.*

Eight

It was Thanksgiving morning. He arrived at Wayne's early, before the women were up. Wayne was at the back of the house, feeding the hunting dog. When he got out of his truck, Wayne led him into the trailer. At the kitchen table, Wayne offered him a beer.

"A bit early to start drinkin'," he said, taking the beer.

"I didn't have to twist your arm," Wayne shot back.

They talked about the last hunting trip the day of the accident. They also discussed Bill's funeral and the tragic end to their friend's life.

"I really miss Bill. He was gonna be here today. He really liked to watch the 'boys' play football, especially their traditional Thanksgiving Day game," said Wayne, referring to the Dallas Cowboy's football team. "Thanks for coming over early so we could talk."

"No problem, Wayne," he said. "I really miss him, too. Even though he wasn't too bright, he was funny at times."

"Yeah, and the poem you said at the funeral made me start to cry," he responded. "Oh, well, let's get over that and think about the future, especially today. The wife is really anxious for you to meet her niece, Deanna."

"Not to be nosey, but where in the hell did she sleep, what with the kids being here and all?" he asked.

"Oh, the kids stayed over at sis's house with her brood," Wayne said. "So Deanna slept in the kids' room. I think I hear one of them stirring now."

The toilet flushed and, a few seconds later, Lulu shuffled into the living area of the double-wide with her hair up in curlers, took one look at the two of them sitting at the table drinking beer, and shook her head.

"You two have got an early start on things, it looks like,"

Lulu said. "I guess you are anxious to meet Deanna. She got here late last night after driving up from Boston. I better go warn her not to come straight out but to pretty herself up first. Maybe you two could get the bird out of the fridge and get it stuffed. That is if you are not too drunk to find the right end of the bird."

"Good mornin' to you too, darlin'," Wayne said. "You look so purdy this mornin' with your best wig on and all that makeup."

"Bite me!" She shot back. And with that, she got a cup of coffee and went back to the bedroom. She knocked on the kids' bedroom door, and they heard her tell Deanna to be fully clothed when she got up to go to the bathroom. They heard Deanna answer that she would.

"Let's see if we can get some pre-game football while we work on the turkey," Wayne said. "You ready for another brew yet? I intend to keep a buzz on all day, but not too high 'cause I want to observe the ol' lady work her magic on tryin' to get you and Dee together."

"I think I'll go slow," he said, "just in case Deanna turns out to be as good as you two have led me to believe. You called her Dee. Is that a name I can use too?"

"Call her Dee if you want. That's the nickname my wife uses. It's a lot easier to say when you're drunk," he said, as he opened another beer and went about the business of preparing the turkey.

"Wayne, where's your remote?" he asked. "Never mind, here it is under the paper." Turning on the TV, he started to channel search. One thing Wayne found money for was his satellite TV with all the sports channels. Surfing, he found the football pre-game show. He really did not care about football anymore. He used to be a big fan, but now he rarely watched a game unless it was with Wayne or in one of the bars he rarely went to while traveling. "You need any help gettin' stuffed over there? I mean the bird, not yourself."

"Funny, funny, funny asshole," Wayne responded. "I think I can do this without you holding my hand. You could take a piss for me."

"As long as I don't have to hold anything of yours," he said.

"Will you two quit talkin' filthy," said Lulu, as she returned

70

with her hair combed out and the housecoat replaced with over-sized jeans and an oversized T-shirt that read "I'm with stupid" over an arrow pointing to the left.

"I didn't know we were supposed to dress up for Thanksgiving," Wayne said. "Otherwise I would have worn my dress T-shirt."

"Is that the only one that doesn't mention bodily functions?" Lulu shot back.

"Will you two quit it for just one day," came a voice from the back of the double-wide. Footsteps were heard and then the bathroom door closed. Water ran in the shower.

"Try to be nice," Lulu said to Wayne. "She doesn't understand our bantering, and I want her to feel at home and try to forget Dedra has been missing for almost two years now."

"She needs to get over it," Wayne whispered. "What she needs now is a good roll in the hay with our friend over there."

"I heard that," he said. "How long would you look for one of your kids if they were missing, a week, a month, a year, two years. Even though I don't have any kids, I think that is one of the hardest issues to deal with. It's even worse than them dying, since at least you know where they are."

Both of them looked at him in surprise.

"We didn't know you were sentimental," Lulu said. "That reinforces that you are what she needs, like I thought all along. Now let's all be happy for today and just enjoy this Thanksgiving. Maybe next year, you and Dee will have us over to your place. You know, I ain't never been, and from what Wayne tells me, it's quite a layout, except for the cats."

"Love me, love my cats," he said.

The sound of the hair dryer replaced the sound of running water just as Wayne finished stuffing the bird. Lulu placed the bird in the oven and started figuring out how long it would take before it would be done.

"We should eat about four o'clock. Now get out of my kitchen so I can get the rest of the food together," Lulu insisted.

"Let's go out for a smoke," Wayne said. Wayne didn't smoke much anymore. Down from two packs a day to three or four cigarettes in the morning and, maybe, one after dinner and never in the house. Lulu insisted he take his filthy habits outside.

"Sure," he said.

As they put on their jackets and ambled out the front door and onto the front porch that ran half the length of the double-wide. It was one of those crisp November mornings that Vermont was famous for. The sky was clear and the wind was calm. Birds were chirping in the distance, and you had a view of the mountains in almost every direction. There was the smell of maple, hickory, and oak burning in the fireplaces of many of the adjacent farmhouses. It was evident why he selected this part of the world to build his mansion. It wouldn't be long however until the first snows started, and that signaled his time to hit the road for the winter. He had several more southern states to add to his collection before his goal of all forty-nine was reached. He shivered slightly as Wayne was finishing his cigarette. They did not say much as they both took in the beauty surrounding them.

"You know, I never get tired of these surroundings," Wayne said, breaking the silence between them. "I know sometimes you head on south for the winter when it gets rough, but me, I look forward to the snow and the change of seasons. Maybe when I'm older and the kids are all gone, me and the missus will winter down south. Although not for the entire winter. Maybe after the holidays."

"I'm here for some of the winter," he said. "I just need to get away every once and awhile to get some sun and exercise."

Just then, Lulu's sister, Elsie, and her brood pulled up with Wayne's two youngest jumping out of the car with their cousins in hot pursuit. Elsie hollered up to the two of them, asking for some help with the pies and other goodies. Elsie was about twice the size of Lulu. Probably one of the reasons her husband left her and her two kids after four years of marriage. She was a sweet woman, but, unfortunately, she was fat as her namesake, Elsie the Borden cow. It was all he could do not to look at her with the gigantic butt, puffed up piggylike face, and undulating boobs when she walked.

He and Wayne both came to her rescue, and he marveled at the quantity of food she had in the trunk of the car. It will not go to waste, he thought, at least not his *waist* as he thought of the play on words.

"How you doin', Elsie?" he asked, as he forced himself to

look at the beady eyes set back in red puffy cheeks.

"I'm doing great," she responded. "You're here early. Is the game on already? Have you met Dee yet?"

"No, not yet," he said, as he followed the swaying mass of blubber up the porch.

Elsie had to turn sideways to get in the front porch door and turned to yell at the kids not to get dirty while they played in the pile of leaves at the end of the driveway. He half expected her to moo a greeting as she entered the double-wide. He was thinking, *A double-wide in a double-wide. When she sits around the house, she sits around the house.* He almost snickered as he followed her through the door and into the living room. He also almost dropped the pies, for what he saw next was Dee.

She looked almost like Dedra, except a little older. He had suspected all along that her missing daughter was the woman from Florida. From his collection, her soul cat was named Dedra. The circumstances of Dedra's disappearance explained to him by Lulu and Wayne were very familiar to him. The last she was seen was the day after her midterms. The next Monday, she did not show up for her classes. No one knew where she went or what she did for that week. She disappeared without a trace.

Dee was as short as Wayne had told him, very petite and athletic looking. She had the same narrow chin, puffy lower lip, and dark brown eyes as her daughter. Dee's hair was the same color, but longer and played around her face like a frame on a beautiful picture. Needless to say, he was attracted to her, not only from the curiosity of meeting one of his victims' mother, but from her chemical makeup, which he found appealing. He had the same feelings about her daughter, but that was changed by the business he had to perform at the time. This should be a very interesting day.

In the ruckus caused by the arrival of Elsie, they were ignored. He walked over to Dee and introduced himself.

"You don't mind if I call you Dee, do you?" he asked knowing what the answer would be. "I might add that you are every bit as attractive as they described to me."

"Thanks," she responded, so coyly, she almost blushed. "And my friends call me Dee. Are you a friend?" She was immediately attracted to him. After all, he was good looking, single, and according to Lulu, had lots of money. Although the money did not matter to her a whole lot, it sure did put her at ease. She was surprised at the shallowness of her own thoughts that money would make a man attractive. But that was a basic instinct, especially for someone like herself who had started out poor and ended up with nothing but her own cash reserves.

"I'll be as much a friend as you want. So, what's a nice girl like you doing in a place like this? Excuse me, a woman like you," he said, with a half-smile. Just then, Lulu, Elsie, and Wayne broke away from their hugs and kisses to notice they were ignoring their guests.

Elsie grabbed Dee away and gave her niece a bear hug.

"Well, I see you two have met," said Lulu. "Is it love at first sight?"

"At least maybe lust at first sight," said Wayne.

"I don't embarrass easily," said Dee pulling away from Elsie. "But you two sure are pushing the limits."

"Why don't we both go out to the front porch and let them discuss their family matters, as disgusting as they are?" he suggested. She nodded agreement, and they proceeded to leave the three relatives to themselves. "You better put on something a little warmer because even though the sun is shining, it is a bit brisk."

She went back to her room to put on a sweater while he went out on the porch. There were two well-weathered wicker chairs and a wicker love seat under the corrugated fiber-glass roof that covered the wooden, raised floor of the porch. He sat on the love seat, hoping she would sit beside him. The kids were still jumping and diving into the pile of leaves. The pile was quickly becoming less of a mountain and more of a plateau. The dog was barking and howling in the back, begging to be let out to play. However, as Wayne told him once, "You don't let good huntin' dog play with children. It ruins 'em for the hunt." It was the same thing that he heard from his uncle's friend a long time ago.

The front door of the double-wide swung open, and he took a glance at her silhouette against the morning sun. Even with the sweater and somewhat baggy jeans, she projected a look of prowess. She reminded him of the bobcat in the forest. Much like the bobcat, she slowly turned to notice him, but instead of backing away, she walked toward him much like a cat moving toward an object of curiosity. She almost sat in one of the chairs, but gave him a cute smile and sat next to him in the love seat.

She started the conversation with an apology about Bill's death.

"I'm sorry you and Wayne lost one of your friends a couple of weeks ago. Did you know each other long?"

"I only knew him for the last five years," he responded. "I met them during the construction of my house, but Bill and Wayne grew up together, so it wasn't as much a loss for me as it was for Wayne. But that's all over now. I understand you lost your daughter last year," he immediately regretted his choice of words at saying lost rather than missing, although this was probably a Freudian slip, since he knew what happened.

"I haven't lost her," she corrected. "She has been missing for two years in February, and although the authorities tell me that the chances of her walking back into my life are nil, I have never given up hope. I guess that is one of the faults of being a parent. Do you have any children?"

"I guess they neglected to tell you I've never been married. I do apologize for my choice of words. I know how bad it is to lose a pet and can't begin to imagine what it would be like to miss a child. Again, I apologize for my apparent display of a lack of sensitivity."

"No apology is necessary. I do miss her so and will never give up looking for her. I do realize I must get on with my life though. That is why I agreed to come here for Thanksgiving. It's so peaceful in this part of the world. It might help me to relax and get her off my mind if only for a few days. So let's change the subject, and please promise to not bring this up again. At least for the weekend."

"Agreed. So what do you do for exercise. It's obvious you work out in some capacity. It's hard to believe you are related to Lulu and Elsie."

"I go to a workout center three times a week for some aerobics and weight training. The other four days a week, I either jog or ride a bike, depending on the weather. I am not one of the lucky ones who can eat what they want and not gain an ounce. If I don't watch what I eat, I'll blow up like a balloon. Both my parents tended to be on the heavy side. I think after this weekend, I'll need to run all the way back to Florida. How about you?"

"I bike a lot." He noticed a slight squint in her eyes when he said that. "I also have a home gym. Vermont, being mostly rural, doesn't have a lot of workout centers. If you are interested, I have a tandem, and if you have never ridden in this part of the world, it is a workout. I know some not-too-bad routes we could ride, but from what you tell me, you could handle some of the more hilly sections." This was déjà vu all over again for him. This is the way he cajoled her daughter for her last ride into oblivion.

"I would like that very much. When? I'm ready to go right now, since I didn't do a bit of exercise the last two days, and it looks like today will bust my waistline. What do you do for a living? And if you don't mind my saying so, you don't look like you are almost forty."

"Thank you, and you don't look like you are in your mid-forties. I try to keep in shape, and I must have inherited some good genes. I guess you could say I'm retired now. I was lucky in the lottery in Texas a few years back, and now I live off the investments. Nothing risky, but I do like the lifestyle I have now. I used to have to bust my ass for everything I had. Before graduating from college, I worked at fast food places, factories, offices, you name it."

"You sound bitter. What about your parents?"

"How about tomorrow for the bike ride? We could make it an all-day affair. An early morning ride, some lunch at a general store, an afternoon goin' hot and heavy on the bike, and then an evening of culinary delight at one of the finer Vermont diners."

"That sounds like a winner to me. You don't want to talk about your parents?"

"Not at all. I just wanted to get the bike ride in there before you changed your mind. I never knew my father, and my mom died the day I graduated from high school. What a bummer that was. She was a good woman, worked hard all her life and then was killed in an auto accident." He could not keep from lying a little bit. It was in his nature, and no one in Vermont knew the truth.

"I lost both of my parents in a car accident," she said, turning on the chair sitting sideways and looking surprised. "What a terrible thing to have in common." There was a moment of silence as she turned, sitting with her back to the seat, but inching a little closer toward him.

"And you never married?" she continued.

"Nope, never even came close. I was shy as a child and never even had a girlfriend until college. That's when religion got in the way of my having the time of my life. I was saving myself for marriage, being a good Catholic boy and all. The problem was none of the women I dated were saving themselves. As soon as they could, they would dump me and pursue someone who could help them spend their love freely. Or as Wayne said earlier, lust. I don't know why I'm telling you all this, but so infrequently, no pun intended, I meet someone who piques my interest, like you have, that I'm dumping all the information on you I can. Thanks for asking and listening. How did you end up in Florida?"

"I took a job there after college. My mom and dad moved to Florida from Vermont and lived there until they died in the accident. I was in college then at the end of my senior year and was somehow able to finish. I met my husband at the Pensacola navy base."

"Hey, you two lovebirds," Wayne said as he stepped out onto the porch. "It's time for a little breakfast if you want." Turning toward the pile of flying leaves and children Wayne yelled. "Hey kids, want something to eat?" At this, the four red-cheeked youngsters responded in unison with an enthusiastic yes!

"Let's go on in and face the music," Dee said. As she got up, her thigh brushed against his shoulder. He felt a tingling he had not felt in years. More like a shiver than a tingling. It started where she brushed up against him and continued to his spine. It felt good, and maybe, just maybe, he could enjoy this woman for what she was and be able to suppress his other desires. Desires that needed to be satisfied. Desires that were deep in his soul. Desires that were animalistic.

The rest of the day was a typical Thanksgiving: eating, watching the Cowboys play football, eating, drinking, eating, and at least once giving thanks. Dee and he were placed together at the table, and Lulu, Wayne, and Elsie kept glancing at the two. Comments were made about how they looked so good together. They also were glancing at each other occasionally, and more than once a smile would break across their faces. Dinner music consisted of blue grass and some Country Western. He was wishing he could listen to a little Vivaldi or Mozart, but the host picked the music. Dee feigned an interest in the football game, He watched and commented on some of the plays, but he could not keep his mind off Dee and tomorrow.

At the end of the day, after all the games were over, the dishes were all done, Elsie and her two had gone, it was time for him to leave. She walked him to his truck, and although they both wanted to give each other a light kiss, they knew there were eyes peeking from the double-wide's graying curtains. Instead they gave each other a light hand-squeeze.

"I'll pick you up tomorrow at 8:30 and please eat some breakfast, since, I assure you, we will be burning it off," he said as he got in and started the diesel.

"Don't worry," she said. "See ya."

Nine

He awoke early, got ready, and made himself a leg of Dedra bagel sandwich for breakfast. He was sure it was Dedra, since he dated all the goodies in his freezer. He had to check the tag on the cat named Dedra, which had the date, name, and state where obtained. He took Dedra, the cat, and placed her in a back room, where she would not be seen should Dee accompany him home tonight. Although the thought of Dee stroking her daughter's namesake was intriguing, it was way too dangerous. It would be hard to explain that coincidence and then what would happen? Too many people have seen them together, and Dee's disappearance would lead directly to him.

He packed all they would need for their bike ride. He brought an extra helmet for Dee, water, and some power bars. He noticed the day was going to be a repeat of yesterday, crisp and cool, with some clouds moving in by afternoon, but no chance of rain. It would be a wonderful ride. The tandem was a Cannondale hybrid, made for the road or semi-rough terrain. It could go on rougher terrain, but it would be uncomfortable and hard to control. Also, it might make Dee's pretty little ass sore, and he had other plans to do that.

At precisely 8:30, he pulled the truck into Wayne's driveway. It did not appear that anyone was up and moving, but within seconds, Dee bounded out the front door wearing bike pants, a sweatshirt, helmet, and a red vest. He was impressed, since she also was wearing riding gloves. Also, she seemed anxious to see him. He got out to meet her, and she gave him a hug and a peck on the cheek.

"Good morning," she whispered in his ear.

"And good morning to you," he responded. "I take it you slept well. Where did you get the bike clothes?"

"They were...are my daughter's," she corrected herself. "I

brought them with me to give to Lulu for her kids when they get old enough. If Dedra misses them when she gets back from whereever she is, I can always get her new ones. I wasn't sure what type of pedals are on the bike, so I'm wearing shoes that have clipless mounts on the bottom, but can also go with plain straps."

"Those will be fine," he responded. "Actually the pedals have toe straps on them so you are all set. I thought we would ride out from here. This road is not too hilly, the traffic is light, and the scenery is some of the best in Vermont."

"You lead, and I'll follow, since I'm just along for the ride," she said.

He went to the rear of the truck and unloaded the tandem, reattached the front wheel, made some adjustments to the brakes, and straddled the front wheel.

"Get on the saddle, and we'll size you up. I already set it to where I thought would be comfortable for you." Actually, he had not adjusted it since Dedra went for her last ride. When she got up on the saddle, the fit was perfect. *Like mother like daughter*, he almost said. "I guess we're ready to ride. Do we need to say good-bye to anyone?"

"No. Only the kids were up, playing in the living room. Anyway when they get up, they'll see the truck and know you did show up as promised."

He noticed one of the curtains on the bedroom window was pulled back slightly, but he did not wave, since he wanted to get moving. After the peck on the cheek, this might prove to be a very interesting day and evening.

"All you have to do is sit there, look purdy, and pedal for all your worth," he said as he got on and straddled the cross bar. She got on the saddle, put her feet under the straps and said she was ready. "I'll call out any bumps, start, stop, and shift changes so you won't get caught by surprise. When I yell out left or right turn, give a hand signal even if there aren't any cars around. You'll get the hang of it in no time. Ready, go," he said as he pushed off and sat down on his saddle.

The first stretch was downhill, but in Vermont, you don't go downhill for very long. The next stretch was slightly uphill, but the road was smooth, and they cranked it up and cruised at 15-

plus most of the time. He took her on a ride along one of the many rivers in this section of Vermont. The road snaked along the side of the river which was coursing its way in the opposite direction. Although it was up hill, neither of them tired. It was just a fine ride. Neither of them talked, since it was difficult to discuss the problems of the day while trying to maintain good oxygen intake.

They stopped for lunch at a small general store. They shared a sandwich and a power bar. They also swilled down lots of power drinks, filled their water bottles, and headed back out after an hour's rest. They both wanted to burn off the calories from the day before. As they flew, so did the time. At 3:30, they were on the way back to the trailer. After six hours of riding, they had gone fifty-five miles. Not a bad pace for Vermont roads, considering they had stopped for lunch and rest breaks four times. They had accomplished their goal and were now hungry for a good dinner. As they pulled into the driveway, Lulu and Wayne waved from the front windows.

"That was a great ride," he said, as they both got off the bike. "I've got a meal planned back at my place if you would like to accompany me there. I can visit with Wayne and Lulu while you get cleaned up." He hoisted the bike into the back of the pickup as he said this.

"I have a better idea," she responded. "Why don't I get my clothes and overnight bag and freshen up at your place if you don't mind. The bathroom in that trailer is like getting cleaned up at a truck stop. I've heard your place is more modern, and I could use a little more pampering."

"I understand and would be delighted to have you see how clean I live. At least your feet won't stick to the floor in any of my bathrooms. I'll be on the porch when you're ready."

"It won't take but a second," she said, with a smile, hurrying past Wayne and Lulu and into the double-wide.

"Hey, Wayne, I'm going to steal your house guest for a while longer if you don't mind," he said, as he approached the porch.

"Oh, hells bells," said Lulu, "we would be disappointed if she didn't go with you and also spend the night, if you catch my drift," she said with a wink.

He caught her drift all right and a little of her stench too. He wondered if Dee was going with him just to get away from them or because she really liked him. Oh, well, he thought it didn't make much difference to him either way.

Not a second later, Dee was out of the double-wide and ready to go.

"You two enjoy the rest of the day," Wayne said. "Me and the missus won't wait up neither." He chuckled as he elbowed Lulu in the ribs.

He unlocked and opened the passenger's side door, and Dee bounded in, holding a small bag. She reached across the driver's seat and pulled the lock up and placed the bag in the back seat of the extended cab. She had a Cheshire cat's grin by the time he checked the bungee cords holding the bike down and got in on his side.

"How long could you have put up with them had I not rode in on my white horse?" he asked.

"In the mood I was in before you showed up yesterday, maybe another week," she responded. "But after yesterday, and especially today, not more than two minutes. I think I'm getting over some of my depression, and the ride today helped me forget the past a little."

"Glad I could help," he said, as they backed out of the drive.

The drive to his mountaintop home was quick. She was amazed at the remoteness of the home, and as they were pulling into the garage, she wanted to ask him how much it cost. He would have told her, but she refrained from asking. Somehow, she thought he would mention it sooner or later, so she kept her curiosity in check. She could not help grinning the entire length of the trip, in anticipation of the evening ahead. She had not been with a man in a long time, but tonight she was willing to let him take advantage of her re-aroused feelings. "Tonight's the night," as the old joke goes.

"So, what do you think so far?" he asked, not really wanting to know the answer. He had not had a woman to his house with him alone that was not a victim.

"Not a bad looking bachelor pad," she responded. She was anxious to see the inside.

"You sure you're not allergic to cats, because I have a lot of them," he said. "I guess you could say they are my harem. I certainly love them all."

As they walked into the main entrance, bypassing the tunnel to the meat lockers, butcher rooms, and all the other fun places, he ordered the security system to turn off. Instantly, the reply came back in a 2001 Hal voice that it was complying.

"Now I am impressed," she said. "I have never seen one of these systems in action except in the movies. What else does it do?"

"Everything I program it to do and have the equipment connections for. I find it convenient to have an automated house, since I live alone and am gone a lot."

"What if there is a power outage and your computer shuts down, and how do you get water and heat this high up?" she asked.

"Whoa! One question at a time. See those cells out there. Those are solar electric panels. They turn over and face the sun when there is sufficient light to generate electricity. They are upside down when there is too little sun and when it gets dark. Turning upside down also keeps the snow off them. When there is enough light, they track the sun and produce electricity which is stored in large batteries. When there hasn't been enough sun for several days, a propane generator kicks on and charges the batteries. In short, I generate my own power. The heat is a combination of propane and electricity. Sometimes I burn wood, too. The fireplace has a system around it to circulate air, taking as much of the heat from the logs as possible. Combustion air for the fireplace comes from the outside, so the system is very efficient. Water comes from a well powered by an electric pump. Except for the propane, this place is self-sufficient. Propane is delivered at the bottom of the hill and is pumped to the top tanks as necessary. All the buildings at the bottom of the hill are powered by the power company."

"So, you are basically self-contained like an RV," she said.

"That's right. Any other questions?"

"What if your computer fails?" she asked.

"There is a back-up computer and a system that calls me on my cell phone to let me know of any real problems. This home is about as self-sufficient as the president's emergency residence under the White House. Would you like to take a tour, or would you like to get cleaned up first?"

"Maybe you should just show me where the shower is, and I was going to suggest we should get cleaned up together. I wouldn't want to say the wrong thing in the shower and have a computer-operated scrub brush drop down out of the ceiling and start scrubbing me raw."

"In that case, the tour can wait and I will take the place of the computer for your scrubdown. Just let me get something simple started for dinner." He took her to the master bedroom and introduced her to the bathroom. "You can get started in the shower, and I'll join you in about five."

He went to the kitchen, took a foil-wrapped prepared frozen lasagna from the freezer and placed it in the stove. He pushed the casserole bake button on the control panel and headed for the bathroom. In the bedroom, he turned on the TV and placed the satellite channel to easy listening music piped through wires in the walls to the surround sound system and to the five speakers placed around the room near the ceiling. The lights were on, and he dimmed them with the remote control next to the nightstand on the left side of the bed.

He opened the bathroom door and like a fog bank rolling in over San Francisco, a rush of steam greeted him. He could see the shower stall through a dream-filled cloud. Behind the pitted glass was a pink shadow moving seductively. He was starting to get an erection as he removed his biking clothes and placed them in the hamper, which led directly to the laundry room. He could smell the sweet scent of the body wash and hear the inviting spray of the multiple showerheads.

"Have you got room for another bod?" he said, as he reached for the shower door. Somewhat embarrassed with a swelling penis, he entered the shower.

"I think I can make room," she said. "Are you happy to see me or is that a hard-on between your legs?"

"It's just something I carry around with me for special occasions," he responded. "Now, can I wash your back, or are you going to stare at it all night."

"If it stays like that all night, I'll do more than stare at it. I'm nearsighted and would have to stare at close range, however."

With that, she grabbed his penis with a soapy hand, making it swell to the point of near pain.

"Don't wash it too quickly, or it could lose some of its power," he said. Giggling, she playfully pushed him back to where he bumped into the shower seat and sat down. Kneeling down she looked up at him and smiled seductively. He could only throw his head back in pleasure as she placed his throbbing manhood into her mouth and slowly stroked him with her left hand as she caressed him with her tongue. It was over in a matter of seconds. He had not been with a woman for sex in a long time, and holding back was not an option. As he finished, she slowly took him out of her mouth and looked at him again and smiled.

"Thank you," he said. He cradled her head in his hands and, bending down, he kissed her. The taste of her mouth was sweet and sensual. She noticed he was still aroused, so she straddled the shower seat, kneeling, on each side of him. Squatting down, she got him inside of her and they slowly made love with the tepid water raining down on them both. She was gasping as she climaxed, and a moment later, he came. They remained on the shower seat, spent for another three minutes, breathing deeply in each other's ears. Their bodies, numbed by the heat of passion, suddenly made them aware of the uncomfortable position they were in on the shower seat.

"You're welcome," she said responding to his earlier comment. She slowly stood up, and he followed suit. They finished their showers too spent to talk. He washed her with the sponge all over, rubbing her on the breasts and crotch ever so gently. Likewise, she sponged him all over.

He opened the shower door, grabbed two warm towels off of the towel warmer, and handed her one.

"I don't usually do that on a first date," she said, "but it has been so long, and I am attracted to you, not to mention the obvious size of your maroon harpoon. I was hungry for it, but now I'm hungry for some real food."

"Where did you pick up that term, maroon harpoon?" he asked as he handed her a white terry cloth bathrobe from a hook on the back of the closed door.

"My ex was in the navy. Some of his lingo has stayed with me over the years, and it comes out from time to time."

Taking his robe from the same place, he decided not to comment further. He was not interested in her past, only what she could do for him in the present.

"I have some lasagna and can toss a salad for us. Of course, there is a bottle or two of wine around here some place. So, do you want to dress formally for dinner, eat in the buff, or stay in these robes?"

"I already ate in the buff, or don't you remember?" she responded. "And since I left my dinner dress back at Lulu's, this robe will do just fine."

He liked her sense of humor. It was refreshing and tart. He opened the door and led her from the bathroom through the bedroom and toward the kitchen. "I noticed the soft music playing in the bedroom," she said as she pinched him on the butt. I have to be careful I don't get seduced. After all, I hardly know you."

He thought that was ironic. If she only knew he was the one who had abducted, dissected, and devoured her beloved Dedra.

He introduced her to the sub-zero refrigerator as she volunteered to put the salad together. He checked on the lasagna, which was ten minutes from being a perfect bubbling mass of cheese and marinara sauce.

"Is a Pinot Grigio all right with you?" he asked.

"Sure," she said. "Forgive me for being ignorant about these things, but is that a white or red?"

"White," he responded. "I found it at the local general store. It's not expensive, but some of the better wines are the least expensive. You don't have to have a lot of money to drink well. In France, the local table wines cost less than bottled water, and are just as good as the wines costing ten times as much."

"So, when were you in France?" she asked, as she cut the tomatoes.

"Right after I won the lottery, which I'm sure Lulu has let you know. I wanted to see the world, but got as far as Italy, when I decided the U.S. was better than all the rest. I settled on Vermont because of the privacy and rural setting. I'm not threatened by urban sprawl, my neighbors leave me alone, and when I get tired of the winters, I have my RV to go south or west."

"Do you travel a lot in the RV?" she prodded while tossing the lettuce and tomatoes.

"About five or six times a year. I'm gone for several weeks."

"What about your cats that I heard so much about? Who looks after them, and where are they now?"

He was getting slightly annoyed by her probing but decided to give her as much information as he could without revealing what he really did.

"The cats are in a different part of the house right now. I didn't want them to bother us, which they are sure to do, since they own this place. I merely reside here at their whim. The computer feeds them, changes their litter box, and keeps their water dish full while I am gone. They have each other for social comfort, but I do miss them when I am gone."

"What dressing do you want on the salad?" she asked. "How many cats do you have?"

"There is some Green Goddess dressing in the fridge," he responded. "I pick up a cat in every state I ride in. I have twenty-four so far." He went to the wine cooler and selected the Pinot Grigio from the twenty-five bottles neatly lined up on their sides.

"How do you remember their names?" she queried as she poured the dressing on the salad and tossed it again to coat the vegetables.

"They have tags, and so far, I can remember them all. Enough about my cats. Are you willing to talk about your daughter? Maybe I can help you find her."

"Not much to tell, except she told her friends she was going for a bike ride with a guy she just met and never came back. What is puzzling is she did not take her bike. She either used someone else's bike or never went for the ride. The police looked for her, but since there are so many missing women, they lost interest when they couldn't find any evidence. Now they treat her as a statistic, and I'm left to do the searching. I have hope that she is still alive, but we were so close, she would have contacted me. It's been almost two years, but I will never give up hope. I have decided to get on with my life and live with my own anguish. That is why I'm glad you came along and made me forget temporarily. I really enjoyed being with you today."

"I hope I didn't ruin the evening by asking about Dedra.

Well, the lasagna awaits, the wine is ready, it looks like you have the salad done, so let's replenish our depleted resources."

The music was trickling from the bedroom like water from a summer brook. Warm and soothing, tickling the ears and stimulating the senses. They ate almost in silence with an occasional smiling glance. They finished nearly all the lasagna, all the salad, all the wine, and a goodly part of the French bread, which he produced from the breadbox. They had had a long day and were both tired. After they took care of the leftovers, the dishes were placed in the dishwasher.

"Intruders, southwest sector," droned the computer.

"What is that?" Dee asked. "A burglar alarm?"

"Sort of," he responded. "Let's see what's out there."

"Cameras on, kitchen," he said in a voice similar to the computer's. "Pan southwest sector. It must be something big, since I have the sensors set to ignore anything smaller than a turkey. Otherwise, it would be a nonstop alert."

The TV in the kitchen came to life, and the view was of the woods. Even though it was dark, the trees were quite visible. "Pan left," he commanded. The camera view started to sweep left and immediately picked up a large shape, dark and very close. "Stop," he said. "Zoom out." The camera responded, and the shape of a very large black bear was soon discernible. "Switch to infrared," he commanded the computer. Immediately, the scene changed to green on black, and the outline of the bear was complete. The bear was foraging in the leaves under a large oak tree. Hearing the whir of the camera's sync motor, the bear stopped long enough to look at the camera, although it was not too concerned.

"I would say he is a male about 450 pounds and stands about seven feet," he said.

Dee stared at the screen, her eyes almost as wide open as her mouth.

"Holy shit!" was the first thing she said, followed by "I'm glad we're in here."

"He would probably run if he saw us," he responded. "Unless they are used to the human scent, they are very skittish and will bolt when they get a whiff. Not that you smell bad, but bears have a terrific sense of smell and will know you're near

88

before you see them. I put up the sensor system all around the property to detect man more than the animals, but it's nice to know if there is a bear or a stag out there before you go for a walk in the woods. Deer can be dangerous too, especially during rutting season. During hunting season, it's especially nice to know there is somebody about with a weapon. Some of these hunters around here are not too bright and will shoot toward the house if there is an animal this way."

"I'm impressed, but what do you do if you see a hunter?" she asked.

"Watch this," he said. "Microphone on, speaker on." There was a slight crackle, which the bear must have heard, because he stood erect. It was obvious he could do bodily harm if he wanted to. "Go away," he said, which was repeated back to the TV screen via the speaker and microphone in the woods. The bear wasted no time. He was on all fours, crashing through the woods, more startled than scared.

"This place is a fortress," she said. "Do you also have a guard tower out there with guns and boiling oil?"

He laughed.

"I can't tell or show you everything, because then I'd have to lock you up in my dungeon. I don't know about you, but I have done enough for today. That bike ride took a lot out of me, since I had to do all the work. On top of that, you sucked out all my vital bodily fluids, leaving me totally exhausted. Unless you want to watch a movie and see me fall asleep, I'm ready to hit the rack."

"I see you know some nautical terms, too," she said. "I'm really tired, too, but didn't want to say anything because you might think I'm a wuss. I wasn't reading a book and eating ice cream on the back of the tandem. So I'm just as tired as you."

"Camera off, speaker off, microphone off," he said in a voice devoid of inflection. "It resets itself in fifteen minutes if I don't reset it myself. It also is trained to my voice, so no matter who speaks, it obeys only one master. Oh, one last thing, dishwasher on." Immediately there was the sound of water entering the dishwasher at the start of the fill cycle.

He then took her hand in his and led her to the bedroom. He gently removed her robe after dropping his to the floor. He hugged her and they both melted into the bed, where they remained embracing until sleep overcame them both. The lilting flute and soft drums of John Huling's "Spiritlands" was playing as they drifted deeply out of the realm of consciousness.

Ten

He awoke first. A glance at the projection on the ceiling from a clock on the opposite nightstand revealed that it was 6:30. He felt her head on top of his shoulder. Her arm was around his stomach. Her leg was over his thigh. They had remained entwined through the entire night. Her warmth aroused him and soon his penis was poking against her arm. He was remembering the feel of her lips around him in the shower the night before. She started to stir, obviously awakened by the maroon harpoon. She started to moan softly, and then reached down and grabbed him ever so gently.

"Good morning, Mr. Penis," she said in a gravelly voice. "Is your owner awake, or is he just dreaming of a past love?"

"I'm awake for sure now, and it's payback time."

She lifted her head and looked at him puzzled, at first, but then smiled sleepily. He pulled her toward him with his left arm and gently kissed her. He kissed the tip of her nose, the side of her cheek and the soft flesh of her chin. He pulled his arm out from under her and ran his lips down the side of her neck, flicking his tongue to get the taste of her inside him. He kissed her shoulders and followed the soft lines of her arm down to the tips of her fingers. He inserted one of her fingers into his mouth and sucked it while encircling the tip with his tongue.

He continued to the palm of her hand and onto her wrist. He returned to the softness of her shoulders while she started to moan in anticipation. He continued down to the soft, warm swell of her breasts, gently cupping both of them while kissing all around one nipple, which was responding with a warm firmness. Extending his tongue, he licked a circle around the nipple and then gently kissed and pulled the nipple into his mouth with an ever so gentle sucking motion. She responded by arching her back to allow him more access to the sweetness of her breasts.

He continued to the underside of her breasts and tasted the sweet saltiness left there by the heat of her passion. He continued down her chest to her navel, kissing and using his tongue to taste and tickle her. She held the sides of his head in both hands, guiding him with gentle pressure. As he arrived at the beginning softness of the hair protruding from between her thighs, he resisted the pressure from her hands and continued to the outside of her hips. She let go of his head and tossed her own head back in anticipation.

His tongue and lips moistened her as he continued down the outside of her leg to the underside of her knee. He continued in a line to the side of her ankle. As he kissed the underside of her foot, she started to giggle until he reached her toes. She was squirming and writhing with a feeling she had never before experienced. He was able to get three of her toes in his mouth at the same time. He sucked them and used his tongue to add to her ecstasy. He kissed and suckled all her toes until she begged him to stop.

He then continued back up the inside of her leg. She was arching her back uncontrollably and opening her legs. He kissed the inside of her thigh and felt the heat of her radiating toward him. She gently resumed her hold on the sides of his head while he used his hands to massage and open her so that his lips and tongue had full access to the part of her which was vibrating and becoming moist and sweet. She was moaning now, and he wanted her more than ever, but was now gently circling her clitoris with his tongue while occasionally crisscrossing the top of it with his lips.

She continued to arch her back and moaned while he placed his hands behind her on her soft buttocks and pulled her ever closer to him. She was guiding his lips with pressure on the sides of his head. She steered him to where she felt the most sensation while he kept gentle pressure on the cheeks of her butt. He was her love machine now, and his tongue and lips were at her beckoning. She tasted sweet and moist, arousing him to a stiffness that was approaching pain. She continued moaning, but was able to say, "I want you in me, please, now."

He did not want to disappoint her, so he moved over her and slipped easily inside her. He was able to last a lot longer than the night before, and she was able to climax more than once. They were both too busy feeling the moment to count how many times. Then it was over. He exploded into her, and they screamed together. Moments later, he fell on his left side exhausted, he continued to caress her with his right hand. He kissed her shoulder and the swell of her right breast. She fell back into sleep while he continued the caress. It was twenty minutes before she stirred again.

"Good morning," he said.

"It certainly was" was her response.

"When are you going back?" he asked.

"Trying to get rid of me already? Wham bam, thank you, ma'am."

"Another navy saying no doubt," he teased. "I'm not trying to get rid of you, just concerned about how many times we can do this before one of us says uncle. I hope, at least, you stay here as long as you are in Vermont."

"I have to get back to work on Monday. I'm not as financially secure as some people in these here parts, in this here house, in this here bed. My flight is this evening at 9:00, believe it or not. I was lucky to get a flight this weekend at all, so I took what I could get. I didn't plan on meeting a stud here in Vermont. Let's just enjoy this for now and let it rest a bit. Then get back in touch with each other to see if we want to continue. This Thanksgiving has been the best that I can remember, and I haven't felt this good in a long time. And I still have a daughter to find."

"I said I could help, that is, if you want help. It's not like I have a lot to do. Maybe with a mission, I could feel a lot more useful."

"We'll see. Let me sort through this weekend on my own, and we can discuss it in a week. Is that acceptable to you? I mean the sex was the best I've ever had, but this is moving too fast for me. I have never jumped in bed this quickly before or felt this way."

"A deal," he said. "I need to think this over too. There is some unfinished business I need to attend to before we take any more steps. At least let me take you to the airport this afternoon."

"I have a rental car, and need to turn it in. Because of the holiday, getting in and out of the airport is going to be a mess," she said and then moved close to him and kissed him gently on the cheek.

"Talk about wham bam," he said. They both laughed.

After a quick shower, she was ready to go. It was a long trip back to Boston Logan Airport. She still needed to get the rental car and pick up her things at Wayne and Lulu's. On the way, they discussed the possibilities of getting together again and settled on after the New Year. She was not sure how she would react the rest of the holiday season without Dedra, and she did not want him to see her in a crying mood. They both knew it was a long time between now and then, but that would allow them to think about how fast this relationship was going. Pulling into Wayne's drive, she kissed him on the cheek. Wayne and Lulu were immediately at the front door, both smiling wide grins. They looked like one of those cartoons with the character's teeth blacked out.

"Are you ready to get razzed?" he said.

"I don't care at this point. At least I'll be gone shortly, and you have to live around here," she whispered.

"I think it's time for me to take a road trip. I like to go to the southwest this time of year, and then I'll swing back around to meet you after the holidays. Here is my card with my home phone, cell phone, and e-mail address so you can get in touch with me. When I'm not home, I check my e-mail and home phone at least three times a day. If I'm not in, leave me a phone number, and I'll call you back. If you change your mind about seeing me again, e-mails are a good impersonal way to dear-John me."

"I will get in touch as soon as I get back," she said.

On getting out of the truck, they noticed the wind had started to blow and there was a bit of a wind chill. Not unusual for Vermont this time of year, although winter was still three weeks away.

"How you two love birds doin' this morning?" asked Wayne. "I don't see either of you walking bowlegged, but that don't mean you didn't have a roll in the hay."

"We stayed up all night watching horror movies," Dee lied.

"It reminded us of you two, so it was like I never left for the night."

"Yeah, I bet you were watchin' TV," said Lulu. "Do you have one on the ceiling in your bedroom, or did you just starch the living room rug?"

"This conversation is getting too intellectual for me," he said. "I think I'll head on back, since I want to get ready for my trip south in a day or two. Wayne, I'll call if I need you to tend to my cats. I will be monitoring the house with my computer while I'm gone. The Hummer is in the garage at the bottom of the hill, and you have the keys in case there is a lot of snow or ice."

"You have a Humvee?" Dee asked. "I guess there is a lot we need to talk about next time."

"Next time?" intoned Lulu. "What are you two planning here? Girl, we have to talk."

"I'll fill you in in due time," Dee responded. "If there is anything important, you will be the first to know."

"Talk to you later," he said directing his comment to all of them. With that, he got in the truck and backed out of the drive, heading back to the mansion. There would be no bump-and-run this time as happened to Bill. He would have to get rid of her some other way if things got serious or she found out too much. Playing the game of dating the mother of one of his victims was going to be fun, but the outcome was inevitable. What fun this would be. He had to decide what state to go to next.

Arriving back at the mansion, he consulted his magnetic state map. Looking at the remaining states, he noticed that Washington, D.C., was still missing.

He remembered the first time he was in the D.C. area, in an aborted attempt to add to his map. It was his birthday, July 13, 1996. He used a trailer park off I-270 and drove to Rock Creek Park. He had parked at the planetarium, off Military Road. The park was forested and had a lot of trails to run on. He headed south, ran to Bluff Bridge, and headed back north. Near the Western Ridge Trail, he saw a woman ahead of him wearing headphones and carrying a cassette player. He slowed so as not to overtake her, at least not yet. Rounding a bend in the trail, she was no longer in front of him. She seemingly disappeared. There was a man walking toward him, and he ran past without a glance. Taking a few more steps, he looked behind him to see if the woman had ducked into the woods and back out again. The man was now missing, too.

He stopped and looked to see if anyone else was in sight. There was no one, so he ducked into the woods to his right and very carefully worked his way back to the bend in the trail. Hearing some rustling in the brush, he crouched down and continued to advance. Peeking out from behind a large oak, he saw her. It was all he could do to keep from laughing, for not twenty feet away and facing toward the trail, he saw the woman, squatting like a cat taking a dump in a litter box. It was funny to him, but not uncommon. There is something about the jogging process that stimulates bowel movement. He had the same problem himself a couple of times. She was doing the only thing she could, short of shitting down her leg.

He decided right then not to pursue her as a possibility. How could he keep a straight face when he introduced himself. "Hi, I saw you take a crap in the woods. Would you like to go to dinner with me?" He bit his lip to keep from making any noise. Rather than sneak away and risk making a noise, he waited until she had finished. She took out Kleenex from a pocket in her running shorts and wiped her ass as best she could from a squatting position. She stood up, pulling the cassette player from her other pocket. She started to walk away, when from behind her and to her right, the man he had passed moved toward her with a rock in his hand. He must have been watching her from the other side.

He hit her hard across the back of her head. She dropped to the ground. The man bent over and hit her again. The man picked up the cassette player she dropped and put it in his pocket. Instead of leaving, the man looked around, grabbed her by the hair, and dragged her through the woods. He decided to follow. He waited until they were out of sight. The track left by the dragging was not hard to follow. The track went up a knoll and then down toward a dry ravine. The trees and brush were dense enough so that he could stay hidden. When he heard grunting, using the trees for cover, he squatted down and crawled along, like a soldier moving under the barbed wire with machine gun fire above. The grunts were getting louder, and when he rounded a large maple tree, he saw the man on top of her. She lay on her back, her face to one side, eyes open and staring blankly toward him. There was a tear in one eye. While the man was humping the girl, he crawled to his left so that he would not be in the way if the man retreated in the same direction that he dragged the body. Just as he felt he was a comfortable distance from the trail, the man climaxed and went limp. After what seemed like an eternity but could only have been five or six seconds, the man jumped up, still hard, and pulled up his underpants and jeans. He had a disgusting look of triumph on his face.

He raised his arms halfway and, twisting at the waist, he turned to the right and then the left as if eliciting applause from some unseen audience. The asshole must have thought he was a gladiator in an arena. Then looking around at the ground, the man bent over and picked up another rock. He then proceeded to bludgeon the woman on the head, striking her again and again. When the man was satisfied she would not get up ever, he threw the rock away and retraced his steps back to the trail. When he was sure the man would not see him, he got up and walked to the woman's side, squatted down and felt for a pulse. There was none. Her face was smashed in beyond recognition. He stood up and carefully found his way back to the trail.

On running back north, he saw the man ahead of him walking as if he hadn't a care in the world. As he passed the man at as fast a pace as he could and keeping his eyes straight ahead, he said in a low voice, "I saw what you did, you sick fuck."

Ahead were some other joggers coming toward them. As he let them by on his left, he glanced back. The man was not chasing after him, but walking along with a smile on his face. "I guess he wanted an audience after all," he said under his breath. When he got back to the truck, he wasted no time getting to the fifth wheel and heading back to Vermont, where he incinerated the running clothes he had worn. He checked the *Washington Post* and the *Washington Times-Daily* on-line versions for an entire week, but found no mention of a dead woman at the park. He knew he would not want to hunt at that park again for his D.C. victim. He also knew he would never forget that asshole's face.

So it was decided, D.C. for another try. He could get there in a day. If he was lucky, in another day or two, he could get back to the mansion, take care of his victim, and then head out to the Mexican border. The border trip was necessary every so often so he could replenish his supply of Rohypnol and dispose of the fifth wheel. He sometimes liked to "permit" his fifth wheel to be stolen and taken to Mexico. That way any evidence of his encounters would get lost across the border forever. It was a simple process, where he would drive across the border, park the fifth wheel, leave it, and return to the States with the plates and identification. The fifth wheel would be gone in a day or two, never to be seen again. He would then simply buy another one and not renew the registration on the old one. This time, he wanted to try a different way to dispose of the evidence.

He was hungry and decided on a Mexican-style bagel sandwich, but first a workout on the stationary bike, some weightlifting, and stretches. After all, keeping in shape is what made him attractive to his victims. He let the cats out of the back room as soon as he entered. Some of them came out right away and rubbed against his legs. The others just looked at him in that nonchalant way that cats will do. He thought it unusual that Dee never asked to see the cats. Maybe she did not like cats. If she was allergic, she would have had a reaction, since they have the run of the house most of the time. As soon as he had one for every state he could drive to, he was contemplating what to do with them. Attrition may take care of the problem for him; however, house cats can live a long time.

On completing the workout and a shower, he gathered supplies for the trip to D.C. He also consulted the RV campsite directory and found several sites close to the D.C. area. He did not call ahead for reservations because they would ask for a credit card to hold the site. Credit cards leave trails. He drove the truck down to the fifth wheel with the supplies he would need. As always, he was sure to take plenty of sandwich meat for the bagel sandwiches that would sustain him for most of the trip.

At the garage at the bottom, he hooked up the truck to the fifth wheel and walked back to the cave to get the Hummer. The walk back took over an hour, but was good exercise. He did not use the road. He used a trail that was a more direct route, but was also steeper. Along the way, he looked for his sensor units and cameras. They were difficult to detect even if you knew where they were. He did not see them. *Good*, he thought. By the time he reached the top, he was breathing heavily, but not exhausted. He was in very good physical condition.

Before leaving for D.C., he got on the computer and transferred some additional money to the offshore bank in the Bahamas. This was his getaway money in case he needed to get lost in a hurry. He had several passports, and different license plates for the truck and fifth wheel. Money will buy anything the dishonest person requires to get lost. He was not going to be caught or leave any evidence behind. All the destruct systems in the house were ready to respond, and if the house was about to be destroyed, he would be notified by the automatic dialer and e-mail. He used the same disposable cell-phone number he gave to Dee. After this trip, he would destroy the phone.

It was getting dark by the time he arrived with the Hummer at the garage. He pulled out the RV and parked the Hummer in its place where, if necessary, Wayne could use it to check on the house. Pulling out onto the highway, he put Willie Nelson's "On the Road Again" on the CD player, and he headed south.

It was better to travel at night, although even at night I-95 was a real bitch, but it was the only direct route. He liked this time alone on the road. He listened to his CDs, ate his bagel sandwiches, and looked at the people going nowhere fast. Also, traveling at night attracted less attention. His fifth wheel was one of the smaller ones, but it still took up a lot of space on the highway. With the two fuel tanks filled, he would stop only to piss, and that he would do in the fifth wheel.

Driving all night, he was able to get through D.C. at 4:30 in the morning. Even at that early hour, traffic was heavy with 18-wheelers taking supplies into and out of the city. It was a terrible place to visit, but you wouldn't want to live there. He headed south to Stafford, Virginia, hoping to stay at the Aquia Pines campground. They should have plenty of empty spaces, since it was after Thanksgiving and before Christmas.

As he pulled into the campgrounds, the sign told him to pick out a spot and come back when the front office was occupied at

8:30. He grabbed a map and drove to the back area, which looked isolated. The grounds were quite empty. He settled on a site that had no campers on either side for three spaces. He backed into the flat, paved parking area. It took only ten minutes to level the fifth wheel and connect the electricity. With any luck, he would not be here long enough to connect to the water and sewer. The fifth wheel was self-contained. The water tank was full, and the gray and sewer tanks were empty.

After pulling the truck out away from the fifth wheel, he went into it, lay on the bed, and fell immediately into a deep, dreamless sleep.

Eleven

He awoke at 1:30, refreshed and ready to start his search. He dressed in his running clothes instead of bike clothes. He wanted to run part of the parkway along the Potomac first. It was more difficult to find a victim while running, but it had worked before. On exiting the fifth wheel, he was greeted by a cloudy afternoon, a typical day in Washington for early December. He got in and started the diesel engine and headed for the RV park exit.

Stopping by the office on the way out, he greeted the woman behind the counter.

"Hi, I'm in space 134 and am going to be here for a short visit. I'll pay for three nights now, and if I stay longer, I'll let you know in advance."

"I have to charge you for last night, even though I heard you come in at about 5:00," she said.

"No problem. How much for three nights, then?"

"With tax, it's fifty-five dollars a night. Last week, before Thanksgiving it was seventy-five dollars a night, but we're on winter rates now," she informed him.

He counted out $165 from his wallet and handed it to her. He wasn't going to bring up registration, but in case she wanted all his stats, he was prepared to give them to her, all fake of course. He had changed the plates on the truck and fifth wheel at one of his piss stops along the highway. "I don't need a receipt," he said as he left the office.

"Have a nice day," she said, without really meaning it.

I will if I find my quarry, he thought. Pulling away from the office, he thought how easy this all was. "The U.S. really was the home of the brave and the land of the free," he said to himself. All you had to do was have a few million in a couple of banks, both here and in the Bahamas, but far more off shore.

He drove back into the D.C. area on I-95 taking the Route 1

exit. He worked his way east to the waterfront and parked near the Woodrow Wilson Bridge. He got out of the truck and walked to the Mount Vernon trail. After some stretching and checking out the area, he began a slow jog toward Mount Vernon. It was still overcast and would get dark early as evening approached. From the trail, he could look east across the Potomac to downtown D.C. The trail was paved and used by joggers, walkers, bikers, skate boarders, etc. This late in the afternoon, there were a few bikers and some joggers. He was looking for that special someone. She was not in sight, but he had not completed a mile yet, and there was always tomorrow. This time of year, many of the government employees would be taking their annual leave. He had hoped to attract one of them, since he had no government meat in the freezer.

The trail was narrow and winding in some places and lined with trees, which afforded some places to hide should he need to. He had not been on this trail before, and a leisurely run would make him feel more comfortable with the area. In a way, he was hoping not to meet anyone today because a bike ride tomorrow would be exciting and great exercise. He picked up the pace a little as he entered the second mile.

Twenty minutes later, he turned around and headed back to the bridge. Most of the people now were walkers, and because of the darkness, they were thinning out. He would get his wish and ride tomorrow. For now, he would head back to the RV park and boot up the computer, connect it to the disposable cell phone, check his e-mail, have some dinner, watch a movie from the satellite dish on the fifth wheel, get a good night's rest, and see what the morrow brings.

After arriving at his campsite, he took a shower while the computer was booting up. This campsite had all the amenities: cable TV, water, electricity, and sewer. He could stay awhile if needed, but too long in one spot would be risky.

After his shower, he poured a glass of wine while the computer connected to his home computer, using the cell phone and the toll-free calling card number. Checking his e-mails, he noticed there was one from Dee, asking him to call her at home. She thanked him for the wonderful two days, made it home after leaving Logan Airport three hours late, and thought about him for the entire trip. She said she was late getting in but had to e-mail him as soon as possible. "Pleeeease call me," was her last entry.

He disconnected the cell phone and dialed Dee's home phone via the calling card. It rang four times, and her answering machine picked up.

"Hey, is the Vermont Vixen at home or are you already out on some hot date with my replacement?" he said after the beep.

Immediately Dee picked up.

"Hey, yourself," she answered. "I was monitoring the number on my caller ID and saw 'unavailable' and thought it was a salesman. It's that time of night, and they never list their number. So where are you?"

"About four miles from your house and on my way to see you," he teased.

"You liar. But if you are, I'm waitin' on the couch with nuthin' on but my merkin," she said. "Where are you really?"

"Wish I were a fur piece closer," he said, a pun to her reference to a merkin. "Actually I'm at a roadside rest in Pennsylvania heading to Arizona. I'm toying with the idea of getting a new fifth wheel. This one needs new tires, so time to trade it in. I'm planning on visiting in a couple of weeks as we planned. Are you still up for it?"

"The question is, are you up for it? So far I haven't changed my mind, but it has only been a couple of days. It seems like another lifetime away. By the way, I'm trying to organize a group of mothers who have lost a daughter in the last two or three years. I'm doing it on the Internet and have four contacts so far. Any suggestions of how to proceed with this?"

"Try the site for America's Most Wanted. They may offer some assistance. Also, search for missing children on the net and see if you can locate mothers that way. Other than that, I don't know what else you can do. Keep me informed via e-mail how you are doing, and I will try to come up with some more ideas."

"Good suggestions. I have some time now until after the holidays to work on this. It helps to redirect my grief, and who knows, I may turn up something on Dedra."

"I always have some time. I'm independently wealthy, or have you forgotten already?"

"I'm not interested in your money. I'm after your bod. You can fill me in on all the boring financial details later."

"We will see," he responded. "Meanwhile, I must get back on the road to Phoenix to take care of some financial business and all that boring stuff."

"Call me tomorrow if you can. Good night and sleep well."

"Good night," he said, and pushed the end button on the cellular.

He thought about getting into a chat room, but decided to get a good night's sleep. He took a melatonin and a Tylenol PM to ensure he would not wake up until morning. After shutting down and turning off the computer, he climbed the stairs to the bedroom, got naked, and crawled under the covers. He dreamed.

He was walking down a dark alley between two tall brick buildings. Although he could not see the buildings very clearly, he could tell they were old from the musty smell. Shadows played on the brick like swaying black ghosts moved by the wind. Light was coming from behind him, but he could not turn around. He was afraid to turn around. What was following him? He knew something, or several somethings, were behind him, pursuing him. He felt trapped, but he must keep going deeper into the alley. Whatever was behind him was quiet, very quiet, but he could feel the presence. The hair on the back of his neck stood out, and the scalp at the back of his head tingled. He needed to keep going away from it, them. They were gaining, and he knew now there was more than one, perhaps many. He tried to run but couldn't. His feet felt heavy. He was able to move only with effort, not knowing how deep the alley was. The light was still behind him and the shadows were getting smaller, closer. He stumbled and almost fell, but he kept going, deeper into the alley and darkness.

Finally he reached a third wall, directly in front of him, blocking the way. He looked for a door, but there was none. Time to turn around, he thought, turn around and face whatever it was back there. He placed his palms up against the wall in front of him. It felt cold and damp and slimy like a dead fish just out of a cold mountain stream. He turned his head over his shoulder and looked for his pursuers. There was nothing. Nothing but a dark alley, except there on the ground was one alley cat or were there more. It was hard to see in the dimness, but there was at least one. He turned completely around. The cat wore that smirky smile that all cats have, but it was silent, staring, and waiting for its prey to make the next move. "Dedra," he said. The cat turned and walked away. He was not sure, but he thought he sensed other cats further back turning and also walking away. He then dropped into a deep sleep and had no more dreams that night.

Twelve

Barely remembering the dream, he started to stir. He was groggy and dry-mouthed from the pills. He lifted his head slightly and looked at the alarm clock. It was almost 6:00. He had slept for nine hours. He sat up and stretched. "I have a feeling this will be a successful day of hunting," he said, out loud to no one. Taking a page from one of Wayne's favorite books of backwoods sayings, "I'm so hungry, I could eat the ass end of a menstruating skunk this morning." Only Wayne would pronounce it "menastratin."

Turning on the CD player, he fixed himself some coffee, and while it was brewing, he fried up an egg for his first bagel sandwich of the day. He was making an egg McSusan or McWhoever it was. He was losing track of who was left in his meat locker. Playing through the speakers was "Navajo Rug." "Two eggs up on whiskey toast, home fries on the side. Wash it down with some roadside coffee that burns up your insides" sang Jerry Jeff Walker.

He ate standing up. By the time he gulped down the second cup of coffee, he finished the sandwich and was ready to ride. He put on bike clothes, attached the fanny pack around his waist, took the camelback out of the refrigerator, grabbed his shoes and helmet, and stepped out of the fifth wheel. The reddish orange sun was coming up, casting a fiery glow on the bare trees on the west side of the park. It was as if an artist was painting a psyche-delic picture with the trees red halfway down. "The sun cometh up in russet mantel clad," he remembered from his high school Shakespeare classes. That was about as descriptive as he could get. It looked like this would be a beautiful morning to ride.

There was no wind, and it was cool. After placing his camel-back, helmet, and bike shoes in the cab of the pickup, he removed the bike from the storage bin under the gooseneck of the fifth wheel and placed it in the bed of the pickup. He pushed the button on the remote, and the alarm on the fifth wheel was armed. The alarm was not only to deter burglars, but it would let him know if anyone had entered or attempted to enter it.

He started the big diesel and pulled out of the campsite, down the park road, and out past the empty office.

As he did yesterday, he parked near the Woodrow Wilson Bridge. He took the bike out of the back of the truck and after a few cursory stretches, donned his bike gear. He was anxious to get started. It was early, but there were already a lot of bikers, joggers, and walkers on the trail. He headed north this time. The trail was eighteen miles long. He could ride the full length of it twice if necessary. Carrying his own water in the camelback and a few power bars, "shingles" as the bikers called them, he could last three or four hours.

The trail was perfect. It wound around trees and grassy areas along the Potomac with a great view of downtown Washington. He was amazed that people would want to live here. He remembered an old description of D.C. that compared it to a Hershey bar, ninety percent chocolate and ten percent nuts.

This would be a great place for someone to disappear. Technically, D.C. was not a state, so would it contribute to his goal? Hell, yes, he thought. He can kill two birds here since he did not have Maryland on his magnetic board yet. He was almost finished with the eastern seaboard and the New England states. Vermont would be his last, just before he moved to the Bahamas. As Wayne was apt to say, he did not want to "shit in his own backyard," at least until he was ready to vacate.

He rode along, not noticing he had picked his pace up until he came up on some other bikers. He braked hard, and went around them to the right, startling them. He yelled back "sorry." Remembering why he was here, he slowed down. The trail was so flat, it was easy to go fast, considering he was in great shape and used to the long, grinding hills in Vermont. He would have to scope out the two he just passed on his way back. The trail snaked lazily along the river, and he reached the northern end in less than thirty minutes.

He stopped and got off the bike to stretch and prepare for the return trip when he saw a lone jogger stretching against a tree. She was wearing tight black running pants and a white jersey.

Her dark hair was pulled back and held in place with a large sweatband/ear warmer. She was leaning against the tree with her right hand. In her left hand she held her left foot behind her stretching her quads. The big "N" on the side told him they were New Balance running shoes.

She smiled at him. No doubt noticing the bulges under his tight biker shorts. His shirt was also tight around his chest. His physical condition attracted most of his victims to him. It was like Ted Bundy's eyes. Only Ted Bundy made too many mistakes. He let one victim get away, and he did not make the corpses completely disappear. He also shit in his own back yard too many times.

He smiled back and pushed his bike over to where she was stretching.

"Didn't your mother ever tell you not to smile at strangers," he chided.

"No," she said. "She taught me karate instead. That way I can smile at anyone I like."

"So you like me," he responded. "And we hardly know each other. Too bad you aren't a biker. Bikers do it in the saddle."

"Too bad you're not a runner," she said. "Runners do it on the track."

"With their shoes on, no doubt," he said.

She laughed.

"You don't waste much time, but I must get a leg on, so to speak. See you around." At that, she started her run. He noticed she had nice legs and was obviously in great shape.

Getting back on the bike, he started after her.

"See you on the return trip," he said, as he passed her.

"Maybe, if you're lucky," she said as he passed.

I feel lucky, he thought.

Going back the way he came, he kept looking for another opportunity. The two women he had startled earlier were heading in his direction. They were both butt ugly, but had nice bodies. Although ugly was okay, good looking was more appealing; however, if he had to settle for ugly, he would. *I guess ugly could taste good too*, he thought as he nodded his head and smiled at them. They smiled back, either not recognizing him from the front, or forgiving him for his breach of bike etiquette.

He continued back along the path passing his truck and continuing on toward Mount Vernon. No other prospects interested him. Most of the other people on the track were either too old, too fat, or the wrong sex. He reached the southern end of the trail in less than an hour. He must have been cranking at twenty-plus miles per hour. This time, however, he was more alert. Some trail users were known to turn in reckless bikers to the police. If that happened, he would have to leave and abort this plan.

On the way back, he passed the two butt uglies on their way back. He smiled again and noticed in his helmet mirror, that the outside rider turned as he passed and checked him out. If the jogger was not available, he would try to find those two again. He wanted to get his business done today if possible. It was almost another thirty minutes before he saw the jogger heading back to her stretching tree. She had been running for over an hour or had taken a rest. He slowed down and approached her as carefully as he could.

"We're going to have to quit meeting like this," he said from behind her.

"How else should we meet?" she asked.

He pulled up along her left side.

"I could meet you for dinner," he countered. "That is, if you won't karate chop me to death. You should be hungry after running for over an hour."

"I run so I can eat. So why are you in D.C.? Assuming you don't live here."

"You are correct. Like ninety percent of this city, I'm here on business."

"What kind of business? And don't give me that If-I-tell-you-I'll-have-to-kill-you routine, because that is true of the same ninety percent of the city."

"Okay, I'll tell you, but I'll still have to kill you. Maybe I'll try killing you with kindness, or with a high cholesterol, high calorie dinner at one of D.C.'s fine dining establishments."

"I can handle both. So what brings you here?"

"I'm writing a book on recreational trails. This is one of the best around here. I bet it's really nice in the spring and summer."

"It's beautiful in the spring, I haven't seen it in the summer yet, but I bet it's too hot to enjoy except in the morning."

"I bet you're right," he said, as pulled behind her to let two joggers go by in the opposite direction. "So why aren't you here in the summer?"

"I'm an intern for a senator, and he was off this past summer for the recess," she said.

They were approaching the end of the trail, so she slowed to a walk. He got off his bike and walked beside her.

"Which senator?" he asked.

"You know too much already, and it's my turn to ask. Which restaurant?" she queried as she sidled up to the same stretching tree.

"You don't give me much chance to think," he said, as he laid his bike down and sat beside it on the ground. "I know an Italian place in Georgetown. If I remember right, it's called Papa Razzi's."

"Never been there, or to Georgetown, for that matter. Isn't that where the university is?"

"Yes, there is also a strip there called M street, where a lot of students and others hang out, but I'm not proposing we go that route."

"I know you haven't thought this through, but did you have a time in mind?" she teased.

"I could pick you up at 7:00, and we could be there, depending on where you live, by about 7:30 or so. I don't like to eat too early, and traffic gets a little better after 6:00."

"I'll meet you there at 7:00," she said as she finished her stretches. "No offense, but I don't know you that well, and the world has some pretty strange people in it. For all I know, you could be the next Jeffrey Dahmer."

"That's all right with me. How will I know it's you? Can you give me a name to go on?"

"And yours is?" she asked.

"Jeff," he said with a smile.

Her eyes widened and then she smiled.

"Linda," she said, as she trotted away.

"Okay, Miss Linda, and by the way Jeffrey only went after boys," he called after her. Under his breath, he muttered, "and he let one get away."

He smiled as he got himself and the bike up. *That was the*

easy part, he thought. *Now to get down to business.*

He rode back to the bridge, feeling assured and comfortable. This one could be tricky, but if she was an intern for a senator, she might not be quickly forgotten. It was almost 10:30 and he had some plans to make. By the time he got back to the fifth wheel, it was almost noon.

He booted up the laptop, dialed his home number, and logged onto the computer. A quick glance at the status screen told him everything was normal. There had been an intruder alert. He replayed the digital recording that the sensor's camera made and saw one buck and three does. It had snowed last night on the mountain, verifying that winter was already on the way. The deer passed by the camera and then headed back down the mountain away from the mansion. Checking his e-mails, there was a note from Dee to call. The usual Spam e-mails were deleted. He logged off and shut down the computer.

Her phone rang the obligatory four times before the answering machine picked up.

"Dee," he said. "Dee, pick up if you are there."

"Hello," she said, a little out of breath. "I was in the back room with the computer and came running as soon as the phone rang. How are you?"

"I'm great. I couldn't wait until tonight to call. I stopped in Little Rock to do some business and decided to call. Now I have nothing to look forward to before I go to sleep."

"I have some good news to tell you, and you have permission to call me more than once a day."

"So what's the good news? Win the lottery so you don't need me anymore?" he teased.

"No lottery, I'm forming a group of parents who have lost children, only I'm limiting it to situations similar to mine. There is a lot of information on the web. I found one mother in Dallas who is just recently missing a daughter. Her situation sounds similar to mine. I'm going to call her tonight and get some more specifics. So, if the phone is busy tonight when you call, I'll probably be talking to her."

"That sounds great," he said. "I have some maybe bad news. I might not be able to call tonight. I'll most likely be on the road if all goes well here. I should be done earlier than I thought and

111

when I finish, I'll be heading back to Vermont. If so, I'll call as soon as I can from home."

"Okay, I'll keep you informed by e-mail as to what happens. I'll try your cell phone first, but I haven't been able to reach you by phone yet. When do you think you'll head to Florida?"

"I don't keep my cell phone on while I'm driving or in meetings. It's too much of a distraction. At other times, I just forget to turn it on. E-mail is the best way to keep me informed. As far as coming to Florida, I'll keep to the original schedule of after the holidays, if that's all right with you. That way I won't have to buy you a present."

She laughed. "Well, you can expect the same from me. After all, what do you get for a man who owns a mansion and a Hummer?"

"I could always use another hummer," he said. "Oh, you're talking about my Humvee. I thought you were talking about that thing you do so well in the shower."

"Well, I can see that this conversation had deteriorated quite rapidly," she said. "Let me get back to my computer before you get both of us all excited."

"Too late," he said. "I do have to get back to the big world of finances, though. Don't want the other guy to take a million away from me because I waste my time talking about sex with you. If I don't call tonight, you'll know I'm on the road and will definitely call tomorrow."

"Wham bam," she said.

"Thank ya, ma'am," he replied.

After he hung up, she sat for a moment on the couch thinking about where this relationship would be in a month from now, if it would be anywhere. "Oh well," she said to herself. "If it doesn't go anywhere, that would be better than a bad relationship. I've already had one of those." The only good thing that resulted from her former marriage was Dedra, and that now appeared to be lost.

With a tear in her eye and her heart aching, she got off the couch and went back to her computer, taking the wireless phone with her this time. She reread the e-mail from the woman in Dallas. Her missing daughter's case was so similar to Dedra's, it gave her goose bumps. The only difference other than the location was that Alice was missing for only a month, Dedra almost two years. Alice and Dedra were the same age approximately, they both were athletic, and both had met someone on a bike ride. Dee replied to the e-mail, asking the Dallas mother if she was available to join her in a chat room tonight. They would then discuss specific details of her case.

Dee was checking other missing children postings on the net. There were so many hits, she decided to limit her search to women about Dedra's age. There were still a lot of hits. Her earlier research about missing women divulged incredible statistics. There were over three thousand missing women every year. Many were never investigated. It seems, law enforcement officials have a lot more to do than look for missing women, especially ones vanishing without any apparent foul play. Law enforcement must write them off, believing that the missing women have run off with a boyfriend and will return when they are ready.

Dee made some notes on some of the posted missing people web sites that were listed. She planned to visit them one by one and contact the ones that looked encouraging. She then posted her own message on several bulletin boards, asking that anyone with a missing daughter with similar circumstances as Dedra's e-mail her.

She decided to check some of the chat rooms for man_iac. Logging into a chat room under Dedra's "orangejewce2," she opened the find-friends screen and typed in "man_iac." There were no hits.

After talking with Dee, he decided to have some fun on the computer. He had not been in a chat room for a while, but needed to keep his skills sharp in case he ever wanted to use this tool again.

He logged in and chose the name "elusive_boy." He had many names. The one he used to find Dedra was long-ago deleted. He entered a thirties something chat room to see what was going on.

No_body_else: hi, elusive boy
elusive_boy: hi, chat room

No_body_else: where u from e-boy?

elusive_boy: all over

No_body_else: LOL, living up to your name huh?

elusive_boy: basically, trying to stay in the shadows, just wanna watch

No_body_else: you should be voyer_boy

elusive_boy: depends on what there is to peek in on

No_body_else: anything u want in here except the chat police may expel u

elusive_boy: I'll just evade them then

No_body_else: LOL, ok, watch away

A window popped up announcing a friend was on line and listed orangejewce2. This must be Dee on Dedra's computer. This was going to be more fun than he thought. He joined the chat room that she was in.

orangejewce2: hi, elusive

He did not respond

aintjusweet: hi elusive

No response

orangejewce2: we are discussing missing children, know any?

No response

orangejewce2: this is serious, if u don't want to participate, please leave

No response

aintjusweet: probably the chat police

orangejewce2: maybe

aintjusweet: so oj, when was your daughter missing?

orangejewce2: two years in February, and yours?

aintjusweet: october 26 was the last day she was seen by her friends

orangejewce2: I'm sorry, any leads?

aintjusweet: no, she just vanished, her dog was found dead in her apartment the next day the vet said it was poisoned

orangejewce2: may I ask what she was doing just before she vanished

aintjusweet: she worked that morning, went home and that was it

orangejewce2: in your e-mail u said she was athletic

aintjusweet: yes, she had been riding the day before with a friend. the friend said she met someone while on her bike, but he was not seen with her the next day when she vanished

orangejewce2: did the police get a description?

aintjusweet: not a good one, he was in biking clothes. you know, helmets, sunglasses. all she said was that he was good looking and had an athletic build

orangejewce2: not much to go on

aintjusweet: you say your dedra had a similar experience before she disappeared

orangejewce2: yes, the bike ride, met someone, then gone no other clues

aintjusweet: it's frustrating

orangejewce2: tell me about it

aintjusweet: have you found any more missing women cases that are similar?

orangejewce2: a few promising, but not yet, but I'm looking it's a big country and there are thousands missing

orangejewce2: elusive are you still eavesdropping, this is supposed to be a private chat room

Lying, he responded:

elusive_boy: yes, I'm sorry, I logged into this room and then went to get a cup of coffee

orangejewce2: how much have you seen?

elusive_boy: just the last bit about missing women I scrolled up to see what you were chatting about.

orangejewce2: and?????

elusive_boy: I sympathize with you, I met someone recently whose daughter is missing under similar conditions

orangejewce2: really, do you have a name or e-mail address? I would like to talk to her.

elusive_boy: I do, but I need to talk to her first to see if it's ok

orangejewce2: I understand here is my e-mail
orangejewce2 @ hotmail.com
what is yours?

elusive_boy: I will provide that privately. I don't like to give out e-mails in chat rooms

elusive_boy: I peeked at your profile and you look too young to have a daughter who is very old

orangejewce2: you must have found a picture of my daughter, this is her computer

elusive_boy: ok, that explains it

elusive_boy: I have to go now. it's been nice and I will get back to you if she wants you to contact her.

orangejewce2: ok, bye and thanks, hated to be so rude at the beginning, but we are still so sensitive about our missing daughters.

elusive_boy: I can understand bye

orangejewce2: bye

aintjusweet: well, I have to run now too. keep looking for more missing women

orangejewce2: I will and keep in close touch. maybe we can stir up some interest if there are enough of us

orangejewce2: hopefully yes. bye

aintjusweet: bye

Dee made a mental note to ask her computer friend Joe how to delete Dedra's profile. Somehow, Mr. Elusive was able to see a picture of Dedra, and she needed to get rid of that ability. There was so much about computers and chat rooms she did not know, but she was learning. Just as she was about to log off, there was a ding sound from the computer. She knew from before that there was a new e-mail for her. She switched over to outlook express and opened an e-mail from an *msjenkyns @ aol.com*. The subject was a missing daughter.

Dear ms Jewce,
    I am responding to your bulletin board memo about a missing daughter. My daughter has been missing for three years. She too was athletic, rode a bike, but on the day she disappeared, she was roller blading by herself. There were no clues except her friends say she went out with someone she had met that morning in the park. My husband and I have been devastated and, as you, frustrated by the lack of concern by the local authorities. I understand

you want to form a group to look into this type of disappearance. If so, call me and we will help however we can.

Mary Jenkyns

Just before signing off and shutting down, Dee fired back a quick note giving out her phone number. Something she did not like to do, but it could be changed later if this turned out to be some sort of weirdo; however, her intuition told her this was genuine. There may be some hope after all. This may be just a coincidence, but she wondered how many it would take to get some attention from, if necessary, the FBI.

That was interesting, he thought. It seemed like Dee was making a little progress in her pursuit to find more missing women's parents. He needed to fuel the fire by finding the e-mail address of one of his victim's parents and feed that to her. He could remember some of the names and, for sure, the cities. Feeding another name to Dee and remaining close to see how things progressed was a game he did not expect from his efforts. This was like holding onto a lit firecracker and tossing it just the second before it went off. The bigger the firecracker, the bigger the thrill. He could lose more than his fingers, but he did not think so.

He did a quick search of names in Oklahoma City. One of the women was an Indian with the last name of Satepahoudle, a name not likely to be very common. There was only one, and the search revealed an e-mail address. This should be the mother of Janie, one of his early victims. He sent an e-mail to Dee, using the elusive_boy e-mail address in Yahoo. He then got rid of that identity, logged off and shut down the computer. It was almost 4:30, time to get ready for more fun and games.

Thirteen

He had never been to Pappa Razzi's, so he arrived early, at 6:00. He checked with the maître d', if you could call her that. She was in her early twenties and most likely working her way through the university. Although if she could afford to go to Georgetown, she probably did not need to work. It was nice to know there were still some people who had to forage in the woods of life just to keep from going hungry. She was able to get him reservations for 7:30, the earliest open time. He used the last name Grave, first name Digger. It went right over her head, or else, she had no sense of humor. If Linda was the punctual type, they could hang around the bar and talk until the table was ready.

The restaurant had high ceilings, was noisy, and poorly lit. There was a stairway to the upstairs, where all the smoke from the bar area floated like mist from a swamp. Music from the speakers was barely audible, but he could make out the voice of Sinatra. He assumed they would play Dean Martin's "That's Amore" next.

He worked his way to the bar, hardly noticed, and lit on an empty seat. Everyone there had someone to talk to. This was not a pick-up bar or "meat wagon," as Wayne would say.

He got the barmaid's attention and ordered a glass of Merlot. He had put on a pair of glasses before entering the bar. They were nonprescription plastic lenses with minimal correction. He used them more for disguise than for reading. They would be incinerated within two days. He noted the location of the men's room and the emergency exits. While fingering the packet of Rohypnol tablets in his jacket pocket, he picked up a menu from the bar and buried himself in it. No use attracting attention. He was sipping his wine when she tapped him on the shoulder.

"I came a little early," Linda said.

"You scared the shit out of me. Excuse my French," he said, as he wiped the spilt wine from his hand.

"Sorry, I suppose my point count is negative now," she said.

"I don't assign points," he said as he looked her over. Even the black leather mid-length coat belted at the middle could not hide her large breasts. At least a "C" size, maybe even "D," he thought. When he saw her earlier in her running clothes, her dark hair was tied back with the ear warmers. Now it flowed down to her shoulders in gentle waves of midnight black. Her eyes, dark as coal, gave her a dark, blank look, much the opposite of Little Orphan Annie's white stare. Her pointed nose on any other woman would have been considered large. On her, it added a noble look. Her lips were full with the upper one slightly parted showing sparkling white teeth, like a cute chipmunk. She wore little makeup and needed none. "I must say, you clean up really wonderfully."

"I almost didn't recognize you without your bike clothes," she said. "You look like Clark Kent with those glasses on. Is Superman in there somewhere?"

"If you can find a phone booth, I'll let you help me change," he teased.

"Not so fast, biker boy, I still have to have my guard up. Also, I need at least one of those," she said, nodding toward the wine.

"Merlot?" he asked. "As long as you don't slip me a kryptonite cocktail, I'll gladly get you drunk."

"I feel like getting drunk after the week I've had," she said. "Can you get that wine as fast as a speeding bullet?"

He caught the bartender's eye and held up his drink and two fingers. The bartender nodded that he understood and reached above him to pull down two wineglasses. When he turned back around, she was pulling up a stool to sit next to him. Her left breast rubbed against his arm. She smiled coyly like a high schoolgirl who just got caught looking at a boy's bulge.

"So, what evil befalls the beautiful intern that I can leap the tallest building to rescue her?"

"I'll tell you later if I feel I can trust you," she said. "When do we eat?"

"I have reservations for 7:30, and it's now 7:00," he said,

119

glancing at his watch. Time enough for a couple of glasses of wine, since you are in need."

"I have to visit the little girls' room. I told the cab to pick me back up at 9:00. Do you think that is enough time?"

"It should be. If it isn't, you can always catch another. They shouldn't have trouble picking up another fare here at that time if you don't show. If necessary, I could always take you home."

"No, I'm a big girl now and can take care of myself. Like I said this afternoon, I don't trust you just yet," she said as she headed for the ladies' room.

While waiting for her to return, he looked carefully around the bar and restaurant. There was no one paying attention to them. They looked like most of the diners and would be hard to distinguish from others if the police came asking questions.

Ten minutes later, she returned.

"Whatever happened to potty parity? There was a line to get in. I hope you brought your gold card. I'm starving."

"Oh, didn't I mention this was Dutch treat tonight. I always do that on the first date."

"Don't get many second dates, do you?"

"Not many. I think I'll make an exception tonight, however, and pick up the tab."

"Good, because I was almost out of here."

"Table for Mr. Grave Digger," said the naïve maître d', who started to blush as she realized the name she had just called. Several of the patrons waiting for a table started to laugh.

Realizing he would now draw attention to himself should he answer the page, he decided to ignore it.

"That was funny," said Linda. "Probably some fraternity prank."

The maître d' did not repeat the name and returned to her station, still embarrassed.

"Let me check on our reservations," he said, as he lifted his wineglass and went to the front of the restaurant.

"I'm sorry," he said to the girl and slipped her twenty dollars. "That was a cruel trick I played. Could you forgive me and take us to our table?"

"Okay," she said, looking at the twenty dollars. Being too

embarrassed by the joke, she did not look at him. "This way please."

"Let me get my date, and we'll be right back," he said. He went back to the bar and got Linda. "I bought Mr. Grave Digger's place, since he was apparently not here to be seated."

She sipped the last of her wine and led the way to the front where the maître d' with her head still bowed, took them to their table next to a window. The window's heavy drapes were closed, preventing passersby from looking in on the diners.

He held the seat against the window out for her. After she was seated, he took the seat to her left with his back to the other diners.

"I need another glass of wine," she said. "I told you I had to drown my sorrows tonight. I hope I'm not making a bad impression."

"I don't mind. Here, have the rest of mine," he said, as he handed her his glass. "Save room for dessert, though."

The waiter brought them water. He ordered another glass of wine for both of them and told the waiter they already had run up a bar tab.

"So, you have had quite an experience as an intern," he said, really not interested in a response.

"You bet and you'll be able to read all about it in the papers soon. News at eleven as the old saying goes."

"There is another saying that 'hell hath no fury like a woman scorned,'" he offered.

"You got that right," she said, in response. "So tell me more about yourself. You dress well and seem to not have a care in the world."

"Do you want the Michener version, or shall I start more recently and go from there," he said, stalling for time to get his lies straight.

The waiter came back with the menu and went through his specials' spiel, giving him more time to think. After finishing, the waiter said he would be back to take their order when they were ready. *Right*, he thought. *When we are ready. More likely when you are ready.*

"Okay," he said. "Where was I? Oh, yes, like I said this morning, I'm traveling as many bike trails as I can to write a

121

book about the best ones. It's a good way to spend my time, and I meet some nice people."

"Let me see your left hand, please," she said, unexpectedly. "I want to look for traces of a wedding ring. That sounds like a story to me."

He held out his left hand for her.

"Satisfied, or do you want to look through my wallet too for pictures of my wife and family?"

"You pass," she said, without emotion. "Can you make any money at that?"

"Not really. I'm doing this for the fun of it. I already have enough money. Do you know what you want to eat yet?"

"I'll have what you're having as long as it comes with wine," she said, as the waiter glided to their table and hovered like a hawk searching for a mouse in the field below.

"Are you ready, sir?" the waiter asked.

"Yes. We will have the antipasti as an appetizer, the Caesar salad for two, the gnocchi with pesto sauce, and a gallon of your finest wine."

Linda almost choked on her wine as she held back a laugh.

"Very well," said the waiter, looking down his nose at nothing in particular. "I'll bring your bread sticks with the appetizer. The wine list is on the table."

"No sense of humor in this place," he said, shaking his head.

"No, they probably don't understand someone having fun in this city, Mr. Grave Digger," she said with a smirk. "You embarrassed that poor girl half to death with that one."

"So you saw through me, did you? I thought that was really clever. One time at an Outback Steakhouse, I used the name Gozinya, Peter. You should have seen the reaction when they called that name."

"Wish I could have been there," she said, smiling. "I like a man with a sick sense of humor. They seem to have more fun than the rest of the world."

"I haven't been thrown out of a place yet. If it wasn't an Outback, I probably would have got booted if I'd have answered. Most of the people who run these places are young and naïve. They really don't throw themselves into their jobs. They want a paycheck, and that's it."

"And so who gives you a paycheck, Mr. Gozinya?"

"I earned my money the old-fashioned way. I inherited it. You could say I'm filthy rich, since my father was in the refuse removal business."

"So, we can have a bottle of Dom Perignon tonight?"

"If they have it and you want it. I've had it, and it's not worth the price. Sure, it's bubbly and expensive, but I've had better house wines."

"Well, I'm satisfied with the wine we're drinking. Do you suppose it's available by the gallon?"

"Whatever you want, my dear." The waiter brought the appetizer and bread sticks. The antipasti was fresh mozzarella slices with tomatoes, prosciutto, red and green peppers, pickled eggplant, and various other delectables. They both were hungry, and the breadsticks and antipasti were both disappearing fast.

"When do you have to go back to work?" he asked.

"Not for another week. I'm taking advantage of the break to paint my apartment." She was starting to slur her words slightly.

"So what sorrows are you replacing with wine?" he asked. "Did a boyfriend leave you high and dry?"

"You're close," she said. "My boss, the son-of-a-bitch bigshot senator. Won't leave his wife for me, even though he promised to six months ago. I don't mind telling you this because I made up my mind to go public with it next week."

"That may be more information than I want to know, but who is this wonderful public servant? Didn't they all learn a lesson from Clinton?"

"I'll save the details for the press. I don't want you to scoop my story."

The waiter brought the gnocchi, took the appetizer plates away, and asked if they wanted more bread sticks.

"Yes, and two more wines," he said

"You know how to please a woman don't you? But I'll be too wasted for you to take advantage of tonight. These are really good," she said as she tasted another forkful of gnocchi. "I have never had them before. They have lots of garlic in them. Makes me thirsty." She took another sip of wine.

"I'm glad you like them. But they have a tendency to swell up, so try not to eat too many. You are painting your apartment, are you? I'm quite good at that. Need some help?"

"By the time I get to trust you enough to let you in my apartment, I will have to be back at work," she said, as she put down her fork. "You are right, these things are filling. I don't think I have room for dessert."

"Perhaps a cup of decaf cappuccino and a glass of sherry?" he asked.

"I think I can handle that, especially the sherry. If you will excuse me, I need to use the little girls' room again," she said as she started to get up. She was a little tipsy from the four glasses of wine but was able to make it to the restroom without attracting too much attention.

"How was everything?" asked the waiter.

"Wonderful," he said. "We are finished except we would like two decaf cappuccinos and two Adonis's made with Jerez sherry."

"Very well," he said, as he cleared the table.

Within five minutes, the waiter returned with the sherry cocktails and cappuccinos. The waiter walked away from the table. He reached over, grabbed her cocktail glass, and dropped in the Rohypnol. As he moved the glass from the right side of her cappuccino to the left, he swirled the sweet drink, distributing the powdery drug so that it was all dissolved. Two minutes later, Linda reappeared.

"Another line in the ladies' room. Sorry I took so long. What time is it?"

"Not a problem," he said, as he looked at his watch. "It's twenty till nine," he lied, It was 9:15. Hopefully the cab had come and gone.

"Well, as soon as I finish this, we, I mean, I have to go," she said, as she cradled the sherry in both hands as if it were the finest brandy. She took a drink. "Tastes sort of nutty and sweet. What's in it." But it came out "wazinit."

"It's the type of sherry. It should taste a little like raisins, too. It also has sweet vermouth and bitters."

"I can taste the raisins, a little bit," she said.

"Could I have your phone number just in case you need a drinkin' buddy to tell your story to? I have the nicest of intentions and would like to see you again."

"Give me yours, and I'll call you if I survive the night," she said as she pulled out a pencil and paper from her handbag. "I'll call you tomorrow as soon as I can. I have a bike and maybe we can go for a ride away from the city."

"Sounds fair enough. It's 555-1001," he said, making up a number. He noticed her eyes were starting to get a glassed-over look. The drug must be taking effect early because of the alcohol. "Do you want to finish your cappuccino before we leave?"

"Sure," she said, but it came out like sthure. She finished the sherry and then attacked the cappuccino. She was not drunk enough to attract attention, at least, not yet. If too many people noticed, he might abandon his pursuit.

"Is there anything else?" asked the waiter as he approached from behind him.

"No, just the check please," he said. Looking at Linda, he smiled. She smiled back at him, but she was drifting into another world. This would be the last thing she would remember, if the dead have memories. She was sort of melting now. The wicked witch of the west wetted down with drugs and alcohol. She was his, now and forever.

"I never asked you where you were from, what state?" he asked.

"California," she said, in a dream. "Los Angeles." She forgot all about the rest of the cappuccino. The cocktail was gone.

The waiter brought the check. It was a little under seventy dollars. In restaurants he wanted to be remembered, he would leave a hundred-dollar bill. In this case, he peeled away four twenty-dollar bills, not too much, not too little.

"Linda," he said. "Are you ready to go? I want to show you my fifth wheel."

"Yes, fifth wheel. What's a fifth wheel?" she said, not expecting an answer.

He stood, held her by the arm as she stood, and then placed his hand on her back, between the shoulder blades, guiding her out of the restaurant and toward his truck. She spoke no more. All the way to the park and up to the fifth wheel she was semi-comatose. Soon she would be in shock from loss of blood, staying like that all the way to Vermont, the mansion, the cutting table, oblivion.

He decided not to get a cat this time. D.C. was not a state, and he already had a California kitty. He fed her internal organs to all the cats. There was enough to go around. The next day, he talked to Dee, and every day after that. Three days later, he headed to the Mexican border. Time to get rid of this fifth wheel and any evidence therein.

Fourteen

The headlines and the news stories broke two days after Linda was supposed to start back as an intern. They read "Intern Missing, Senator Under Scrutiny." Dee took immediate notice. Her eyes jumped around the story, noticing: young, athletic, last seen jogging, no trace, no suicide note, apartment not disturbed. It was several minutes before she could settle down and read the story from beginning to end. Her parents lived in California, but there were no addresses given. However, the senator's name was there. He vehemently denied any involvement and vowed to help find the missing intern.

After breakfast and a run in the neighborhood, she decided to e-mail the senator's office, explain her newly formed group (she did not mention that so far only three were in the group), and asked his help in contacting the parents. She explained that speed was of the essence to keep the trail from getting cold. She then e-mailed her "group" to tell them that they may just have a new member. She also e-mailed Vermont to see if he had read about the missing intern.

She received an e-mail from elusive_boy about the missing woman from Oklahoma. She saved it to respond to later.

He pulled up to a small motel outside of Deming, New Mexico, registered under an alias, paid in cash, and drove to the back set of rooms to settle in for the afternoon and part of the night. He placed his laptop on the table, sat down and booted it up. Logging onto his home computer, he received Dee's e-mail and decided not to call her until later that night. His main concern now was in getting rid of the fifth wheel.

He spent the rest of the day going through the fifth wheel, making sure he had any identifying marks taken off. After a thorough search, he was ready for a nap. The room was clean, but one where you would not set your suitcase on the floor. Doing so would ensure you took home at least one and maybe several cockroaches, maybe even a scorpion. He had only a small hand-carry suitcase, which he took into the room and placed it on the chair next to the table. He closed the heavy, brightly colored yellow drapes, cutting the sun down to a knife blade of bright light from the seam where the drapes did not touch.

He called Dee.

"Hi," she said, picking up on the second ring. It was 6:00 in Florida, two hours later than New Mexico.

"Did you know it was me?" he asked.

"I guessed. The caller ID indicates unknown, and that usually is you. Did you see the news about the missing intern? Her case is similar to Dedra's, and I'm trying to contact the parents. I have two more members in our group since I e-mailed you this morning. I have contacted the *Today Show*, and they may give us a spot next month. Then the word will really get out."

"You ought to name yourselves MOMY-Gs, Mothers of Missing Young Girls," he said.

"I like that. Mind if we borrow it?"

"Not at all, glad to lend my assistance. You didn't ask where I am. Have you given up asking?"

"In a way. I figure you'll tell me if you want me to know and then kill me before I give away all your secrets."

"Just so you know, I left Vermont yesterday and am on the way to Phoenix to trade in my fifth wheel for a newer model. After I'm through wheeling and dealing, no pun intended, I'll be off to see a beautiful woman somewhere in the southeast."

"Well, if she lives somewhere around here, stop in and see me so I can kick you in those wandering nuts. Why go all the way to Phoenix for a fifth wheel?"

"Ouch!" he said. "I'll be sure to stop by. You sure know how to make a guy feel homesick. Phoenix is a great place to get a used RV. There are plenty of snowbirds willing to trade or sell. I'm really tired from driving almost nonstop from Little Rock, so I can't talk a lot. Gotta get me some shuteye, as they say out West. I sure am glad this MOMY-Gs thing is working out for you. Please keep me informed. I can kick in some cash if you need a donation."

"Thanks for the offer. We may need some money for rewards or travel later on if this thing gets rolling. I'll keep you informed by e-mail. Thanks for calling."

"I'll talk to you later when I'm not so tired," he said. "Bye."

"Bye," she said, and let out a sigh.

As he hung up, he stretched out on the bed. He slept, dreamlessly. The two-day trip to New Mexico left him tired.

He woke without an alarm at three A.M. There was no noise from the highway. The time was right to take a leisurely drive across the border to do what was necessary. He showered; drying off with the threadbare towel, which was not much bigger than a face cloth. It smelled from the hard water it was washed in. He could have stayed in an expensive hotel with all the pampering he could stand, but this made him feel like he was blending in and returning to his roots. He was also not as likely to be remembered under these circumstances.

Before shaving, he started the little pot of coffee on the bathroom sink. At least he had some amenities, although the coffee smelled like old running shoes as it perked noisily through the premeasured packet of ground beans. He poured the coffee into a Styrofoam cup and put a lid on it for later.

Gathering up his computer and overnight bag, he headed to the truck for his drive south of the border. The diesel made its usual racket starting and warming up. There were no other patrons on this side of the motel who would be awakened. By the time he idled around to the front and out on to the highway, the big engine was purring like a kitten, albeit a large kitten.

Heading south on one of the roads that would take him across the border, he reached in the cooler and pulled out a cold Mexican bagel sandwich to go with the tepid stale-tasting border motel coffee. "Yum yum," he said to himself. "What a day to dump a trailer."

It was still dark as he entered Mexico, having stopped at the border crossing just long enough to answer the questions from the guard at the gate, who had been sound asleep when he approached. He passed through as the guard stared at the fifth wheel. He would probably be sound asleep again before the fifth wheel was out of earshot. He would return by a different route without the fifth wheel of course, so there would be no record of it.

After driving into Mexico a few miles, he took a side road that the map showed would lead him to another road to re-enter the States. It was pitch black under a moonless night. When he stopped to unhitch the trailer, he could hear coyotes in the distance. He first changed the plates on the truck and took off the plates from the back of the fifth wheel. He then entered the fifth wheel for the last time, long enough to set the timer on the small incendiary device and to turn on the gas stove. He did not light the burners. In an hour, he would be across the border and heading west to Phoenix, when the morning sky would explode like an overinflated balloon, shoving a bright ball of orange fire toward the morning rays of sun. The fifth wheel would be in a thousand pieces over a wide portion of the desert. Any remaining parts would be burned into tangled ashes, giving some Mexican a late Christmas present of usable scraps.

He smiled as he worked his way back up to I-10 and headed toward Phoenix. Blowing up the fifth wheel instead of letting someone steal it was a last-minute decision. This certainly was faster, although it might attract more attention. While stopping at a convenience store in Tucson for some much better coffee, he bought a paper with headlines about the missing intern. The story indicated that the senator was romantically involved with the missing intern, but the senator denied any knowledge of her whereabouts. *What the fuck did he mean "romantically involved?" It would be an easier thing if he could just say they fucked each other's brains out and even easier if the paper could print it,* he thought.

The story went on to say that the FBI was working the case. He supposed the extra attention was due to the senator's involvement. Well, good luck, FBI. They won't find a body, unless they are looking for a slab of Linda in his freezer, or a Linda sandwich in his ice chest. "I wonder if there is DNA left in cooked body parts?" he asked himself. "I suppose it depends on whether it's well done or rare," he answered. "I never eat rare meat anymore. You don't know what you can catch from tainted meat." *Maybe madwoman disease,* he thought, smiling.

He pulled into Phoenix and checked into the Best Western in Awatuki, just south of town. After a short nap, he went to the lobby and picked up a copy of the local swap sheet. There would be plenty of used fifth wheels that the snowbirds were willing to get rid of. He went to the bar and pulled up a barstool.

"Bloody Mary," he told the approaching bartender.

"You got it" was the response.

The bar was a small room attached to the hotel/motel. It had a C-shaped bar along the wall, away from the windows. His eyes needed to adjust to the dimly lit interior. Even in late December, the Phoenix sun was bright, causing temporary blindness when you went inside. Slowly, he was able to see only three other patrons, and they had their eyes focused on CNN's Lynn Russell on the TV hanging from the corner to the left above the bar. He always thought she was unbelievably sexy, with her deep voice, puffy lips, and large deep eyes. I *wonder how big her tits are,* he thought as the bartender brought his drink.

"Run a tab?" the bartender asked.

"No," he said as he opened his wallet and placed a twenty on the bar. "Just keep 'em comin'."

"You got it," the bartender said. This must have been the bartender's favorite phrase, a man of few words caused by years in the same dead-end job. The desert sun may have fried some of the gray matter in his frontal lobe, too.

After the bartender returned with his change, laying it in the same spot on the bar.

He turned his attention to the RV section of the swap sheet. He circled several possibilities, all of them fifth wheels, all of them less than three years old, and all of them stating "must sell." Money was not a problem, but must sell means he could get it tomorrow, have them sign the title over to him, pay cash, and be gone before nightfall.

"More on the missing Washington, D.C. intern after the weather," stated Lynn. *Lynn Russell is one of them women you don't know whether to eat up your fuckin', or fuck up your eatin',* he thought. *I wonder what her lips taste like! I mean all four of them.*

"Here ya go," said the bartender.

He had finished one Bloody Mary and not even realized it.

The desert air must have made him thirsty.

"Thanks," he said, and grabbed for the drink.

"You got it," parroted the bartender as he grabbed the empty glass and enough cash from the pile to pay for the second drink.

"In an interview this afternoon, Senator Lane expressed his deepest regrets to the parents of Linda Amory for the disappearance of their daughter," announced Lynn. The scene switched to the senator standing outside the senate building with several microphones thrust in his face.

What a cocky-looking little man, an asshole, to put it bluntly, he thought. *How could a nice person want to fuck him, or for that matter elect him? Oh, well, the government is full of people who are full of themselves. There is no hope for this country with them running things. Perhaps I should head for the Cayman Islands sooner than I want to.*

"How's that?" asked the bartender.

He didn't realize that he was actually talking softly out loud now.

"Just wondering about the state of the state is all. One more, and I quit," he told the bartender. He had to call the owners of the fifth wheels tonight to arrange seeing them tomorrow.

He turned his attention to the TV as the senator was making his statement. The senator was pledging his full support and help to the FBI and reiterating how he had no knowledge of Ms. Amory's whereabouts. It was amazing how politicians could keep the same straight face whether they were lying or not. In this case, he was telling the truth, at least about the disappearance. Whether or not he was sincere about helping was improbable. He was more than likely relieved as hell that she was not around to tell the sordid details about their affair. Now he could lie like hell to his wife and say all she did was give him a blowjob or three, and sweat nights, wondering if she would show up and expose his lies. Had this not been a high-profile case, Linda's disappearance would already be forgotten.

He finished the third Bloody Mary, took two five-dollar bills and left the bartender a $3.50 tip. He did not want to leave too little or too much, so the bartender would not necessarily remember him. He already had a stock of Arizona bagel sandwiches, which were a couple of years old. But always staying in a

132

stealth mode (as he liked to call it) kept him from messing up when he had to be unnoticed.

On returning to his room, he made five calls and had four appointments, all of them in the morning. The fifth one was an answering machine, which he hung up on. He connected his laptop to the phone and checked the status of his mansion. All was in order. He then called Dee.

"Hi," she said picking up on the third ring this time.

"Hi, yourself," he said.

"I've got some good news." She sounded ecstatic. "I'm going to be on the *Today Show* next week, interviewed by Jane Peasly. I also received a phone call from Mrs. Amory, the mother of the missing intern who has been on the news a lot lately. The senator gave my information to her, and she wants to join our group, which, by the way, has grown to nine. More want to join, but I'm restricting it to just those with missing daughters and circumstances similar to Dedra's. And—"

"Slow down," he interrupted. "When next week, and should I postpone my visit until after you get back?"

"No, the interview isn't until Thursday, so I'll be free until then. When are you planning to show up?"

"If I finish tomorrow, and I don't see why not, I can be there Friday morning. Is that acceptable?"

"Friday will be wonderful. Just call if you will be later than noon. I have a hair appointment at one. Will you stay for New Year's Eve?"

"Of course. What will we do?"

"There is a nice restaurant in town that is advertising a set dinner and live music. I have never been, because it's very expensive. Since you are a man of untold wealth, we could go there. Afterward, we can watch the fireworks in my bedroom."

"The last part sounds like a winner," he said. "I could bring the Roman candle."

"I could light it for you. Make sure you bring a big enough one."

"I sure will," he said, laughing.

"Sounds great," she said, laughing in return. "See you in a couple of days then."

"See ya."

After she hung up, he held onto the phone for a few seconds. He thought he could feel some stirring inside, but he shook it off. *Can't fall in love now*, he thought. *But I also can't get rid of her. This MOMY-G thing of hers has gone too far. Besides, if she is gone, there are others to carry on the search. We'll see what happens.*

That night, he slept and had another alley dream:

It was the same alley, dark, damp, and close on both sides. It was quiet except for the drip, drip, drip of water hitting shallow puddles from an earlier summer shower. He was sweating from the closeness and the humidity of the still night. There was a dim light ahead of him, and he floated to it, not being able to control his legs. They were not moving, but he was. Ever closer, but slowly, he drifted to the light. The light did not get any larger. It remained as distant as a star, not moving, not getting any brighter. Then there were two. Two lights in the distance. He could make out a wall at the end of the alley, but the source of the lights was not apparent.

As he drifted closer, he heard the soft noise of padded feet behind him. He tried to turn around, but couldn't. His eyes were fixed on the lights at the end of the alley. He tilted his head to one side as he noticed a change in the lights. They were going from white to pink and then to red. As he got closer, being drawn as if by some magnet, he noticed a glistening. He also was aware of the patter of feet behind him. He could not tell how close it was. Was it a dog, a cat, as before, or some other beast?

Then he saw the end of the alley clearly, and on it was a mirror. As he squinted, he could see the lights were eyes. The eyes were staring at him. Piercingly red and looking straight at him, no mistaking it. The eyes were fixed on him, but there was no emotion in them, the eyes of a cat, unblinking, burning, fiery red.

Strangely, his reflection was not in the mirror. He was close enough to touch the mirror, and as he reached out, it was gone, and so were the eyes. His feet hit the ground. He could feel in control now, but the sweat was pouring off him. He quickly turned his head around and saw a shadow retreating, back toward the beginning of the alley where his dream started.

"Dedra!" he shouted.

The shadow turned around, and two red eyes looked at him without emotion, and then it all disappeared as he sat up in bed. The bed was soaked with his sweat. His muscles were all tensed, and he felt like a compressed spring. He got up and checked the air conditioner. It was working. He got a glass of water and sat down in the chair by the round table his computer rested on. "Jesus Christ," he muttered. "Must have been the Bloody Marys."

He went to his night bag and took out a bottle of pills he got with the Rohypnol in Mexico. The label read "carisoprodol," the generic name for Soma, a muscle relaxer. After downing the pill with water, he crawled back into bed, on the other side from where he got up in a cold sweat. In twenty minutes, he could feel the drug at work. He started to uncoil as though a giant hand was squeezing the tension out of him from his head down to his feet. Squeezing the last drop of tension as if squeezing a lemon to get the last bit of juice from it. He then eased into a drug-induced sleep, dreamless this time.

When Carlos Gallegos got out of bed that morning as the rooster crowed, he felt his 65-year-old body groan from head to toe. He didn't hear the rooster, because age had taken most of his hearing. He just knew from years of getting up before dawn that it was time to go to work. He was getting too old to do manual labor, but he had to eat. His grandchildren had to eat, too. His son-in-law was a no-good drunk, leaving Carlos's daughter and their five children, his lovely grandchildren, to fend for themselves. So Carlos had to haul vegetables in his old Ford pickup from the farm to the market. Some of the produce always seemed to fall off along the way, landing in Carlos's kitchen and supplementing the eggs from his chickens. The misappropriated vegetables were a small benefit from a job that paid him five dollars a day American. The cash money bought rice and flour, so the seven of them got by.

He stumbled out of the strawlined cot that had been his bed for as long as he could remember. A bed he shared with his wife Maria until she died five years ago. They made love countless times in that bed, but only one child survived. His heart ached for Maria more than his poor old tired bones.

There was no time for breakfast. That he would get on his way back from the farm with a load of vegetables. Carlos put on his worn shoes a clean shirt and a not so clean pair of pants. He yawned and combed his gray hair with his callused hands as he shuffled out of the hut to the pickup. The pickup started on the third try. He blinked the desert dust out of his eyes and headed down the dirt track that led to the highway. The dim headlights of the pickup barely lighting the way.

A mile down the main highway, he saw a shape in front of him, a large box, he thought. In the dawning light, he could not tell exactly what it was, but it was there and looked odd by itself in the desert. Still a mile or so from the box, he saw a truck pulling away. He stopped his own truck until the other one was out of sight leaving a trail of dust. He then went forward cautiously, looking in all directions and noticing no one. As he got closer, he saw that the box was a trailer, but one with a funny front end. It had what looked like a big hook on the front, and it looked abandoned. He stopped behind the trailer and walked all around, looking for signs of life. Knocking on the door, he yelled out, "Ola. Quien esta aqui?" There was no answer. He opened the door and yelled again. Still no answer, so he went in. He had never seen anything like it. It was a casa with everything in one place. *What a palace on wheels*, he thought. *Que bien*. The inside smelled like rotten eggs. Maybe something died in here. *This must be why the stranger got rid of it*, he thought. *It smells so bad, but I could find the dead animal and get rid of it.*

He sat down on the couch and thought for a minute. He could not hear the hiss of gas escaping from the stove. What if he just took it back to his house and kept it for the stranger. What harm could that be. He would be doing them a favor. He would have his daughter write a note, which he would bring back and place on a stick at this exact spot. It would tell them where to find the casa on wheels. If no one came looking, then he would keep it . Of course, he would have to make sure it was safe at night by sleeping in it. He looked around some more and found it had everything his little adobe shack was lacking. "I have to get out of here, it smells so bad."

He went back outside and pondered over the hook. How

could he get it back to his house. He pulled the pickup around to the front and backed under the gooseneck. He closed the tailgate to his truck and cranked the handle on the side of the fifth wheel. The gooseneck lowered onto the bed of his pickup, causing the old springs to sag, but they held. He got back into the truck and slowly pulled forward until the gooseneck held against the tailgate. He pulled slowly ahead. The trailer came with him. He turned around heading for home with his treasure. In thirty minutes, he was pulling alongside his shack.

His daughter and five grandchildren ran out of the shack to see what he had brought them. He joined them at the door to his palace on wheels. *"Que es esto!"* they all shouted. As he opened the door, the element on the incendiary device clicked once. A small electric spark ignited the gas fumes. Carlos did not have to worry anymore about food for his family. His family did not have to worry anymore about eating.

Fifteen

It indeed had been a banner day for Dee. First the phone call from the *Today Show*, setting up the day for the televised interview at her home in Florida. Then the call from the mother of the missing intern. The circumstances of Linda's disappearance were similar to Dedra's. Dee mentioned the spot on the *Today Show* and Mrs. Amory was hopeful that more attention would now be given to her daughter's circumstances. Mrs. Amory's fears that less and less attention was being devoted to her daughter were becoming a reality now that the senator was officially cleared. The police and FBI were suggesting that Linda must have run off with a boyfriend or went on a trip to forget her heart-breaking relationship with the senator. After all, there were thousands of missing people reported every year, and some of them eventually turned up. They did not add that a large number never were found alive or otherwise.

Also, she received a call from him, and she had a date for New Year's Eve, the first one in many years. She was starting to have real feelings for him. His voice was soothing, and he was the best lover she ever knew, not that there were a lot. She had experienced very few orgasms. Remembering the one morning with him, when she had multiple ones, left her weak in the knees and her heart beating fast. In two days, he would be here with the teasing and pleasing that she so wanted.

For now, she was going to immerse herself in this project, organizing this, so far, a diverse group of parents with missing daughters. They all thought that MOMY-G was a good name for the group, another reason she was glad she met him. With the exception of California, all members of the group were from different states. Linda and another woman were from California; however, Linda disappeared from D.C. and the other woman from Sacramento. The woman from Oklahoma with the hard-to-pronounce name, was a puzzle. After asking all her friends, she did not know anyone who called himself elusive-boy on the Internet. When Dee went back on line to find elusive-boy, he had disappeared. The name was not in use anymore. Elusive boy was turning out to be just that.

Another piece of the puzzle was the time span among the disappearances. The earliest was five years ago, and the latest was Linda. Only two of the parents had given up hope of finding their daughters alive. Even Dee was wrestling with the possibility that Dedra would not be found alive, or found at all. But they all wanted to bring closure, no matter what the outcome. Life changes had taken place for all the parents. There were divorces, lost jobs, savings spent on trying to locate their daughters, a lot of sleepless nights, a lot of antidepressants, and MOMY-G had located only ten members so far.

Dee was at her computer, opening a spreadsheet she had developed with all the information gathered so far. She checked her e-mail. There were sixty-five e-mails to download, so she just sat back and watched them pop up. Almost all had the same subject, missing daughter. Going through each one would be tedious and gut-wrenching. Reading the individual stories brought her to tears and sometimes a sob or two, but it had to be done. She felt bad about telling most of them that their missing child did not fit the profile. Most were either too old or too young. Some were not physically fit, and some were not women. She answered each e-mail. Only three fit the profile that was in her growing spreadsheet.

Dee also needed to start worrying about going back to work. She had a lot of annual leave accumulated, since she did not take much time off in the last year and a half. She was lucky she could accumulate enough to be off from before Christmas until the week after New Year's. She was also worried that she would not be able to devote as much time to her project when she started back to work.

There was a lot of work to do, and it took money as well as time. So far, none of the members of MOMY-G were wealthy. They had spent most of their resources trying to locate their missing daughters already. But surprisingly, or not so, they were willing to do what it took if the results looked good. Some pledged to remortgage their homes or sell them to get the money. There was always the possibility of fund-raising activities, but that would take a lot of time. "I will do what it takes," she told herself.

After sending all her e-mails, she noticed that she had ten more downloading. "I can't answer any more tonight," she told herself. "I just can't."

That night she read herself to sleep, dozing off with the reading light beside her bed still on. An hour later, she sat straight up in bed, awakened from a nightmare. She had dreamt she was crawling, no, walking on all fours. Actually bouncing along following a prey like a wolf. No, she was a cat, she was sure of it. An alley cat prancing in a long corridorlike alleyway, trying to stay out of puddles, which dotted the alley from a recent rain. She was moving forward, not like a cat ready to pounce, but like a cat on a mission, looking for something or someone. In her cat transformation, she could see through the darkness with ease. There was someone ahead near the end of the alley. She could smell fear on him but could not identify him.

Getting closer, she saw a mirror at the end of the alley. It was tilted up so that she could see the top of the person's body. It was a man, or manlike. His face was not clear. She stopped moving and stared at the mirror. Stared hard, but could not see any clearer. Then he reached out toward the mirror, and it moved, downward. She saw her own image. Her body was catlike, only the face was human. She was Dedra. She was so startled, that she turned around and started back down the alley. The man thing shouted, "Dedra," and she turned around and looked right at him. He had no face, just an empty black hole in a hood shrouding his face like a death veil.

She remembered the dream when she re-awoke in the morning. She would tell him the dream and see if he could help her understand it. He was coming tomorrow, and she needed to clean the house. She also needed to check her e-mails for any more potential members. Her life was suddenly getting very busy, and she liked it. She also wanted to look through her cookbooks for something special to fix them for their first night together since Thanksgiving. *Something with oysters*, she thought. *Aren't oysters supposed to be aphrodisiacs?*

He bought the third fifth wheel he looked at. The couple selling it had moved into a retirement assisted-living complex in Sun City. They had been snowbirds for fifteen years. She was showing signs of Alzheimer's, and he did not want to be a snowbird any longer. The fifth wheel was two years old, and they asked a better than fair price. He paid them with cash as they signed the title over to him. The registration and plates were good for ten more months. Except for the year of manufacture, the fifth wheel was identical to the one that lay in scattered pieces next to Carlos's blown-apart shack. At the storage facility, he hooked it up to his truck, grateful that it had full propane and water tanks and empty sewage tanks. As he pulled away, he noticed tears in their eyes. No doubt their memories of the years of snowbirding were still intact. In less than an hour, he was heading out of Tempe, south toward Tucson. After Tucson, he would head east on I-10 through a small part of New Mexico, then drive the long stretch across Texas working his way non-stop ever eastward toward Dee.

After a nonstop drive, Friday morning he pulled the fifth wheel into a trailer park outside Pensacola. After plugging in the electrical cable, he called Dee to say he would be there in the late afternoon instead of the morning. She was disappointed, but understood. She gave him directions to her house, although that was unnecessary, since he already downloaded a map from the Internet. He then turned on the two air conditioners, climbed up to the bedroom and fell into a deep dreamless sleep.

At 5:00, Dee was starting to worry about him. She had tried his cell phone several times, but there was no answer. She could only leave e-mail messages. She also did not know where he called from this morning. If this was going to get serious, she wanted a more positive line of communication. *If he is so wealthy, why doesn't he have a good cell phone?* she thought. She turned the evening news on TV. She was watching but not listening. Her mind was drifting toward him, the MOMY-G group, and the dinner she had ready to pop in the oven. "I hope he likes raw oysters for an appetizer," otherwise she would have to toss them. Oysters did not taste good unless they were fresh.

As the weather announcer came on, she heard the unmistakable sound of a diesel pulling up outside. She grabbed the remote as she shot out of the chair and clicked the power button. She peeked out the glass window on the front door as she heard the door slam on the truck. Her heart was pounding, as much from the sudden dart to the door as from seeing him striding from his truck to the sidewalk leading up to the house. He was carrying flowers, a bottle of wine, and a gift-wrapped box in a paper bag. "Damn!" she said out loud. "I forgot to get him a Christmas present. Oh, well, I'll just have to give it to him orally."

As he parked the truck in the driveway, he looked at the outside of the ranch-style home, so much like all the other homes in the area. It was tan stucco on about a quarter-acre surrounded by palm trees, saw palmettos, and Bermuda grass. The roof was flat and extended out over an array of jalousied windows. He got out of the truck and walked up the concrete driveway past a blue Subaru to the side door.

As he reached for the door, she flung it open and grabbed him around the neck and placed a lip lock on him; letting a moan come from deep in her throat.

"Are you happy to see me, or is that a banana in your breast pocket?" he said, backing away slightly.

"That's my line," she responded. "And it better be more than a banana in your pocket. At least it better be bigger than a banana. I'll take your line and ask what's in the bag, bitch?"

"My dirty laundry. I've been on the road for days you know. So where is your washing machine?"

"You'll be doing the hand laundry if that's what you brought me. Do you like oysters?"

"You mean passion berries? Why don't you get right to the point instead of saying hello or something more romantic, like you missed me."

"Excuse me. Was that a kiss I gave you or an exchange of germs. If that's what you want, hello, sir. May I take your coat and hat; and shirt, jeans, and jockeys, too?"

"Don't you think I better eat lots of oysters first, and yes, I do like oysters. I know you like wine, so here is Seven-Eleven's finest. It even has a screw-on cork so it can be resealed for later," he said, as he handed her the wine. "I guess you can have these flowers, too. They were on special at the Wal-Mart. Nuthin' but the finest for my lady friend."

"Well, come on in before the nosey neighbors call the cops for lewd and lascivious behavior."

"You don't need to ask twice," he said, as he went up the stairs and through the doorway leading to the kitchen. She closed the door behind him as he set the wine, flowers, and bag on the kitchen table. When he turned around, he took her in his arms with a bear hug and lifted her off the ground. They embraced for a long moment while he kissed her long and hard. She was kissing back just as hard.

"I didn't know how badly I missed you until I saw you get out of that truck and walk up the driveway," she said. "I'm sorry I got attached after only one day together. I told you it had been a long time since I felt for anyone, and now you walked into my life. I guess the timing was just about right."

He smiled at her, a smile that melted her heart.

"I didn't realize how much I cared for you until two nights ago when I told you I would be here today," he said, with some sincerity. "Hopefully we can get this worked out this weekend. I could stay all week, but I know you have your interview on Thursday with Jane."

"Please stay. The interview is here, and I can hide you in the guest room. Besides, I will need some moral support to talk about Dedra. So it's settled then. You will stay."

"Yes, ma'am," he obeyed. "Oh, I forgot. Here is the dirty laundry I mentioned. It ain't much, but what the heck, I ain't much either." He handed her the package wrapped in Christmas paper, red with snowflakes on it. A red bow was stuck on one corner with a label that read "To a Vermont vixen, from a horny buck."

"I'll let you unwrap your present after dinner," she said, attacking the present like a child on Christmas morning. On opening the box, she found two smaller boxes inside. She picked the larger one to open first. Inside was a watch. A simple watch, but obviously all gold. It was not a Rolex, but a gold watch, just the same. Her eyes started to mist over as she looked at him. "I can't accept this. This is too expensive. I didn't get you anything. You'll have to take it back."

"You deserve this, Dee. You are a special woman, and I want to treat you that way. I can't take it back now anyway. I got it in Houston on my way through yesterday, so taking it back is not an option. I don't expect a gift from you anyway. After all, you hardly know me," he said, with a smile.

She grinned, tears welling up in her eyes.

"If you insist. I don't deserve anything like this."

"Sure you do after all you've gone through. Please keep it."

Without saying anything else, she started fumbling with the other package. She let out a gasp as she pulled out earrings that matched the watchband.

"Well, if you insist, I guess I'll have to keep these, too," she said, with a smile, and tears running down her cheeks.

He bent down and kissed away the tears.

"No more of this, okay? Now, where are those oysters you've been braggin' about?"

She reached up with one hand around his head and pulled him toward her. She kissed him long and hard. "Maybe you don't need those oysters after all. Let's have a glass of wine first, okay?"

"Anything to please the little lady. I just happen to have a bottle of pussy fussy right here. It's one of your French wines. Not too pretentious, but flaccid just the same."

"You're a hoot" was all she said as she led him out of the kitchen and into the living room. "Have a look around while I pour us some wine."

"I would like to find the restroom. Now that my hard-on is going down, I think I can empty my bladder," he said.

"Don't let it get too soft," she said as she returned to the kitchen.

He walked through the modest living room that had a couch, an easy chair, and the obligatory television on a TV stand in the corner. It was plain to see she was neat and had nothing out of place. Pictures of Dedra and Dee lined both sides of the hallway leading to two bedrooms. He passed by one bathroom and went into the larger of the two bedrooms. There was a queen-size bed on the opposite wall and the door to an adjoining bathroom to the left. The bathroom was large with double sinks and a shower tub against one wall. He relieved himself in the toilet, careful not to splash too much. He replaced the seat like a perfect gentleman, and then washed his hands..

On his return to the living room, he peeked into the spare bedroom. It had a full-size bed against the near wall and looked like it was awaiting Dedra's return. There was a computer stand in the corner with what looked like an older style computer with a monitor set on top of it. Speakers were on each side of the computer. When he returned to the living room, she was sitting on the couch with two glasses of wine beckoning him.

They sipped wine while she told him all about the MOMY-G group and how they now had fourteen members. They decided to have dinner before pleasure. While she got dinner ready, he retrieved a rolling suitcase from his truck and set it in the living room. He returned to the kitchen, and they sat down at the table. The oysters were fresh and delicious, followed by the main course of salad and breaded veal Parmesan. The veal was her food allowance for the week, but it was the holidays. She would worry about money later. When she wasn't looking longingly at his blue eyes, she stared in amazement at her new watch. This was the nicest present she had ever received, and it came at a time when she needed to be pampered. Maybe this was her knight on a white horse every little girl dreams about when growing up. Looking at him made her tingle inside her chest. She was almost giddy by the time they were done eating.

They made love that night and fell asleep in each other's arms. In the morning, they made love again. The lovemaking was gentle and sweet. He was good, and she needed that at this time. He was strong, but held her as if she were a fragile china doll. It was 10:00 before they both were awake again after the morning session.

"I think I'll go for a run this morning, unless you have the tandem with you," she said.

"I could run with you," he said, "but you wore me out this morning."

"I'll try not to wear you out tonight," she said.

"It feels good to be tired from making love," he responded. "Let's go before you-know-who wakes up."

"Who, my neighbors or the one-eyed anaconda?" she said, as she groped for him under the covers.

"Too late. It's awake and stretching. Better get up soon."

"Okay for you," she said, as she let go of him. "Tonight we'll have to try whipped cream on a stick."

"Talking dirty will get you nowhere with me. Actions could speak a volume though," he said, as he started to get out of bed.

"You're a tease," she said, as she got out on her side of the bed. She headed for the bathroom, and he went out to the living room, where his rolling suitcase still remained unopened on the floor by the front door. The dishes were still on the table, pots were in the sink, and their clothes were on the floor by the couch where their lovemaking began.

He put on his jockey briefs, located his running pants, shoes, and a T-shirt. He noticed the weather was overcast, but the neighbors were out across the street in shorts. "It's nice to be in a climate where you can run, bike, or golf, year round," he said to himself. As he was putting on his running shoes, she came out of the bedroom wearing her running gear less her shoes. She looked great, lithe with a nice body. He remembered Wayne telling him about her big boobs as he looked at them. They were large, but not grotesquely so. Even with the athletic bra holding them tight to her under the running shirt, they stood out. Her hips were narrow and her legs were smooth and tight looking. He was starting to get excited again.

"I'll clean this mess up when we get back," she said. "I hate to leave it like this, but if we don't get out there now, it will get too hot and humid to enjoy the run. If you have never run in this climate, drink lots of water now before we get out there. There are some places in the park to drink, but the water tastes like shit."

"I want to brush my teeth before we head out," he said, as he headed toward the bathroom in the hall carrying his toothbrush.

"There is toothpaste in the cabinet," she called after him.

In five minutes, they were out and jogging toward the park about a quarter of a mile from her house. An hour later, they returned. Both exhausted, but somehow refreshed. After cleaning up last night's mess in the kitchen with his help, she showered in the master bath while he used the shower off of the hallway. Neither shower was big enough to accommodate two. When finished, they sat at the table and drank coffee and nibbled on toast with strawberry jelly.

"I need to know more about you," she said. "For starters, what church do you go to?"

"I don't believe in organized religion," he said, which startled her.

"You don't? Why?"

"There have been more people killed in the name of and because of religion than any other nonnatural cause. Since the beginning of time, people have been killing each other because they didn't tolerate the other person's belief in God. The Roman Empire, the Crusades, the Spanish Inquisition, the Jews in World War II, on up to today's crises in the Middle East. All those people murdered in the name of religion. I just believe religion has done more harm than good."

"I can see your point, but where would we be without it?"

"A lot better off" was his response. "Religion had its purpose, but has become an evil unto its own. Don't you know we're not supposed to discuss religion or politics. Why don't we just agree to disagree on that issue?"

"Agreed, but what about politics? Are you as set against politicians as you are against religious leaders?"

"Even though I have money, I'm a conservative Democrat, if you want to label me. I can't stand the religious right that has taken over the Republican party, especially the stand on abortion. Nothing is worse than bringing an unwanted child into this world. If there were no way for poor people to abort a pregnancy, there would be a lot of unadoptable children running around with no one to love them. Also, I believe the Republican party is full of racists. Just after Johnson's many equal rights initiatives is when the Republicans started to take over Southern politics. The old Democrats in the South switched sides because they thought the Republicans could put an end to racial equality. Any other questions, or are you going to kick me out?"

"No, I'm also a conservative Democrat. Can't stand the Republican party for the reasons you have mentioned. On a lighter note, where are you taking me New Year's Eve? I know I mentioned a place, but there are still a few others advertised in the paper that have open reservations. I would like to go to one that has dining and dancing. Entertainment is not important. Would you like to take a look?" she said as she picked up the morning paper and turned to entertainment section.

"Any place is okay, as long as we don't have to be too dressy. I left my tux in Vermont."

"Well, that leaves out the place I had in mind earlier. I'm sure they have a dress code. Here's one that's C&W, so we could wear jeans," she said, handing him the paper. "It's not too expensive either."

He took the paper and glanced at the advertisement.

"Looks great to me. I just happen to have a set of boots in my truck that will do if you want to dance the two-step. I don't have a cowboy hat though."

"Great. Let me call and get a reservation," she said, as she took the paper back from him. Walking to the phone, she did a little shuffle, imitating a dance step. "I'm ready to enjoy a New Year's Eve for a change, even if it's with a Democratic heathen," she teased.

"You won't hurt my feelings," he shot back. "I need to hook up my laptop to a phone line so I can check on Vermont."

"You can use my computer if you don't go to any porno sites," she said.

"I'll use my own, it's all set up to connect with my main computer at the house and download the info I need. Thanks anyway."

He connected the computer to the phone jack next to the counter in the kitchen. She came up behind him and placed her right hand on his right shoulder and rested her chin on his left shoulder.

"Watch this," he said as his laptop logged onto the main computer.

"Is this a long distance call?" she asked.

"No, I used a credit card. Even if it was long distance, I would make it up to you by paying your phone bill for the month. The connection is slow, since we are using the 56K modem instead of a cable or DSL connection, but watch anyway."

As they watched, the computer gave options for camera locations both inside and outside the house. He clicked on one where the cats were usually located, and the computer brought up the image of six of his cats lounging on the sofa in the sun-room on the south side of the house. "They like to lie in this room in the sun, even in the winter." He then clicked on the alarm console icon and the status of the alarm systems popped up. There were no alarms or abnormalities on any monitored systems. He then checked an outside camera. There was a foot of snow on the ground, and the screen indicated the temperature to be twenty-eight degrees. The sun was shining through the bare trees. It was a beautiful Vermont winter day.

"That makes me shiver," she said as she backed away from him. "I'm glad I'm here. I'm also glad you're here. You do have too much time and money. Maybe you can donate a little of each to our MOMY-G group. Your cats remind me of a dream I had the other night." She told him the dream, and he listened intently. He could remember his dream, but he did not tell her about it. He swallowed hard when she finished. "What do you think it means?" she asked.

"Maybe Dedra was abducted and you will some day be stalking the person who did it. I believe in ghosts and the spirit continuing on after a person dies. If Dedra is dead, and we both hope not, then maybe her spirit is trying to communicate with you, to tell you something. Anyway, that dream sends chills up and down my spine."

"Me, too."

"As far as my time and money, I decided a few days ago to do as much to help as you want. I think you need to do as much by yourself as you can, but I'll be there when and if you need me. I'll set up a trust fund your organization can draw from any time you want. I'll set it up at a local bank next week and give you the checkbook. Don't worry about how much is used. I will monitor it and replenish as necessary."

"I don't deserve you," she said, tears welling up as she hugged him from the back. "You are a wonderful man, and I wish I had met you long ago."

"I was a different man long ago, and I had no money. I'm glad to be of service, ma'am," he said, pretending to tip a hat. Standing up, he said, "I think I'll do a little bit of reading this afternoon if you don't mind. I brought a book along in case you got tired of me."

She smacked him teasingly across the butt.

"I plan on keeping your interest later on, but right now, I have to check my e-mails and plan for our first meeting of MOMY-G's. So far, all the members are from different states except for California. By the way, didn't you bring a fifth wheel along?"

"Yes, I did. It's parked at a campground outside of town. I didn't think your neighbors would appreciate the thing parked in the street, nor would you like it parked in the driveway."

"That's thoughtful. Well, bury your face in your book while I tend to my business on the computer." She gave him a kiss on the cheek as they separated for the rest of the afternoon.

After three chapters in his book, he laid it across his chest and closed his eyes for a little power nap. He was awakened forty-five minutes later by a loud "oh, no!" emanating from what used to be Dedra's bedroom. He jumped to his feet and headed for the room.

"What's wrong?" he asked as he approached her from behind.

"I got the blue screen of death. I tried to reboot, but it's not recognizing the hard drive. Can you fix it? I have all my e-mails on it and information about MOMY-G stored on the hard drive. Shit, shit, shit."

"Let me try. Where do you keep your backups?"

"I never backed it up," she said.

"Mind if I look around in the desk. I bet that Dedra made at least an emergency disk when she first got the computer. At least that will be a start."

"Be my guest," she said. "Please don't tell me that everything is lost. Please."

"Nothing is ever lost on a hard drive unless it's written over. There are ways to get it back. Just let me do some magic."

"I can't stand to watch. I'll go out in the kitchen and fix us a little happy hour."

"Let me get my laptop. It has some recovery software on it." He went to the kitchen and got the laptop. He set it next to the ailing computer and searched in the desk for a start-up disk. He found it in a stack of other disks. At least Dedra had enough sense to make one. He put it in the A drive and pushed the "on" button. Seconds later, the diagnostic tools were loaded and he was able to access the hard drive. He did a scan-disk and was able to repair some damaged files.

She stuck her head in the doorway.

"Do I need to get another computer?" she asked.

"No. Give me another fifteen or twenty minutes, and I think it will be back and running." This was the opportunity he was looking for. He knew that Dedra must have saved some of his e-mails and that they could be traced back to him with the right type of software. The FBI had that capability, and if they got involved with Dedra's disappearance, they would surely confiscate this computer and trace the info back to him. He had not communicated via e-mail with any of his other victims, even though he used the computer. Therefore, this was the only link from a victim to him.

"Okay, I'll get some dinner together for us. I hope you like pasta."

"Love it. I'll call you when I'm done."

She left the room. He rebooted the computer, and it was up and running without a hitch. He had disconnected the speakers so she wouldn't hear the startup sound. Entering into outlook express, he found the damaging evidence in a backup file. Even if she made hard copies of the messages, this is what the FBI needed to trace the e-mails. He pulled out a floppy disk from his computer bag and inserted it into Dedra's. He ran the erase program, essentially removing all traces of the e-mails. He then went to the ICQ program he and Dedra used and erased the references to his screen name. Doing a search, he found all the text files Dedra had saved and obliterated them, too. He next installed a spy program, which, running undetected in the background, would e-mail him all the activity on this computer from now on. The spy program also would hide itself among other programs and reinstall itself if any detection software was used on this hard drive. He was through now, but for good measure, he defragmented her hard drive, essentially rewriting all the data. He now felt that the only link between him and Dedra was now gone. He was wrong.

While the computer was defragmenting, he went out to reassure her.

"All is well. As soon as it's finished doing some badly needed maintenance, you can get back to work. I'm sure some files got destroyed when it crashed, especially the ones in the program you had open. You won't know until you look for them. Now where is that happy hour you bragged about?"

"Right here, big, tall, and handsome," she said, smiling and handing him an ice-cold, long neck Coors. "I owe you so much."

"Ah, shucks, ma'am," he said, in his best Texas drawl as he shuffled his feet. "T'wern't nuthin' at all." He took the drink and clinked it against hers. "Here's to the computer and a lasting friendship."

"Back at ya, pardner. Here is a little something to get us started," she said as she reached in the refrigerator for a plate.

"Not more oysters. I don't think I need them with you."

"No, a few shrimp and some crackers. We're having pasta primavera and some garlic bread. It will make our breath bad, but with both of us eating it, only others will know, and I ain't expecting company. For dessert, we have whip crème."

"Whip crème and what?" he asked, realizing what she intended to do with the crème. "Oh, silly question on my part. Can we have whip crème first?"

"No, we need to eat so we will have more energy so we can eat, if you catch my drift."

"I'll go out on the couch and do some tongue-stretching exercises while I sip beer and eat these shrimp." They both went out to the couch and sat down. When he sat down with his beer, he turned, and she was inches from his face with full, parted lips. He could only wrap himself around her and kiss her long and hard. Her tongue darted in and out of his mouth, and in response, he tasted the inside of her mouth, tickled the roof of her mouth, and traced around her teeth with his tongue. In seconds, they were both writhing and drawing themselves together. He could smell her hair and the lingering scent of her late morning shower. She could feel him against her, hard and warm. It was if they were two twisting sandstorms in a desert rushing toward each other and joining into one, then slowly dancing in the wind.

He reached under her top and unsnapped her bra. Slowly he pulled the top straps off and down her arms and out of the sleeves. As he removed the bra from her, he lightly rubbed her nipples, which were hard and felt like two olives attached to her swelling breasts. She reached under his shirt against his chest with both hands and, in one easy motion, stripped his shirt up and over his head. He did the same to her and then they held each other close, skin to skin, chest to breast, stomach to stomach. They kissed until they were both almost out of breath. She pushed away for a second.

"Be right back," she said.

He looked confused for a second, but smiled as she returned from the kitchen with the can of whip crème.

"What, no cherries?" he asked.

"The whip crème won't be on long enough to put cherries on top, and how do you balance a cherry on a hard cock anyway?"

With that said, she put the can on the floor next to the couch and reached for his belt buckle again. She pulled his pants down his legs slowly in a tease that was having the desired effect. He was very hard and was poking out of the top of his briefs. With one hand, she pulled his briefs down and off his legs while grabbing the whip crème with the other. "I hope it's not too cold and shrivels you up," she said, with pouting lips.

"I'm willing to tough it out if you are," he responded.

She popped the top off the can and let it fall to the floor. Straddling him, she shook the can, teasing him unmercifully. Then she pointed the can down.

"Brace yourself," she said, and foamed him from his balls to the top of his penis. His erection was pulsing with anticipation. "I'll have to get more, since it took a lot to coat old baldy there."

With that, she bent down and licked the crème from his balls. Slowly she licked up one side of his penis and then down the other. He was writhing now in pleasure and anticipation. Then she held the base of his penis with one hand and slowly placed her lips around him. She slowly went down until he was at the back of her throat. She did this again, and he was arching his back. He placed his hands on either side of her cheeks as she slowly sucked the crème off of his throbbing penis. She caressed his penis with both hands slowly sliding him in and out. It took less than three minutes until he felt like he was turning inside out. As he came, she slowly sucked him inside her and down her throat. He let go a guttural scream as the last of him exploded and then collapsed back down onto the couch.

"Jesus Christ," he said. "I think I'm having a coronary."

"I thought you might like that," she said, as she moved up and rested on top of him. "Maybe you can return the favor."

"Give me a few minutes, or maybe an hour or two after that," he said as he held her toward him and stroked her body with his fingertips.

They lay together for twenty minutes without talking while he touched her ever so gently. Her skin was tight from working out, but soft just the same. Her hair was soft, long, and silky. It was a joy to just touch her all over. He had gone soft during this interlude, but was starting to get aroused again. He started kissing her on the ear and then around the back of her neck. She started to moan a little. "I think I found a sensitive area," he said as he continued to nibble at the back of her neck. She started to wiggle a little as she moaned, but did not pull away. "Yes, indeedy, I think this is the place to start."

"I'll give you an hour to cut that out," she said, with a giggle.

He gently rolled her over so that she was beside and slightly under him. He continued to nibble at her neck and then back on the ear. She angled her head back toward the couch as he moved down to the top of her left breast. Her nipples were hard. He teased them with his mouth, tugging gently with his lips. He then kissed under the breasts. She arched her back and put her hands on either side of his head and pushed him down her stomach while he kissed and tasted her skin. There was no time now for whip crème for her, and he did not care. She was spreading her legs and bending her knees in anticipation.

She continued to urge him down toward her. He wanted to tease her some more, but she was not going to let him. As he got to where she wanted him, she pulled him toward her, guiding his tongue to where she was getting the most pleasure. He moved his hands behind her buttocks and pulled her even closer as he used his tongue and lips to taste deep inside her. She was moaning and twisting her head back and forth as he pleasured her. His tongue was soon replaced with his fingers, and he probed even deeper inside until he was massaging the spot that made her moan even louder. At the same time, he was sucking her clitoris, and she was obviously enjoying this attention to her body. She climaxed more than once until she told him she wanted him inside her.

He wasted no time in placing his very hard penis inside and as deep as he could. It felt that he had reached all the way to the back of her uterus, and almost at the same time, he started to come for the second time in less than an hour. She climaxed again as he finished. This time, he collapsed against her. She seemed as if she had passed out, but he too was spent. They lay like that for half and hour before they had the strength to pull apart.

"I'm a little hungry," she said.

"I think we both worked up an appetite," he replied as he rolled off onto the floor. He groped for his jockeys. She sat up, gathered her clothes, and headed for the bathroom. "I'll pour us a glass of wine."

"Turn the burner on under the pot of water while you're at it," she said, as she closed the bathroom door.

While the pasta was boiling, they devoured the shrimp and crackers. The pasta they ate like bears awakened from a winter's sleep. While eating, they probed each other with questions, learning a little more about each other's likes and dislikes. He helped her with the dishes while they continued to talk. She told him all about Dedra's childhood, Dedra's father, and her growing up in Florida after they moved there from Vermont.

She told him that her ex was not much of a father or husband. He had wanted a boy, and when Dedra was born, he withdrew from them both, finding solace in booze and other women. Finally, after staying away for one entire weekend while she sat up with a sick Dedra, Dee went to a lawyer and filed for divorce. There was no fight for possessions, no fight for custody, and no regrets on her part. Soon after the divorce, Dee reverted to her maiden name and stayed in Florida, where Dedra grew up with no knowledge of her father. Dee made no attempt to notify him of Dedra's disappearance and was sure he was not involved. "As far as I know, he's never seen her since the divorce," she concluded.

After they were through in the kitchen, they went to the bedroom. She read a little while he watched her until his eyelids were too heavy to keep apart. Shortly afterwards, she turned out the light and joined him in a deep dreamless sleep.

It was New Year's Eve when they awoke.

He lay awake, staring at the ceiling, wondering what was happening to him emotionally. He was always in control, but with Dee, he felt uneasy. Could this be the companion he used to look for before he began his just-for-fun adventures. Maybe, but what was the next step. Continue this relationship and lose emotional control of his life. Do as he had planned, making her one of the others, or call it off before he lost control completely. If she just disappeared like the others, he would be a suspect, since their relationship was known, and by how many, he did not know. The sexual part of their relationship was very appealing to him. It was wonderful, and the closeness was something he had wanted in his youth. Also, being in close contact with her would assure him that he would be kept up on MOMY-G. There is time yet to decide. There may be other options too, as befell Bill in Vermont. As he lay there contemplating his options, she stirred in his arms and awoke.

"Good morning, your sweetness," he said.

"Umph," she replied, not wishing to discuss the break of day until she started to breathe some more.

"Feel like a morning run?" he asked.

"Right now I don't feel like anything but brushing my teeth. All that garlic" was the muffled reply.

"Well, I have to get up to drain the dragon," he said.

"I'm glad you aren't going to drain it here. I guess I gotta drain the clam, then," she replied.

He laughed, got up, and went to the bathroom, leaving her half-uncovered. "I guess I might as well get up too," she said, sitting up and throwing her legs over the side of the bed.

She put on her robe, brushed her teeth, and went to the kitchen to make some coffee. Feeling like a wild animal trashed his mouth, he brushed his teeth, too. He then followed her to the kitchen after donning his jeans that he retrieved from the crumpled pile they made on the floor, where he tossed them the night before.

"After the interview on Thursday, why don't you come to Vermont with me and stay a few days at my place. It will allow you to relax for awhile. You can check your e-mails on my computer, and I'll help you write a web site for MOMY-G."

"You can make a website?"

"Of course. Actually you should have one up and running for your interview with Jane. That way you can tell the world about it. I could start today if you want. First you need to register your domain name."

"That would be great. But as far as going to Vermont for awhile, I have a job to return to next week. If I don't, I will lose my only means of support and my ability to continue with MOMY-G."

"I have a suggestion," he said. "Why don't you ask your boss for a leave of absence for a month or two? I think I can come up with the necessary money to keep you alive until then in addition to the MOMY-G trust. You are doing such a good thing with this MOMY-G that I don't think he will be able to say no, especially after you thank him and his company on national TV."

"It's worth a shot, but you have done so much so far for someone who you just met a month ago. I can't ask any more of you."

"Fahget about it," he said in his best imitation of an Italian gangster.

"Okay, let's plan it out after I beat you in a morning run," she said as the coffee finished percolating. "We can have coffee when we get back."

"You probably will beat me after you wore me out last night," he said, "but we'll see."

They went for the morning run starting and finishing side by side. When they cooled down, they had coffee and decided not to go anywhere for New Year's Eve. Instead they would watch the celebrations on TV, work on the design for the MOMY-G web pages, and make love until they both passed out.

157

Sixteen

Thursday morning dawned with the palm trees in Dee's front yard rustling from the humid haze blowing in from the gulf. Even in January, Florida weather could be uncomfortable. The constant breezes made the humidity more tolerable, but just barely. Dee was up before the sun. The interview crew from the *Today Show* was there at 5:00, setting up with their van parked in the driveway. Cables were run to the inside of the house through the open front door, letting in the humidity. Cameras and lights were placed in the living room. The air conditioner would run constantly up to the time the televised interview was to begin, shortly after 8:00. It would be turned off during the interview to lessen the background noise. Dee was given a quick makeover by one of the crew. He was staying out of sight in her spare bedroom, fine-tuning the MOMY-G web site. He expected the site would be getting thousands of hits after and during the show. He zeroed the web site's counter and cleared the guest book.

Five minutes before the interview, Dee was a bundle of nerves. She sought him out, and he gave her a reassuring hug. They had been very intimate in the last week, and she was beginning to rely heavily on his broad shoulders. Her boss was very cooperative with her request for a leave of absence. She did not have to play her publicity trump card to persuade him. She intended to thank him on TV anyway. She also intended to thank her new best friend even though he requested otherwise.

He gave her one last squeeze, and she retreated back to the living room where her name was being called. He went back to the computer and checked in with his computer in Vermont. There was a problem.

"We're back," came the familiar voice of Jane Peasly, "and

with me now is Deanna Mayfield, the founder of MOMY-G, which stands for Mothers Of Missing Young Girls." The screen showed Dee sitting on the living room couch with her name and the organization name superimposed at the bottom of the screen. "Tell us about your organization and what you are doing."

"Well," Dee started without holding back, "we are a group of women who have in common the frustrating problem of trying to get law enforcement to give serious attention to our missing daughters."

"What makes your organization different from hundreds of others?" interrupted Jane.

"If I may finish," countered a feisty Dee, "we are the mothers of missing young girls, most of college age who have disappeared without a trace. They are all athletic, pretty, and bright women. They did not take anything with them when they disappeared, and there is no evidence of an abduction or foul play of any type."

"What do you hope to accomplish with your organization?" asked Jane.

"As I said, we want to get the attention of law enforcement, which, until we added Linda Amory, was minimal." While Dee was talking, the pictures of the missing women were flashed on the screen. "These are the daughters who are missing, and you can see that they are from different states, making law enforcement cooperation that much more difficult. We now have an FBI agent assigned to us who is helping coordinate our efforts. While we number only fifteen so far, I would like to point out that we have been contacted by hundreds of mothers and fathers with missing children. Our organization is specific to the descriptions I gave earlier."

"Why are you limiting your group to only those who fit a specific description?" Jane asked.

"Because we believe there is a connection among the missing girls."

"You mean perhaps serial abductions of girls fitting only a specific description," stated Jane.

"Precisely that," said Dee. "We feel if we limit our group to those commonalities, we stand a better chance of finding out what happened. For instance, all the girls were avid outdoor types who were cyclists, runners, or both. Most were last seen jogging or cycling the day before they disappeared. The authorities have told us all that they were probably runaways and would come back some day. There are thousands of missing girls every year we have been told. We all know our children and know they are not mere runaways."

"And you said the mother of the missing intern, Linda Amory, is among your members?" asked Jane.

"That is correct, and until she became a member, we were not taken seriously. We hope that this program and *America's Most Wanted* will bring more attention to missing persons. We also hope that more mothers who have missing young girls will come forth and join us in our search. We have a web site, *www.momy-g.org,* where they can go to get more information. We appreciate this opportunity that the *Today Show* has given us to further our cause. I would also like to thank my employer, Pensacola Air Delivery for granting me a leave of absence to pursue my missing daughter."

"We also have with us this morning, Agent Paul Ford of the FBI," said Jane as the screen split to show Agent Ford and Deanna together. "Good morning to you, Agent Ford."

"Good morning, Jane," Agent Ford said, in that typical emotionless FBI agent tone.

"Could you add to the statements that were just provided by Ms. Mayfield?" asked Jane.

"The FBI has and will provide any assistance we can to find these missing youths. As Ms. Mayfield has stated, there are thousands of missing children in this country every year. However, in this case, we have been presented with a set of circumstances that we believe to have merit leading to abductions across state lines. That is why I have been assigned to help coordinate the various law enforcement agencies' efforts."

"What about the charges that no interest was shown until Ms. Amory was included in the list?" asked Jane.

"We were working on the disappearance of Ms. Amory and shortly after were given the evidence of the other similar cases," responded Agent Ford.

"I would like to say that since Agent Ford has been assigned, we have received more attention then before," intoned Dee. "Although we are making little headway, we do appreciate the efforts of the FBI."

"Well, we are out of time. We wish you the best of luck, Deanna, and would you please give the web site address again?" asked Jane.

"*Www.momy-g.org*, answered Dee, "and thank you."

"Thank you," stated Agent Ford.

During the interview, using his calling card and Dee's wireless phone, he made a phone call to Wayne to ask him to look in on his cats. Wayne did not work much in the winter, so he was home when he called. The main automatic feeder for the cats was empty and the backup was malfunctioning. Although he was sure the cats would not starve, he would not be back for at least three more days and his guests would not be happy when he finally did get there. Armed with a temporary code to disable the security system, Wayne anxiously agreed to "...go fix the damn thing."

"Nuthin's worse than a hungry pussy," said Wayne. "Besides, I wanna drive the Hummer up and down the mountain," which was his real reason for the enthusiasm. "The missus and I are watchin' your girlfriend on TV," Wayne continued. "She looks good enough to eat, don't ya think?"

"I have, and behave up there, because I'll be watchin' you with my remote," he reminded Wayne.

"You have what?" asked a befuddled Wayne.

"Never mind," he responded, as he pushed the end button on the phone.

Just then Dee walked in.

"Who was that?"

"Wayne," he answered. "The backup cat feeder is not working, and I asked Wayne to go fix it. He jumped at the chance to drive the Hummer. I leave it for him when I'm gone. His old Chevy can't make it up the side of the mountain, especially with over a foot of snow on the ground, so I leave the keys to the Humvee for him. I watched you on the TV, and you looked stunning."

"That wasn't the image I was trying to project. I was hoping

161

for a more caring mother impression," she said as she left to check on the status of the equipment tear down.

Within fifteen minutes, the crew was gone, the front door was closed, and the air conditioner was turned back on. The crowd that had gathered outside dissipated like the moisture being wrung out of the house by the air conditioner. As she returned the house back to a reasonable semblance of what it was before the invasion of the camera people, he connected his laptop to his home computer. Within seconds, the Humvee came into view, climbing effortlessly up the snow-covered driveway. He could see a big shit-eatin' grin on Wayne's face and also that he had Lulu with him. *Shit, what did he bring her along for?* he thought. He did not tell Wayne to go alone, but he did not intend for her to be there, too. She was a bit of a snoop. She had never been to the house as far as he knew, but probably got a good description from Wayne.

He followed their progress up the road, which was barely discernible, covered with all the snow. In some places, there were three-foot drifts. The Hummer never hesitated as it ate its way up the mountain. Wayne was probably pissing himself with joy while Lulu looked terrified. They finally got to the top, and Wayne punched in the temporary code. The large garage door opened, and the garage camera showed them pulling in the heated space. The doors of the Hummer opened and Wayne and Lulu got out.

"Woowee," said Wayne. "That was some ride."

"Fuck you," said Lulu. "I was scared shitless. I thought we were going to slide backwards in that thing. I shoulda never agreed to come along."

"Ah, shut your trap," Wayne said, in the same tone he would address his old huntin' dog. "I can drive that thing any-where. The ride down should be more fun than up."

"I'll get out and walk if you make me too scared," said a defi-ant Lulu.

Ma and Pa Kettle on the mountain, he thought to himself, *but they're good people. Jesus Christ, I'm starting to get senti-mental now.*

"What ya doin'?" asked Dee, as she returned from the task of straightening up.

"Watching Wayne and Lulu in my house," he said. "Come and see for yourself."

She pulled up a chair next to him, and they sat side by side like two voyeurs peeping into a neighbor's bedroom.

They could hear everything that was said by the two visitors as they made their way along the corridors leading to the main house. As they passed the butcher room, Lulu's inquisitiveness got the best of her.

"What's in there?" Lulu questioned.

"That's where we cut up deer, turkeys, bear, and anything else we hunt," Wayne told her. "It's really somethin' else. I'll show it to ya on the way back. Let's do what we came here for, and then we can explore."

"I've never seen that room," said Dee. "Will I get to see it next week?"

"Sure," he said, hiding his anger that Wayne was going to snoop around with Lulu. There was nothing to find except some strange looking meat in the freezer, but that still made him feel uneasy, especially now that Dee was watching also. He could have turned on a speaker and through the computer connection told them to behave because they were being watched, but decided against it. Telling them not to go into the butcher shop would raise suspicion.

As soon as they entered the main part of the house, mewing, hungry cats surrounded them.

"I knew you had cats," said Dee, "but so many."

"Boy, there sure is a shitpot of cats in here," commented Lulu as they walked toward the feeder. The cats followed them mewing and roaming about underfoot, rubbing against their legs.

"Yeah," said Wayne. "I've seen 'em before, and they seem to have the run of the place. Let's get to the feeder. I don't like the way some of them are lookin' at us, as if we were their next meal."

"Look," said Lulu, "they all have tags." She bent down to examine one of them. The camera angle exposed her ample ass from behind. The voyeurs looked at each other and laughed. But just then he realized what was going to happen next. Lulu began to read the tags out loud. After she read four state names with the associated victim's names, she asked Wayne if they were all named like that.

"I think so," said Wayne, as she followed him into the feeding room. "I believe he gets them from the states he visits when he travels."

Lulu bent down again and picked up one of the smaller cats.

"They must all be females," she said, as she cuddled the one cat that had a state and a victim name.

"I think he likes only female pussies," said Wayne, and they both laughed.

Lulu pulled the cat's tag toward her to read it.

"Florida," she said, and there is another name under it I can't quite make out."

As she was staring intently at the tag, Wayne succeeded in opening the feeder. The cat Lulu was holding, Florida/Dedra, jerked around and wiggled out of Lulu's grasp and leaped to the floor, making a beeline for the food.

Goddamn that was close, he thought. *I need to pull that tag as soon as I get back.*

"Shit," said Lulu. "That cat got me with its back claws. Got me good, too." She held up her left hand so that Wayne and the voyeurs could see a deepening crimson color emerging from her palm.

"Shore did," said Wayne. "That'll teach ya to play with a pussy other than your own. Put some pressure on it while I make sure this thing is workin' okay, and then we'll get a tourniquet for your neck so we can save your head."

The voyeurs laughed out loud, but Lulu was not amused.

"Fuckin' funny, Wayne," said Lulu, as she applied pressure to the wound with her thumb of her right hand.

Wayne assured himself that the feeder was indeed working okay, but he secretly hoped it did not so that he could get another chance to drive the Hummer. "Let's go find a bandage for your hand, and then I'll give you the cook's tour."

The voyeurs followed them from one camera to another until they were in the bathroom opposite the kitchen. Wayne rummaged around in the cabinet until he found a box of bandages while Lulu washed her hand. After drying her hand, Wayne put the bandage on her wound. They looked strangely attached to each other, even though they were at odds most of the time.

There was a gleam of affection in the old boy's eyes for his hefty wife of many years. Dee got the same impression as she looked at him and smiled. The two voyeurs touched foreheads together, and then resumed their clandestine watch.

"There, that ought to keep you from bleedin' ta death," said Wayne. "Now I'll go check on that poor cat to see if it's still alive."

"Asshole," shot back Lulu.

"Let's see if I can find our way outta here," said Wayne. "What part of the house do you want to see? I ain't never been through the whole thing. He seems to keep some of the rooms locked up, at least the doors are always shut when I was here."

"I would like to see the bedrooms and the other bathrooms, but I wouldn't feel right about snoopin' around the whole house. You said he also has cameras installed everywhere so he might be able to tell if we've been lookin'. I would like to see the butcher room at least. Since you seem to have bragged on it so much."

"Shop, butcher shop," he said, correcting her. "Okay, let's go. It's on the way out anyway."

On the way back through the kitchen, Lulu spied the stairway down to the computer room. "What's down there?" she asked as she started down the stairs.

"I think that's where he keeps the computer that operates the house," Wayne said following his wife.

"Door's locked," said Lulu, as she tried to twist the knob, first right, then left, then right again.

"They ain't nothin' else down here," Wayne said, as he headed back up the stairs with Lulu in hot pursuit.

The cameras and two sets of eyes in Florida followed them back toward the garage. At the door to the butcher room, they stopped and Wayne reached down and gave the handle a twist. The door opened slowly, and automatically the lights came on as they entered the room.

"Holy smoke," declared Lulu as she looked around at all the stainless steel tables, cutting surfaces, band saw, and other cutting implements. "What is that, a furnace?"

"It's an incinerator," said Wayne with pride. "It gets rid of the evidence."

"What evidence?" she asked.

"The deer parts we can't eat. You don't think all those deer we get are legal do you. We have to get rid of the head and hooves and other parts. Otherwise we could go to jail for poaching."

"Look at that door. Is that a refrigerator in there?" asked Lulu, still in amazement.

"Sure is," said a proud Wayne. "Wanna look inside?"

He was acting like a proud parent showing off pictures of his newborn son. Wayne walked over to the stainless steel door and opened the walk-in freezer. A mist billowed out when the sub-zero vapor condensed as it rushed out to meet the more humid air of the butcher shop. Wayne switched on the lights from the outside switch.

"Jeez zu pete," commented Lulu. "I ain't never seen a freezer so big in a house in all my life. How much stuff is in there?"

"Lots and lots of deer, moose, turkey, and even some bear," boasted Wayne. "He could feed the town for months on this. Some of this belongs to us since we din't have any room to store it at home. Some was Bill's too."

"Let's take some home for this weekend so I can make some jerky," said Lulu. "Can you tell which is which since it's all wrapped in butcher paper? It looks like it's marked with the cut and dated. Look, here is some hindquarter and some leg. Let's take one each."

"I don't know which ones belong to me or Bill, but I guess it don't matter, since we killed them all together and Bill is gone. Go ahead and grab a couple of packages, and then we can go."

Lulu pulled the two packages close to her chest as they walked out. Wayne closed the door and turned out the light. They left the butcher shop, turned right down the corridor leading to the garage, and left the mansion.

"They took something out of the freezer," she told him when he returned from the kitchen with a cup of coffee for both of them.

"It must have been some of the meat from our hunting trips. Some of that meat belongs to Wayne, some to me, and some was

166

Bill's. It's okay if he took some of it. *Damn*, he thought. *I hope he didn't grab some of the special cuts. Oh, well if he did. All the special meat is cut up and not recognizable as human.* "How much did he take?" he asked her.

"It looked like two packages," she said. "Lulu had them close to her chest when they came out. The camera was not in the freezer, so I couldn't tell for sure."

"There is no camera in the freezer. I guess I'll just ask him when I see him again if he doesn't tell me first."

Lulu didn't say anything on the way back down the mountain. She was scared to death, and Wayne enjoyed driving the Hummer so much, he was concentrating on every bump, twist in the road, and jostle of the four-wheel drive behemoth and its 6.5L diesel turbo-charged engine. Wayne felt like he had all the power in the world at his control. Lulu felt like they were going to careen down the mountain, roll over, and be squashed like two fat rats in a large trap.

At the bottom of the hill, Lulu made the sign of the cross as she got out of the Hummer as soon as it was parked in the garage. Wayne stayed a few moments, grinning like a kid on Christmas morning. At last, he got out and rubbed his hand across the lines of the Hummer as he made his way out of the garage. Pushing the temporary code closed the garage door again, and he walked morosely back to his beat-up old Chevy pickup.

"You said there were cameras in the house, din't you?" Lulu asked, as soon as he got in the car.

"Yep," sighed a dreamy-eyed Wayne. "Got them everywhere, even outside. I guess he wants to know if anyone fools around up there, only I don't know who in their right mind would walk that far just to rob the place. I guess it's because of the dope he grows there sometimes. Only I ain't never seen it."

"Dope, what kinda dope?"

"Marijuana, that's about the only dope you can grow around here."

"Well, the reason I asked is I din't wanna say anything in the house, or for that matter in that jeep."

"Humvee," Wayne was quick to correct.

"Well, anyway, I saw the name on that cat's tag. It was

167

Dedra. I wonder what that is all about. Dedra is Dee's missing daughter."

"I know that. He probably named the cat after he met Dee is all. Probably intends to give it to her later. I don't see anything wrong with that."

"The tag had a date on it. It had 1996 stamped on it, the year Dedra disappeared. What do you think of them potatoes?"

Wayne looked at Lulu, but said nothing. They both said nothing during the drive back to their place. It was snowing harder now, but they made it back before the roads got too bad to drive on. It snowed the rest of the day.

As he and Dee made plans to leave the next morning, Lulu was thawing one package of the meat to make jerky.

Jerky needs to be cut thin and then marinated overnight. Lulu opened the package of meat just before dinner. It looked strange to her, nothing like any wild animal meat she had ever seen. It still had the bone in it and looked like a part of a leg. It had been sawed into one-inch pieces with the bone in the middle. The meat was pink and not gamy looking. It also had a membrane around it that looked like skin. She sliced it against the grain into one-eighth-inch-thick pieces and placed it in her special marinade. She put it in the refrigerator, where it would stay until she took it out to dry tomorrow. She then fixed supper for her family. She thought about the meat and the cat named Dedra until she went to bed for the night.

She was awakened three hours later from a dream. In the dream, she was watching herself and Wayne hunched over an object on a dark night. She was watching as if she were another person. There was also a tail between them. The tail of some creature also crouching, but she could not make out what the three of them were doing. The view changed to a closer look, but the light was so bad, she saw little. There were crunching noises. Crunch! Crunch! Crunch! It was a disgusting noise accompanied by a sucking sound. The scene switched around to the front of the two of them and the crouching animal that looked like a cat. The scene zoomed in like the eye of a camera and three crouching animals looked up at the same time.

Like a scene from the movie *Night of the Living Dead*, their faces were covered in blood and strings of bloody meat hung

168

from their mouths like moss from a tree. Dangling, dripping. Their eyes were wide open and the catlike animal seemed to be grinning. There was a tag on the cat and from a glint of light from behind, her dream's eye could see the name. It said Dedra. The three ghouls resumed their bent posture and ripped flesh from what looked like a body lying on the ground. Zooming in even closer, the scene revealed what they were tearing with their teeth and chewing with that crunching sound. It was the body of a young girl, a young girl that looked a lot like Dee. There was a necklace around what remained of the girl's neck. The light reflected back in gold letters D-E-D-R-A. That's when she woke up.

Lulu could not get back to sleep that night. She tossed and turned, listening to Wayne snore like a bear. At four-thirty, she got up, took the meat out of the marinade, dried it between two paper towels, and placed it in the oven on low to finish the drying process. It was almost six when she turned on the oven. Soon the house would be filled with the sweet smell of jerky. She wondered what the strange looking meat would taste like. *I'm definitely going to ask him what type of critter that was,* she thought to herself. As she put on a pot of coffee, she heard Wayne relieving himself and hacking up a luger to spit in the toilet. "The habits some men have," she said to herself. "Makes me wonder why women ever get married. Well, time to get the kids up for school." She decided not to tell Wayne about the dream.

Seventeen

They forestalled their morning run together on Friday. They both wanted to get an early start, and they did. They drove out to the park where he had left the trailer, hitched it to the truck, and away they went toward Vermont. It was a two-day trip and they planned on parking at a roadside rest that night. Dee had never traveled with a mobile home and was looking forward to the adventure. That night, Dee asked him about the magnetic map in the fifth wheel. He told her it was left from the people in Phoenix from whom he bought the fifth wheel. He said a lot of RVer's kept maps of where they have been. She studied the map for a minute and seemed satisfied. The next day, they got up early and continued the drive. Had he been by himself, he would have driven straight through. He avoided the I-95 corridor from D.C. north by going west of the entire mess. If God wanted to give North America an enema, that is where he would stick the hose, he thought.

Late Saturday, they pulled into the garage at the bottom of the mountain. He left the fifth wheel hooked to the truck as they took their belongings out of the fifth wheel and loaded them into the Hummer for the trip to the house. They were both beat when they got to the top. While she unpacked her clothes, he let the cats out. After a quick soak in the hot tub, they plopped into bed and were out in seconds. The cats were curled up all around them when they woke up in the morning.

She got up first, while he was still asleep, and went down the spiral stairway to the kitchen to make some coffee. Some of the cats followed her. It had snowed during the night, and the trees were covered in white as if cotton had been placed there. She could not believe how beautiful the winter could be. The view from the top of the mountain was breathtaking in the fall. In the winter it was truly amazing.

"Beautiful, isn't it?" he asked from the bedroom railing above the main living room. "As long as you have heat, electricity, and a way to get up and down the mountain, this is as good as it gets."

"You promised to show me the cat house last time and never did."

"Come with me," he beckoned. He took her to the cathouse, showing her the automatic systems. "This is where Wayne was yesterday." She looked around the room for the camera. "If you are looking for the camera, it's hidden in that book on the shelf behind you," he said. "The cats come in here to eat and poop as you say. Behind that door is a giant cat box that combs out the poop and urine and deposits more litter, the kind that clumps up so that liquids can be removed, too. It's all deposited in a composter, which disposes of waste naturally. It's actually quite good fertilizer for growing vegetables, if you can get rid of the stigma that it used to be cat food. The cat box has to be dumped once a day because of all the cats using it. This is the automatic feeder, which holds about a month's worth of feed. This is what usually malfunctions."

"You said before that you got them in every state. Are you going for 50? That's a lot of cats at one time." she said.

"To remind me where I've been, I get one in each state where I have camped and ridden my bike. There are twenty-four cats so far, but I think I might stop collecting for awhile unless I lose some."

"How do you tell them apart, or do you even care to?"

"I get a collar and a tag from the animal shelters with their name on it. They are named for the states, or if the state name is too long like Mississippi, I shorten it to Miss. It doesn't really matter, since I can't give them individual attention, they don't know their individual names. I just yell, here kitty, and most of them respond."

"At least they have a home instead of living or dying in a shelter," she said. "They were all probably unwanted cats, which is sad in itself."

"Yeah, me, the public-minded servant. Oh, well, it's better than nothing."

"Helping me is not nothing. I really appreciate it too, and

I'm going to let the members of MOMY-G know about your generosity. I forgot to mention you during the *Today Show*, interview and I am sorry. That reminds me, I need to check on my e-mail. You said I can do that on your computer."

"Right this way, darlin'," he said, as he took her to the computer in the kitchen. It was a secondary computer, connected to the main computer with CAT5 cabling secured behind the walls and floors of the house. The main computer was in a secure room protected from intrusion by security walls and a halogen fire system. The back-up computer was in the same room. The computer room was also his "escape" room that would protect him from any intruders for several hours if the need arose. No one knew about the escape provision except for the architect/builder. The builder gave him the original drawings after construction. After the house was totally his, he altered the design and made a few additions and changes on his own. He was not about to show her the computer room.

He watched as she downloaded her e-mails. There were 152 of them.

"It looks like I'm going to be here awhile. Sorry," she said.

"That's fine. I have some other things to do and a fire to build. It should be nice and cozy in the living room in about an hour. I'll check back on you then."

Lulu decided to try some of the jerky that she made yesterday. It was odd that she liked jerky and Wayne couldn't care less about it. Besides, she made it too spicy hot for him. He took some with him on hunting trips, but that was about the extent of his association with jerky. She took the smallest piece out of the bag and stared at it like it was a fish in a bowl. Then she smelled it. "Smells like all the other jerky I've made," she said aloud. She placed it on her tongue as if it were the body of Christ and this was her first communion. She chewed it with the remaining molars in the back of her mouth. Jerky is supposed to be bitten off and then chewed, but the last time she had any front teeth that were hers was about fifteen years ago. It was a little chewy for jerky, but did not have the gamy taste of venison or the strong taste of moose. It could be bear meat, but she wasn't sure. The spicy flavor was there, but that was just her special blend of soy,

Worcestershire, onions, garlic, hot sauce, and ginger. She decided to call him that afternoon, assuming they were back from Florida. She smiled as she thought of her role as matchmaker. She loved her niece like a sister and thought Dee deserved a better time in her life. She also did not like there being a rich bachelor loose close by and Dee needing someone at the same time.

"Agent Ford wants me to call him," Dee said as he walked into the room. "Ford said if Dedra had a computer, he would like to take it to the FBI lab for analysis. I e-mailed him back and told him she had one and he could get the house key from the neighbor anytime. I also looked at all the e-mails and narrowed it down to eight more possible missing women. If they pan out, that will make twenty-two. Out of the eight, two are from the same state, so the pattern of one from each state is still pretty much intact."

"I hope you can do most of your work from here, because we are supposed to get what they call a nor'easter tonight. In fact, I think we're seeing the effects now because of our elevation."

"What's a nor'easter?" she asked.

"It's a low pressure area that travels from west to east, but just as it gets to the New England states, it takes a jump out to sea and travels up the coast. It pulls in moisture off the ocean and dumps it inland. Depending on how fast it moves, we could see two to three feet of snow in the next twenty-four hours. The Hummer can get through it without any problem, but in a whiteout condition, you can't see where the hell you are going. So, we just need to hunker down 'til it blows over. I have enough provisions so that we could survive up here for a year if we had to. Now, sorry you asked?"

"No, as long as we can stay warm, I don't care. I can do all my e-mails from here. I sure will miss my morning jog though."

"You weren't here long enough last time for me to show you the exercise room. It also has a steam room. Come with me for a little tour."

She followed him through a door and down a flight of stairs opening out at ground level on the backside of the house. On opening the door, she almost gasped at the large room and the equipment inside. The floor was entirely of the padded material that absorbed noise while cushioning every step. You could do low-impact aerobics in your bare feet. Directly in front of them was a Nordic treadmill with a large deck, heart rate monitor, and power elevation. The treadmill was connected to a computer displaying a computerized course visible on a large-screen TV against the wall in front of the deck. You could also run against someone connected to the Internet. A stationary recumbent bike sat beside the treadmill connected to the same computer system. Around the exterior of the room to the right, were several Nautilus weight machines, a Smith machine for doing legwork, several stations with free weights, preacher curl machine, and Olympic weight bench and barbells. A redwood door to the left opened into the steam room large enough for four people.

"I should have known," she said, wide-eyed. "I can't wait until tomorrow morning, but you'll have to show me how to use the treadmill with the computer attached."

"All you have to do is turn on the treadmill and the computer will ask you what you want to do and take you step by step through the setup."

"What's the longest you've stayed up here without going down to civilization?" she asked.

"Not long. I really don't like to be by myself, since I get cabin fever. The cats tend to keep me company when I'm here for extended periods. I think the longest was two weeks."

"I find it hard to believe you don't have a bevy of women hanging around this place all the time. Am I just too naïve about this, or what?" she said, not really wanting an answer.

"I've had friends from time to time, but I'm not attracted to many of the women here, and the ones I am attracted to elsewhere do not want to live in this harsh of an environment. Therefore, I usually remain celibate when I'm at home. I don't get many visitors, because of the remoteness of the house. The lack of a road makes it hard for someone to just pop in."

"Well, I think I could find this life very interesting."

At three o'clock, Lulu picked up the phone to ask about the strange-looking meat. Also, she wanted to be filled in on how the two were doing together. She figured that they should be done with any hanky-panky by that time of day. She figured wrong.

As the phone rang, they were halfway through a mid-afternoon horizontal mambo session and had no intention of answering the phone. When the answering machine picked up, a suspicious Lulu said, "Pick up, this is Lulu, unless—oh, well, never mind. I just wanted to let you know we took some of the meat from the freezer and you should check it out. I think it may be going bad, because it doesn't taste like any game meat I ever had. Unless it's bear meat, I ain't never had none of that yet. Oh, well, give us a call, and let me know what you are up to. Better yet, just give me a call. I think I know what you're up to." She hung up.

A little before four, he retrieved the message and told Dee she had better call Lulu to let her know they were back and okay. Dee said she wanted a session in the sauna and a nice hot shower before she called Lulu back.

"She tends to be a bit wordy, and I want to be all set for at least an hour with the phone stuck to my ear."

They both went to the sauna and sweat as much as they could stand. She took a semi-hot shower in the exercise room, and he went to the master bath for a cold shower. She wrapped herself in an oversized Turkish bath towel like the ones in a luxury hotel. After drying off, he put on a fresh set of blue jeans. He had some work to do.

It was almost 5:00 when Dee returned Lulu's call. She hoped Lulu would be about ready to feed the troops, which would shorten the conversation.

"Lulu, this is Dee, am I calling at a bad time. Don't want to interrupt supper."

"No," said Lulu. "We are having Kentucky Fried." Even though the name was changed to KFC, most people still called it by the old familiar reminder that they still served artery clogging fried food. "Wayne just went to fetch it. The snow has let up here for the time being and the plows just went by. So it's wings, beer, and belchin' night tonight."

"Save me the vision of that scene," said Dee. "I would have called last night, but we got in late and slept until way past noon." She didn't know if Lulu would buy that story, but it was worth a shot. Lulu wasn't fooled.

"If you say so, girl, but I think you two were bumpin' uglies is what I think. Anyway, I was worried if you got back or not. It's a good thing you made it last night, since this storm is supposed to be a bad one and last a day or two."

"That's what we found out this morning." *Shit* she thought. *I blew that one. Step one, open mouth, step two, insert foot.*

Lulu glossed over the contradiction or wasn't listening that well.

"I just wanted to let you know that one of those cats of his is named Dedra. I saw the tag when we were up there the other day."

She didn't want to let Lulu know they had watched them with the computer, so she did not respond right away. She was a bit put back by this revelation though.

"At first, I couldn't read the tag on the cat, but then I saw it. I didn't say anything to Wayne right away, because there are cameras all over that house, and he may have recorded it. So I told Wayne on the way home. Girl, I'm concerned about this. And that strange meat in the freezer. We just watched the *Silence of the Lambs* last weekend on tape, and I remember that Jeffrey Dahmer thing a few years' back, ya know?"

"Oh, Lulu, I'm sure he named the cat for Dedra after he met me. He hasn't told me yet, but I'm sure he will. And he already told me that the meat probably is bad as you suggested when you called. He said some of that meat is over three years old and he feeds it to the cats. Serves you right for taking meat without asking."

"Girl, that tag was stamped the same year that Dedra went missing. I shouldn't be saying this over the phone, because he may be listening."

He was. In the computer room on the speaker-phone he listened. Dee or Lulu would detect no audible clicks or background noise from here. He was planning on damage control as he listened. He turned off the speaker, but allowed the computer to record the rest of the conversation, and quickly located the cat with the incriminating name tag. He removed the collar. He took the tag to his workshop and re-stamped the tag so the date was changed. It had been 1996, but he added a loop to the 6. It now looked like 1998. He thought about getting rid of the tag, but that might have raised more questions. This way, he could at least buy some time. If the FBI lab analyzed the tag the double dye would surely show up. But he would destroy the tag before then. Just as quickly as he removed the collar, he replaced it on the cat's neck. Dee was just hanging up the phone as he walked up the stairs and through the kitchen on his way to the butcher shop freezer.

"Lulu is really concerned about that meat in the freezer," she said. "Maybe you ought to check it out."

"I was just heading there to do just that. Want to tag along?"

"No, I think I'll just enjoy the view of the storm from the comfort of the living room. Also I would like to catch up on the news if you don't mind."

"No, not at all. I may have to destroy the meat in question, and it might get a little smelly. The incinerator does not draw well when the wind is blowing as hard as it is now. You just go and enjoy the view."

She had no intention of doing that. She was going to look for the cat with the Dedra name on it. In the living room, the cats turned to see who was entering their domain. She approached the couch where she counted six cats in various positions of repose. At least ten other cats were scattered about the room, some slumbering, some playing with each other. As she knelt down on the floor, almost all the cats came over to see if they could get a stroke or a scratch on the jaw from the human in their regal midst. Dee obliged them eagerly. Dee carefully scratched and stroked them with one hand while pulling the tag around for a close look. As he told her, they must have all been obtained from different states. Not only did the state names match the list of MOMY-G members, they also matched the filled-in magnetic map as near as she could remember. At least he wasn't lying about where he got them. But this seemed like an unusual coincidence.

Finally on the twelfth cat, she found what she was looking for. The tag did say Dedra in addition to the state of Florida. It also had a date. She looked closely. It was not really clear, but it sure looked like 1998, not 1996 as Lulu said. Lulu must have misread it when the cat jumped out of her arms. Hopefully he would explain without her asking, why he had a cat named Dedra from Florida. If he said nothing, then she would be concerned.

When he got to the freezer in the butcher shop. He pulled the packages he had that were on one side of the freezer. He always kept the special meat separate from the rest. There was not a whole lot of it left, just about twenty packages of various shapes and in no specific order. Meat will keep a long time at sub-zero temperatures so that he did not worry about having to eat the oldest first. The computer kept records of the temperature in the freezer and would warn him if the temperature had risen to where the meat could spoil. He gathered up the meat in a basket and took it to the incinerator, placed it in the chamber, dialed in the approximate weight of the meat, and pushed the start incineration button. A whirring sound identified the door locking, and there was a faint whoosh as the burners fired up. An instant later, the sound of the exhaust fan could be heard. In two hours, there would be nothing but ashes to identify.

Leaving the incinerator to do its work, he returned to the living room to find Dee playing with the cats.

"I see you are getting acquainted with my house guests. They are very affectionate, considering I leave them to their own devices a lot. There is one that is special."

Thank god, she thought. *He is going to tell me about Dedra.*

"I picked up one on my last trip," he continued, "and named her for Dedra. Although I got her in D.C., I stamped her tag when we got back with this year's date and your state. I hope you don't mind. I thought she could keep you company until Dedra is found. If you can't take her home, she can be here for you each time you visit. I assume you will be coming back."

"I may never leave," she said, tears welling up in her eyes. She reached over and picked up the one named Dedra and held her close to her face. "At least until you get tired of me and kick me out."

"I hope you will stay a long time," he lied. *At last*, he thought. *I'm starting to feel like my old self again. Maybe now I can resume my travels, as soon as I get rid of her. And Ma and Pa Kettle, too.*

The next two days, the storm raged about the mountaintop. They passed the time exercising, making love, eating fine food, and drinking fine wine. She kept in touch with her MOMY-G group, which now had a solid twenty-one members, and with the

California exception, no two from the same state. In the morning, the wind quit blowing, the snow quit falling, and the sun started shining again. The phone rang. It was Agent Ford, and he wanted to speak to Dee. He handed the phone to Dee, telling her who it was.

"Hello Agent Ford," said Dee. She wanted to call him by his first name, but the FBI agents were so stiff, she thought it appropriate not to get too familiar.

He remained in the same room as Dee listening to only one side of the conversation. Later, he would listen to the agent's side recorded by the main computer.

"Hello, Ms. Mayfield," the stiff agent said. "We have found something, but not on the computer. The computer is so clean, it was hard to believe it had been used at all."

"Oh," said Dee. "Well, I did have a crash on my computer, which my friend fixed for me. That could explain it."

"Are you all alone?" continued Agent Ford. "What I mean, is there a chance someone could be listening to both sides of this conversation?"

"No," replied Dee as she looked at him by the window staring at the snow.

"The hard drive seems to have been deliberately wiped clean," said Agent Ford, "but while I was in your house, I looked around and found several floppy disks that I also had analyzed. I notice you are in Vermont, so please listen, and don't repeat what I say. There were some e-mails on those floppies. Do you or your daughter use the on-line name of orangejuice2, only juice is spelled j-e-w-c-e and the number 2?"

"Yes, both me and Dedra used it."

"Well, these were dated 1996, the year your daughter disappeared. There were some chat-room conversations on the floppies with a person using the on-line name of maniac, only it was spelled with an underscore between the man and iac."

"Yes, I'm aware of those."

"We were able to track those chat-room conversations to an Internet service provider in upstate New York, Glens Falls, to be exact. The trace then went to Vermont, but it was bounced around so much, we can't be sure where."

Dee's heart skipped several beats, but she stared straight

ahead and did not look at him.

"Another set of chat-room recordings were traced to Florida around the date your daughter disappeared. This could be because the person was close then and had traveled to meet her.

"This could be only a coincidence. If a computer-savvy person was in these chat rooms, they could have bounced the Internet connection all over the country. We can't really be sure where the connections originated until we find the other computer. But if maniac knew what he was doing, we may never find the smoking gun. Do you feel completely safe where you are now?"

"Yes, completely," although she was starting to have doubts, and if he could somehow hear the other end of this conversation and he is maniac, she may be in peril. She decided to get back to the safety of her home as soon as possible.

"That's all for now," said Agent Ford. "Keep me aware of your location if you decide to go somewhere else."

"I will, and thank you, Mr. Ford."

"Was that good news or bad?" he asked when she hung up the phone.

"Actually, the computer was clean. Could the crash have done that?"

"Well, I had to do some cleaning up of the hard drive when I fixed it. I don't know what they were looking for, but the software I used could have done that. I hope I didn't destroy any evidence."

"Me, too. I probably ought to get back to Florida though in case something else comes up. I want to do some more with the MOMY-G group and would like to do that closer to civilization. No offense to your mansion here, but it is rather isolated, and if there is another storm, I might not be able to go if I have to."

"No offense taken. But you know you are welcome to stay as long as you like," he said, but he was ready for her to leave. He was starting to feel uncomfortable with her here and he had work to do. "When do you want to leave?"

"The sooner the better, but I'd better pay my respects to Lulu and Wayne before I go."

That afternoon, he took her to see Wayne and Lulu on her

way to the airport in Burlington. Although the storm dumped a lot of snow at the airport, the runways were plowed and flights were arriving and departing. He bought her a one-way, first-class ticket on Delta with a connecting flight in Boston to Pensacola. She would take a cab home. She gave him a hug and a kiss and promised to call him as soon as she was home. He told her he was planning another road trip and would stop in to see her on the way. Her eyes were welling up as she walked down the jetway. She believed she would never see him again. He sensed the same thing, but there were no tears in his eyes. He was planning his next move. She left Dedra the cat at the mansion.

As she was making her connecting flight at Logan International, he was listening to the computer-recorded conversation between her and Agent Ford. *That's too bad*, he thought. *I knew we would have to end it sooner or later, but I hoped it would end on my terms. I can't send her to see her daughter now. It would be too obvious. First I need to take care of the remaining bits of evidence.*

The next morning, Dee called Agent Ford.

"Agent Ford speaking," he said, answering on the second ring.

"This is Dee," she said. "Any more information on the chat-line traces?"

"Yes. We are sure now that one of the chat rooms originated from an ISP in Vermont. The others are untraceable. We are searching the data base of known sex offenders in the White River Junction area, since that is where the ISP is based."

Another hit, she thought. White River Junction was a local call from South Royalton. She knew that from using the phone at Wayne and Lulu's.

"Well, I wanted to let you know that I'm home in Pensacola now," she told him, although this was unnecessary. All of the agent's phones had caller ID. "I would like to meet with you and go over some of the information I have from the MOMY-G group if you can come to Pensacola," she added. "We have quite a bit of information. I don't know if it's useful or not, but you can decide that."

"I can be there tomorrow," Agent Ford said. "I need to return your daughter's computer anyway, and I need to get away from the snow here in D.C. We'll keep the floppies as evidence in case we need them."

"That would be great," Dee said. "I'll be right here. And thanks for your help, Agent Ford. I really appreciate it. Good-bye."

"Good-bye."

She added up what she knew: the ISP close to South Royalton, the U.S. map with the states matching the missing women's last known locations, and the cats with the name tags. She was hoping this was just coincidental, but her intuition was telling her otherwise. If he had something to do with the disappearances, how could she live with herself knowing she had been so close to him? She had been distracted long enough. Finding her daughter was all she could be concerned with now.

She called him that morning to let him know she arrived okay. She apologized for not calling him last night, but she got in very late. He would not get the message until later that day.

Getting into their double-wide was easy. Most people did not lock their doors in Vermont. Waiting in the snow in sub-zero conditions until Lulu went to pick up the kids at school was the hard part. Rigging the furnace was easy, too. He did not find what he was looking for in the freezer or kitchen cabinets. Ransacking the house was not his intent anyway.

He was back home and loading the fifth wheel for a trip before Lulu got back from school and Wayne got back from work. He called and left a message on their answering machine that he would be out of town for a few days. He would leave the keys to the Hummer in the same place as always. He intended to be several states away when the "accident" happened. The valve control and timer were set for Saturday morning at 3:30. He would be in sunny Florida leaving an evidence trail just in case an alibi was needed.

Eighteen

Dee had finished her morning run and was sitting down to a cold glass of ice tea, when the phone rang.

"Hello," she said.

"Hi, it's me," he told her. He was using his home-billed cell phone which would provide a record of a call.

"Where are you?" she asked, as a chill ran up her spine. They had not talked since they parted in Burlington. They were playing phone tag, which was all right with her. She was apprehensive about another encounter with him and had mixed feelings on hearing his voice again.

"I'm in Tallahassee and will be in Pensacola around lunch time if you are free."

"Oh, no, I have a hair appointment at 11:30 and won't be done until about 1:30," she lied. "Can you stay for dinner?"

"Oh, babe, I'm sorry. I have to be in Phoenix in two days and can't stop very long. I will be coming back this way in a few days if you are free then."

"That would be great, but give me more than a couple of hours' notice. I'm really busy now with MOMY-G. I need to have a serious talk with you, anyway."

"Not the ol' brush off is it?"

"No, I need to discuss where we are going. I am a planner and have to look to the future, with or without Dedra."

"Now you have me worried, but I can wait a few days. I'll call you the day before I get back. Later, then?"

"Later, you bet."

Alibi established, with cell phone records and a witness.

Wayne and Lulu got the kids in bed that Monday evening before the explosion flattened their double-wide like a firecracker set off in a pile of dog shit. The whole family was sleep-

183

ing soundly. Wayne and Lulu were both snoring, Wayne loud enough to scare away a bear if one had been nearby. A small electronic device was waiting until the furnace turned off the first time after 3:30.

They never heard the faint click that directed the propane gas from their furnace into the house. The furnace room was in the middle of the pre-manufactured home, so that the gas quickly left the louvered combustion openings in the door to the furnace room and spread along the floor like a nest of snakes escaping from hell. Since all were raised, on their beds, they did not smell the methyl mercaptan gas placed in the propane to give it a rotten-eggs smell.

Ten minutes later, the plastic combustible valve switched back to furnace. The gas then lay in wait for the thermostat to call for heat and start the sequence that ordinarily would heat the house. The furnace worked flawlessly as it had a thousand times before.

Blown from her bed, miraculously, Lulu survived. Wayne, the kids, and a half-dozen nesting rodents did not. The hunting dog was the only member of the family not injured by the blast. He was sheltered behind the storage shed, which was scorched, but left standing. Neighbors heard the explosion, saw the smoke and yellow glow from the fire, and called 911 immediately. In rural Vermont, that meant the state police were the first ones on the scene. The volunteer fire department got there about twenty minutes later, long enough for the house to be completely incinerated, including any evidence, had anyone cared to look. Lulu's sister, Elsie, was called after Lulu was transported to the hospital by care-flight.

The explosion and deaths were called a horrific accident by the *White River Junction Valley News*. Lulu was in intensive care for three days after the explosion. The doctors said it was her corpulent nature that saved her from being killed. Her body fat had absorbed the shock wave. Her position against the outside wall enabled her to be blown free of the consuming fire. This was no consolation to someone who had just lost her husband, children, and home in the blink of an eye. A week later, still in the hospital, she was able to talk without pain, so she told Elsie to have Dee call her at her room phone. Lulu did not think this

184

was an accident. They had just had the furnace serviced before the heating season.

Dee was devastated by the news of the explosion and fire. She cried the entire time she talked to Lulu.

"The strange meat," Lulu whispered painfully through scarring lips. "I didn't have room in the freezer for the un-opened package, so I put it in the storage shed. Unless some animal got it, it should still be there. The bones left over from the jerky, I fed to the dog. See if your FBI friend can find out what kind of animal they were from. Don't worry about me. They say I will be just fine. Elsie's been here the whole time. You take care, girl."

Dee fought back tears long enough to sob a good-bye to her aunt. After an hour, she was able to call Agent Ford. He agreed to get the meat from the storage shed. He went to Vermont four days later.

"Dee," he said, "what's wrong?" He called her that evening from Kentucky and told her he was in Phoenix.

She was able to tell him the story, and he seemed to tear up a little.

"I'll be done here tomorrow with my business and then I'll head back to see what I can do for Lulu. That poor woman. My God, I loved that family. Do you want me to pick you up on my way back?"

"No," she said. "There is nothing I can do that Elsie can't. I'll go to Lulu as soon as she is out of the hospital. I need to immerse myself in MOMY-G more than ever now. The anniversary of Dedra's disappearance is a week away, and I need to be alone. If I change my mind, I'll give you a call. Give me a number where you can be reached."

"I'll have the hotel phone tied up most of the day, so use my cell phone. I promise to keep it on. I may leave this evening instead of tomorrow."

"Okay, talk to you later," she said.

Agent Ford arrived at the scene and shook his head at the devastation a little propane gas can cause. Charred wood, insulation, appliances, and the remains of the double-wide were strewn all over the property. Neighbors had picked up what little there was to salvage, including the hunting dog, and were holding all of it for Lulu. The storage shed had been opened and most of the contents removed for safe keeping. He found some of the butcher paper from the package that held the meat. Raccoon tracks were in the snow and had likely carried it off.

He searched the dog pen and found some bones. He picked them up with protective rubber gloves and placed them in a plastic bag for testing. He also looked at the furnace, or what was left of it. It was blown apart, and the gas line leading to it was twisted into a pose like a striking cobra. If any device was used that caused the fire, it was completely destroyed and scattered about the site. Without an exhaustive search of the area, the only conclusion was the one the local authorities made, which was an accident. There was little else to do here, so he got back in his car to return to the airport.

She didn't call him, and by the next morning he was already back in Vermont with number 25 and a new cat named Kentucky. He was back on track to his goal of filling up the map. The incinerator burned again that night.

Because of media attention and that of a senator being involved, the FBI was politically motivated to put more of its resources behind the investigation. A profile was being developed from the information that the MOMY-G group had put together. The FBI had no other leads, and the missing intern fit the characteristics of the other missing MOMY-G women. The profiler believed the abductor, as they were calling him now, was a male, attractive to women, a runner/biker/athletic type, smart, mobile, and with the monetary resources to allow him time to do the abductions. This fit Dee's friend. A quick background check on him by the FBI showed he was a lottery winner, but they found less than one million in banks in the States under his name. Their conclusion was that he must have the rest of the money in stocks, at his home, or in offshore banks. If he had other identities, he could hide the money, but he would need fake Social Security numbers.

It took the lab just one day to determine that four of the bones Agent Ford found were human. He only needed to talk to Lulu for confirmation that she had given the bones to the dog and that she had gotten the bones from his freezer. When this was done, Agent Ford had the evidence to get a search warrant for the house in South Royalton. He called Dee and gave her the news and asked her to get DNA samples from the members of the MOMY-G group. He explained that a hairbrush, toothbrush, fingernails, and other personal items could provide DNA matches. The lab would compare their samples to the bones to see if they came from any of the missing women. This would be a long shot, but they had to try.

Dee told him of the cameras and sensors in and around the house. Agent Ford said he was obtaining a warrant to search the house and would use the direct approach. That was the last time she talked to him.

Dee got busy contacting the members of MOMY-G. There were only eight members who could provide some type of DNA, mostly hair from brushes saved when their daughters disappeared. The others said they would look, but they did not save much, or there was not much to save, since their daughters were not living at home at the time. She asked them all to mail the samples to the FBI directly. As Agent Ford told her, this would be a long shot.

She checked her e-mail and found a message from a woman who had visited the MOMY-G web site and had a missing daughter. They were from Kentucky, and her daughter had been missing for six days. The description of her daughter matched perfectly with the other missing women on the MOMY-G site. Dee copied down her telephone number. "Six days," she thought out loud. "Wasn't that the last time she talked to him, but he was in Phoenix. Agent Ford would just have to check his alibi, if he had one."

Mud season came early to Vermont. By the time Agent Ford had obtained the search warrant. It was March 15. Two days later, he was in Vermont with one other agent and two Vermont State Police agents. Rural Vermont and most villages and towns did not have a police force. The state police had jurisdiction and accompanied federal authorities on searches and potential arrest situations.

It had been unusually warm the last week, and the snows were melting. When the snow melted on ground that had been frozen four feet down, there was no place for the water to go. It stayed on the surface unless there was adequate drainage. With piled up snow blocking the flow pattern, the water created a spongy layer of soil. Driving over the dirt roads of Vermont, can be quite an experience. Four-wheel drive is a necessity, especially if you want to get to the top of a mountain. The FBI agents did not have a four-wheel drive car.

Following the freshly made tracks of the Humvee, they got half-way up the road to the mansion before they got stuck in the mud. There was no going backward or forward, "...at least not in this car," said Agent Ford. One of the state police agents called in for a state tow truck.

"Bring the biggest four-wheel drive truck you have," the agent told the dispatcher. One of the state agents went back down the road to direct the tow truck. Agent Ford and the other two started to walk up to the house. The agent returning down the road had instructions to direct the tow-truck driver to take the agent and the rest of their equipment from the trunk of the stuck vehicle to the top of the mountain. Agent Ford intended to serve the warrant and search the house today.

Before they were in sight of the house, he was watching their every move. He laughed as they trudged along in the mix of snow and mud in their working shoes. He noticed that it was starting to snow, not heavy, but a steady, light snow. *They will be mad as hell when they get here and I don't even let them in*, he thought. When they started to bust in, as he was sure they would, he would be secure in the one room of the house designed to withstand, if he wanted it to, bullets, fire, and a lot worse if they decided to try to get him out. First they had to find the room, and he would let them search for a little while before he sprang his trap.

Before they got there, he had to get rid of the only evidence that would implicate him if he was ever brought to trial. He went to the butcher shop and took all the special meat out of the freezer from his latest victim and placed it in the incinerator. Since it was frozen, it would take a while to burn, but he figured it would be at least an hour before they found the room. By then, the evidence would be ash. He set the incinerator for a hundred pounds of meat and hit the start button. He then went to the living room to say good-bye to his guests. He picked up the one named Dedra/Florida and decided to save her from the fate the rest of them would share with the unsuspecting agents. He felt sorry for them, but there was nothing else he could do. Letting them go outside would be a worse fate. Wild animals would kill the ones able to survive the cold and starvation. He carried the cat back with him to the safe room.

"What the hell is that smell?" asked Agent Ford, although not really expecting a response.

"Smells like burning hair or meat," commented one of the other agents as the smoke from the incinerator wafted down on them from the chimney. The wind was blowing from the other side of the mountain causing a downdraft that carried the smoke toward them. It was starting to snow harder and at the elevation they were at now, it was below freezing. Down on the access road, where the garage housing the fifth wheel was located, it was still above freezing. The snow was falling there as well, making a sloppy mess of the road. Up on the mountain, the agents were still cursing the mud and the snow blowing in their faces.

The incinerator was using a large amount of propane. So much so, that the low-level trip was reached. The computer sensed the low-level condition, notified him, and sent a signal to the controls at the base of the mountain. The pump inside the garage at the base of the mountain turned on, transferring propane from the large filling tanks beside the pump up to the tanks outside the mansion. The pump could have filled the tanks in ten minutes, even with the incinerator going full blast, if it were not for the power going out.

Tim Clayburn had just finished his eighth beer, drinking alone at the Royalton Raid VFW Post #7673, when he decided to head home. Like many Vietnam era veterans, he was trying to forget all the friends he lost in 'Nam. He had been trying to forget for thirty years. He didn't feel drunk, so when the bartender asked if he needed a ride, he replied, "Naw, I'm okay." He wasn't.

He walked as steady as he could out of the VFW, across the parking lot, through the wet falling snow to his beat-up 1986 Chevrolet pickup. He never locked his truck. "What the hell is there to steal anyway," he always told himself. He never carried insurance and got his inspection sticker from his buddy who owned an auto repair shop. He hauled his fifty-four-year-old, overweight, 240-pound, 5-foot 10-inch frame into the driver's side by holding onto the roof and sliding in. He had a day-old stubble of growth on his face surrounded by alcohol-induced red nose, cheeks, and ears. Deep lines etched his forehead and radiated out from the corners of his eyes. He had smoker's wrinkles around his mouth. What little hair he had curled out from under his red hunting cap in a black matted mess.

The old Chevy started, but not without protest. He pulled out of the parking lot and headed across the bridge and then north onto Route 14. Route 14 snaked its way along the north side of the White River. It would have been a beautiful ride home on a nice day; however, a wet snow was falling. This was not going to be a nice day, and a last one for Tim Clayburn. The wipers were original equipment, so it was not a surprise when he turned them on and the hardened rubber groaned a muddy streak across the cracked windshield.

"Godamn shit," he muttered as he dug into his dirty camouflage jacket and pulled out a cigarette. The cigarette lighter in the car would have worked if it had the element that fit in it. So he was forced to dig in his other pocket for a Bic lighter. He had to take his eyes off the road long enough to light the cigarette. Just long enough for the car to enter another turn in the road. He looked up and was able to turn the wheel to the right just far enough so the bald tires lost traction, putting the truck into a slide. At sixty miles an hour, the truck crossed to the other side of the road and sideswiped a utility pole. The pole survived, but the power line did not. Neither did Tim.

The power line snapped at the top of the pole. Dropping to the ground, the line moved around like a rattlesnake with blue-white fangs biting the pavement. Electrons etched a charred path across the blacktop where the snake had been, coughing a plume of ozone and smoke into the falling snow.

The force of the sideswipe spun the truck counter clockwise and down an embankment. A state police officer, traveling in the opposite direction, witnessed a spectacular crash as the truck rolled over four times throwing the unbelted Tim into its path.

190

The Chevy came to rest on top of the veteran's lifeless body. Within seconds, a fire truck, rescue equipment, tow truck, ambulance, and a power company bucket truck were dispatched. The state tow truck called in to help the agents was delayed getting around the accident. It would be two hours before lost power could be restored to the South Royalton area.

The three agents were experiencing a near-whiteout condition as they approached the garage to the mansion. He could see them from the cameras on the roof. They were not having the time of their life. "Propane gas dangerously low," said the computerized voice. "Shit!" he said out loud. He could have screamed it and no one would have heard. He checked the indicators and controls at the base of the mountain and determined that the power was out. "Shit!" he yelled again. "Oh, well, Dedra," he said to the cat, "we'll just have to see what happens next." He turned his attention to the three agents. In addition to not having boots, their coats were not heavy enough. They were warm enough from having climbed halfway up the mountain, but soon they would feel the cold wind. "Propane tanks empty," droned the computer.

Without propane, the sensors on the incinerator shut the supply valve. The contents were scorched and starting to ash over from the outside, but because the load started out at sub-zero temperature, the meat at the center of the incinerator was not yet thawed. The incinerator in the automatic mode would turn back on when propane pressure returned to normal. Until then, the contents would smolder some more and then go out.

"What now," asked state Agent Drake, who was the heaviest among his present companions. He wished he were the one sent back to the road to direct the tow truck. The walk up the mountain took almost all the strength in his six-foot 200-pound frame. They were approaching the garage with a door in the middle between the large overhead doors. There was no obvious main entrance to the house, nor could they detect a sidewalk or pathway leading up to one from the garage. The snow obscured the way to the side entrance to the house. The side entrance was seldom used, especially in the winter. There were no windows in any of the doors to the garage. There were two sides to the garage but they too had no windows.

"We knock," said Agent Ford. "Unless you can find a door-bell." By this time, they were feeling the cold, biting wind at the top of the mountain. The sweat on their shirts from the climb was now making the chill that much worse.

Agent Ford ungloved his right hand and knocked loudly, and he yelled.

"FBI agents. We have a search warrant. Open up." He was not about to wait any longer. "Break it down," he told Agent Drake.

Agent Drake reared back and kicked the door at the knob with the heel of his shoe. The door did not give way. It was a steel door and frame welded to the steel frame structure. Two more kicks and the door started to buckle but still it held like the vault to a safe.

He was laughing all safe, warm, and secure in his room. If the incinerator had finished its job, he would have let them in, using the remote garage door opener, and saved them some aggravation. If all went as planned, in a very short time, they would not be feeling the cold, or anything, for that matter.

Another kick, and it was obvious they would have to wait for some of their tools from the car. The state agent called the dispatcher and found the tow truck had been delayed getting around the accident, but was on its way. It was in fact, loading up the equipment from the stuck FBI car. In ten minutes, it was at the garage doors at the top of the mountain. Agents Ford, Drake, and Crane climbed into the front seat of the tow truck, with the heater on full, while the tow truck driver and state Agent Mallard attacked the garage door with the heavy ram. It took five solid hits before the door gave way. The agents sent the tow-truck driver back to the stuck car with instructions to return as soon as the car was safely at the base of the mountain. They were not going to walk back down. It was still snowing.

He watched them gain entry to the garage. The alarm system was of no use, so he had it disabled.

"He must be here," said Agent Ford. "Our information is that he always armed his alarm system when he was gone. Also, here is the Humvee he uses to get up and down the mountain."

"The keys are in it," commented Agent Crane. "Why don't

we confiscate it as evidence to go back down the mountain."

"Perhaps," said Agent Ford. "Perhaps." They would be returning down the mountain by other means and, except for Agent Drake, not today.

The door to the corridor leading to the main house was of similar construction as the one they just battered in, but under warmer conditions they were more enthusiastic. They were through it in a few hits with the ram.

Off the corridor was the butcher shop. Dee had e-mailed Agent Ford a description of the house, and they were all briefed before they started up the mountain. The door to the butcher shop was not as substantial as the other two, but it was locked. As they busted it down, power was restored at the base of the mountain and the pump started transferring propane from the garage tanks to the house tanks.

"There is the source of the smell," said Agent Ford pointing at the incinerator. He approached the incinerator with his hands out like a blind man feeling his way in an unfamiliar room. "It's still warm, but looks like it's off." He grabbed at the handle and turned it. The door came open and a pungent white smoke was pushed back into the room from the wind blowing on the outside exhaust.

"Jesus Christ," said Agent Drake. "Shut that fucking thing before we all choke to death."

"No, there's something in there that hasn't burned yet," said Agent Ford. "Find me something to pull it out with."

While the other agents looked around in the drawers and tables of the butcher shop, Ford opened the freezer. "This all needs to be confiscated, too," he said.

Brandishing a butcher's hook used to hold a carcass for cutting into smaller pieces, Agent Drake approached the incinerator. He was able to pull out one of the packages of meat, but closed the door to prevent any more smoke from entering the butcher shop. Since the gas pressure had resumed, the incinerator safety switch was only waiting for a signal that the door was closed before it resumed its cycle. Before he could realize his mistake, the door safety latch closed, similar to the latch on a self-cleaning oven, and the burners turned on. The temperature quickly jumped and burning resumed. No one could easily open the incinerator again until the temperature had returned to a safe level.

"Godamn it, what the fuck did you do?" said Ford, not needing an answer. "Well, I see you at least got some of the contents out."

Agent Drake was holding the smoldering, scorched, and still partially frozen meat on the hook staring at it like a kid looking at his first Popsicle.

"Set it down in the godamn sink and see if you can save what's left of it," said the infuriated Ford. "And then see if you can pull the plug to that thing."

His anger while watching them retrieve evidence out of his incinerator gave way to a smile when he saw their Keystonian antics as Drake closed the door to the incinerator. "Propane levels returning to normal," stated the computer. They had a piece of one of his victims, but would it make it to a lab to be analyzed? From the spy program he had placed in Dee's computer, he knew they had bones from the meat the bitch Lulu had taken from the meat locker. So what if it was human? There was no chain of evidence linking him to a crime. If DNA was not obtainable, what could they convict him of, but the meat in the sink, was a different story. However, they would have to get him in addition to the evidence. He would let them advance a little further before he sprang the trap.

The agents could not find any valves or power cut-off to the incinerator. They were all neatly concealed in the crawl space under the butcher shop. Punching the keys on the coded controls of the incinerator resulted in frustration. Without the number sequence, the incinerator would complete its job, which was only ten minutes away. They set aside a suggestion to break into the incinerator while it was operating, correctly surmising that this would be very dangerous.

"Hell," said Ford. "Drake, stay here and watch the evidence while we see if we can find him."

They left the butcher shop and, with guns drawn, were slinking toward the door at the end of the corridor. That door, Agent Ford knew led into an alcove that adjoined the kitchen and main living areas. The door was not locked, and they charged through one at a time. Ford first yelling, "FBI, come out with your hands raised."

Cats scattered in all directions. Some just crouched as low as they could, waiting for the next move. Watching all this with amusement in the computer room, he was preparing for his last hurrah. He waited until the indicators told the computer the incinerator was starting its cool-down process. The agents were methodically searching the bedroom, exercise room, living room, and the cathouse. They started toward the computer room stairs after checking out all the other rooms. Given enough time, they would find him, but their time was up.

He opened the hatch to the tunnel that would give him access to the side of the mountain opposite the garage. Inside the tunnel, there were clothes, snowshoes, and a backpack with all he would need. Before he entered the tunnel, he checked the monitors. It was still snowing and the propane tanks were full. "Incinerate," was all he said to the computer. He then picked up Dedra/Florida and entered the tunnel and donned the winter gear and the knapsack. He tucked the cat into the coat next to his shirt. She stuck her head out between two of the buttons, seeming to enjoy this new adventure.

The computer, not knowing its own fate was sealed, obeyed the command as it had been programmed to do. After a five-minute delay, it opened valves leading to the crawl space and all the rooms of the house. It directed the valve on the tanks at the bottom of the hill to dump the remaining gas into the RV garage. It then turned off all the main power to the house, throwing the rooms without windows into darkness. Because of the darkening storm, not a lot of light entered through the windows. A split second later, the main valve opened from the propane tanks. Gas immediately flooded the house as 120 gallons of unregulated propane expanded to atmospheric pressure.

By that time, he was out of the tunnel and heading down the side of the mountain at a safe distance. Expanding rapidly, the gas created a fog mixing with the air in the mansion. All Agent Ford had time to say was "What the hell is going on?" His brain never had time to react as the computer ignited the death cloud. Ten seconds later, the propane cloud in the garage at the bottom of the mountain ignited when the heater turned on.

Safely on his escape route, heading down the south side of

the mountain, he felt the shock wave as the roof of the house above him launched into the air. Debris was jettisoned all over the top of the mountain as the force flattened the structure. Dedra/Florida squirmed at the sound. The tow-truck driver about to start up the mountain again, having safely retrieved the agent's car, heard the explosion and looked up to see debris raining down toward him through the snow clouds. Although he could not have seen it because of the storm, he missed the spectacular fireball. The sound took five seconds to travel the distance from the top. His truck was hit with pieces of metal, and siding shattered his windshield. Agent Drake, or what was left of him, landed on the hood of the truck, denting it to the top of the air filter.

The explosion from the garage behind the driver blew out the rear window of the tow truck, but by that time, he was on the floorboards, hiding from the rain of debris. Another explosion from the top of the mountain signaled the end of the Humvee when its fuel tank ruptured, lifting the Hummer ten feet in the air and depositing it upside down, roughly where the butcher shop had been. The top and sides of the mountain looked like a scene from "Desert Storm," where a smart bomb had found its target in a sea of snow instead of sand. Of the group of five, the tow truck driver was the only survivor that had gone to the mansion that day.

The heavy evergreen tree cover on the south side of the mountain shielded him and the cat from any of the fallout that the wind had not blown in the other direction. The snow was still coming down but was letting up. Close to the base of the mountain, he was able to jettison the snowshoes and head for the old barn, where he had an ordinary looking blue 1995 Ford F150 pickup truck waiting. Four days earlier upon his return from Kentucky, he verified that it had plenty of fuel and a good battery charge.

He dialed in the combination to the padlock and opened the door. He put the cat in the truck, took off his jacket, and tossed it aside. Another lighter jacket was in the cab of the truck. He donned the jacket and lifted the garage door, got in the truck, and headed south. He pulled to the side of the road as emergency vehicles came toward him, heading the other way. "They're going to need a lot more trucks," he said to the cat. A tilt of the head is all the response he got in return.

Response to the mess on top of the mountain was slow. The FBI replacement team was not there until the next day when the temperature went above freezing. The melting snow caused the road to the top to be impassible except for the largest of four-wheel drives. State and federal agents were soon swarming the area, looking for clues. A helicopter was brought in to aid in the search. The exit from the tunnel was not found until the third day after the explosion, and the melting snow and wet conditions hid the fact that it had been used at all. When the snow-shoes on the south side of the mountain and the discarded coat in the barn were found, suspicions were raised; however, it would be two more days before they started a fruitless search for the suspect.

Dee watched the news on CNN, about the explosion and loss of two state police and two FBI agents. She wondered why they did not start searching for him immediately. She went to bed on the night of the third day and dreamt:

She was out jogging on a morning heavy with green fog. She felt like a dull knife moving sideways through lime gelatin. It parted as she approached and closed behind her. She must have been jogging forever and was getting tired. Behind her, she heard the tapping feet of someone following her. She turned her head to see who it was, but the fog was too dense and the view was shimmering. She looked forward again but could not tell where she was. The steps were getting louder. Whoever or whatever the thing was, it was getting closer with every step she took. The faster she tried to go, the more drag the green, dense, gelatinous fog put on her so that she could just barely maintain a pace above walking speed. The taps were getting louder now, but they were softer than her own and had a distinctive tappidy-tap, tappidy-tap sound, as if the jogger was four-legged instead of two. She tried to stop but could not. She tried to move to her right and then left, but could not. She tried to speed up, but could not.

Tappidy tap, tappidy tap, tappidy tap came the steps. The hairs on the back of her neck stood up as she felt hot breath. Surely she would be caught and carried off by some beast. As she closed her dream's eye to keep from seeing her own tortured death, the heat on the back of her neck was gone. The tapping came from her left side. She opened her eyes and looked to her left. She let out a scream, a scream that was silenced in a cloud of condensed vapor, captured in a green super bubble in the saturated atmosphere that surrounded her. She was being paced by a large cat the size of a man, but with a man's head, a feline centaur. It had his face, and he was smiling, almost laughing, as he passed her, looked back, and then disappeared in the gelatin. The bubble of a scream, which had been floating beside her, burst and let out the captive shrillness of her own voice waking her. She sat upright in bed and started to hyperventilate. Only after she lay back down on the sweat-drenched sheet did her breathing return to normal.

Nineteen

He had not shaved for three days when he and the cat arrived in Mobile. He had passed through Pensacola earlier that morning, thinking of Dee and what her reaction would be if he just showed up at her doorstep. It would have been fun to see her reaction and the fear in her eyes, but he did not want to leave a trail. She was having a dream at that time. A dream she thought would last the rest of her life. He had slept peacefully in the truck one time during the trip from Vermont. He took his time getting to the gulf area, since he did not want to attract the attention of any ticket-happy state troopers.

In the morning newspaper, he found what he wanted. He called the number and made an appointment for ten that morning. He bought a hat with a full brim that hung down all around his head partially hiding his beard-stubbled face and hair. To hide his eyes, he wore a dark pair of sunglasses. His face had not yet been broadcast, but just the same, he was disguising himself as much as possible.

The boat captain greeted him at the entrance to the dock. The captain was a salt from the old school with a weather-beaten face and hard, callused hands. He had a squint to his eyes from many days staring at the horizon. The rays of the sun bouncing off the sea etched deep lines on the sides of his face radiating out from the corners of the slit of his eyes beneath heavy brows. He wore a T-shirt adorned with a well-faded picture of Jimmy Buffet and loosely laced deck shoes. The shoes were connected to a pair of many-pocketed khaki shorts by dark thick hairy legs that looked more like the tops of wooden piles.

As they walked down the pier and onto the boat, he emitted an air that told you "this was his boat, godamn it, and if you didn't like it, you could take a flying fuck at a rolling doughnut." They stepped onto the foredeck of the boat, an old fifty-foot-single-masted yacht in well-kept condition. He turned around as they stepped down to the main deck.

"The name's John Potter, but most just call me Cap'n Johnny," he said from between teeth clenching a well-chewed stogie. "Me and the boats for rent for a day, week, month, or several years if you need it. I require cash up front for a week or less. Over that, is negotiable. On the phone, you indicated an extended period. Can you be a little more specific and where do you want to go?"

"I want to sail the Caribbean, maybe even through the Panama Canal, the coast of South America, North America, and maybe up to Alaska. I have come into some money recently and have always wanted to sail the seas on a small ship. I know little about sailing but am a quick learner. You appear to be the man I'm looking for, and if I like the ship, then we will be gone for at least a year."

"We can handle that," Captain Johnny said, meaning he and the boat. "It's a boat, not a ship. She's called the *Fisher Cat*. Do you know what that is?"

"It's a cousin to the weasel that has a cat-like body and a face like a bear," he said. "It lives off fresh water fish and is known for being able to kill a porcupine by repeated swift attacks to the face and head. After killing the porcupine, the fisher flips it over on its back and starts eating the belly."

"Sorry I asked, but, at least, I ain't gotta explain it," Captain Johnny said. "Let me show you around."

The schooner was as self-contained as any home. There were three bedrooms and two heads. It had all the latest in sonar, radar, GPS, and radio equipment. There was a TV with a VCR and a well-stocked video library. "You can't get CNN out at sea," Captain Johnny explained, "The satellite dish ain't stable enough, but if you want to get the news and especially the weather, we got radio. We can get satellite TV when we dock, if you need it."

"I want to get away from everything for a change," he told him. "You know, escape from it all."

"Ain't nothin' like it," Captain Johnny agreed.

The kitchen had all the appliances you could ask for in a modern home. There were storage spaces everywhere, although they would pull into ports often enough to get fresh supplies. The longest they would normally put to sea, Captain Johnny explained, would be about two weeks.

"I'm sold," he told Captain Johnny. "However, do you allow pets on board? I have a cat, and she goes with me everywhere."

"As long as she don't poop on the poop deck," said Captain Johnny, at an attempt at a joke. "Cats do well at sea. For a year, it will set you back $170,000 plus expenses. That's $50,000 up front and $10,000 a month when we pull into a port where I can wire the money to my bank. If we go more than a year, we renegotiate, my terms of course. I got a contract, if you want paperwork, otherwise we shake. We can leave as early as tomorrow, as long as the money is in my bank." Captain Johnny was a business man first and a sailor second.

"I gotta tell you up front that this is an old boat, and she's special," said Captain Johnny. "She acts a bit strange at sea. You have to experience it first hand to know what I'm talkin' 'bout."

"As long as we stay in one piece and make it back to shore safely," he said.

"Oh, we will that," Captain Johnny replied.

"Then it's a deal," he said and extended his hand.

Captain Johnny shook his hand, sealing the deal. On the way back from the bank, they stopped to donate the truck to the Red Cross, who gladly gave them a ride back to the boat.

Captain Johnny made some phone calls. The supplies he did not have already on board were delivered that afternoon, paid for with cash. He, Dedra, and Captain Johnny spent the night on board, and at 6:30, after buying a paper from the dispenser at the head of the dock, they left on the morning tide. There was no mention of him in the paper. Leaving the coast of Alabama behind, they headed south then southeast toward the rising sun. Jimmy Buffet was playing "Son of a Son of a Sailor" over the speakers on either side of the helm. They wouldn't set foot on American soil for another six months.

The morning after they left, his face was all over the morning news, but there is no CNN out at sea.

PART II

Twenty

When Deanna watched CNN the day after the explosion that destroyed the mansion in South Royalton, she couldn't believe it. The pictures from the news helicopter showed a leveled site. There was debris scattered everywhere, and the ruins were smoldering. The FBI had the area cordoned off restricting access to the site. She immediately called Lulu, who was still recovering from her injuries at the Dartmouth Hitchcock Hospital near Lebanon, New Hampshire.

"Hello," said Lulu.

"Hi, Lulu, this is Dee. How are you doing?"

"I'm healing," said Lulu. "The doctor's said I can go home in a week if I continue to recover like I been doin'. Only I don't have a home anymore except for Elsie's place."

"If you are well enough, you are welcome to stay with me. I could come and get you."

"I might consider that," said Lulu. "This place has too many bad memories now. It has some good ones too, but they are fading. We'll see how I feel after I get released."

"The warm sunshine here might help you forget and I have plenty of room. Have you seen the news?"

"About what?" Lulu asked, puzzled.

"It's on CNN. The mansion exploded yesterday, killing Agent Ford, another FBI agent and two state police."

"You're kidding," Lulu said.

"No, I'm serious. The place was flattened. There is nothing left but a pile of smoldering debris. I don't know if our friend was in it or not. The Hummer was in the pile at the top. The fifth wheel and truck in the barn at the bottom of the hill blew up too. If he wasn't there, he must have walked out or had another car."

"I just turned on the TV," said Lulu. "I see what you're talking about now. My God, what a mess. It looks like what happened at our place." Lulu started to tear up and sniffled into the phone remembering what happened to her family. "I'm sorry, it will take me a long time to get over what happened. I still don't think it was an accident."

"I don't either," said Dee. "I think he was trying to destroy evidence. There must have been something about that meat you found in his freezer."

"What would be so important about a few poached deer that he would have to destroy his house and ours, too?" asked Lulu.

"I don't think he was trying to cover up illegal deer meat," Dee responded.

"What would be so bad to have to kill Wayne, me, and the kids?" Lulu sobbed.

"I can see I am upsetting you, Lulu. I'm sorry for this, but I have to tell you. The FBI, and I too, believe he had something to do with the disappearance of young women. Some of the bones Agent Ford found in the dog pen were human. You said you gave the dog the bones from the jerky you made with meat you got from his freezer. I can tell you that we were watching you on camera the day you went to fix the cat feeder. God, I hate to think he had human remains in his freezer."

"Maybe that's why he wanted to blow up our house, but why kill us?" Lulu was still sobbing.

"I don't know. Maybe he looked through your house and couldn't find the meat you took and got mad. You and Wayne were the only ones who could definitely say the meat came from his freezer. I don't know what to think or who to trust anymore. Look, I have to run, Lulu. Call me, or have Elsie call me as soon as you are released."

"I sure will, Dee," Lulu said. "I love you, girl."

"I love you too, Aunt Lu," said Dee. "Bye."

"Bye," sobbed Lulu.

As soon as Dee was done talking to Lulu, she dialed the FBI number that Agent Ford used to answer.

"FBI, Agent Brinks speaking," said a female voice.

"Hi, this is Deanna Mayfield. I talked to Agent Ford several times in the past and—"

"I need to tell you I am recording this conversation, ma'am," said Agent Brinks.

"That's okay," said Dee. "I am so sorry about what happened to Agent Ford in Vermont yesterday."

"Thank you. I didn't know Agent Ford personally, but I have been assigned to the accident along with two other agents. We were just going over the events of the last several weeks. We have your name on a list of contacts. We intended to call everyone on the list as part of our investigation. Would you mind if I called you later this afternoon to ask some questions?"

"That will be fine, but I don't think the explosion was an accident," said Dee.

"We are still investigating and can't comment about that," said Agent Brinks. "As I said, we will get back to you this afternoon. Thank you for calling. Is your number 555-9804?"

"Yes, it is," said Dee. "I will be waiting for your call. Good-bye,"

"Good-bye, Ms. Mayfield."

On setting the phone down, she remembered that he promised to set up an account for her to use in her search for Dedra and for the MOMY-G group. She went to Dedra's room and grabbed the folder labeled "Finances," opened it, and searched for the information he had e-mailed to her. There it was, an account number, access code, and password for a local bank. She went back to the living room and looked up the number of the bank. It was after banking hours, but they had a 24-hour number for over-the-phone service. She dialed the number. Following the instructions, she entered the account number and then the access code. "Your balance is fifty thousand dollars," droned the computerized woman's voice.

"I can't believe it," she said out loud. Fifty thousand dollars was hers. She was not sure what to do about the money now. He also said he would keep the account full. It would be interesting to see if that happened.

"Hello," Dee said, on picking up the phone.

"Hello. This is Agent Brinks from the FBI. May I speak to Deanna Mayfield please?"

"This is Dee, Agent Brinks. Thanks for calling back."

"Ma'am, would you be able to get a sample of hair or anything else that may contain DNA. We have some unidentified body parts at the explosion site and need to compare samples with the remains. Some may be his."

"I doubt it. He always used his own hairbrush, and I have cleaned the house, towels, and other items he touched while he was here. I will look to see if there is anything he used that would still have some DNA."

"I will have a local agent come out tomorrow and help you search, if you don't mind. We have people trained to look for DNA in the most unlikely places. Just don't clean or move anything else until they get there."

"Okay," Dee responded, feeling guilty about not having cleaned the house in three weeks. "What time will they be here?"

"About nine A.M. Is that too early?"

"Nine o'clock is fine," Dee said.

"Okay. If you can think of anything else that may help us identify him, let me know. You have the number. Good afternoon, Ms. Mayfield."

"Good-bye Agent Brinks," Dee said and hung up the phone. She thought about telling Brinks about the bank money, but decided not to. They may confiscate the account, and she needed the cash, having spent a good deal of her own money on the MOMY-G venture. If his body parts were not found, she might hunt him down, using his own money.

The FBI agent came the next morning and searched Dee's home. They took samples under the lip of the toilet, found some hair under the bed, took prints from her computer, pulled hair from the shower P-trap, and emptied the contents of the P-trap under the sink in the bathroom into a plastic bag. Agent Brinks was right, they knew places to look she would have never thought about. They also took samples of Dee's DNA to eliminate her from the other samples.

Two days later, Agent Brinks called Dee back to tell her they found an escape tunnel and evidence that he may have left the area from a barn on the other side of the mountain.

"Do you know if he had another vehicle other than the Humvee and the Dodge truck?" asked Agent Brinks.

"Not to my knowledge," responded Dee.

"We found several dead cats and some live ones in the woods near the explosion. They had tags on them correlating to the states, names, and years of most all of the missing women's names in Agent Drake's files."

"I was aware of the cats," she said. "He told me they were from states he visited with his fifth wheel. Look in the fifth wheel. There should be a map of the States with the same states filled in. What happened to the cats that lived?"

"Some had to be put to sleep. I think only five or six could be saved. They were taken to an animal shelter nearby. The trailer was blown apart in another blast. We found a twisted magnetic map, but all of the metal states were blown off it."

"Am I in any danger?" Dee asked.

"We already thought he might try to contact you. There are agents watching your house twenty-four/seven just in case he shows up. With your permission, we would like to tap your telephone line in case he calls." She neglected to tell Dee that the FBI obtained a court order two days ago and were already monitoring her phone. They had recorded the call to the bank.

"You have my permission to tap my phone," Dee said as she walked to the front room. "How long will the agents be there?" She pulled aside the curtain, but did not see any cars with agents inside.

"Until we find him or are certain you are not in any danger," Agent Brinks said, "you might want to consider getting a cell phone for when you go out."

"I might do just that," she said.

"That is all the information I wanted to pass on to you," said the agent. "I will call you if anything breaks in the case."

"Please do," said Dee. "And thanks for giving me the heads up on his possibly being on the loose. Talk to you later."

"You're welcome. Good-bye."

"Bye," she said, and hit the end button on the phone.

Later that day, she wrote a $30,000 check for cash on the account he provided and put it in her personal account. She rationalized that the money was reimbursement for all the expenses she incurred in the past several months. She then purchased a cell phone. "Business expense," she said to herself. She wanted a cell phone for a long time, but put off committing to

209

one because of the cost. Now with his money, she could afford it.

She called her boss and asked for an extended leave of absence from her job. He granted it reluctantly, but Dee was an excellent worker, and she did give him a plug on national TV. He told her to keep in touch in case he had any questions that only she could answer. She said she would and gave him her new cell phone number.

Twenty-one

The *Writer Aboard* as the *Fisher Cat* was first named, was built in 1966 for a wealthy semiretired couple. It was to be their retirement home until one or both of them could not sail anymore. *Writer Aboard* was a beautiful boat, of the Catalina line. She was fifty feet five inches in length overall, with a tall rig. Her mast height over water was seventy-four feet ten inches. Her nearly fifteen-foot beam could sleep ten adults if necessary. Two people had all the room they needed. For David and Adrienne, it was luxury at sea. *Writer Aboard* could cruise at nearly nine knots forever on her sails. The seventy-five horsepower diesel used a little over one gallon of fuel per hour. With her two fuel tanks full with eighty-eight gallons of marine diesel, she could travel on her own power for nearly eight hundred miles. *Writer Aboard* had a single mast with a mainsail and jib. She also had a spinnaker for the experienced sailor. She had an LPG stove and oven, but most of the food consumed was canned. There was a small ice box on board that could keep perishable items fresh for a limited time. She held four hundred gallons of water and an eleven-gallon water heater. Two fifteen-gallon holding tanks for sewage were dumped at sea and used mostly in port. After several lessons from some experienced friends, David and Adrienne took off on their own.

They just wanted to sail and have fun, meet new friends, and take old ones with them on trips to ports in the Caribbean, South America, the East Coast, the Panama Canal, the West Coast, and even Alaska. Their dream trips were interrupted halfway through when they were boarded by unfriendly parties and disappeared.

David was a writer. He made a few million dollars before they decided to take a long break from his publisher. They had the boat customized for their lifestyle.

He met Adrienne at the Mardi Gras in 1949 while on spring break from the University of Texas, where he was using his World War II GI Bill. Adrienne was a bastard child of mixed race. Her father was white and a son of an old Southern slave-owner family from the Deep South. He raped Adrienne's mother, a professed Voodoo lady from Jamaica, one night in a back alley of the French Quarter beating her senseless. She took a year to recover, during which time she gave birth to Adrienne and cast a deadly spell on her assailant. Her rapist was never prosecuted for his crime, but soon after the spell was cast, he died from a broken neck when he was thrown from a horse. Adrienne was brought up believing in the power of Voodoo, convinced by her mother that she, Adrienne, had the same special powers. "Use your powers only for good. Save the bad juju for serious business. Your powers will multiply when used sparingly," she said.

Adrienne's skin was a beautiful coffee with heavy cream color. She inherited some recessed gene from her father, having long, wavy, red hair. Her black facial features were from her mother. Her nose was broad, but not overpoweringly so. Her lips were slightly full. She was often mistaken for white most everywhere she went. When she met David, they fell in love at first sight. She then worked her magic to keep him spellbound the rest of his life.

He was aware of Adrienne's special powers and respected her for it. Adrienne's rituals blessed all his books before they went to the publisher. David was a good writer, but it was no coincidence that they became best sellers.

The next six years on the yacht were sheer bliss. Having no children, they were free to come and go whenever they felt like it, traveling throughout the Caribbean, the Gulf, and up and down the East Coast. They were planning the next trip that would take them through the Panama Canal and then up the Pacific Coast to Alaska. They were a day out of Kingston, heading toward the Yucatan Channel on their way to New Orleans, where they planned on visiting Adrienne's mother, take on supplies, and pick up some friends who were to accompany them on the six-month cruise. Pirates were known to be in the area, and usually, David and Adrienne traveled in a group of other boats for safety and for companionship. This time they were alone.

Everything was going their way in a sea with three-foot swells. They were flying the American flag, indicating to all that the *Writer Aboard* was a documented boat of U.S. origin. They thought that would keep them safe if pirates were about, but also knew it was useless to try to outrun or outgun pirates. The pirates had fast boats and were much better armed. That was why they did not alter course when they saw the speedboat approaching from the south. David looked through the binoculars for signs of danger, but the bad guys with the guns stayed away from sight. Adrienne was manning the ship-to-shore radio and was able to get out a mayday signal with their location as soon as the gunman appeared. The speedboat pulled up alongside, and David offered no resistance. These were drug cartel members, and they wanted the boat to run drugs from Colombia to the United States. As soon as they were on board the yacht, they shot David in the head, killing him instantly and threw his body overboard. Adrienne screamed, and they tracked her down in the forward bedroom.

They did not kill her outright. The pirates wanted to have some fun, which was a mistake. Adrienne started casting the spell as soon as they all had their way with her. They held her down while each pirate went at her, but she lay there without resistance and without emotion. While they rested, waiting to take another turn, she started the incantations casting the bad juju on them and on the boat. They thought she was just hallucinating, but she was speaking in the Cajun tongue taught to her by her mother.

"This boat will be where these pirates meet their fate,
Fifteen miles from shore back to an early date.
This boat will always be doomed to sail that way
The speed she goes will determine how far she may
Pass through time and on her return to shore again
She will re-enter the present from which she came."

As the pirates mocked, her she suddenly stood, ran out of the cabin, up the ladder, past the pirate standing guard, and jumped into the sea. The last they saw of her was her red hair floating beneath the surface as she sank down to join David.

The pirates waited in the area another fifteen minutes, making sure she did not surface before they headed back to Colombia on the *Writer Aboard* now flying the gold, blue, and red striped flag of Colombia.

On their first and only trip aboard the newly named *El Tiempo del Fuego*, the pirates left Turbo, Colombia, late at night, hauling five hundred pounds of marijuana and five hundred kilos of uncut cocaine. The pirates did not see the shimmer as they passed through at nearly nine knots. Two of them were experienced sailors and were using the stars to guide them purposely avoiding any land. They also kept a close watch for other ships, but they did not have to worry about that. The yacht had traveled back in time to 1561, and there were very few other boats in the Caribbean. They could not believe how lucky they were, having not seen another boat as they approached within thirty miles of the U.S. coast. They lowered the sails and were going to finish the trip on the diesel engine.

As the leader, Miguel Campo, searched the horizon while the others ate breakfast, he noticed a large object in front of them. He called to the others, and immediately, the pirates were up on deck with their guns out. His brother Eduardo picked up the binoculars and trained them toward where Miguel was pointing. Eduardo's mouth dropped when he finished focusing.

"It's a ship, an old ship. It looks like an old galleon," shouted out Eduardo.

"Take the helm," commanded Miguel. "Let me see what the hell you're talking about." Miguel's reaction was no different from his brother's. "Shit, whatever that is, it's headed right toward us and coming fast. Get the antitank weapon and rifles." The other two pirates went below to retrieve the weapons.

The Spanish seaman in the crow's nest of the *Nuestra Señora de la Mercedes* could see much farther over the horizon than the pirates, who were only ten feet off the water. Upon sighting the yacht, long before the yacht could see them, the seaman was as confused as Miguel and his brother. His captain, confirming through his spyglass what the lookout told him, wanted to get a closer look at the strange little boat flying the unknown flag.

Back on board the yacht, Eduardo spoke to his brother.

"Maybe it's one of those ships the Americans sail for special occasions. You know like the Fourth of July."

"This is the middle of April," stated Miguel.

The other two pirates arrived topside with the antitank rocket launcher and two AK-47s. They set the automatic rifles on the deck of the cockpit and set up the rocket launcher on the foredeck. Miguel cut the engines.

The galleon was closing the gap fast having all her sails raised. Within a half-mile of the yacht, the sails on the galleon were lowered. Within a tenth of a mile, the yacht and the galleon were adrift in the same current. The galleon swung her bow to the east so that her starboard side was parallel to the yacht. The pirates on board *El Tiempo* were looking at five cannons loaded with twelve-pound balls. The two vessels drifted to within two hundred feet of each other. In addition to the cannons, the deck of the galleon was lined with at least fifty armed soldiers who were being transferred back to Spain after explorations in the New World. They all had loaded muskets ready to aim at the men on the yacht if directed to do so. Miguel and his brother stood in the cockpit with their pistols at their sides. The other two were on the foredeck holding the rocket launcher aimed at the galleon.

A man on the galleon hailed the men on the yacht.

"We are going to board you," he said, in Castillian Spanish. Miguel and his men looked at each other and almost laughed at the pronunciation. They had never heard Spanish spoken that way.

"What the hell was that?" Eduardo asked. "I ain't heard no one talk that way before. Are we going to tell them to fuck off?"

"We'll answer them with our rifles if they get too close," said Miguel, not taking his eyes off the galleon. A small rowboat appeared around the bow of the galleon with five men aboard. Two were rowing, a third was manning the tiller, and the other two were standing holding flintlock pistols. When they were within fifty feet of the yacht, Miguel gave the order to fire the rocket. A flame shot out of the back of the launcher. A snakelike trail of smoke briefly connected the yacht to the galleon, where the rocket tore through its hull amidships and about halfway up from the waterline. The Spaniards all ducked for cover. Even in the rowboat, the standing men joined the other three, ducking below the gunnels.

What happened next confounded the pirates on the yacht. Nothing happened to the galleon. No explosion ripped open the hull. No firestorm raged inside the ship from the warhead of the rocket. There was just a deafening silence. Miguel was the first to react by picking up the AK-47 and squeezing off a short burst at the men in the boat. The 7.62-mm shells ripped the rowboat apart. The men in the rowboat screamed in agony as they too were hit. Two of them, dead on impact, the other three, mortally wounded. "That's more like it," said Miguel. Eduardo was aiming his rifle at the deck of the galleon. He misjudged the distance, and the shells hit the galleon three feet from the rail. Two of the cannons on the galleon belched forth a plume of fire and smoke chasing the cannon balls toward the yacht.

The galleon was too close to aim that low and the twelve-pound balls sailed over the yacht ten feet above the deck. As the pirates on the yacht ducked, the men on the galleon opened fire. The two pirates dropped the antitank launcher overboard as they were hit with a volley of musket balls. Bleeding, they made it back to the cockpit. Miguel and Eduardo fared no better. Miguel was hit in the shoulder, causing him to toss his rifle backward and into the water. Eduardo was hit in the forehead and was dead before he hit the deck. Miguel turned toward Eduardo's dropped rifle and was hit again in the chest. He fell limply to the deck, not dead, but mortally wounded. The other two bleeding pirates stood up with their hands in the air.

The captain on the galleon shouted something to them, but they did not understand. They sat down defeated and awaited their fate. Another boat was launched from the starboard side of the galleon, and it made it to the yacht. The soldiers tied up the pirates and loaded them with the weapons they found in the rowboat. Eduardo's body was tossed overboard to feed the fish. A line was tossed from the galleon to the yacht and was made fast around a cleat on the bow. The captain decided to tow the yacht close to the shore, where he would effect repairs to his ship while his men boarded and searched the yacht. For now, he was satisfied to leave it unmanned towed behind the galleon.

The other pirates were taken on board the galleon. Miguel was laid on the main deck and left to bleed to death. The other two spoke a strange form of Spanish, so they were left to sit on the main deck, tied up next to the bleeding Miguel. The captain planned on making another attempt to interrogate them when the galleon was anchored near the shore. They would then be shot. All available hands were sent below to patch the holes caused by the strange looking cannon ball lodged in the bulkhead of the ship's magazine.

The sails were raised on the galleon, and she headed toward the coast of America. Fifteen miles from the coast, the seaman, watching the yacht trailing the galleon, yawned, closing his eyes. When he reopened them, the yacht had disappeared having been catapulted forward to the present time. The seaman looked around startled and shouted, "The boat is missing. The boat is missing."

Three other sailors came up and verified that. Trailing the galleon was nothing but the line that used to be attached to the yacht. They ran to port and starboard, looking for the yacht. They yelled to the seaman in the crow's nest to use his spyglass to see if he could find the strange little boat. After scanning the horizon, he yelled back down that it was nowhere in sight. By that time, the captain was topside, asking questions that no one could answer.

As the captain scratched his head in disbelief, the gunners mate was hitting the strange cannon ball with a mallet, trying to dislodge it from the bulkhead. When the warhead went off, it set off a chain reaction, igniting the stacked barrels of gunpowder. The explosions peeled the galleon like a banana. In less than two minutes, the pieces sank, taking all those on board to the bottom of the Gulf of Mexico.

The next day, when the Coast Guard found *El Tiempo Del Fuego* drifting toward the coast three miles offshore, she was boarded. They found the marijuana and cocaine and immediately impounded the yacht. The report from their investigation stated that she was probably used in illegal drug trafficking. Those on board must have had a gunfight with persons unknown, and from the amount of blood, probably were dead or met an undetermined fate. The report also revealed that she was actually the documented boat, *Writer Aboard*. They even found the outline of the original name under a fresh coat of paint. The report mentioned the musket balls found lodged in the hull, but made no conclusion on how they got there.

The Coast Guard could not find any heirs to the lawful owners, and because she was found with illegal drugs aboard, she was held for twelve years and then finally put up for auction in 1984. Captain Johnny bought her, spent the next four years patching her up and making her seaworthy. Because he liked to have ice with his rum and cokes, he replaced the icebox with a twelve-volt battery-operated refrigerator he got from an RV dealer. He took out one of the crew cabins and added an additional 80-gallon fuel tank, increasing her cruising range on the diesel engine to 1,500 miles. He connected power winches to the sails so he could raise and lower them by himself from the pedestal.

He did not care whether he made a buck or two from his charter service. His retirement from the navy and his savings was sufficient to keep him afloat for the rest of his life. He would like to be rich, but lacked the ambition to work hard. His philosophy was that he wanted to go out of this life the same way he came into it, "Poor, ignorant, and naked, and two outta three ain't bad," he would say to anyone who would listen.

The gulf was calm on his and Captain Johnny's first day at sea after leaving Mobile aboard the *Fisher Cat, AKA Writer on Board, AKA El Tiempo Del Fuego*. The sun was about ten degrees above the horizon and shined brightly. The water was like glass, and the sky cloudless. Captain Johnny was tending to the helm. Because of the calm winds, they were still on the seventy-five horsepower diesel engines.

"I do want to learn to handle this boat, Cap'n," he said climbing up from below decks with two cups of coffee from the galley. He was barefoot, wearing jeans he had cut off above the knee that morning with a knife he found in the galley. A gray Dallas Cowboy's T-shirt from when they won Superbowl XXVIII completed his sea ensemble. His beard was starting to fill in, offering a disguise in case his picture made it to foreign ports. He handed one of the cups to Captain Johnny, who was wearing the same thing he had worn yesterday. He backed away and sat down on a bench seat in the cockpit.

"Where's that cat of mine?"

"Dedra's up on the bow deck, trying to get her sea legs," Captain Johnny responded, taking the cup of coffee.

He looked forward and saw Dedra cautiously exploring the boat staying as far from the edge as she could. She would be a good sea cat as soon as she got her bearings.

"You said that this boat acted funny at sea," he asked. "What did you mean?"

"I said strange, not funny," Captain Johnny responded. "You'll see what I mean as soon as we get out about fifteen miles or so. It happens pretty quick so don't take a nap."

"Don't worry about me, I don't sleep all that much. In fact, I wouldn't mind driving this thing at night if you show me how."

"You *steer* her. You don't drive this thing," Captain Johnny corrected. "We'll most likely anchor at night unless I teach you how to drive her."

"I'd love to sail her at night and let you take her during the day. Are we out fifteen miles yet?" he asked.

"Not quite," said Captain Johnny. "According to the GPS, we're right about here." He pointed to a location on the chart not far from where they left Mobile.

Dedra completed her inspection of the bow area of the ship by jumping down into the cockpit. She walked over to him and jumped up in his lap, meowing. She did what most cats do before getting really comfortable. She started pumping with her paws into his lap. He called it making biscuits because it was a kneading action. Probably a throwback to their kitten days when they pumped their mothers breasts for milk. After several pumps, she lay down while he petted her. She started to purr quite loudly.

"See that up ahead," Captain Johnny said pointing slightly off the starboard bow. "That's where we pass through."

"Pass through what?" he said. He cupped his right hand to his forehead, like he was giving a bad salute, squinted his eyes, and looked ahead and to the right.

"You'll see," said Captain Johnny. "You'll see."

"I see a line of heat waves above the water," he said. "It's shimmering from horizon to horizon from the water up as high as I can see."

"That's it," said Captain Johnny. "We'll be heading right through it. Not too fast this time, so the effect won't be as bad."

"You said yesterday that there was no danger," he said. "I guess I'll just have to trust you. But what's causing that. I've seen areas like that in the desert, caused by heat waves that are called mirages, but they go away when you get near them. This seems to be getting closer. In fact we're about to get into it."

There was no response from Captain Johnny, but Dedra reacted. Suddenly she stood up and jumped to the floor looking around as if in a nightmare. They were now within twenty feet of the mirage and heading right into it. Dedra arched her back. She started to hiss as all the hairs on her back stood up. She looked like a Halloween fright cat. This in turn made all the hairs on the back of his neck stand out, and he got goose bumps. Captain Johnny was relaxed and smiling at both of them as the bow of the *Fisher Cat* entered the mirage. It was like looking through a mirror at the carnival as the boat passed into the ripple of air distorting her from bow to stern. In a second, they were through the shimmer. He looked back to see if he could see where they went through, but there was nothing out of the ordinary, and the shimmer was gone. Dedra looked around and then relaxed as if nothing had happened. She pranced over to the hatch and then down the ladder, going below decks, no doubt looking for something to eat.

"What the hell was that?" he said, looking at Captain Johnny.

"You'll find out in time," was the only hint Captain Johnny gave him.

"Want some more coffee?" he asked.

"Sure," said the captain.

He went down to the galley and found Dedra lapping up water at her bowl. "Sorry I don't have any organ meat to give you, Dee," he said, realizing, seconds after he said it, that he shortened her name . "I think I'll call you Dee from now on."

After pouring a cup of coffee for himself and Captain Johnny, he reached over and turned on the radio, hoping to get some news. He doubted if any coastal stations would mention a house explosion in Vermont. He was willing to take that chance. One of the radio stations came on, playing oldies music which was piped above decks to speakers in the cockpit. He went back topside carrying both cups held by the handles in one hand. Captain Johnny was singing along to "Alabama Rain" as he handed him his cup with the words "my fuckin' cup" printed in blood-red, bold letters. He reminded himself that Captain Johnny's cup was Captain Johnny's, and to get caught using it, could be a fatal mistake. The cup hadn't been washed since the first time it held coffee, attested to by the dark brown stain on the inside. The outside of what used to be a cream-colored cup also had coffee stains, where dribbles from Captain Johnny's mouth ran down the sides. The half-moon stain on the outside to the left of the handle indicated that Captain Johnny always held the cup in his right hand and put it to his lips in the same place every time.

He sat down in the same seat, sipping his coffee and enjoying the oldies.

"Well, that wasn't so bad," he said referring to the mirage. "Are there many of them at sea?"

"They come and they go," Captain Johnny said, with a chuckle.

The song was over, and the announcer came on telling them about the song they just heard. "That was 'Alabama Rain' by request in memory of Jim Croce from his fourth album 'Life and Times.'"

"I remember when he died, in September 1973," he said to Captain Johnny. "I remember it well."

"We'll play another dedication to Jim after this commercial," said the announcer. The commercial came on, touting a local grocery store running a special on coffee at $1.50 a pound. He half-listened, staring out at the horizon.

"Turn around," he said to Captain Johnny. "That's the cheapest coffee I've heard advertised in thirty years. We ought to stock up and sell it up and down the coast. We'd make a killing. Must be some promotional gimmick."

"Could be," said Captain Johnny. "Could be."

The announcer came back on, giving the weather, which was the same as they were experiencing miles off the coast. "Our next song is 'It Doesn't Have to Be that Way' from the same album. It also is in remembrance of Jim Croce who died last night in a plane wreck in Natchitoches, Louisiana, along with five others."

He looked at Captain Johnny, who was grinning about as wide as one could.

"What the fuck was that?" he said. "Did he say last night? That happened almost thirty years ago."

"No, if he said it happened last night, it probably happened last night," Captain Johnny said. "I told you strange things happen on this boat."

"Okay, explain it please," he politely demanded. "This is something that only happens in 'Star Trek.'"

"Oh, it's real all right, and this ain't 'Star Trek,'" said Captain Johnny. It happens every time I get out this far. It happened the first time I took her out. I was alone and didn't understand what was going on. I went through pretty fast, and must have ended up a long time ago. Nuthin' worked. No radio, no GPS, no TV. I tried the ship-to-shore transmitter and got nuthin' but static. I marked the spot on the map, thinkin' I hit some sorta Bermuda triangle or somthin'" (Captain Johnny pronounced it Bamuda).

"Obviously, you got back to the present time, or are you some future person that doesn't exist yet?" he said, with skepticism.

"Oh, I exist all right," said Captain Johnny. "I exist. You exist. That cat exists. We just ain't in the present no more."

"Tell me more," he implored.

"Well," Captain Johnny continued. "I didn't know what happened. I didn't believe that all the electronics had gone out at once. I thought maybe there was a power surge from the generator that musta done it. So I checked with my battery-operated emergency radio, and all I got was static. I turned her around and headed back toward shore. No use tryin' to hit the exact same spot, 'cause there weren't no way to find it. It was overcast and nothin' to take a fix off of. All I had was my charts, so I used the compass, my speed, and watch. But ya know, out here there are currents and speed is hard to tell. I guess I was about a mile beyond the shimmer, lookin' hard to find it. Then, all of a sudden, I passed through. I didn't see the shimmer like before, but everything started workin'. By the GPS, I was way off where I went through headin' out. I was a Navy SEAL in 'Nam, but I was a little shaken by what happened. I went back, docked her, and got real drunk the rest of the afternoon and stayed that way until the next mornin'."

All he could say was, "You were a SEAL?"

"Oh, yeah, retired," Captain Johnny said and went on with his story. "So I put out to sea again as soon as I got rid of my hangover. I headed for a different spot toward the southwest this time. About the same distance out, I saw the shimmer again. I slowed way down and went through very cautiously at just about a tenth of a knot. When I got through, everything still worked, so I did what you did. I turned on the radio. I was gettin' year-old news. I checked the GPS and was only a few feet away from where I passed through. I turned around and headed back. A few seconds later, the radio got full of static, and then the news was just like it was before I passed through."

"Did you go through the same spot?" he asked.

"Almost, but not exactly. So, I headed back toward shore aways. I turned around again when I could see the shimmer and took a run at it, doin' three knots. When I passed through, every-thing still worked like before. When the static cleared on the radio, they were announcing news that was ten years old. I turned around, went back to the present, and headed out through the shimmer again, this time at six knots. This time nothin' worked. I got scared, so I went back through, and it was as if nothin' had happened."

"What were you afraid of?" he asked.

"I thought if I went back too far in time and went too far from the shimmer, I couldn't get back to the present. I went back to the dock and didn't sleep all night. Then I decided that the next time, I would go through real slow and see how far back I went. If I lost only a month or two and couldn't get back, I could live those few months all over again without being too much older."

"What do you mean too much older?"

"I noticed that every time I went back in time, I didn't get any younger. If I couldn't get back to the present, and I had gone back forty or fifty years, I could be dead by now. After I made sure

223

I only went back a few months, I'd head east a few miles and then back toward shore."

"When did you try this out."

"I waited till a very calm day," Captain Johnny continued. "Three days later, it was like it is today. I headed out, and when the shimmer appeared, I just drifted through, barely makin' headway. The radio was on, and the static thing happened again. From the news, I determined I only went back four months. I headed east, staying more or less twenty miles out from shore. The radio was still givin' the same news. I'd gone about twenty-five miles east when I turned north. About five miles later, no shimmer, but the static returned, and then the news came back on the same as when I left that morning."

"So, it appears the time warp is fifteen miles out and at least twenty-five miles long," he said thinking aloud and tugging on his bearded chin.

"Oh, it's bigger than that," Captain Johnny said.

"How big?" he asked.

"I ain't found no end to it yet. It appears to be attached to the boat and goes wherever she goes."

"Foreign ports, too?" he asked.

"Yep. I've been to San Juan, Martinique, Belize, all over the Caribbean, with the same results. As soon as I get close to shore, bingo. Like nothin' happened."

"You've had others on the boat. What did they say?"

"I ain't never told them we went through a, whadja call it, warped time?"

"Time warp," he corrected.

"Yeah, time warp. Most of my charters have been within the twelve-mile limit, so I never took her through. Those that did go out further and saw the shimmer, I told them that was a heat inversion. I learned that on the Discovery channel one night. Sorta like mirages. I told them that was where warm water met cold water, so we have to go through real slow so the boat won't shrink too fast. I made sure the radio was not workin'. Nobody was the wiser."

"Why did you tell me?" he asked.

"Shit, you're gonna be on this boat for a year at least. You're bound to notice it sooner or later."

"Who owned the boat before you? They must have known."

"She was confiscated by the Coast Guard from drug runners. Seems she was stolen from the previous owners who were done in by the druggies. The government sold it at auction. Still had bloodstains in the cockpit here. It also needed some repairs. It had bullet holes in it. I got it purdy cheap, got rid of the blood stains, fixed her up, put in an extra fuel tank, and that's that."

"So no one knew the previous owners?"

"Didn't care and didn't ask," said Captain Johnny.

"So you were a Navy SEAL?" he asked again not being able to get the thought out of his mind. Captain Johnny did not look like he could swim under water for miles, coming up only occasionally for air. And at the end of the swim, crawl up on shore armed with only a knife, wreaking havoc on the enemy, undetected.

"Yeah, sure was," Captain Johnny responded. "It's been a few years ago and a few pounds. I still have the skills, but not the stamina. Here, take the helm for a bit while I do something." He took the helm and the captain pulled out a length of rope from the storage compartment under the bench, tied it to the cleat at the stern, and tossed it overboard, letting it trail behind the yacht.

"You forgot to put a hook on the rope, CJ," he said.

"It's called a 'line' at sea," CJ said. "And it ain't for fishin' "

"Oh, excuse the fuck out of me. What's it for, then?"

"It's a lifeline in case your sorry ass falls overboard and I ain't here to pull you out. Even if we are going only a knot or two, that's faster than you can swim, so you just swim toward the rope, grab it, scream for all you're worth and maybe I'll come to your rescue. You might even be able to haul yourself back up."

"Why didn't you put it out earlier?"

"I used to, but every time I went through the shimmer, I'd lose a piece of the rope. It seems to get cut off somehow."

"That's strange. Well, on to something more interesting. Where we headin' first, Cap'n?" he asked.

"You got a passport?" Captain Johnny asked.

"Yes, sir, in my black bag," he responded.

"In that case, how's your French?" Captain Johnny asked.

"I speak all languages but Greek," he replied.

"Voila," said Captain Johnny.

"That's Greek to me," he said.

"Magnifigue, let's head to Martinique," Captain Johnny replied, as he turned the *Fisher Cat* due south toward the Yucatan channel.

Twenty-two

After only three days at sea, Captain Johnny let him know he was becoming a first-rate sailor.

"You're doin' better than most. I think I'll let you take the helm tonight for a few hours. Just wake me when you get tired or if the winds pick up."

"I think I can handle her," he said, with confidence. "Hell, everything is powered. I can just put her on auto-pilot, sit back, kick my feet up, and look at the stars."

"Take the helm while I go get us a couple a drinks and dinner," said Captain Johnny. Dedra followed Captain Johnny below decks and into the galley.

"Don't forget the dinner," he chided Captain Johnny.

The captain liked his rum and Cokes with a lot of lime juice and diet Coke. "Why waste the calories on sugar," he liked to say. "With diet Coke, I can have more rum. I used to drink Cuba libres, but it took too long to add the gin and bitters."

Ten minutes later Captain Johnny appeared with his "un-Libre" (in a large spill-proof insulated mug), an open bottle of wine, two well-filled ham-and-cheese sandwiches, and chips. Tagging along behind was Dedra.

"I think you stole my cat from me," he said, taking the sandwich and bottle of wine.

"I kinda like that cat," Captain Johnny confessed as he took a bite from his sandwich, followed by a swig of his un-libre. "When you took the helm this morning and I went to bed, she curled up in my crotch. I woke up later with her sittin' on my chest starin' at me."

"You snore like a bear. She was just probably tryin' to figure out where all that noise was comin' from."

"After I fell back asleep, she woke me up, touching my eyelids."

"You must have been having a high REM episode, and she was attracted to your pupils moving under your eyelids."

"Havin' a what?"

"Rapid eye movement episode. Dreaming with your eyes movin'."

"I don't remember dreamin'," Captain Johnny added.

After taking a drink from the wine bottle and a bite of the sandwich, he changed the subject.

"I have to get some exercise soon if I keep eatin' like this. When we get to Martinique, I'm going to look for a riding bike I can use on board."

"We got room if it ain't too big," Captain Johnny replied, as he downed the rest of his un-libre.

That night, Captain Johnny went to bed, leaving him at the helm. Dedra went to bed with the captain. He was all alone topside. It was a moonless night and crystal clear. There were no ships nearby, so he turned off the navigational lights and the green night lights on the helm. In the absence of artificial lighting, the full spectrum of the heavens could be seen. It was similar to a foot that becomes numb and tingles when it slowly regains feeling. Only it is the eyes that are slowly awakening to the tingle from pinpoints of light millions of miles away. He spent the rest of the night admiring the sky and thinking about what he did with his life so far.

The next morning Captain Johnny came on deck with coffee, while he went below to get some sleep. Dedra came up with the captain, but went back down two hours later as they passed over Adrienne and David's resting place.

His dream was similar to one he had before, but this time it seemed to play in reverse. He was already at the end of the long dark alley, but he was turned around, facing away from the dead-end brick wall. There was a musty, wet smell with the dampness. What little light there was played off the puddles on the ground and moisture clinging to the brick walls. He realized then that the light was shimmering. A rippling wave he felt was oddly familiar. Looking down in front of him, there were cats. They were hard to count in the darkness and wavering light, but at least a dozen or more pairs of eyes were staring at him. They seemed to beckon him to follow. His legs started to move although he was not making a conscious effort to walk. The cats led him on toward the source of the light he could only assume was the beginning of the alley.

As he followed the felines, he passed through the shimmer, as if walking through a veil of gossamer. As his vision became clearer, he noticed lines on the walls of the alley. Greenish lines interspersed with writing. He counted the lines between the writing. He counted ten before he came to the first words. He squinted to see, mouthing the word, "mickmix," no, something similar, "micmixcik." It made no sense. He kept walking, almost floating now, counting the green marks. "Nine, ten, eleven, twelve." Then the same word, "micmixcik," no, a different word, "mcmxcviii," but all in capitals, like MCMXCVIII. *Roman numerals*, he thought. Looking back he read the word he passed before. "MCMXCIX. Yes, Roman numerals."

Turning back toward the cats, he continued moving after them. It was like he was floating, floating on wet pavement, floating on water. In the waning darkness, he could see the cats, which seemed to be dwindling in number. Or did he just think they were.

Remembering his grade school days, he replaced the letters with numbers. "MCM, two thousand less one hundred. XC, one hundred less ten. IX, ten less one. 1999 was the first," he whispered. "After that was 1998. The next should be 1997." He floated after the cats. As he passed by each of the green lines one, then two, and then three of the cats faded and disappeared.

Twelve lines went by and then, "MCMXCVII, 1997," he mouthed. The end of the alley was becoming clearer now. There was light, not bright, but light streaming in through the opening caused by the walls and ground. Only it wasn't ground, it was rippling like the surface of a narrow channel. He was standing still now, not walking, but still moving toward the light. Mouthing out the years, 1996, 1995, 1994. He looked down, and there were only eight cats left. 1993, 1992, and the cats were gone save for one standing beside him.

The beginning of the alley was in front of him now, and it

opened into a sea. He was standing behind the wheel of a boat floating out to sea, a single cat beside him. There was someone swimming in the water on the starboard side of the boat. It was a woman smiling at him. She was beautiful, with long red hair floating on the water beside her light tan-colored face. As he approached her, she looked up at him and smiled. He smiled back and wanted to say something, but couldn't. Instead, she spoke to him. "Point five," she said, followed by something unintelligible. He strained to hear her as they passed a little closer. She was within inches of the boat. He bent over the rail and tried to grab her, but she swam away and repeated what she said before, "Point five, point five, and all will be alive." Then she sank down into the water, trailing strands of red hair until she was gone. He looked down at the cat. The cat's eyes were glowing red now, red like the woman's hair.

He sat straight up in bed, wide awake, repeating, "Point five, and all will be alive." He laid back down and floated into a deep dreamless sleep. In the morning, Dedra woke him with a gentle touch to his eyelids. He vaguely remembered a dream, but it faded as he gradually shook off sleep.

Ten days and many un-libres later, they were within twenty miles of Martinique. They had been sailing nonstop taking turns at the helm. Otto pilot, as they called him, actually did most of the boring routine work of steering when the winds were light and the seas were smooth. The onboard radar warned them when there were ships approaching.

As they got within fifteen miles of the coast, Dedra did her frightened-cat routine again letting them know they came back to the present.

"Will thirteen days have passed, or are we returning on the same day we left Mobile?" he asked Captain Johnny.

"Time passes the same as if we never went back," Captain Johnny responded.

"Why don't we see the shimmer when we approach land?"

"I ain't figured that one out yet, but I always pass through, shimmer or no."

"Where we goin' in Martinique?"

"A place called Le Marin. Its bay is the best mooring spot on the island. It's around the southern end. We should be there before nightfall."

The first part of Martinique that came into view was Mont Pelée, sticking 4,600 feet above the sea. As they got closer, the island started to take shape. The terrain was mountainous with indented coastlines. It looked like a green emerald held in the hand of a blue sea. Sails and white masts dotted the coastline almost everywhere.

Captain Johnny pointed out a town off the port bow.

"That is Saint-Pierre," he said. "When Pelée erupted in 1902, 30,000 residents were fried. Only one man survived. He was in a prison protected by its thick walls."

"Amazing," he replied. "It sure looks like a beautiful place now. No offense, Captain Johnny, but when we get to Le Marin, I'm going to find a nice hotel with a nice hot bath and hot tub. You can join me if you want, my treat. Dedra can stay on the *Fisher Cat* by herself for awhile. I don't think she'll go anywhere."

"No, thanks. I like it here. I can join you for sight-seeing if you want, but I also have some places of my own I want to go to. There are some rum factories on the island. Make some of the best rum in the world here."

"No wonder you wanted to come here first," he said.

"Don't worry about Dedra either. Her and me will do just fine by ourselves, won't we, little one?" Dedra looked up from Captain Johnny's lap at the mention of her name and meowed.

As they pulled into Le Marin harbor, he saw what Captain Johnny meant. There were more yachts than he could count all anchored in neat rows. The sun was going down in the west, casting a golden curtain on the white masts and the mountains in the background. Although he was anxious to get to a good hotel, they all three spent one more night on the yacht. He slept deeply and peacefully. The first night of full sleep in twelve days.

The next morning, they took the raft to shore. Leaving Captain Johnny to his own devices, he took a taxi to the Soleil Levant hotel. The going rate for a week was just under $2,000, but he negotiated $6,500 for a month. On checking into his room, he plugged in the laptop and connected to the phone line. "Time to move some money around," he said aloud.

After moving some of his offshore assets to Costa Rica, he checked to see if Dee had touched the money he left her. He noticed it was down by $30,000. He wanted to keep his promise to her and continue to play the game, but he wanted to wait until just before he left to replenish the account. The rest of the day he planned on starting to get back in shape, but first a trip to the barber to trim his beard.

After five days on land, five trips to the hotel's exercise room, and twenty-five miles of running on the beach, he felt he was back in reasonable shape. He kept in contact with CJ just to make sure the boat was still in the harbor. He was starting to get a tan and felt it was time to find a woman to release his pent-up urges. After a shower and shave, he was ready to take a walk along the beach.

Within an hour, he was watched by two bronzed bikini-clad beauties. They were sitting up on beach towels, supporting their upper bodies with arms behind them, as only women can do, with their elbows bent in at odd angles. He waited until he was well past them and glanced back. They were unabashedly still staring at him from under broad-rimmed straw beach hats. He was amused that he was a little embarrassed at the attention. They must be European, because American women don't act that way, at least not the ones he was used to. He continued his walk along the beach, and as soon as he was sure they were no longer looking in his direction, he circled back well in from the beach. He approached them from behind, stopping a moment to observe their actions.

"Hello, ladies," he said, when he was close enough to startle them.

They let out a little noise that sounded like two frightened mice and jumped a little forward on their towels. The brunette turned back toward him with a coquettish smile.

"Oh, you are an American." Her accent reminding him of a Maurice Chevalier movie.

"Yes," he said. "I am sorry to intrude, but this is my first trip to Martinique. I have been at sea for the last three weeks and am a little in need of some human contact."

"You were alone at sea?" the blond asked. They looked almost identical in size and shape, like clones except for the hair color. They were wearing what looked like identical red bikinis pulled down so as to expose as much of their breasts as possible. They were also well tanned from long hours at the beach. They must have had a bikini wax, since the bottom part of their suits were skimpy and covered little with no hair showing. They also had no leg hair as so many other European women have.

"Not alone. The captain of the boat and I are the only passengers. We sailed from the States a couple of weeks ago and I'm just starting to get used to being on land again. So what is there to do on this little island?"

"A lot if you have the money," the blond said grinning. "Would you like us to show you? We have been here for two weeks and are getting bored."

"Well, I didn't mean to impose," he said, somewhat embarrassed by their candor. "I think I can afford most anything, at least for a month or two."

"What about your friend?" the brunette asked. "Would he like to come along?"

"He's not really my friend, more like my employee, but I'll ask him. I believe he is more interested in touring the rum factories. He is a bit older than I and a bit rougher around the edges." Later he did ask CJ, but he was not interested.

"Not yet anyway," said CJ. "I want to tour the rum factory by day and play blackjack by night. I've started to win at the tables and until my run of luck changes, I think I'll trust the cards rather than the ladies. I can always buy a woman and pay a whole lot less than you will."

CJ was right. The two women cost him a small fortune, but he enjoyed the nightclubs, casino, zouk, and jazz music, and the women themselves for the next two weeks. When their holiday was over and they had to return to France, he was ready to return to the sea. CJ's luck ran out, and he lost most of what he won earlier. They took the next week getting the boat ready.

During that time, he thought about how he was able to enjoy the company of the two French women without any desire to hurt them. "I think my time with Dee ruined me," he said to himself one night while trying to get to sleep. The day he checked out of the hotel, he transferred money into Dee's account bringing the total back up to $50,000.

Twenty-three

Deanna awoke in the morning six weeks to the day after the explosion in Vermont. She did her morning run, followed by stretches and some light weight-lifting with a set of weights she purchased with some of the $30,000. She updated her wardrobe with a thousand more. Another $1,500 bought her a new computer, and with the newly installed cable modem, she was able to work at home. There was still plenty of money left for the MOMY-G organization if it was still needed. She went to the office three days each week. Her boss was delighted she had returned to work.

Deciding to check to see if any money had been replenished in the account, something she had not done for a week, she booted her computer. She decided to use the bank's online system, since the FBI was still monitoring her phone. Besides, it was easier to use than punching all the account information into the phone and getting a droned response. If he didn't replenish the money soon, she was going to transfer the rest to her personal account. After logging into the bank account with her user name and password, her account menu popped up. "Bingo," she said aloud as she noticed the account was back at $50,000.

She had mulled over whether to tell the FBI about the account or not. She felt it was her money and a gift. She had gone to the Texas lottery web site and found he did win the money after all. Since it was not stolen money, why should she take the chance that the FBI would confiscate the account. She may even be considered an accessory to the crime by hiding the account from them. She considered calling her computer-savvy neighbor, Joe, to see if he knew how to track money using the Internet, but he was still the letch he had always been, so she decided to see if a private investigator could help. She thought it ironic that she would be using his money to find him.

She did a search in Google for private investigators in the Florida, Pensacola, area. There were several, so she narrowed her search to those who could find missing people. Looking through the list, she found that almost all claimed to be able to use banking records to locate missing people. She settled on four firms and e-mailed them to see if they would be interested. She left her computer on as she took her shower and got ready for the day.

After lunch, Dee checked her e-mail. All but one of the PI's returned an e-mail. Two said they could help, but stopped short of saying they could access bank accounts. The other said they could with the owner's permission. She selected the latter to call. She set an appointment to meet with an investigator at 10:00 the next morning.

She arrived promptly at 10:00. The office was located in a small strip mall on the north side of town near Interstate-10. She parked her car, walked across the parking lot, and through the glass door painted with the sign J. Carp, Investigator, Licensed in the State of Florida. An older woman in a plain white blouse and black pantsuit looked up at her through black-framed glasses. She was of average build, not overweight, with short-cropped dark hair.

"Yes, may I help you?" asked the woman with a slight southern drawl. A computer with monitor sat on top of the chrome-and-glass desk. A nameplate announced her as Hillary Carp in white letters embossed on a black background. *Must be a mom-and-pop operation,* she thought. The remainder of the desk was neatly ordered with stacks of files, a stapler, pens, and pencils. A small laser printer/fax/telephone sat behind the secretary on a chrome-and-glass bookcase. The rest of the office was sparsely decorated with plastic plants, a gray metal filing cabinet next to a door adjacent to Hillary's desk, and a bluish color short-pile carpet. Against the opposite wall from Hillary was a blue couch. Above that hung a G. Harvey painting of a cowboy riding a horse on a dark snowy evening, strangely out of place in Florida.

"I'm Deanna Mayfield. I have an appointment with Mr. Carp at 10:00."

"He is expecting you, Ms. Mayfield. I will let him know you

are here," she said as she picked up the telephone from the cradle on the printer and dialed a number.

"Ms. Mayfield is here to see you," she said, and then awaited a response.

"He'll be right out," she said.

"Thank you," Dee said. *They seem very efficient,* she thought as she headed for the couch. She was admiring the painting and was about to sit down when a tall young man came out of the closed office door. His white dress-shirt sleeves were rolled up two turns exposing dark, curly arm hair. She assumed he was one of those men who looked like a bear naked with thick, black hair covering his body. He had a stocky build, not very athletic, but he looked like he could handle himself in a fight. His dark blue dress pants broke neatly over black loafers, which protected rather large feet. She guessed the shoes at a size twelve or thirteen. He had a pleasant smile filled with white teeth under a black Clark-Gable-style mustache. His brown eyes were hidden under black eyebrows, which were connected in the middle by more hair. His head was topped by more black curly hair. *He probably leaves a mat of hair in bed when he gets up in the morning*, she thought.

"Ms. Mayfield, I'm Jake Carp. Please come on in," he said, in a deep, raspy voice.

He led her into his office, decorated similarly to the lobby area. The bluish carpet continued through the door and into his office. His computer sat on a back work surface, which was like his desk, glass and chrome. The wall on the left had a door partially open revealing black and white tile *which*, she thought, *must be the bathroom.*

"Please sit down," he said indicating an armchair in front of his desk covered with similar material as the couch in the lobby. Another blue couch sat against the wall on the right. She looked at the picture above the couch for more than a second. It was another oddly out of place painting of two cowboys on a stagecoach driving lathered up horses through a snowy night.

"A G. Harvey print," he commented, noticing her interest. "I have always been a fan of his. The snow helps to make me feel cool on a hot humid day."

"They are interesting," she replied. When she turned around abruptly, she noticed he had just lifted his eyes from looking at her butt. She walked to the chair and sat down.

"Would you like a soda or cup of coffee?" he asked.

"No, thanks."

"How can I help you?"

"I had someone transfer money into my bank account, and I need to know where it came from."

"You want to know who transferred it?"

"I have a pretty good idea who. I want to know where they were when the transfer took place," Dee said, with authority.

"I have to ask if this money is legal. I do not want to jeopardize my license or reputation by getting involved in an illegal operation."

"I understand, and the money is totally legal as far as I know. I have set up an organization to find missing women, and there is an anonymous donor sending me money. I just want to be able to find out where they are and thank them in person."

"Have they asked to remain anonymous?" he asked. "What I mean is, they might stop donating if they are exposed."

"They haven't said anything, but I intend to honor their wishes when I find them."

"You said you thought you knew who they are. Is that correct?"

"Yes and no. I think they have a missing daughter, and because they have money, are reluctant to be exposed to all the publicity. If I am able to locate their daughter along with some of the other missing women, then I feel they may come forward," Dee lied. She was spitting out a story she had rehearsed in the car on the way over.

"You are the MOMY-G organizer?" he asked.

"Yes, and congratulations on doing your homework," Dee responded.

"Why don't you just go to the media and ask the donors to contact you?"

"I think that may scare them away."

"If I find out where the money came from, how will that help?"

"At least I will know where they are and if it is who I think it is, then I can go there and meet them. If I do this discreetly, then I have a better chance of talking to them."

"I will help you," he said. "My terms are $150 per hour plus expenses. I don't expect too many expenses, since I should be able to do the investigation from here. But if there are any, they will be itemized. I don't guarantee results but will give you all the information I can find."

"Agreed," said Dee. "I would like a report in three days if you are unsuccessful, sooner if you are. After the three days, I will decide if you need to go any further."

He pushed a button on the speakerphone.

"Hillary, please draw up a standard contract with a three-day renewal clause and have Ms. Mayfield sign it on the way out."

"Of course" was the response.

"Now, give me the information you have on the banks," Jake said, with a half-smile.

Fifteen minutes later, Dee left Jake's office after signing the contract. When she got back home, there was a message on her answering machine. It was from Agent Brinks, asking her to call back. "We have some information for you," was the rest of the message.

Agent Brinks did have some information. There was some DNA found in her house that did not match Dee's. It also did not match any of the DNA found at the crime scene, which they were now calling it. Agent Brinks said they had proof that the explosions were not an accident. They were now investigating the murder of federal agents. She added that the DNA found at the scene of Lulu's double-wide matched DNA of three of the missing women on the MOMY-G list, but not Dedra's. Dee had a lump in her throat and tears in her eyes when she hung up. "Dedra will never come home now," she sobbed. "I will find that son of a bitch, if it's the last thing I do, and I will use his own money to hang him."

Two days later, Jake Carp called Dee and said he had some information for her. In an hour, she was at his office.

"The money transfer was from a bank in the Bahamas," he calmly told her. "I was able to determine the transfer was done electronically from a computer modem in a hotel in Martinique."

"Where is Martinique," she asked.

"An island in the Caribbean," he said. "The phone number and name of the hotel is in my report along with the accounting of my time and expenses. Is there anything else I can do, otherwise I can close this file."

"Keep the file open for a while until I get back from Martinique," she said.

The next afternoon she landed at Fort-de-France Lamentin Airport in Martinique, three days after *Fisher Cat* left. She went to the hotel and found he had checked out and left no mention of where he was going. After bribing the day desk clerk, she was told that he arrived on a boat and was seen occasionally with another man and, yes, at least two other women. "Can you describe the other man?" she asked.

"He was an older, rougher looking man and did not wear appropriate attire. He was always in ragged shorts and a T-shirt and smelled like the sea. He was called CJ. Sometimes he had a cat sitting on his shoulder. He also spent a lot of time in the bar," he said, nodding toward the far end of the hotel lobby. "He was tolerated despite his lack of manners because he tipped quite well. They both seemed to have a lot of money, but I'm sure it was not family wealth."

"Did they both spend time in the bar?" she asked.

"Occasionally, but the one called CJ stayed well into the night."

"*Merci beaucoup*," she said, thanking him.

"You are welcome," he replied with a slight bow of the head.

Her next stop was the hotel bar, where she found a bartender willing to talk. She ordered a glass of white wine and left the change from a fifty sitting on the counter. The bar was empty and had one side open to the hotel pool. After she described Captain Johnny, the bartender eyed the money in front of her drink. "I tip well if the conversation is interesting," she told him, noticing his glance. "Do you know where they were going next?"

"The one called CJ, which I theenk was short for Captain Johnnee, did not say directly, but he was fond of the rum," he replied in a thick French accent.

"Did he mention anything at all about his boat?"

"Oh yes, he talked about it like it was a woman. I theenk he said it was seventeen meters or so long and could cruise around the world if he wanted to."

"Seventeen meters. How big is that?"

"I theenk that is like maybe fifty feet Amereecan. I theenk he called it the 'Feesher Cat' or something like that."

Writing the information down on a bar napkin, Dee asked about the cat. "Yes, he had a cat weeth him sometimes. A cute leettle cat that sat on his shoulder almost all the time. When the cat peed and pooped in the sand outside the bar, that is when we asked him not to bring it in here no more. But that was four or five days ago, and I have not seen them seence."

"And there was no mention of where they were going?"

"The capitan said he thought the rum here was very good, but in Belize, it was the best in the Caribbean."

"How far is Belize," she asked.

"About 600 kilometers, or 1,800 miles Amereecan, maybe more, maybe less."

"How long would it take to get there by boat?" she asked.

"I don't know, maybe a week or ten days, depends how fast you go."

"*Merci beaucoup,*" she said and left the bar, not touching her wine or the change.

"Thank you, madam," he said scooping up the money.

She left Martinique the next morning, heading back to Pensacola.

Twenty-four

Captain Johnny pulled up anchor on a fine afternoon. The tide was heading away from Martinique, and so were they. They had a new supply of canned goods, fresh tropical fruits (plenty of limes), diet Coke, fresh vegetables, cat food, water, wine, and rum for CJ (as he was now called) all stowed aboard. To keep in shape, he bought a stationary bike that folded up and could be stowed in the crew cabin. CJ said he might even give it a try as long as there was a place where he could put his un-libre. A cup holder was then attached to the handle bar stem.

"Let's get out in the middle of nowhere and do some fishin'," CJ declared.

"Sounds good to me," he responded. Dedra just looked up at the two of them and meowed. At any rate, Dedra was a sea cat of the first caliber. She only went in the ocean one time, when they were in Martinique, and spent a half-hour trying to clean off the salt water, gagging the entire time, until CJ washed her off with fresh water.

They went through the shimmer at about two knots. From the radio stations, they figured they went back to 1966. They followed fifteen-degree latitude until they came to seventy-five degrees west longitude. They were again close to where Adrienne and David were attacked by pirates. CJ lowered the sails and broke out the fishing gear. Dedra's curiosity peaked as she sniffed at the remnants of past fishing trips on the items laid before her.

"CJ, what are we usin' for bait?" he asked.

"I picked up some packages of frozen scrod bait fish at the head of the pier," CJ replied. "We just hook it and throw 'em out. If we catch somethin' we eat fresh fish. If we don't, we eat the rest of the scrod. Go get one of the packages, and we can get started."

He went below and retrieved one package from the freezer. Once topside with it, CJ took one of the fish out, hooked it, and tossed the line overboard. Dedra was all over the package as he baited his hook and tossed the line over the other side. CJ placed his rod in the holder and he did the same. He took the rest of the fish back to the freezer, much to Dedra's dismay.

He picked up a book and started to read, just happy to be away from it all. After reading the same paragraph three times, he put the book down and looked at the beauty that was around them. There was nothing but blue-green water from horizon to horizon. There was a slight swell in the sea, giving the boat a slow, pitching roll that was hypnotizing as well as soothing. The only sound was the slapping of the water off the sides of the boat and the sound of the rigging slapping against the mast as the boat rolled with the motion of the swells. The sky was a hazy blue with some high cumulus clouds billowing up thousands of feet. It was peaceful. He started to think about Dee and if only he could have met her before he started killing innocent women. *If only I could go back and start over, knowing that she was out there,* he thought. Then he jolted upright as an idea hit him. Just then, a fish, like the thought he just had, hit his bait, jerking the pole.

"Got one," he said to CJ, who had fallen asleep but now jumped upright like the fishing pole did. Holding onto the thought as tightly as he held the pole, he let the fish take the bait and run with it a little.

"Don't let it run too far," CJ advised. "It could work loose and get away."

There was nothing like hooking a fish. You held onto a line connecting you to something you could not see. Your imagination played with images of whatever was tugging on the other end, especially in the ocean where there were numerous possibilities. It wasn't until you had it in close and visible that the mystery was solved. Your heart rate increases even though there is no strenuous activity. One wonders if the fish is playing the same game, only if it loses, it dies. Pulling back and then leaning forward while winding the reel, slowly the line was brought in. CJ got the net as the last bit of line brought the fish toward the surface.

"It's a king mackerel," cried an excited CJ. "I ain't never

seen one this far south. It's a big one, about fifty pounds." CJ dipped the net into the water and pulled out the fish. After he dropped it in the cockpit, it started to flap around vigorously. Dedra headed for below decks, apparently wanting no part of this game. CJ hit it on the back of the head with a spar. It quivered a little as it lay dying, gasping for air. When it was still, they could see what a truly magnificent creature it was. Its back was an iridescent bluish green and its sides silvery. Its body was streamlined, giving it an appearance of motion even when lying still. This was a fish built for speed.

"It put up quite a fight for a fish that size," he said to CJ.

"They are fighters," agreed CJ. "Looks like we'll eat good tonight."

Dedra mustered up some courage to peek up over the top step. Cautiously, she slinked toward the dying fish. The fish gave one last flip sending Dedra straight up in the air about eighteen inches. She landed and turned in one motion and headed for the safety of below decks.

That night, they dined on pan-fried mackerel, while Dedra ate her fill of scraps.

"Let's go to Belize," said CJ.

"Do they make rum there?" he asked.

"Does a cat have an ass?" smirked CJ, just as Dedra turned tail and walked away to go sleep off her fish feast.

"That one does," he said, looking over to see her going down the ladder with her tail up and ass showing.

They both laughed.

CJ went below decks to clean up and call it a night. He took his position for the night watch, put on a headset, and listened to whatever station he could find on the radio.

Their routine in the morning was the same. CJ fixed breakfast, and then they ate topside. CJ took over the helm. He went below to get some sleep. Dedra followed the captain and stayed with him on deck for three hours and then headed below decks for her mid-morning nap.

At 12:30, as he was getting up and putting on shorts to ride the stationary bike, CJ hollered for him to come topside quick. When he got there, CJ had the sails lowered and was holding the binoculars looking to the south.

"What's up?" he asked.

"We may be in for trouble," CJ said. "I noticed a blip on the radar coming at us kinda fast. It looks like a speedboat, but I can't make it out just yet. It could be pirates."

"Pirates," he said, puzzled. "What do they want from us?"

"The boat. They want to use it for smuggling. We are expendable to them. We better get prepared just in case. Take the helm and bring her about so that our bow is headed right at them. That way, they can't see if there is anyone on board. I'm going to hide Dedra and get a welcoming committee ready for them."

CJ went below decks, carrying Dedra. He put Dedra in the forward head, locked the door, and then closed it. He could open it later from the outside with a special key. In his bedroom, he pulled out a drawer from under the bed and took out a thirteen-inch hunting knife and heavy-duty Kevlon sheath. The knife had an eight-and-a-half-inch stainless steel, razor-sharp, surgical blade. He looped his belt through the sheath, tightened his belt, and placed the knife in the sheath. He took out another smaller dagger and attached it to his ankle with a strap and sheath. Next, he grabbed a pistol from his nightstand. He took off his shoes and went topside.

"Damn, CJ, you look like Lloyd Bridges. What's the plan?"

"Can you shoot one of these?" CJ asked, holding the Glock 30, .45-caliber pistol in the air. "If not, I can handle it all."

"Yeah, I am a pretty good shot with rifle or pistol."

"Where are they?" CJ asked, leaning over the port side and looking south. "I see 'em. They're still coming straight for us. Here's the plan. We can't shoot it out with 'em. There are probably more of them than us. If they are pirates, and I'm pretty sure they are, they will take this boat and kill us as soon as they see us. Here's what we do. We slip off the boat at the stern and wait for them in the water. Use the yacht to hide behind. They can approach the boat only from one side. We'll be on the other. They will tie up and go on board, looking for occupants. I will slip into the speedboat and take care of anyone there. If I get spotted, use this pistol; otherwise, let me handle it. Got any questions, ask in the water. Let's go." He followed CJ to the stern where they crept over the side and into the water.

"What if they start the diesel before we can stop them?" he asked.

"I disabled the engine as soon as I saw them," CJ said.

"What about sharks?"

"Which sharks do you want to fight. Them or the ones you can't see? Make sure you keep the gun out of the water. We're dead in the water, but use the lifeline if you have to."

He didn't ask any more questions as they both moved to the stern, holding onto the boat trim. He held the gun up and out of the water as they heard the approaching craft.

The powerful engine on the speedboat cut back to a garbled growl as they approached from the starboard bow. They could hear the wash against the bow of both boats as the speedboat came alongside the yacht.

As soon as they heard the boats touch, CJ went underwater and headed for the speedboat.

As CJ swam away, he worked his way around the portside, holding onto the handholds with one hand, the pistol in the other out of the water. His heart started to beat faster and his ears started to ring. The tunnel vision came, and he heard the voice. Only this time, it was a woman's voice, a woman's voice with a Southern, no, a Cajun, accent, but the pirates interrupted her.

"Eduardo, get down below and see where they are," said a man in Spanish.

"Miguel, I don't like this," said Eduardo. "It's too quiet. Where are they?"

"Damn it," said Miguel. "I'll go with you. What are you, a woman?"

He heard two sets of squeaking shoes on board the yacht.

The woman's voice came back, whispering in his ear. "I will guide you," she said. He felt almost as if there was someone in the water pulling him around the stern to the starboard side of the yacht. As he rounded the stern, he saw that the powerboat had turned and was tied up portside to starboard and about halfway down the side of the yacht. He could see the heads of the two pirates on the yacht. They were heading for the ladder to go below decks. One pirate in the speedboat was behind the wheel, and another was holding a rifle with the butt to his hip and the muzzle pointed up. The boat motor was making a lot of noise, sounding like a giant gargling with salt water.

CJ's hand came slowly out of the water and up to the side of the speedboat. As he aimed the gun toward the men on the speedboat, the woman's voice said, "Wait, I will guide you." He felt a slight tug on his arm. The boats looked like they were far away. CJ's head emerged with the knife between his teeth, like something from an Errol Flynn movie. CJ hauled himself on board the speedboat slowly and deliberately. He still had the Navy SEAL in him, after all. The noise from the engine masked any noise CJ was making as he seemed to glide across the deck, then grab the man with the rifle by the hair, yank his head back, and sliced his throat. The man never made a sound, but the rifle did as it hit the side of the boat and bounced overboard. The driver was alerted, but it was too late. CJ had already had him by the hair and dispensed with him summarily. Just then the other two came up the ladder of the yacht and saw CJ. who was already on his way to the yacht, but they had the drop on him.

"Now," the voice said, and he felt as if he was being lifted out of the water. His gun arm was leveled toward the two pirates. He later remembered thinking to himself, *I'm too far away to hit them.* He felt as though the gun was aimed as if a magnet held it toward the two on the yacht. He didn't hear the two pops from the pistol because his ears were ringing. As if in a distant dream, he saw his hand jerk twice and smoke belch from the weapon. He saw two bullets in slow motion, one slightly behind and to the left of the other, ripping through the distance between them and toward the eyes of the two pirates who were now staring at him. Their heads exploded from the impact of the .45-caliber slugs, and they were knocked back down the ladder below decks. "Yes," the voice said. "Now we live again."

As the ringing in his ears went away and his vision returned to normal, he saw, or thought he saw, two forms float out of the water in a northerly direction. One was trailing long red hair. In an instant, his dream came back to him, but disappeared when CJ yelled, "Good shootin' there, mate." The tunnel vision returned to normal and he was back alongside the yacht.

CJ disappeared for a minute.

The speedboat stopped sputtering. As he was trying to pull

himself back into the yacht, still holding the pistol out of the water, CJ's head peered over the side and a hand came down to lift him into the boat.

"Heads nearly blowed off both of 'em," CJ said, showing a lot of teeth. "Why din't you say you were a marksman, an expert, at that. And what was that thing you did on the water. Christ, you was outta the water to your waist when you shot, both hands on the pistol. Your feet must a bin goin' a mile a minute. Shit, you spooked me out, boy. Well, we got pirates to feed to the fishes and brains and blood to clean up."

"Just like when you first got her, huh?" was all he could think to say, as he followed CJ down the ladder.

"What the fuck does that mean?" asked CJ as they lifted Eduardo's body up the ladder and threw it overboard.

"You said you had to clean blood from the boat when you bought it from the Coast Guard."

"What Coast Guard. You must of hit your head on somethin' in the water. I ain't never told you that. I bought her from an old couple. Weren't no blood on board. Let's get the other one and then scuttle the speedboat, and stay outta my rum. Better yet, maybe that's what you need 'stead that pussy fussy wine you drink."

He followed CJ down the ladder, and they fed Miguel to the fish. His head was spinning. He had to sit down as CJ chopped a large hole in the side of the speedboat. It slowly sank with the other two pirates showing a bloody ear to ear smile from their throats.

That night they both stayed topside and got drunk.

David and Adrienne completed their goal of sailing the Caribbean, South America, the East Coast, the Panama Canal, the West Coast, and, yes, even Alaska. David did not remember anything of their lost moments. In fact, they picked up where they left off. Adrienne remembered it all and what could have happened. David wanted to sell the *Writer Aboard* in 1982 and get a new yacht, "She's sixteen years old and needs to be worked on," he said.

Adrienne convinced him to keep *Writer Aboard* just a couple more years and then sell her, "Let's wait just a couple more years and see if we want to keep sailing," she said, with her smile that still melted him even after thirty-three years. She knew some day in 1984 in Mobile, they would have to find a retired Navy SEAL named John Potter and sell him the boat. If not, all the corrections of the past will be overturned. She knew they would succeed, since they had made it this far. They gave John Potter a great deal, which David objected to, "He's getting this boat for less than half of what she's worth," he said.

"Look at it as an investment in our past," she said, with a smile. He frowned at her, but sold the ex-SEAL the boat. They never bought another boat, but moved into a retirement community in Sarasota, Florida. He wrote about their sailing adventures, his first book in eighteen years. It became a best seller after Adrienne's blessings, of course. They went on a book-signing tour in 1998. That's when she met one of the pirate slayers for the second time.

When the sun blazed darts of pain into their eyes the next morning, they were glad they were facing west. It was amazing that they kept the boat on course for Belize. Otto pilot did most of the steering, while the diesel hummed at the lowest speed that kept them in a westerly direction. They slowly started to recover over cups of hot, dark, thick coffee. Even Dedra seemed hung over. She had both front paws over her head as if trying to keep it from falling off.

"Jesus," CJ said. "I hope we don't have to go through that again."

"What, the pirates or a rum dumb drunk?" was the muffled response.

"I can take the rum drunk," said CJ.

"You know, we probably made a mistake killing those men," he said.

"What the fuck do you mean?" asked a dumbfounded CJ.

"We altered the future by doing it. We were in the past where we shouldn't have been. We killed someone and may have had an effect on the future."

"Oh, you mean one of those slimeball assholes might have been working on a cure for cancer and just wanted this boat for research money?" jeered CJ.

"I don't know what future role those two could have played. Maybe they would have been destined to kill someone worse than they were. I just don't know. When we get back to the future, we may find things different."

"If it had an effect on us, wouldn't we have just disappeared?"

"I would think so, but maybe it's a delayed reaction. We'll find out when we go through the time warp. How close are we to Belize?"

"Don't know until I shoot the sun, and I ain't ready to do that just yet," he said with a painful squint to the east. "I think we are pretty close, maybe fifty miles or so. We're in the past far enough that the GPS doesn't work. I say we just keep on due west and see what happens."

"Okay by me." They drank their coffee in silence. CJ went to the galley and fixed them some dry toast to settle their stomachs. They kicked the speed up to nine knots, and three hours later, Dedra announced the passage back to the present. They looked at each other to see if either of them disappeared. Then they looked at Dedra. The cat cocked her head and looked back at them as if to say, "well, what did you expect?" The three of them continued on toward Belize.

Dee contacted Jake Carp a week after she returned from Martinique.

"I want you to find someone in Belize," she told him. "A man who goes by the name of CJ or Captain Johnny. He would have sailed into Belize on a fifty-foot yacht, named the *Fisher Cat,* with another man. Captain Johnny is fond of rum and often has a cat on his shoulders when he visits the bars. If you locate them, let me know, and I will go to Belize myself."

"I'll do my best," said Jake, "but need some up-front money to do that type of long-distance investigation."

"How much?" Dee asked.

"Five thousand should be sufficient," he said. "I'll let you know if I need more."

"The check is in the mail," she said.

Eight days later, he had some information for her.

"They are in Belize. It took quite a few phone calls. I hired a local private investigator, which took a good deal of your deposit, but I located the one called Captain Johnny. The yacht is docked in the harbor. He spends quite a bit of time in the bar at Captain Morgan's Retreat, a resort in Ambergris Caye, and he does have a cat with him." After hanging up the phone, Dee thought Captain Morgan was named appropriately for a person who likes to drink rum.

Dee left for Belize three days later. She arrived at the Philip S. W. Goldson International Airport late in the day and found a room at Captain Morgan's. The resort was like a picture out of paradise, with open pole structures and thatch roofs. There was a 400-foot-long pier jutting straight out from a milky white beach. The water was crystal clear and calm. Little waves were lapping at the sand like a cat drinking milk. It was a long trip to get here, but worth it, she thought, *If only I weren't just looking for some son of a bitch.* She decided to rest in her room for what was left of the day and night.

The next morning, she started her search. She walked to the pier and with binoculars from her beach bag, she searched the moored boats for the *Fisher Cat.* It didn't take long. She found her anchored, bow and stern, about half a mile out with a small dinghy tied up on her starboard side. There was movement on the deck, but it was too far away to tell who it was. She walked to the beach and sat under one of the grass-thatched shelters. Occasionally checking the yacht with the binoculars, she let the tropical morning sun trickle under the shelter washing over her already-tanned skin. She listened to the sea gulls constant din and the subtle swishing of the waves gently caressing the shore.

Just before noon, she heard the faint sputtering of an outboard motor. She picked up the binoculars and spotted the dinghy slowly cutting through the water toward the pier to her right. She watched the small craft until it beached at the base of the pier, where there were other similar boats beached at a rental place. She walked toward the pier and watched as what must have been Captain Johnny got out of the boat and headed toward her on his way to the resort. Captain Johnny had a full beard and was wearing a T-shirt, baggy tan adirondack shorts, and sandals. She saw the cat astride his shoulders similar to a parrot she once saw in an old pirate movie on late-night TV. The cat was not sitting upright, but draped around the back of his neck, like a mink shawl.

She passed by Captain Johnny, who did not even look in her direction, but the cat did. Dedra seemed to stare at Dee in recognition and, at the closest point, Dedra rose up and mewed. Captain Johnny reached his left hand up and held Dedra by the back of the neck in anticipation of her falling. Dedra did not fall, but shifted her stare to the other side of Captain Johnny's shoulder as Dee passed behind them. Dedra looked back from time to time as Dee followed at a safe distance. Soon they went into the retreat bar and out of sight.

Ten minutes later, Dee entered the bar. Although she was wearing sunglasses, she needed to wait a few seconds so her eyes could adjust to the change from the noon sun to the semi-darkness of the bar. As her vision slowly improved, she walked past the bar on her left to a table at the far corner near a large opening overlooking the harbor. The bar was open to the beach on the opposite side she entered from. The light was at her back. There were a few other patrons sitting at tables scattered about the wooden floor. The dress was obviously casual, as most of the patrons were in beach attire. She felt a little out of place in her shorts and tucked in blouse. She pulled her blouse out and tied it in the front at her waist. She took out a book from her beach bag and pretended to read until a slim, blond waiter approached her with a menu.

"American?" he asked, handing her the menu. He was dressed in a white, short-sleeved shirt draped over khaki shorts. She thought it odd that the waiter wore sandals.

"Yes," she said.

"Would you like to hear the specials?" he said in the king's English.

"No," she responded. "The menu will be fine, and please bring me a glass of Chardonnay."

"Very well," he said, a little disappointed that he could not rattle off the specials and show off his waiter skills.

Using the menu as a shield, she peeked around the room. She found Captain Johnny at the bar alone with the cat. The cat was staring back at her. She was going to wait all day if necessary to see if someone joined them. When the waiter returned with her wine, she ordered a salad and breadsticks, then busied herself in her book.

Captain Johnny was deeply involved in a conversation with the female bartender, while Dedra stared at Dee from his shoulder. Soon a plate of some type of chicken and fries finally distracted Dedra. Captain Johnny fed her as much as she wanted from the plate. He smothered the fries in vinegar, which made Dedra sneeze from the acrid vapors.

Just as Dee was finishing her salad, her patience paid off. He walked in from the beach side of the bar, sporting a neatly trimmed beard and mustache. His hair was a shade or two lighter than she remembered, probably bleached from the sun. He had on an unbuttoned, blue, short-sleeved shirt partially covering white swim trunks. His skin was bronzed from days of tropical exposure. He must have been jogging or walking on the beach, for his feet were bare. He took off sunglasses and looked around. He too was blinded by the darkness of the shaded room and did not recognize Dee. He walked straight for Captain Johnny and Dedra as if that part of the bar belonged to them. Even though she suspected him of murdering her daughter, she still felt a tingle throughout her body. *If only he had not done such terrible things...*, she thought. She lifted her book to hide her face as tears welled up, blurring her vision.

When she looked up, he was gone. Rather than risk attention by jumping up and seeing where he went, she waited for her check. At least she knew he was here and where to find him.

When he walked into the bar, he had déjà vous. It was like the last time he went hunting with Wayne and Bill. He could not recall exactly what it was, but it felt eerie. CJ and Dedra were in their usual place at the end of the bar. CJ was probably on his third or fourth un-libre. As he approached, Dedra did not acknowledge his presence with her usual meow and stretch. Instead, she was staring at the back of the bar. Blinded from being out most of the morning, running along the beach, his eyes were not yet adjusted.

"That running stuff is gonna kill you," CJ said, without even looking at him.

"Those fries and rum are going to get you first. Good after-

253

noon, you old fart. What's with Dedra?"

"I don't know. She started acting strange the minute we got ashore. Maybe she don't like this place anymore."

"Maybe she don't like sittin' at a bar all day long, watchin' you chug rum."

"Then why don't you take her for awhile to that hotel you're stayin' at?"

"You two always start that way, but end up leavin' like you were long-lost buddies," chided in the bartender.

She must have been beautiful fifty pounds and fifteen years ago, he thought. *Now she is just a bleached blond ex-patriated American who came here years ago and fell in love with the place.*

"It's a love-hate relationship, Suzie" he told her.

"I guess so. Want your usual white wine?" she said, over her shoulder as she walked away.

"Yes, please," he said, as he sat on the stool next to CJ, who was distracted by some of the fries that had gone soggy in a bath of vinegar. He felt the sensation again, this time, stronger. He felt he was being stalked just like when he saw the big cat in Vermont. He glanced over to the mirror behind the bar. The mirror reflected the back of the bar toward the area Dedra was staring when he first came in. His eyes were now adjusted to the darkness, but he squinted just the same. As he focused toward the back of the room, the image of the wild cat from his last deer hunt in Vermont came into focus and quickly faded. He squinted harder, trying to focus deeper into the room, and then he recognized her. Dee was staring in their direction.

"How did she find us?" he said in a low whisper.

"Who find who?" CJ said, finally leaving his fries alone. "Geez, you look like you seen a ghost. What the fuck is it?"

"Someone I'm trying to forget," he said, as Suzie brought his wine. "We need to leave tomorrow morning. When does the tide go out?"

"Not till eleven. We just got here, but you're the boss. Who you lookin' at?" CJ asked, as he started to look over the shoulder that Dedra was sitting on. When Captain Johnny turned back around, he was gone.

Dee left right after she paid her bill. Captain Johnny was looking in her direction, but there were at least twenty people sitting at tables in that part of the bar now. She walked out through the entrance she came in, trying to hide her anxiety. As she left the bar, she was followed. She went back to the hotel to cry. Maybe tomorrow she would be able to confront him, but not today.

As soon as Dee went up to her room, he approached the front desk.

"I would like to leave a message for Deanna Mayfield, please," he said.

"As you wish," said a slightly snooty clerk, an attitude out of place in this tropical paradise. The clerk was tall and thin and dressed in a flowery tropical shirt and long white pants. He placed a note pad with the hotel emblem and a pen on the counter. Thanking the clerk, he picked it up and went to a stuffed chair located between two large tropical plants and an end table. He wrote:

Dee, please forgive me. I have been thinking a lot about you in the past few weeks. The time we spent together made me realize how badly I screwed up my life. I don't know how I can ever reverse what I did, but I will try. If you ever see me again, you will not know who I am or what I did in the past. However, if we do meet, I hope we can start over and surpass the level of care we had for each other. I know this does not make sense, but trust me, go home and wait. I will be either gone forever or with you for eternity.

He did not sign the note. There was no need to. He simply folded it and handed it back to the clerk with a fifty-dollar bill. The clerk gasped at the tip and started to blurt out a thank you, but the generous American was heading out the door.

When Dee read the note that evening, she was angry and confused. How could he say such things? How could she ever forgive a man who did such terrible things to Dedra? She decided to go to the *Fisher Cat* in the morning and let Captain Johnny know the identity of the person he was ferrying around the Caribbean.

At ten-thirty the next morning, Dee went back to the pier where the day before she spotted the *Fisher Cat*. Since she knew nothing about boats, she had to rent one and convince the man with a crisp American $100 bill to take her to the yacht. As they were approaching the yacht, the *Fisher Cat* was getting underway. She could only see Captain Johnny at the helm, steering the boat out of the harbor and toward the open ocean. They gave chase for a short distance, but the little outboard was no match for the large diesel of the yacht. They had to turn back. "Do they go out very often?" Dee asked.

"Not since they came in two weeks ago," the sailor said. "I think they are gone for good, since they turned in their rental boat this morning. When they first rented it, they said they would keep it for a month or so."

"Did they say where they were going?" Dee asked.

"No, not to me. You may want to ask Suzie at the bar. The captain was there a lot."

"I will, thanks," she said, as they pulled in next to the pier. Dee did ask Suzie, but she did not know either. All Dede could do now was to go back to Florida. When she got back, she had a visit from Agent Brinks.

"Who is it?" asked Dee, as she walked to the front door, drying her hair with a large velour bath towel. She had slipped on her robe when the doorbell rang.

"Agent Brinks" was the droned response. "Dee, we want to talk to you."

"Just a minute," Dee said. "I just got out of the shower. Give me five minutes to blow dry my hair and put on some clothes." She took ten. "Come on in," she said, holding the door open to the two agents sitting on the front porch steps. Agent Brinks was five foot ten inches in a well-toned female body. Her hair was short, chocolate brown, and close-cropped. She peeled off what looked like government issue pilot's sunglasses to reveal coal-black eyes. She had no facial makeup that could be seen. Her pursed, thin lips were unadorned. There was no smile on her face, but here was a nasty scar frim her forehead across her nose to the center of her cheek. She reminded Dee of a taller version of the female KGB agent in the James Bond movie, *From Russia with Love*. She even dressed the part in a navy blue suit. Her partner was a short black man in an FBI suit complete with earphone and wire running behind his neck to some transmitter. He did not speak the entire time, but his eyes darted around as if he were guarding the president.

"Would you like some coffee?" Dee asked, hoping the answer would be no since she had not made any yet. She was not disappointed.

"No, thank you," said Agent Brinks. "Ms. Mayfield, we'll get right to the point. We are aware you have made two trips recently, one to Martinique and one to Belize. We also are aware of your drawing several thousand dollars from one bank account and putting it in another. We would like to know where the money came from and who you visited in the Caribbean. We also are aware of your association with a private investigator by the name of Jake Carp. If you refuse to talk, we can do this in the FBI offices here in Pensacola."

Dee told them the story amidst sobs and pleas for understanding. She said she was going to tell them about it as soon as she found out where he was. She got off with a stern lecture on obstruction of justice and how she should let the FBI do the investigating. She promised to pay back all the money she "borrowed" from the account he left her. Agent Brinks said that others in the department would determine what needed to be done with the account and the money. After an hour and a half of discussion, the two agents left Dee alone with her own guilt.

Twenty-five

When they left Belize, CJ noticed the small craft chasing after them. With the seventy-five-horse diesel cranking at full power, they were doing nearly ten knots, fast enough to outrun the small outboard. After the little boat turned back, CJ kept it at full throttle for awhile and then eased back on the power, preparing for cruising through the shimmer. As they went through, announced by Dedra, he came up the ladder with their morning coffee.

"How fast were we going that time?" he asked.

"About one point five," CJ responded.

Point five, he thought, *Where have I heard that before?* Then he responded by saying,

"We should be back in the sixties then."

"About that," said CJ. "Back before GPS, 'cause that ain't workin'. By the way, we were followed out to the open ocean. Think it was your friend from the bar?"

"She was a friend once," he responded, without realizing he gave CJ more information than he was willing to divulge.

"So we are running from a woman, are we?" said CJ

"Yeah, somethin' like that, and I want to run far. Can this thing make it across the Atlantic?"

"If you're serious, I guess we can try. I need to know what time of year it is so I can tell how rough a trip it will be."

"Well, let's turn on the radio."

After an hour, they determined it was June 15, 1969.

"June is okay for a run across the Atlantic. Not too much bad weather then," CJ announced. "We have lots of supplies, and the fishin' should be good. Let's go for it."

The next fifteen days went by quickly and without incident except for Dedra falling asleep on the foredeck and rolling overboard. CJ was at the helm. "Dedra fell in," he yelled out, as he grabbed a life jacket and jumped overboard after her, with a loud splash.

"Goddamn, CJ!" he said, as he came running out of the galley and up to the cockpit and grabbed the helm. CJ already had Dedra and was swimming for the lifeline trailing behind the yacht. CJ grabbed hold of the line as the mainsail lowered. They were still moving at five knots, but were slowing. CJ was holding Dedra in one hand, his arm threaded through the life jacket. With the other hand, he held on tight to the lifeline.

As he pulled the line up to the stern, with CJ and Dedra attached, CJ held a nearly drowned cat up to him. He lifted her safely onto the boat as CJ pulled himself up

"CJ, are you fucking nuts?" he asked. "If I had been asleep or not heard you, you both could have been lost. You could have died for that cat."

"Blow it out your ass," spluttered CJ. "I couldn't have lived with myself if I didn't try. Give her to me and take the helm. I'm going to dry her out and see if she is okay."

He handed Dedra to CJ and took the helm, shaking his head. Dedra used up one of her nine lives that day, but was none the worse for the adventure. She never went on the foredeck again.

On the morning of July 1, he was at the helm, getting ready to turn the watch over to CJ, when he spotted a sail on the horizon. When CJ came up on deck, he pointed out what was now a sail attached to a small boat of some kind.

"What the hell is a sailboat doing this far from land?" he asked.

"Jezus fucking Christ, asshole," said CJ, "we're a fuckin' sailboat, too."

They approached cautiously not noticing anyone on board. As they got closer, CJ, looked through the binoculars. "That's a trimaran."

"A who?" he asked. "Who the fuck is a trimaran?"

"Not a who, a what. It's a three-hulled boat," CJ said, not taking the binoculars off the object. "Holy shit, that's the *Teignmouth Electron*, Donald Crowhurst's boat. He tried to sail around the world back in 1968 and never made it."

"I never heard about that," he said. "It's 1969 here. What happened?"

"Well, he left from England in late October 1968 and sailed around the Atlantic until June 1969, or so they figure. His boat was found in July, abandoned. They speculate he jumped or fell overboard, since all they found was his boat and no trace of him. He left all but one of his logbooks behind. He was a bit of a perfectionist and braggart. He told everyone he would make it faster than anyone else could. In fact, he was in a contest that he wanted to win for the money and fame. Seems his business was on the fritz."

"You said he just sailed around the Atlantic from October till June? Why did he do that"

"He had a lot of problems with the trimaran and didn't know if he could make it through what is called the roaring forties at the Cape of Good Hope."

"At the tip of Africa. I remember reading about that in grade school. It's supposed to be pretty rough seas."

"You bet," said CJ. "That's why it's called the roaring forties. It's at forty degrees latitude. It's also got some southeast trade winds, difficult to sail into. Anyway, he sailed over to South America, patched up his boat, waited for awhile, and then started back to England as if he went around Africa, through the Pacific, around Cape Horn and back into the Atlantic. Then he disappeared where we are now." They were within a half-mile of the trimaran and closing quickly. CJ lowered the sail and started the diesel. The noise brought some activity in the trimaran. "Look," said CJ. "There's someone on the stern."

There on the stern was a man naked from the waist up. He was very thin and burnt from the sun. He also was staggering, not from the rocking of the boat, but was either drunk or delirious. He had something tightly tucked under one arm much like a fullback with an armful of pigskin, heading for the goal line. It looked like a book. As suddenly as he appeared, he walked to the bow of the boat. What he did next would be argued about for many years. He transferred the book to his left hand and tossed it into the sea. He staggered to the edge and either fell or jumped overboard.

The yacht was within two hundred feet of the trimaran and CJ was steering a bee's line toward it. As they pulled within fifty feet, CJ cut the throttle and ran to the bow of the boat. "Take the helm," he said, as he dove head first into the sea.

"Jesus Christ," he said. "Here we go again. Goddamn crazy SEAL."

As he brought the stern of the yacht around toward the front of the trimaran, he saw CJ coming up for air, and then dive down again. He came up again and then dove one more time. When he surfaced this time, he had Donald Crowhurst around the chin in a headlock. Donald was not putting up a fight and looked lifeless. The book he tossed in the water before he went in was floating away from them both. CJ was back pedaling toward the yacht. "Throw me a life jacket," he shouted as best he could with seawater splashing into his mouth.

He tossed the life jacket to CJ, cut in the diesel, and brought the boat up beside them. CJ had Donald's arms in the life jacket and was fastening the front Velcro straps. He steered the yacht around the two men in the water so that the trailing lifeline curled in their direction. CJ grabbed the line and, just like he did with Dedra, CJ lifted Donald toward the boat. With Donald safely aboard, CJ climbed into the yacht. He was breathing hard but was all right. Donald on the other hand was not breathing at all. After five minutes of CPR from both rescuers, Donald started to cough up seawater. CJ turned him on his side and Donald vomited more seawater. In spite of the tropical heat, Donald started shivering. A blanket was brought up from below and placed over the thin man, who looked like a skeleton in brown shrink-wrap. He had sunken eyes, a dark mustache, and curly long hair. He hadn't bathed for awhile and smelled of booze and puke. It had been difficult to give him CPR and CJ almost gagged doing it.

They were both exhausted from the ordeal and sat back to see what happened next. Dedra just watched from her seat on the cockpit bench, where she had been throughout the whole ordeal.

"You said he was lost at sea. Now we've altered history, you godamn dummy. Well, CJ, what are we going to do with him now?"

"You and your goddamn altering history speech. I couldn't let him drown."

"What about the trimaran?" he said. "It must be a mile off the port stern and moving away from us."

"We'll let it go. It was found abandoned about where we are now, so we won't be altering your goddamn history."

As they finished their discussion, Donald started to move and babble incoherently. He seemed to be in a drunken stupor but was able to get to his feet and allowed them to help him below decks and into a bed. "I'll watch him and you go mind the helm."

Four hours later, CJ came up on deck.

"This guy needs help," he said. "I think he went insane out on the ocean by himself. He keeps babbling about how he died and has now achieved status as a god of some sort. He is taking water, but no solid food yet."

"So what do we do with him?" he asked. "We're out in the middle of the Atlantic with a nut case. If he needs help, where is the closest place to take him?"

"To get to any serious help, I believe Puerto Rico is the best bet. We're closer to Africa, but I'm not sure where we could take him if we went there. At least, in San Juan, there are Americans and good doctors who speak English."

"How are we going to explain thirty years of absence?" he asked.

"If his condition doesn't change, we won't have to. They'll lock him in a loony bin. If he comes to later, he just becomes crazier if he tries to tell them what happened. Chances are, most people who remember him are dead or in their seventies and eighties. How could they believe he never aged all the time he was missing."

"What if we just dropped him off somewhere in Africa or South America? If he dies or gets lost for awhile, then we are off the hook."

"What hook?" CJ asked. "He doesn't know us from Adam. We could just keep him liquored up till we get to shore. He's in such bad shape, it will take him until we get to land just to be aware of us. I can't live with myself if we're responsible for his death. I couldn't let Dedra die, and I can't let him die."

"All right, you win, CJ. Let's turn this thing around and head to San Juan. Isn't there a navy base there?"

"Yeah, Roosevelt Roads. I think the sailors call it Rosy

Roads. There's also a hospital there, where they could keep him until transfer to a civilian hospital. We can sneak in at night and leave him on the beach. Make your heading due west. Then we can drop south when we get close."

"Aye Aye, Captain," he mimicked. "Due west, it is."

Donald's condition did not seem to improve the rest of day. His rescuers took turns watching over him. The next morning, however, was a different story. Donald emerged from below decks, scaring CJ and Dedra while on watch, and who were looking over the stern, admiring the golden morning sun.

"Where is the *Teignmouth*?" he asked CJ in a raspy voice.

CJ jumped more quickly than Dedra at the unexpected inquiry.

"Jesus," CJ said, whirling around to see Donald standing at the top rung of the ladder, swaying a little. Donald was still clad in shorts, but with a blanket wrapped around his shoulders. "You scared the shit out of me."

"Americans?" Donald rasped.

"Yes, we are Americans. We pulled you from the sea after you fell overboard. The trimaran drifted away, and we let it. You were in pretty bad shape and almost drowned. You want some food?"

"I'm Donald Crowhurst," he said. "And who might you be?"

"I know who you are," said CJ, not realizing how he was going to explain his insight. "I'm Captain Johnny, but you can call me CJ. Everybody else does."

"My reputation must precede me," said Donald. "You said we. Are there others on board?"

"Yes, one other man. This is my boat, and he hired me and my boat to take him sailing. We ran into you on the way across the Atlantic."

"Where are we headed now?" asked Donald, pulling himself the rest of the way into the cockpit and sitting down heavily on the portside bench seat. "I mustn't go back to England. A fate worse than drowning awaits me there. Have you got a Marconi?"

"If you're hungry, we have almost everything else, but not no macaroni," said CJ.

"He said Marconi, fuck nuts," a voice from the galley said. "That's another way of saying two-way radio."

"I dare say," said Donald, "who is the foul-mouth gentleman belonging to the voice I hear."

"Let's just say I'm CJ's first mate," the voice from the galley said. "And yes, we have a Marconi." He did not want to give away his identity to someone who was sure to get some press when they left him off in Puerto Rico. "I'm making some coffee, want some?"

"Do you have any tea aboard?" Donald asked.

"In the port side cupboard, top shelf," yelled CJ. "And make the coffee strong."

"Aye aye, cap'n. Strong it be, matey."

"To answer your other question," continued CJ. "We are takin' you to the navy hospital in Puerto Rico. You was in pretty bad shape when we found you."

"Is there anyway I can convince you to leave me on the next deserted island we pass?" asked Donald with a half-smirk from shallow cheeks. "I don't want my fate to be known. Please don't announce where I am over the Marconi."

"Don't worry," said CJ. "No one has known where you have been for the last thirty years, and we ain't about to tell them."

"What are you talking about?" asked Donald. "Thirty years indeed. I haven't been adrift for that long." At that, CJ commenced to tell Donald all about the time warp while they had tea, coffee, and toast and jelly, the latter of which Donald consumed avidly. Surprisingly, Donald did not look perplexed at the prospect of traveling ahead in time. He listened with great enthusiasm to the stories about the advances made in computers and space travel. He was actually eager to be a part of the present and allow the past to go with the trimaran.

"I have one request," said Donald after CJ was finished. "And that is to be put ashore on the American continent. I can rather get lost there. The island of Puerto Rico is too small a place."

"How about Brazil?" asked CJ. "We ain't ready to go back to the States just yet, and they have some good rum there."

"Brazil is fine with me," said Donald.

Donald filled the rest of the voyage with explanations and

stories of his failed attempt to sail solo around the world. He admitted to having been on the brink of insanity. Although he would miss his wife and children dearly, the shame of having to face the world and explain the fraud he had attempted was too much to bear. So he would take his chance on obscurity. He was offered cash and took less than what was offered. Twenty days later, they said good-bye to Donald at Georgetown, British Guyana. "Don't drink any purple Kool-Aid," said CJ. Of course Donald did not know what that meant, since he skipped 1978 and the Jonestown disaster when he went through the shimmer. They kept the yacht in port long enough to take on supplies and, of course, more rum.

They left port at night and cruised toward the fifteen-mile time warp. He was at the helm and slowed to one knot in anticipation of passing through the shimmer. He did not want to go back too far and encounter more pirates. Drug smugglers preferred aircraft in the late eighties and that was where he wanted to go back to this time. CJ was in the galley, making some sandwiches with canned tuna. Dedra was audible, all the way to the cockpit, begging for a chunk. She suddenly stopped her begging, indicating CJ had given her the juice and any leftovers.

He was looking at the speed indicator, which was glowing a pale green for nighttime sailing. The marks between the numbers were green lines. One, two, three, four, five lines, the number one repeating up to twenty knots. He was staring at the green lines trying to remember something, a dream maybe. Or maybe it just reminded him of an old car he used to own with a speedometer illuminated with a green dash light.

CJ came up from the galley carrying their dinner, on a tray, no less, snapping his thoughts back to the boat. As CJ arranged the sandwiches, chips, and drinks, Dedra sauntered up and sat on her haunches, licking her paws and cleaning the tuna juice from her face. She went into her scared-cat act as they passed through the shimmer, all but invisible in the failing light.

"I know we pass back and forth through the time warp on the boat," he said to CJ, "but what if we got off the boat and went ashore before we passed back through. Would we be stuck in the past, or would we return to the future as if we had stayed on the boat?"

"I ain't never thought about it, but I would think we would end up back where we started from."

"When we got in the water and went away from the boat when the pirates attacked, we stayed in the past, but we didn't go too far from the boat. I wonder how far out the time warp extends. You said you lost a piece of the lifeline when you trailed it behind going through the warp. How much did you lose?"

"Well," CJ interjected. "I could see the pirate boat a long way off and the radar picked it up before that. So I would say it goes to the horizon anyway. I never measured the length of line that was left, but it must have been at least ten feet off a fifty-foot line."

"I think you're right about the horizon when we're far from land, but when we get close to going through this next time let's tow the inflatable raft behind us on the lifeline and see what happens to it. If it disappears, then it stayed in the past. If it stays with us, then we have to assume we will always go forward even without the boat."

"What about the distance thing you mentioned. I mean, what if we don't tow the raft far enough back."

"Then we get a longer line and try it again. How long a line do you have?"

"I got another fifty-foot we could use."

"That will have to do for now," he said.

CJ took the tray and trash and headed back down the ladder to go to bed.

"Keep her headed due north. We'll turn east in the morning and follow the signs to Costa Rica. Good night," CJ said, as his head disappeared below decks. Dedra was right behind him.

Ten days later, on a dark moonless night, they approached within twenty miles of Costa Rica. CJ brought the raft topside. CJ pulled a cord, inflating the two-man raft with CO_2 cartridges. He then tied it to the stern, put it in the water, and played out fifty feet of line. "Now we'll find out if your theory is correct," said CJ.

They could barely see the raft trailing the yacht, but with

the sails still up and diesel turned off, they could hear the water splashing around it. "Get a flashlight," he said to CJ.

"No" was the response. "The white light will ruin our night vision." Five miles later, on cue, Dedra announced the passage back to the present. They both stared back toward the raft, collectively holding their breath. The line went taught. They both ducked out of the way, thinking the line would part and snap back into the boat. Shielding his face, CJ looked back toward the raft.

"She's gone," CJ stated. "The line is slack, and I can't hear or see it."

"Turn around and go back," he demanded. "Let's go back through the time warp to see if we can find it."

"We could," responded CJ. "But I wasn't watching the speed indicator to see how fast we were going. Even if we knew the speed, it would be hard to hit it exactly. Point five either way and we could be off a month or two."

"What did you say?" he asked startled by the comment. "About the point something or other."

"Oh, you mean point five." CJ said. "Point five knots. You know, half a knot either way and we could miss by months."

"Point five and all will be alive," he said, remembering a dream.

"Who will be alive?" asked CJ.

"I don't know. It was a dream I just now remembered."

"Well, spare me," CJ said. "Nuthin's more boring than someone else's dreams."

That night, they anchored a half-mile from shore. They planned on entering the port of Colón, Costa Rica, in the morning. CJ went to bed first, followed by Dedra. He stayed topside, just staring at the stars and lights on the shore. He started to wonder if he could go back in time just like the life raft and erase all the wrong he did. The woman in the dream seemed to indicate so. She even gave him the speed that would take him back, but how far. If he went too far he would lose the money from the lottery? If he didn't go far enough, some of the women could still be murdered. If he carried back a lot of cash, would it disappear? "It's worth a chance," he told himself. "Our next destination will be the Texas coast. I will ride in a raft behind the boat. I'll

267

give CJ some of the winnings, and if something goes wrong, we can arrange to meet when I catch up to him in the future."

The next morning, as they were heading for shore, he told CJ his plan. He would leave most of his cash with CJ, and meet him when CJ got back to Mobile. Of course, if his plan works, he will be older than he is now.

"What the fuck do you want to do that for?" CJ asked.

"I will have a chance to correct some wrongs of my past. It's a golden opportunity."

"If that's what you want to do," CJ said. "I certainly like the part of leaving me with lots of cash. What if you don't show up?"

"The cash is yours to keep. If I don't show up, then you will know something went wrong."

"What about the cat?"

"I think you should keep her. She seems to prefer you to me anyway. I can always get another one."

"Okay," CJ agreed. "If you want to do it, there ain't nothin' I can say to stop you."

They spent five days in Colón, the first of which Captain Johnny topped off the fuel tanks. The next three were spent loading supplies depleted by their trek back and forth to the middle of the Atlantic and up from South America. They left on the morning of the fifth day.

Ann Brinks grew up in a man's world. She was raised by her father after he divorced Ann's mother, who was having an affair. Ann's mother gave up custody without a fight and disappeared from their life. Ann had no siblings or surviving grandparents and her father never remarried. As a consequence, all her values were learned from men.

Ann knew she was different when other girls her age started dating and she wanted to play sports instead. She excelled in field hockey and softball which she played year-round where she grew up in Atlanta. It wasn't until college when she discovered her sexual orientation was for the same sex, but did not pursue any romances. She majored in criminal justice at Gibbs College in Vienna, Virginia. She then went to the University of Virginia Law School in Charlottesville and graduated with honors. She was recruited by the FBI and accepted as an agent trainee. Her academics and ability in sports gave her the edge to graduate from the FBI program in Quantico, Virginia; however, a training accident left her with a scarred face.

Ann was learning how to disarm an attacker armed with a knife. Although the training was supposed to be realistic, it was not supposed to cause bodily harm. The attacker was a trainer who did not like women in the FBI, especially one who was also suspected of being a "bull dykin' ass bitch," as he told his wife. So, it was no surprise when he was aggressive. It was a surprise when Ann was just as aggressive; however, her grip on his arm slipped in part because it was a hot humid day and she and the trainer were both sweating, but also because he was trying to resist a little more than usual. The knife came across her face, cutting her from the center of her forehead down the side of her nose, and across her left cheek. It was not deep because of the dullness of the knife, but it was wide and long. It took fifty-five stitches to close the wound and because of an infection, it healed badly. She opted to keep the scar because it deterred advances from the opposite sex, and made her look "bad." Ten years later, when Agents Ford and Crane were blown to bits at the mansion in Vermont, she was assigned the case.

From the information gleaned from Dee, they had sought and obtained the cooperation of various law enforcement agencies throughout the Caribbean and Central America. When and if their suspect went through any Customs checks, they would be alerted. Primarily they were tracking John Potter, alias Captain Johnny, because he had used the same passport in Martinique and Belize. She was angry with Dee for holding back the information, but another department would deal with her later. She was concentrating on catching the man who was suspected of wasting two valuable agents, friends, and fathers. When the call came in from Colón, Costa Rica, she and another agent were on the next plane out of BWI. Arriving in Colón, they were greeted by the chief of police, Captain Emberra, who drove them to the marina where the men were believed to be staying aboard the yacht. The captain explained that it was only by luck the two were detected in Colón. It seems the one named Captain Johnny had to show a passport to buy fuel for the yacht. Had they not needed to refuel, they might have remained undetected.

Arriving at the marina, they located the man who fueled the *Fisher Cat*. He pointed to the area where the yacht had been that morning, but Agent Brinks could see it was not there. Further inquiries gave them the impression they had missed the yacht by one hour. "Goddamn it," Agent Brinks, said embarrassing her partner.

"Can we get a fast police boat to take us out to look for her?" she asked Captain Emberra.

"We have a helicopter that I can get here in about thirty minutes," he replied.

"That would be great," Ann said.

Twenty minutes later, the police helicopter landed in the parking lot of the marina. The two agents and Captain Emberra got on board and they headed out to sea to look for the yacht. Agent Brinks had no idea what they would do if and when they located the yacht. "Can we get a police boat or Costa Rican Navy boat to board her and bring her back?" she asked.

"I have alerted the Coast Guard and they are ready to assist us as long as the yacht is in territorial waters," the captain said.

"I am impressed and very pleased that you are willing to help us," Ann said smiling.

"There is a yacht," the co-pilot shouted over the roar of the rotor blades pointing out the left side of the 'copter. Agent Brinks craned for a view, but they were too far away to see the name on the boat. Using the binoculars, the co-pilot read off the name. "*Fisher Cat*," he said.

"That's the one," the two agents shouted simultaneously.

The pilot banked to the left and headed for the yacht.

"How far out do the territorial waters reach?" Ann asked.

"A hundred and fifty kilometers from shore and we are about thirty right now," the co-pilot said.

"About how far is that in miles?" Ann asked, trying to convert the distance in her head.

"I think it is about twenty miles American," he shouted back.

The pilot drew up beside the yacht hovering about 100 feet off the starboard bow. They could all see the two men on board as the pilot called the Coast Guard for assistance. The yacht was moving at a steady pace and it appeared the two men were not concerned for their safety.

"Does this 'copter have a megaphone?" Ann asked.

"Yes," the c-pilot said, handing her the microphone.

As Ann was about to identify herself to the *Fisher Cat*, the boat took on an eerie appearance. It started to wiggle and then shimmer as if they were looking at the boat through cellophane that was starting to crinkle. Then as they stared wide-eyed and mouths agape, the yacht just disappeared. The pilot circled the spot they were all staring at, but the boat was nowhere to be found.

"What the fuck happened?" Ann said, fingering her scar and embarrassing no one.

They circled for five minutes until they were convinced there was nothing floating where they had last seen the *Fisher Cat*. There was silence as they headed back to the shore. The two agents were on the next plane back to the States.

Leaving Costa Rica, he made sure they were going point five knots as they approached the shimmer. Before passing through, they heard a helicopter approaching from the south. They could hear it and then see it long before the helicopter turned and made a beeline toward the *Fisher Cat*. As the helicopter hovered close by, splashing them with backwash from the whirling blades, they passed through the shimmer. The helicopter sounded like it was in a tunnel and then it disappeared as did the hollow wop wop wop sound from the rotor.

"Was that your fucking girlfriend again?" CJ asked not caring one way or the other. He spared CJ a response as he tuned in the radio to verify it was June, 1992.

The red-haired lady from the dream was right, he thought. It was three weeks before the lottery drawing when he won the fifty-eight-million-dollar jackpot. If they cruised at nine knots they could make the trip to Galveston in less than ten days. He would have plenty of time to replay the lottery. This time he wanted to meet Dee under different circumstances. *Would she remember him? Of course not. Could they get to the point they reached before she found out about him? That will have to be played out. They had the chemistry once. Was it possible the*

271

same ingredients would be there?

Nine days later, just as the sun was coming up in the east, they came within twenty miles of the U.S. coastline. CJ inflated the new raft and attached the small outboard motor. The sea was calm. From fifteen miles out, he could motor to the Texas coast in three to four hours. If necessary, he had oars for rowing. He put a million dollars in cash in the bag he brought on board with him six months ago. The newspaper he bought before he left Mobile was still on the bottom of the bag, so he covered the cash with it. He put another million in a black gym bag and left it with CJ, who insisted it was too much. "Get yourself a new boat," he said. "I can't take it all with me and mine may just disappear."

He said good-bye to Dedra and got into the raft. CJ let out fifty feet of line.

Five seconds after Dedra announced they had passed through, the raft disappeared. CJ thought he heard someone shout "good-bye," but there was no one around. He immediately went to the stash of money to see if it was still there. It wasn't, but CJ was rapidly forgetting what he expected to find in the black gym bag. He also was at a loss as to why he was trailing 50 feet of line behind the *Fisher Cat*. He heard a cat crying, but he looked all around the yacht and found no cats. Scratching his head, he checked where he was on the GPS and steered the boat on a heading to Mobile.

From the shoreline in Sarasota, an old woman faced west over the Gulf and chanted. The spell was lifted from the yacht forever.

When the yacht disappeared, he yelled a good-bye to CJ to see if there was some link to the future. There was no answer. He started the outboard and headed for the Texas coast, using the rising sun for direction. Three hours later, he saw the shoreline. It was another hour before he ran the raft ashore on Galveston Island. Wading ashore, he dragged the raft with him. There were tents and campers dotting the beach. As soon as he could, he opened his bag. He pulled back the paper and saw that the money was gone. "Fuck me!" he said aloud. "I guess I'll just have to win the Lotto all over again."

He noticed a couple watching him from lawn chairs under a

brown awning attached to a thirty-foot brown-and-white Winnebago. There was a small open-air jeep attached to the rear of the motor home. They were 100 feet down the shore to his left. As he approached he noticed a man and woman in their mid-fifties. They must have been health conscious, since neither one was overweight. The man had on a red pair of short-cut swim trunks. His body hair surrounded by a dark tan was either bleached white by the sun or turned white with age. She had on a two-piece white swimsuit, which showed off her modest tan. They were wearing expensive-looking sunglasses and holding tall glasses filled with ice cubes and what could have been lemonade.

"Hi," he said, as he got to within twenty feet of the motor home.

"Hello," they said in unison.

"I'm sort of stranded. A wave from a passing ship capsized my raft while I was out cruising around this morning. I was able to upright it and get the motor restarted, but I lost my wallet in the process. I don't want to try heading back home, since the outboard was flooded and might not make it."

"Oh, no," said the woman.

"Sorry to hear that," said the man. "Can I give you a ride to town, or at least to the nearest telephone."

"You are a life saver, sir. I'm afraid I'll need a ride into town since my wife is working today and not home to answer the phone. The name is John Potter," he said, taking CJ's name.

"I'm Jim Rivers, and this is my wife Janis," he said, standing and offering a handshake. "Janis, get my wallet and keys to the tow vehicle while I disconnect it."

"Also, could I borrow some money. You can keep my raft as collateral," he said, taking the offered hand and shaking it vigorously.

"Of course," said Jim, and he unhitched the Jeep, lifted the tow bar, and attached it to the fender. "Would fifty be enough?"

"Fifty would be fine," he said, noticing the Minnesota tags on the Jeep. "Let me drag the raft over here."

"That's not necessary," Jim said, as Janis brought out his wallet and keys. "I'll drag it over here with the Jeep when I get back. You gonna be okay, honey, till I get back?"

"Sure," said Janis. "I'll fix us some lunch while you're gone."

He tossed his bag in the back of the Jeep. They both got in and headed away from the campsite.

"Where to?" asked Jim.

"I need to get to the other side of Houston, so someplace where I can call a cab or get on a bus would be fine. My wife dropped me off in the ship channel on her way to work this morning."

"There's a nice restaurant five miles from here," Jim said, as he got on Highway 45 heading toward Houston. "The wife and I ate there last night."

Five minutes later, they were in the parking lot of the restaurant. He got out, thanked Jim and went to the telephone hanging on the outside wall. Jim sped away, not aware that he was the proud owner of raft and outboard motor.

The cab took him to the Greyhound bus station in downtown Houston. From there, it was a three-hour ride to San Antonio. He took another cab to his apartment, which was as he left it in 1992 after he picked up his Lotto winnings. He had to get his spare key from the fake rock in the flowerbed. It fit. It was déjà vu opening the door and walking in. All his old stuff was still there. All he had to do was go to his job as electrical engineer at the design firm of Peoples Architects and Engineers and wait for the Lotto drawing in less than two weeks. Of course, he also had to remember the lucky numbers.

He hesitated about going to work, but was curious to see if it was as he left it. It was. No one noticed that he was six years older, but were curious about his tan. He was able to get through the next two work weeks easily. He had already designed the two projects six years before, so doing them again was a piece of cake. He enjoyed going back to the old office and the friendships he once cherished. The night of the Lotto drawing, he bought his ticket just as before. He was sure he remembered the numbers, but he didn't. He was off by one number. It still earned him $150,000, enough for him to move to Pensacola to find Dee, but he decided to wait. There were too many what-ifs in play. What if she was not as anxious to meet someone? What if she was still

274

concentrating on raising Dedra. What if she was in a relationship? By waiting until Dedra was in college, he would be in a better position to start again. He would have to wait four agonizing years. Meanwhile he would take the Lotto winnings and invest it. He could remember some of the stocks that did well in the mid-nineties so he was sure of at least quadrupling his earnings.

Twenty-six

He did well in the stock market. He quit his job four years later on his birthday, after making an anonymous call to the Washington, D.C., police department. This time he thought it appropriate to alter history to save a life by reporting a potential rapist and murder he had witnessed. The man's looks and clothing were etched in his mind, so the police were waiting when the woman was assaulted. On the way to Pensacola, he bought a copy of the *Washington Post* and read all about the apprehension of a man the police suspected of five other rapes and murders in the D.C. area. The woman would recover from a blow to the head, but that was better than what could have been. There was a reward for the informant if he would just call the police and identify himself. The reward money went unclaimed.

Once he was set up in Pensacola, it was easy to meet Dee. Having had to relive four years of his life, they were now the same age. Dedra was running along on a street near her home. He simply played the role he had honed when he used to pick up victims. Albeit a bit rusty, he could still turn on the charm. Dedra did not fall into his arms this time as she did in that far away dream. She consented to a date, and then another, and then another before she even kissed him goodnight. When she did invite him in for a cup of coffee after a romantic dinner, she wanted to talk more than anything else.

"You know I have a daughter," she said.

"Yes, you did mention it a time or two," he responded. "I'm sure you have a picture of her around here somewhere. May I see if she is as beautiful as her mother?"

"As a matter of fact, she sent me a digital picture in an e-mail this morning. Follow me, and I'll let you decide who is better looking." She led him over to the laptop she had on the kitchen table. Hitting the enter key, the laptop came out of the standby mode. She opened Outlook and clicked on an e-mail. As she opened the attachment, he sucked in a small breath at what he saw. It was like those dreams more than four years ago. There was Dedra posing playfully in a cat like pose with her hands up in a pawing motion. But that is not what made him gasp. Her eyes were red. It was only "red eye," the reflection of the camera flash bouncing off the blood vessels of the retina inside the eyes, but they looked like the eyes of the cats in the dreams he had.

"You have goose bumps on your arms," she said, looking shocked. "I guess that tells me who you think is better looking."

"N-n-no, no," he said, with a stutter. "It was just that she reminded me of a dream I once had of a cat with red eyes. She is beautiful but doesn't have the mature handsome look of her mother."

"She almost always has that red-eye look. I was told it was because she has light colored eyes and they don't absorb the light as well. Also her pupils dilate more than normal. I'll take the mature handsome comment as a compliment."

"You should, as it was meant to be," he said.

That night, they made love. It was a gentle session, but with passion. Afterwards they talked about the past and the future. She was starting to fall for him. He was hopelessly in love with her and had been for four years. They were together from that time on.

Two years later, on the day he met Captain Johnny in a faraway dream, he was riding with Dee on their tandem through the streets of Pensacola. At one intersection, they stopped to rest and get some water. There was an old woman standing on the corner looking at a city map. He could tell that at one time she must have been pretty, although she was now showing her age. She had short white hair, but her skin was still a creamy chocolate color. He thought he recognized her, but from where? She was apparently lost, looking at the map with wrinkled brows. Dee got off the bike to stretch her legs and get a drink. She took the bottle from the bike frame and sat on the bench to drink while he asked the old lady if she needed some help.

277

The old lady looked at him and smiled.

"No," she whispered. "You helped me once many years ago, and now it's time for me to help you. You have a newspaper in an old duffel bag. Look at it carefully. Make sure you read it all and pay attention to the dates."

"You are oddly familiar," he said. "Where have we met?"

"At sea," she said. "I had red hair then, long red hair."

He closed his eyes, squinted, and remembered an old dream, or was it a dream. Then suddenly he was aware of a past life. One he tried to forget over the past six years. When he opened his eyes, the old lady was crossing the street. He thought he saw long red hair flowing from her head as she appeared to float across the street.

"What did she want?" asked Dee.

"Directions," he said. "Just directions."

When they got home, he rummaged around the stuff he had stashed in the garage after he moved in with Dee. He found the bag he had brought with him, opened it up, and found an old newspaper stuffed in the bottom. He opened the paper. It was a *USA Today*. He carefully read all that was left of the newspaper. There were several pages missing. What was the old lady talking about, "pay attention to the dates." He looked at the date. It was tomorrow's date on an old newspaper, so?

'Look at it carefully," she had said. He looked carefully. "It must be a typo," he said aloud. "That's tomorrow's date this year." He reread the paper. It contained events that he heard on the news at noon. It also contained the previous day's lottery results for all the states, including Florida. It said there was one winner of the thirty-five-million-dollar jackpot and gave the numbers.

"Holy shit!" he shouted. "Holy shit!" He almost broke the door down trying to get into the house. He flew past a perplexed Dee to the bedroom to get his keys. She followed him into the bedroom as he grabbed the truck keys with a shaky hand.

"What's wrong, and where are you going?" she asked.

"I'll explain later," he said.

That night he showed her the winning ticket. After she got over the shock, they made mad, passionate love on the living room floor. Six months later, in Mobile, he met a perplexed, salty sea captain returning from a trip to the Caribbean. He handed Captain Johnny a cashier's check for one million dollars annotated "Paid in Full."

"Have a good life, my friend," was all he said.